R.

NIGHTS
IN THE
GARDENS
OF
BROOKLYN

By Harvey Swados

NOVELS

Out Went the Candle
False Coin
The Will
Standing Fast
Celebration

SHORT STORIES

On the Line
Nights in the Gardens of Brooklyn (1961)
A Story for Teddy, and Others

NONFICTION AND ANTHOLOGIES

A Radical's America
Years of Conscience: The Muckrakers
The American Writer and the Great Depression
A Radical at Large: American Essays
Standing Up for the People: The Life and Works of Estes Kefauver

HARVEY SWADOS

NIGHTS

IN THE

GARDENS

OF

BROOKLYN

THE COLLECTED STORIES OF
HARVEY SWADOS

VIKING

VIKING
Viking Penguin Inc., 40 West 23rd Street,
New York, New York 10010, U.S.A.
Penguin Books Ltd, Harmondsworth,
Middlesex, England
Penguin Books Australia Ltd, Ringwood,
Victoria, Australia
Penguin Books Canada Limited, 2081 John Street,
Markham, Ontario, Canada L3R 1B4
Penguin Books (N.Z.) Ltd, 182–190 Wairau Road,
Auckland 10, New Zealand

First published in 1986 by Viking Penguin Inc.
Published simultaneously in Canada

The stories in this book appeared earlier in
the periodicals *Contact, Cosmopolitan, Discovery No. 4,
Esquire, The Hudson Review, The Kenyon Review, Midstream,
New World Writing, The Prairie Schooner, The Saturday
Evening Post,* and *The Western Review,* and in the books
Nights in the Gardens of Brooklyn and *A Story for
Teddy and Others* by Harvey Swados.

Library of Congress Cataloging in Publication Data
Swados, Harvey.
    Nights in the gardens of Brooklyn.
    Includes stories from the two collections the author
published in his lifetime: Nights in the gardens of
Brooklyn (1960); and A story for Teddy (1965); plus
two previously unpublished stories. I. Title.
PS3569.W2N6 1986   813'.54   85-40631
ISBN 0-670-80974-8

Printed in the United States of America by
R.R. Donnelley & Sons Company, Crawfordsville, Indiana
Set in Avanta

With love for
Marco and Robin
Felice and Rick
and
Beryl and Megan
Miranda and Julia

CONTENTS

INTRODUCTION

Shortly after my father died, I picked up a copy of *A Story for Teddy* —an arbitrary choice from the dozen or so of his books on my shelf—and began scanning its pages for a thread that might connect me to the father I remembered.

I found that thread in the story "Claudine's Book." As I read it, I recognized a portrait of myself as a child that my father had drawn. Details had been altered here and there, but the story contained a specific reference to a namesake I had resented in my youth, at a time when friends and foes alike took equal delight in the pleasures of name-calling. I was often teased unmercifully about my name. I was referred to as the one who stole from the rich and gave to the poor, the sidekick of a comic-book hero, and the first bird of spring. I remember angrily asking my father how he had chosen my name, and he replied (not without a certain pride) that I had been named for Robin Roberts, a pitcher for the Philadelphia Phillies. I felt his answer reflected the ultimate indignity, since baseball was a sport in which I had no interest or talent.

Why had he never discussed the story with me before it was published? Perhaps for fear of bruising the sensibility of an already thin-skinned eleven-year-old; or perhaps, in the years that followed, because it simply ceased to exist as a source of discussion, as happens to so many points of contention between parents and children. Whatever the explanation, I long ago put aside any residual childhood resentment—either of my father *or* Robin Roberts—and am left now with only a lingering regret that fate never allowed me the opportunity to thank him adequately for this small but precious legacy.

When my father died on December 11, 1972, at the age of 52, he left a body of work that is a unique amalgam of politics and fiction. The books span a seventeen-year period from the publication of *Out Went the Candle,* his first novel, in 1955, to the completion of *Celebration,* his last, in 1972; and range from the essays in *A Radical's America* (1962) to his powerful and now classic portrait of life in an automobile assembly plant, *On the Line* (1957). Two collections of stories published in the 1960s, *Nights in the Gardens of Brooklyn* (1961) and *A Story for Teddy* (1965), are enjoying a renaissance in this volume. They are a distillation of my father's talents as a fiction writer, and they also display his concerns as an astute observer of the American social scene.

Out of vogue for years, the short story seems to have made a triumphant return in the 1980s. It has undergone transformations that occasionally seem as extreme as the changing political and social forces which have surrounded it. It has been pared down to the bare bone, robbed at times of style and at others, of content. Weary of it all, its characters meander through a romantic and sexual void, vaguely searching for a way to make up for spiritual loss. To underscore their authors' alienated sensibilities, the stories are typically written in the present tense, as if neither the past nor the future carried any weight. "Hear my story *now,*" these writers cry out. "Yesterday is gone and tomorrow may never come."

In light of this peculiar literary trend, how remarkable it is to encounter in *Nights in the Gardens of Brooklyn* characters whose common bond lies in their resolute refusal to capitulate to emptiness. Their search to find meaning to their lives and their struggle to connect to one another perfectly encapsulate the imagination that spawned them. Filled with a desire for love, dreams of a better life and a more fulfilling job, and driven forward by an often instinctive sense of optimism, these men and women are the products of one man's creative sensibility—that which belonged to Harvey Swados.

Harvey Swados was born on October 28, 1920, the son of a doctor, in Buffalo, New York. At least until the advent of the Depression, his life was filled with games and music. He and his only sibling, his older sister, Felice (also a writer), spent a great deal of time outdoors; they both played the piano, and he studied the flute as well. But as he once recollected, "throughout the 1930s Buffalo seemed a gloomy, wretched, and dismal place. There were lengthy evening discussions of young intellectuals dreaming and scheming of fleeing the decaying city."

My father was fifteen when he left Buffalo and entered the University of Michigan at Ann Arbor, and before he reached his eighteenth birthday, he had his first taste of success as a writer: a story published in the university's quarterly literary review was included in *The Best Short Stories of 1938*. His fervent and lifelong commitment to the politics of the left began at an early age, too. After a brief involvement with the Young Communist League in the thirties, he chose finally and irrevocably to identify himself as a radical socialist.

Several years ahead of him at the University of Michigan was Arthur Miller, one of the few among his contemporaries to exhibit many of the same political and social concerns in his playwriting that my father did in his fiction. In addition to the writers and actors and musicians who populate the stories in this volume, there are salesmen and census-takers, ordinary and decent men who might very well have joined Willy Loman for a cup of coffee in the Automat—Bern in the whimsical "A Handful of Ball-points, A Heartful of Love"; the reflective narrator of "Nights in the Gardens of Brooklyn"; "The Dancer" 's Peter Chifley, wide-eyed and running desperately from door to door, clutching his Matso Minute Man's kit. These are the people with whom my father's sympathies lay—people who work.

And my father worked, always. After graduating in 1940, he took a job in an aircraft plant as a riveter. After a year of that, he was sure he never wanted to live in Buffalo again, and indeed he never did. Nevertheless, the city frequently served as the locale for much of his fiction, most particularly and effectively in his 1963 novel, *The Will*.

In New York, he spent a year working in an aircraft plant in Long Island City, and, fairly well cured of whatever romantic notions he had about the industrial working class, joined the world of seafaring workers at the outset of World War II by enlisting in the Merchant Marine. After training first as a seaman and then as a radio operator, he served as radio officer on a number of ships through 1945, sailing the North Atlantic, the South Pacific, the Mediterranean and the Caribbean to various ports from Australia to Yugoslavia. His experiences during those years formed the basis for a number of his short stories—"Bobby Shafter's Gone to Sea," "Tease," and "The Letters"—and in a general way were responsible for the marvelous variety of their locales. He also completed an unpublished novel during this period, *The Unknown Constellations.* Resoundingly autobiographical, its story involves a young sailor who settles in New Orleans in the hope of escaping his father's stern and unforgiving shadow, only to become embroiled in a battle of good versus evil with another authority figure—his crooked boss.

At the war's end, two of the most profound experiences of my father's life occurred. His sister, Felice, had published one novel and was at work on another when she died in 1945 at the age of 29. This event devastated him, but it also strengthened his resolve to become a writer.

And in September of 1946, he married my mother Bette.

As marriages go (and many of them went, in the sixties and seventies), it was a long and happy one—always faithful, occasionally turbulent, honest, passionate, and loving. Through it all, my mother remained, in Dan Wakefield's words, my father's "best and most trusted editor, literary confidante and counselor, sometime agent, staunchest supporter, shrewdest and most articulate defender of the man and his work, finest and most faithful friend."

As a child of this extraordinary bond, I was always deeply (if subliminally) cognizant of the frequent instances of public indifference or critical disdain for my father's work, a situation he acknowledged bluntly during the mid-sixties:

> Despite the honors that have come my way in the form of grants, fellowships, and awards, I have never been able to support my family solely from my writing. My books have never sold; and I am sharply aware that my work is seldom considered in critical evaluations of what is presumed best in contemporary American fiction. Nevertheless, on balance, when I consider the miseries of those of my fellow writers who have been treated more like movie stars than creative figures, and whose work has suffered correspondingly, I incline to the belief that my position is more fortunate than theirs. . . . I am concerned with pleasing myself, not with gratifying that vast and shapeless public which consumes not the work of novelists, but news

about them in slick magazines and gossip columns, as it does candy bars. I remain a social radical, too, at once dismayed and exhilarated by my seemingly doomed yet endlessly optimistic native land.

But if my father was distressed by his lack of commercial success, he certainly never voiced this concern to me; on the contrary, I was oblivious to the financial problems that so often characterize the life of a serious writer. As I grew up, the grants, fellowships, and awards bestowed upon my father—and the occasional sabbaticals he was able to take—led to prolonged and peripatetic stretches of time spent in a variety of homes. Over the years, "home" became something of a generic term to us, comprising Valley Cottage, a small town in Rockland County, New York; San Francisco; Iowa City; Cagnes-sur-Mer, a tiny medieval village nestled in the hills between Nice and Cannes; and finally, a white clapboard house high atop a Berkshire mountain ridge in Chesterfield, Massachusetts, the quiet New England town to which my parents moved just one year before my father's death.

Our three sojourns to Cagnes in the fifties and sixties were particularly happy times for my family. We were ensconced on the Mediterranean coast and surrounded by a new and very different set of friends and acquaintances—peasants and artists, American expatriates, Scandinavians, British aristocrats both current and fallen. But the culture shock, however mild, led to certain frictions. In particular, it wasn't an easy move for my mother, who had never been out of the country and spoke no French.

In "Year of Grace," a frightened and generally inexperienced small-town woman whose stuffy academic husband has transported her abroad during a year's sabbatical, discovers, unexpectedly and without a trace of vindictiveness, that there is more to her life than her connection to her husband. Predating the women's movement by more than a decade, this unstrident portrayal of self-discovery appears as valid today as it did twenty-five years ago. It seems perfectly apropos that it is followed by what might be considered its Gallic counterpart, "The Peacocks of Avignon." This brief but deeply moving piece tells the story of a young woman whose sorrow and resentment threaten to destroy her otherwise loving relationship with her mother, a widow desperate to make up for the loss of her husband—and her youth—by engaging in an affair with a man half her age. Alone in a foreign country, she discovers, in a sudden and profound moment of revelation, the meaning of forgiveness.

Although my family spent more than five years in Europe, it was the "seemingly doomed yet endlessly optimistic native land" to which my father always insisted we return. It was America—a country whose political and social mores served as the target for much of his disapprobation—for which he retained his greatest loyalty and deepest affection. It was here that he found his true voice—a voice that spoke out for the great American values, values he felt were all too often perilously ignored by his fellow citizens.

He was often ahead of his time. His 1959 essay in *Esquire*, "Why Resign from the Human Race?", provoked an unprecedented avalanche of mail and is generally acknowledged to have inspired the formation of the Peace Corps. His social concerns were no less apparent in his stories. For example, in "A Chance Encounter," the issue of abortion, possibly more controversial today than when the story was written, produces a surprising and most unexpected victim. Peopled almost exclusively by male characters, it is a subtle, shrewd, and thought-provoking argument for freedom of choice.

My father gracefully balanced the larger social and political concerns in his novels and essays with a tender humanism in his stories. The subject of poverty, for example, plays a devastating role in "A Question of Loneliness," in which an overburdened and underpaid young worker winds up paying dearly for his solitary attempt to rescue his wife from the dreariness of her domestic routine. The cost to him is a future of guilt and recrimination. Their story is sad and chilling.

"Nights in the Gardens of Brooklyn" also presents young people striving to ameliorate their lot in a difficult world, but it takes a far broader and more optimistic (albeit cynical) view of its impoverished group of protagonists. It is a brilliant and stirring novella which might well have served as the progenitor for his long novel, *Standing Fast*, published in 1970. The product of five years of work, the novel chronicles in painstaking detail the history of the American left between 1939 and 1963.

"Nights in the Gardens of Brooklyn," much like the later novel, examines people from a variety of social, political, and economic backgrounds whose lives intertwine. Their early ideals will inevitably and even brutally be compromised with the passage of time. The story will seem all the more touching and timely to a new generation of readers whose lives bridged the gap between the turbulent and idealistic sixties and the radically different—and markedly un-radical—eighties. Little has changed in our entry into the rat race; only the price has gone up. One of the most beautiful of all New York stories, "Nights in the Gardens of Brooklyn" remains a perfectly compressed portrait not only of the generation of young people struggling to find their way immediately following World War II, but also of what is arguably the world's most exciting city, so joyously described in the opening sentence as "my mother, my mistress, my Mecca."

Manhattan also serves as the setting for "The Dancer," a pioneering story whose finale was found, in the early fifties, to be so daring and controversial that no literary magazine would accept it for publication; its eventual inclusion in *discovery,* a paperback collection of new and often experimental fiction, earned it something of a cult status. An extraordinary, hallucinogenic tale that veers off in surprising and unexpected directions, it is filled with a series of bizarre, feverishly surreal images. The point of view is that of twenty-one-year-old Peter Chifley, who leaves his hometown of Elyria, Ohio, to pursue his dream of becoming a dancer. What happens to him upon his arrival in New York provides a truly horrifying portrait of innocence lost, and if Peter seems to be too good to be true, this may say more about the age in which we live than it does about our perceptions of him—an artist destroyed by a shattered dream.

It is no accident that there are more than a proportionate number of stories here about artists. My father's predilections were hardly limited to literature; his passion for music was particularly acute, and he surrounded himself by the sound of it all day. Highly disciplined, he rarely deviated from his routine of waking each morning at seven and getting to his typewriter by eight, even on weekends or holidays. At the same time, it was equally rare for him to work past five. He often relaxed with a late-afternoon Scotch and an attempt to stumble through a prelude or two on the piano. He was better at the flute. The frequent harp-and-flute duets my sister, Felice, played with him—which sometimes turned into trios if by good fortune my brother, Marco, joined them at the piano—brought out the best in my father. They are some of the loveliest (and frequently most hilarious) memories of my childhood.

Just as those ensembles were inspired by a musical give-and-take, so the crescendos and diminuendos of my father's people echo throughout the stories in this collection. We find those echoes in "The Man in the Toolhouse," when Harry the violinist is wooing Rita the harpist; in "A Glance in the Mirror," when rueful bandleader Roy Farrow finally gathers the courage to redress the grievances of his daughter, Kate, an aspiring cellist; in the friends and lovers of "Where Does Your Music Come From?", a beautiful and bittersweet remembrance of the evolution and dissipation of childhood friendships, the tentative stirrings of romance, and the tragedy of war. All are recorded here with the clarity and complexity of a prism hung in a sunlit window.

And then there are stories dealing with writers. It is always easier, I think, to reflect on careers in art other than your own, and if the characters in my father's belletristic gallery seem collectively tinged with the pain that is an inevitable part of the literary sensibility, they are also bathed in the warmth of his obvious affection and admiration for them. Long before I had decided on a writing career, for example, "The Hack" affected me profoundly as a particularly delicate and devastating morality tale. It is a writer's story of a writer's story of a writer's false stories, and its subject is the cost of artistic integrity, a lesson learned in an instant of unintentionally inflicted pain. Harold Banks, the hack of the title, is both hero and victim and one of my father's most vivid and memorable creations—a pathetic, chain-smoking raconteur who weaves not the fabric of life but merely fabrication. Not only the most unforgettable character ever met by Tommy, the story's young narrator, he becomes unforgettably one of ours too—a man at once tragic and noble.

"A Story for Teddy" has as its narrator a successful writer looking back on an early incident in his career—in this case his frustrated but well-intentioned passion for Teddy, a beautiful and innocent young woman from the Bronx. Years later, the narrator stands in a windy, empty parking lot, ruefully pondering the affair that was shattered in a single excoriating moment of misguided morality. His recollection stands in melancholic contrast to the soft and lingering image of the story's young lovers who are "yearning for everything but understanding nothing."

"The Man in the Toolhouse" was written at a time when my father found himself beckoned by Hollywood during his year as Visiting Professor at San Francisco State College. The overtures made to and rejected by him may well have served as the story's inspiration. This is a lacerating portrait of an unpublished but nonetheless self-assured writer whose long and determined struggle on the road to success proves a far greater source of continuing creative motivation than any of its subsequent rewards. A somber reflection on the potential hazards of selling out, "The Man in the Toolhouse" is my father's moral and professional tribute to his fictional hero, whose personal triumph is quite possibly the triumph of his creator's as well.

"My Coney Island Uncle" and "The Tree of Life" serve as a fitting conclusion to the collection. Delicately constructed, the two stories belong together, like a set of faded photographs found by accident. They trace, over a period of some thirty years, the touching and sentimental history of a young boy's love for his favorite uncle. It is a voyage from childhood to adulthood and back, at once magical and dismaying, as it gently but inexorably wends its way to a heartrending conclusion. Separately or together, these last two tales perfectly encapsulate my father's warmth and generosity of spirit. They bring to mind two sections from his first and last novels. In *Out Went the Candle,* he wrote:

> Even if some unimaginable disaster were to wipe forever from his memory the rare and beautiful moments of the past, the girls locked in his arms, the great cities of Europe opened to his senses, the books discovered and treasured, the ravishing music played for his own delight, the sudden revelations of humanity in simple people, there would still be with him forever, until the day he died, those other memories of mankind at the end of its rope. They were the core of his apple of knowledge, whose sharp almost unbearable taste would remain on his lips long after even the recollection of the fruit's flesh had faded.

And in *Celebration,* completed only days before my father's death, Samuel Lumen, the novel's ninety-year-old hero, writes in his diary:

> I used to think that the unique quality of great age lay in its beautiful challenge to refine, to purify, to discover simplicity. Now that suddenly I am terribly old, I have the uneasy feeling that I had been romanticizing, out of ignorance. Because nothing seems simple to me

now. Everything is complex, mysterious, impure, starting with my own motives and conduct . . .

These are not only the prescient visions of a man who seemed often to care more about others than he did about himself. They also serve, now, as a fitting set of prologues to the stories that follow. Where did my father's music come from? From the heart—written though it was on the shores of Panama, or in the fields of Provence, or the gardens of Brooklyn. It came from an age not long ago, and yet seemingly so distant, when messages were scrawled passionately on pieces of paper and slipped under the door; when luxury was synonymous with a cab ride on a rainy afternoon; and when music was listened to high on the steps of Lewisohn Stadium. It was another time. And just as the music of another era has the power to ignite a long-forgotten memory, to rekindle a feeling long since thought lost, so do these stories have the power to haunt, to bring tears, to astonish, and to delight.

Robin Swados
New York
June 1986

NIGHTS IN THE GARDENS OF BROOKLYN

There was a time when New York was everything to me: my mother, my mistress, my Mecca, when I could no more have wanted to live any place else than I could have conceived of myself as a daddy, disciplining my boy and dandling my daughter. I was young, the war (the one that ended in 1945, the only one that will ever be "the war" for people my age) was just over, and I was free.

I had graduated from college in 1943, a bad year for nostalgia or avowals of future reunions. And a bad year for me, because my older brother was killed in North Africa and my widowed father dropped dead four weeks before I got my degree, all alone. I said goodbye to my roommate, my best friend and almost-brother, Barney Meltzer, and entered the ready embrace of the United States Army. Then came several new varieties of education, including the unlearning of my undergraduate radical platitudes in Mississippi, England, Normandy. From there on I sweated it out, was frightened, shot, got shot at, was finally felled by shrapnel, and so acquired enough points to graduate from the army. I headed for New York City from Europe like a bee or a pigeon or a youth who knew what he knew and wanted, hungrily, to find out what he could do with it. It was so inconceivable that there could be any other place but New York to find out that I distinctly remember wondering, strolling the bright and unblasted streets, why it was that all the other American cities weren't depopulated now that their young people were free once again to get up and do as they pleased without governments or uniforms to stop them.

I had mustering-out money, all the time I could use, and the desire for a little more privacy than I was permitted in a Seventy-third Street rooming house. So I arose every morning at dawn to prowl, and one of these mornings I saw a lady putting out an Apartment to Let sign to start out her day on Remsen Street, in Brooklyn Heights. I went up the stoop, admired the two rooms and bath, was admired as a wounded ex-G.I., assured her that the absence of a kitchen was compensated for by the view of the scraggly garden below, paid my two months' security, and walked out smiling into the winter sunlight and through the line that was just forming to appeal for the apartment—my apartment, the key in my pocket.

It was only after you had found a place to live that you faced the questions of how to live and what to do for a living. A couple I knew gave up good music-teaching jobs in Oregon simply because an uncle in Manhattan wired that he was holding a three-room apartment for them. They came rushing back to the apartment and no jobs, they were weak with joy, and they threw a party that I didn't recover from for three days. That was what New York meant to us then.

I wasn't lonely, even though I lived alone and had almost no relatives. I drifted. One day I thought of being a movie actor or maybe director, and made inquiries about studying the medium on the G.I. Bill (I was sour on the idea of going back to college), another day I considered starting an avant-garde music magazine, and from time to time it occurred to me that it might be fun to become rich and patronize the arts in my leisure hours. What I needed was a stabilizer, but not something that would choke off the daydreams. After nosing around in search of work that would not be one big solemn lump of responsibility and commitment, I found it.

I got a job ringing doorbells for the Census Bureau, working out of the old Federal Building on Christopher Street, at the far west corner of Greenwich Village. I knew from the start that it was right for me, even though it involved interviewing strangers and asking them personal questions. The office atmosphere was relaxed, and all of the enumerators—with the exception of two dowdy, money-hungry housewives—were young veterans like me, mostly not looking to climb the civil service ladder but rather wanting a pay check while they thought about becoming poets, accountants, actors, even merchants. They were tall and cadaverous former first lieutenants, short, panting privates happily stuffed with momma's blintzes again, and nondescript ex-noncoms like me, still wearing out the remnants, khaki socks and undershirts, of government issue. It took a while to sort them out, longer than the few days of indoctrination and hero-sandwich lunches that we ate en masse, jammed in, laughing and quarreling, at the Italian grocery down the block.

Just as I was beginning to, I was given my portfolio and shipped out into "the field" (bureaucratic abstraction for meeting the human race face to face). So it was that I found myself swaying out to Coney Island on the BMT, staring anxiously up the parted thighs of squat, somber women opposite me, scared stiff of ringing my first doorbell.

To be honest, I can't remember the first. All too soon they tended to merge, to become anonymous: warm women in warm kitchens, cold men in cold hallways, friendly mouths, lonely eyes, suspicious hateful glares, little brown faces, broad black faces, narrow white faces. What I did learn was something of which the unimaginably monotonous years of enforced barracks existence had made me skeptical: the immense and unquenchable variety of human nature. After the early uncertain days, after I had hardened myself somewhat to rudeness and rebuff and, more important, to undecorated peacetime misery willingly displayed to my stranger's eyes, I looked forward to getting up each morning and going out into the streets. What would I find? Whom would I meet?

For one thing I met Pauline. Not, as perhaps I should have, on the wind-blown top of a double decker (although for a time they continued to make their majestic elephantine way, snout to tail, up Fifth Avenue, with me seated on the front bench swaying, as I shall never forget even when I am an old man, in the howdah high above the gilded scene like the richest rajah in the world). No, it was in the sooty Seventh Avenue subway, she with her briefcase, I with my portfolio.

She was deep in *Partisan Review*. That was what first caught my eye, that and her legs. The girls were wearing their skirts short—it was just before the New Look came in—and her nyloned knees, pressed firmly together as were her little feet in mahogany loafers, gleamed at the points as though they had been sculptured and burnished. I wanted to stroke them. That a girl with legs like that would be reading *Partisan!* Our eyes met once, briefly, as she glanced up impersonally at me hanging from the strap above her; I lacked the nerve to smile. But when a seat became vacant at her side I took it.

I peered. She was reading Isaac Rosenfeld's story "The Colony." I could smell her hair, brown and glossy as her moccasins, freshly washed and brushed to the alpaca collar of her gabardine storm coat. I breathed deeply, trying to screw up courage, I had no idea where I was, the car gradually emptied out, she was lovely, I remained desperately at her side until at last she arose, swaying to the squeal of the brakes as gracefully as Cleopatra on her barge, still apparently unaware of my presence, her index finger slipping between the pages of the magazine to mark her place. There was nothing else to do, I lurched after her as the double doors opened for us.

"What do you make of that Rosenfeld story?" I heard myself croaking in an unnatural voice.

For the second time, she glanced at me. Her face was rather broad and pale, quite Slavic, with prominent cheekbones and a small but proud nose the wings of which now dilated. If she walked away, I was cooked. If she replied coldly, I could at least keep on talking for a while. What she did, after an endless moment, was to smile.

We mounted the steep steps to the street. What was this? Nothing but black faces. One-hundred-and-tenth Street, yes; but not the Morningside Heights I had expected.

"What's the matter, don't you know where you are?"

"It's all your fault. But I don't care, if you hadn't gotten off here I'd have ridden out to the end of the line."

We had coffee in a White Tower filled with leather-jacketed Negro laborers. Her name was Pauline Friede, she was quite fresh out of college, and she worked as an investigator for the Department of Welfare. We couldn't stop talking, we had so much to say. I walked her slowly to her first client, and it took us ten minutes to say goodbye.

The next time we met, I kissed her in the subway, to commemorate our first encounter and salute our mutual courage. Ordinarily I hate that sort of thing, but now everything was fluttering and flying inside me, birds, balloons, pennants, all set loose. She flung her soft hair free from the collar of her coat, and the flesh of her arms inside the sleeves was warm and pulsing beneath my fingers.

Thank God I had the apartment. What did they do, young New

Yorkers in love and needing to be alone together? When I had been a soldier, or visiting as a student, it had been difficult enough, hunting for privacy with a girl—cruising the rainy streets in a taxi, clutching and moaning while the meter ticked away; grappling in the back row of a movie house, trying to work up the nerve to try a hotel; phoning from a United Cigar Store to plead for the loan of a friend's apartment, while the girl waited, wretched and frightened, at the chewing gum counter. With Pauline I couldn't have done those things.

Yet I would have had to do something. Pauline still lived with her parents and a high-school brother on Tremont Avenue in the Bronx. The brother was all right, he was still young enough to be awed by combat veterans, and her mother was actually rather sweet for a big woman, with an air of resigned defeat that invariably aroused in me a lively sense of guilt (she had a way of smiling shyly at me, as much as to say, Since you know that I know that you're sleeping with my daughter, maybe the knowledge will make you chivalrous and responsible). But her father, who ran a small men's-furnishings shop on Fordham Road and was still sweating out shortages (first of customers, now of white shirts), was virtually hump-backed, astigmatic in more ways than one, and monumentally opinionated. I wouldn't have minded so much if it wasn't that the opinions were invariably secondhand, borrowed from the columnists and commentators to whom he was addicted as other men are to girls or gambling. I used to have to listen, bored and needing other news and advice, to Gabriel Heatter, Lowell Thomas, Elmer Davis, Raymond Gram Swing, H. V. Kaltenborn, and Drew Pearson. At the end of the evening, when Pauline and I wanted most to be alone, there would be angry, incoherent letters to the editors of *Reader's Digest* and the *New York Post,* read by that indignant correspondent, Pauline's father, with fervor and sharp snaps of his dentures between sips of tea and swallows of spongecake.

Within two weeks after we had met, Pauline had a key to my apartment. Occasionally we would make primitive dinners there on a gas burner I had on top of the dresser. Invariably we would make love. And talk. Since it seemed impossible that there could ever come a time when we would have nothing left to say to one another, and since the warmth of my little Brooklyn Heights flat as we rocked in each other's arms was infinitely preferable to the clammy chill of the Woodlawn express rocketing us miserably to her parents' home at three o'clock in the morning, nothing was more logical than that we should get married as quickly as possible.

If Pauline had lived alone, if her family were in Cincinnati instead of the Bronx, then perhaps she would simply have moved in with me and we would have put off marriage for a while. But since we also hoped that there were no impediments to our love (Pauline had had a wartime romance, but when she learned by V-mail that her boy friend intended to marry an English WAAF before her pregnancy became too pronounced, she was not only not heartbroken, but enormously relieved), there was no impelling reason for us *not* to get married.

We were self-conscious about appearing corny and cocksure—that was strictly for the squares who had really hurried home to mom's cooking and the salesman-trainee's job, and to their steady girl friends, who had waited bravely for the wagon-wheeled development cottage. Besides, we were more than a little frightened, with good reason. I was too used to living alone or with men in a barracks (which came to the same thing), she was too used to living with her loving family. So our first months together were hard. Yet we stayed in love, a marvel in itself, and meanwhile, other things were happening.

For one thing, I found Barney again. When I went overseas he had apparently gotten my APO number fouled up. His last letter had informed me that he was getting his Master's in math, and maybe he could go all the way to his Ph.D. if I would go on fighting for him, and if his own draft board didn't catch up with him. Then silence.

Pauline and I had gone to the City Center to hear Bernstein conduct the New York City Symphony. We sat with the eager girls, the fans up in the second balcony, yelling "Lenny! Lenny!" as though they were at the Paramount. When we came downstairs at intermission and stepped out into the chill night air of Fifty-fifth Street for a smoke, there was Barney, a head taller than any of the chattering young fairies or serious young couples around him. He hadn't changed at all. His black eyebrows still grew together over that nose like a knife, a little Between the Acts cigar still stuck out between those thin lips.

We caught sight of each other at the same instant, and lunged forward through the crowd that separated us. Then we were embracing, and laughing with sheer delight that the war had not conquered our friendship.

"I knew it," I said happily. "I told Pauline that if I'd go to enough concerts, I'd find you."

"Stop!" he commanded. "Halt! Let's get organized. Meet my girl, while I meet yours. This is Cordelia Spencer."

She looked very fine, the girl he produced as if he were drawing her from his raglan-sleeved topcoat. Tall herself, almost my height, she half-concealed her very blonde straight hair, which she wore long (although long hair hadn't quite come in yet), beneath a wispy silk scarf looped over her head, around her throat, and over her left shoulder. Young, but expensive-looking and enormously self-possessed.

"My roommate, my conscience," Barney was explaining to her as I took her gloved hand. "Always after me about matters political."

"I'm still ahead of you, Barney. Pauline and I are married."

"Dog!" Barney cried. "Dog! Without asking for my approval? But such luck! I don't suppose he told you, Pauline, that he was drummed out of Omicron Nu for cheating at solitaire. Or that he joined the army after he was jilted by a Siamese."

"I am trying to make it up to him," Pauline murmured modestly.

"For that a kiss, even if I wasn't invited to the wedding. Pucker up, Pauline."

He kissed her good, too, in all that crush, and didn't stop until, with everyone around us watching and laughing, Cordelia plucked him by the arm. "Hey, you never treat me like that."

"You're not married."

We were reluctant to separate, even for an hour. Impatiently we sat through the second half, and then went together around the corner to the Russian Tearoom, where we caught up on the years of separation over tea and baklava. We were rewarded for our extravagance: Marian Anderson sat regally with S. Hurok only two tables away from us.

From then on we four were together more evenings than not, and usually on week ends too. Often there would be others—William Jennings Bryan Oberholser (we called him Peerless Willie), who was getting his Ph.D. at Columbia in history, taught at Brooklyn College, and turned up with an infinite variety of girls, of all shapes and sizes; a clever young couple name of DeFee, designer and interior decorator respectively, friends of Deelie's; a reckless cousin of mine called Zack, who was writing a war novel about the South Pacific, where he had led several let's-go-home demonstrations. But we four were the nucleus, or we considered ourselves as such, which was what mattered; for we were the ones who made the big decisions on eating, playgoing, parties, and most important, whom we would invite on our outings.

I have the photos yet of Barney and me in slapstick Abbott and Costello poses, of Pauline and Deelie with their arms linked, of Peerless Willie muzzling a babe in the course of a picnic at Fort Tryon Park when we tramped through the Cloisters and hung from the palisades over the Hudson. I cherish too the snapshot Barney took of me, with Pauline and Deelie on either arm, at the bow of the old One-hundred-and-twenty-fifth Street ferry, trying to look like a New Jersey Viking, but doubled over with laughter. What were we laughing at? I don't remember, we laughed easily and often. And there is a red rectangular folder with eight serrated snapshots, memento of one Sunday when we walked across the Brooklyn Bridge. It started with late breakfast at our place on Remsen Street; then around noon we'd meander over the little Penny Bridge at the foot of Montague Street and on through the broken-down bars and vague-eyed derelicts of Myrtle Avenue and Sands Street (all gone now, replaced by handsome characterless courthouses and office buildings), on to the great bridge. So there are pictures of Barney and me cavorting, of Deelie and Pauline strolling like models on the promenade, of us all lined up before the struts with the marvelous skyline and the springtime sun behind us, our faces half in shadow but leaning forward to the camera's eye in hope and expectation.

But I have no pictures of Barney at work in the North Jersey research lab that was deferring him, of Deelie trying to make it on the Broadway stage without seeming eager or obvious, of the inner texture of Pauline's life and mine.

This last was what was most extraordinary about all our days. Beyond the bickering over my enforced Friday evening visits to the Friedes, where I would sit, a miserable captive of my father-in-law's complaints and commentators, and our slow, almost imperceptible adjustment to each other's private rhythm, we discovered that our work and our play, our jobs and our personalities, came to complement each other so well that we were almost frightened by our happiness.

As the weeks went by and we grew more confident about our jobs, we tried to gain some control over where we would be sent. I could usually switch with several enumerators, if not Dante Brunini, a sharp young Italian actor with a game leg, then Herman Appleman, a ruddy-cheeked ex-paratrooper bucking for a G.I. loan to go into the photographic supply business. With their cooperation I worked out my field schedule so that I could see New York as few people had seen it before or ever will again; and I was able not only to meet Pauline at the end of the day, but sometimes to set off with her in the morning, and often to go with her in the evening after supper while she visited a family or I caught up with some of those in my sample who were out during the day.

So Pauline and I would meet on the streets of the city as we had first found each other below the ground. Briefcases in hand, we would hasten off together to dinner through the twilight of Red Hook, Ridgewood, or East Harlem; and after we had eaten, I would drowse at a bar over television (still a barroom novelty) while Pauline, her heart aching, would be struggling with the problems of bewildered refugees afflicted with cancer and layoffs. If I was the one who had to work, Pauline would read Mary McCarthy in a cafeteria while I mounted the steps and soared in the elevators to enter for a moment the worlds of the New Yorkers of all kinds who opened their doors to me.

They were becoming a very intimate part of my life, these citizens whom I would visit, pad in hand, to inquire whether there had been a change from one month to the next in the household, job status, hours worked, income earned.

An old Italian lady of Bay Ridge with a hairy chin and a blinking smile, who forced jelly beans on me while she answered my questions and continued to work at the kitchen table, wedging bobby pins onto cardboards for the neighborhood notions store.

A youngish woman of the rooming-house type with fine legs and hair dyed the color of newly minted pennies, who always opened her door furtively to me, as though I were a secret lover. After the first few monthly visits, I was just as furtive, because her husband, a slippered, scant-haired crank with a bitter eye and mouth, both pulled down at one corner by a stroke, would invariably kick me out if he heard my voice. "So it's Henry Wallace's stooge again." Useless for me to explain that Wallace was not my boss. "Go on, get out of here. There's no law says we have to answer."

A wholesale diamond merchant in a sunken living room in River House, rising every month to greet me punctiliously across half an acre of Baluchistan carpeting, and to offer me a glass of port while he told me politely of his job status.

A Jewish FBI agent, self-satisfied but wary, who always took me confidentially into his kitchenette to explain that it was a state secret, he couldn't even estimate how many hours he had worked, and that he was always just a phone call away from hardship and hazard. He grew morally outraged, agitatedly fingering his little moustache, when I finally ventured to suggest that it sounded like an ideal job, no questions askable, for a husband who wanted to play around.

A suave importer of Parisian negligees who refused to answer my questions but instead questioned me about my education, my army record, my ambitions, and finally offered me a job at his Fifth Avenue salon with, he assured me, an unlimited future.

This one Pauline laughed about. It was funnier than the pathos she had to live with in her own work. "Imagine somebody asking you what you do, and you saying, I'm in ladies' underwear!" That wasn't the only reason, though. It was more that we couldn't imagine ourselves doing anything else but what we were, or living any place on earth but in New York—and the importer had thrown out as bait that if I came to work for him he would be sending me to Paris on occasion. Paris? I had had my bellyful of Europe, and it was only afterwards, years later, when Pauline and I began to dream of traveling abroad, that we bethought ourselves of the negligee importer, and began to wonder what it would have been like, living in Paris during those years . . .

It was bitter for Pauline, a soft and gentle girl, to meet misery every day; clever and attractive as she was, Deelie hadn't yet found herself, as the saying went (nor had I, for that matter); and Barney was marking time until he could be released to pick up his career. Nevertheless our lives were good. The very air smelled of freedom and hope. What more can you want?

Barney lived at home with his parents in Flatbush, but Deelie had inherited a tiny little place in the Village, on Gay Street, from a friend who had given up the theatre for marriage and Long Island. When the four of us were together in that dark, narrow little alcove it was jammed, but it was a place to go, and I think Deelie and Barney were happy there.

They used often to meet us in Brooklyn Heights, since our place was more or less midway between Flatbush and the Village. Not just for

Sunday breakfast and the walk across the Bridge, but in the evenings too. Deelie would curl up catlike on the studio couch, purring and sleek in her stockinged feet, awaiting the arrival of Barney, his pockets loaded with delicacies lifted from the fancy goods counters of Gristede's and Esposito's. We divided the labor equitably: Barney the burglar earned relaxation with *PM*, while Deelie set the card table, Pauline opened the mulligatawny soup and heated it on the burner, and I worked the coloring agent into a bowl of white margarine. Throughout these unbalanced meals, the anchovies, smoked oysters, and Argentine ham augmented by a Mason jar full of chopped herring from Barney's mother or a bowl of jelly cookies baked by Pauline's mother, we argued politics and hashed over the day's doings.

Deelie had a three-day job at a private gallery, mostly cataloguing and mailing out announcements, and she filled the week with volunteer work for a ladies' organization that did good deeds for wounded veterans. There was neither money in one nor satisfaction in the other, but Deelie's people in Greenwich had money anyway, and she took her pleasure from Barney, his quick mind and cutting humor, and from her theatrical expectations. If she didn't make it in the theatre she was bound to make it somewhere. She was good-looking and had an elegant figure; and even if for me she was not sexy, not as Pauline was, with her brooding eyes and those nostrils which flared as her passion mounted, yet she was undeniably desirable, smelling as she did of money and challenging all men with her self-assurance. She had gone for a while to Bradford Junior College and then to Bennington College; the traditional upper-class upbringing, overlaid with a patina of avant-garde ambition, was captivating to Barney, whose experience hadn't ranged, to my knowledge, much beyond flat-heeled girl radicals and harpsichord players. Deelie was fun. She was also anxious not only to be one of us but to be good to us. And she was, in many little ways: she passed on to Pauline "extra" cashmere sweater sets given her by spinster aunts; she gave us theatre tickets, which she insisted she had gotten for nothing; and one memorable week end she hauled us off in her cousin's jeep to his wonderfully isolated and comfortable summer place out at Southampton.

Pauline and I used to lie in bed and talk about why Barney and Cordelia didn't run off and get married. When you're young and married, you find it hard to imagine that there can be others willing simply to say good night and go their separate ways. Barney didn't seem eager to discuss it, not as we would have done in our undergraduate days, but the way Pauline had it from Deelie, neither was quite sure of the other—or of their families, neither of whom would have known what to make of the other or in fact would have wanted to have anything to do with the other. So for the time they were simply having a love affair and enjoying it.

When we spent our evenings on Remsen Street, Barney and I playing the Bach double concerto or the Telemann two-violin sonatas while the girls knitted and gossiped, everything was as it had been when we were rooming together. We both played badly, but it was a communion that completed the day.

But it was different when we went out. And how sharply I remember the casual restaurant discussions, as we admired the Chock Full O'Nuts girls assembling cream cheese sandwiches with knife and fork, or chewed pastrami deep in the swaying forest of suspended salamis at Katz's delicatessen—maybe because later eating out was to become an occasion of state like going to the theatre, and the axis of your life turned inward, so that at mealtime you argued only with yourself, or, your mouth full of food and your head tired, with your other self, your wife. When we went out Barney was more frank than he was in my own little apartment.

There was an evening in Joe's Restaurant (gone now to make room for more faceless Brooklyn buildings and boulevards), with its white-tiled walls, slowly swinging fans like horizontal windmills and slow-moving black-jacketed waiters who looked as though they had been carrying platters of pigs' knuckles since Theodore Dreiser's youth. Barney and I sat carving lamb fries and explaining to the girls' shivery delight what it was that we were eating with such relish. Larry MacPhail and some of the lesser Brooklyn Dodgers, whose offices were around the corner, were talking baseball at the next table, and under the cover of their voices Barney suddenly turned to me, apropos of nothing. "How long can it go on?"

"What do you mean?"

"Don't you feel sometimes that it's all too good to be true? That we haven't earned this?" He waved his arm negligently.

"No, I don't." The unexpectedness of it made me a little aggressive. "I spent three stinking years in the army, mostly with people I didn't like.

Now I spend my time the way I want, and I don't feel one damn bit guilty about it."

Barney pressed it no further than to comment, "I didn't mean it that way, about feeling guilty. Certainly not in your case. Me, I stayed home and dodged the draft."

But another evening, half a dozen of us were having supper in the Sokol Hall on Seventy-first Street, spooning up our dumplings and chicken soup under President Masaryk's watchful eye, while the athletes leaped up and down thunderously in the gymnasium beyond the wall. In the middle of the heavy food and an argument about Palestine, I felt Barney's bony fingers pressing my knee.

"You remember what I said that night in Joe's?"

I knew what he meant.

"I wasn't thinking about fighting Bevin in Palestine, or even that the food sticks in my throat because the DP's are hungry. That was your pitch in college, and you never sold me. But now that the war is over for most of us, and we want to live it up, I feel uneasy. Have we really earned it, the whole country?"

I was a little embarrassed. I was the one, not Barney, who had been involved at college in left-wing politics; I had been only slowly and painfully disabused of my more adolescent ideals during the war years. So I should have been the one to feel that we were all in a fool's paradise. But I didn't. For one thing, I was happy as he really wasn't, even though I hadn't yet made a long-term work commitment and he was earning almost exactly three times as much as I, at work in his own field. The war was over, but the draft lingered on; and Barney had been forced to break off his graduate studies (no longer reason for deferment) and take up a military research job he didn't want, to stay out of the army. There were moments, I knew, when he was tempted to say the hell with it and sign up as a drunken conqueror in Tokyo or Berlin; but then there was the hope that the draft would die and he would be able to return to graduate school. Besides, there was Deelie.

She was sitting and laughing, not listening to us, between Pauline and Dante Brunini, whom I had brought along despite the fact that he was not one of us. Dante had done me favors on occasion, and even though he wasn't their kind of intellectual, the others did find him amusing.

In fact he dominated the table, different from us in that he was more determined, more insistent, less polite about his ambitions than we could afford to be about ours. If for Deelie the theatre was a game, or a dream, for Dante it was so practical that even the most glamorous clowns and tragedians, Chaplin, Lunt, Olivier, members of a pantheon awesome even while arguable, were to Dante no more than guys who had gotten there before him.

Nothing awed Dante. I looked at him, entertaining us with his version of Jules Munshin in *Call Me Mister*. His eyes, black as currants, snapped in the lamplight, his voice was resonant and happily husky, his hands were shapely as they sped through the air, he battered us with his self-assurance and the confidence that he would one day be paid to do what he was doing now for fun, to ingratiate himself with his new friends. The fact that for us highbrows theatre meant Copeau and Brecht and Pirandello, while for him it meant auditions, Equity, and New Haven, neither daunted nor amused him. It was just a fact, among all the others that he faced every day; and if there was anything to be gotten from mixing with us, he was out to get it.

But if Dante was sure of what he could do, I knew what he *couldn't* do—understand the compunctions that were troubling Barney. There was no point in my interrupting him to argue with Barney, much less in my using him as an example of the very thing that bothered my friend. Whatever I said in direct response to Barney would not only bring Deelie's head up, it would alert everyone at the table to a malaise that maybe, if it was only a passing mood, I had no right to underline at this time and among these people.

So I let it ride. In the weeks that followed Barney didn't bring it up again. We took Pauline and Deelie swimming in the St. George pool, and to hiss Clark Gable (Gable's Back and Garson's Got Him!) from the balcony of the Greenwich Theatre. We rented rowboats in Central Park, and bicycles in Prospect Park, and cycled through the gardens and greenery of Brooklyn all the way out Ocean Parkway to Coney Island. We met dutifully at the New School to hear Meyer Schapiro lecture on Picasso. We even dragged the girls to Ebbets Field, once the season had started, so that Barney could show off his indomitable hero, Pistol Pete Reiser. During all this time that we had fun, we were so far from the matter of Barney's winter uneasiness that Pauline and I never thought to discuss it alone together.

We talked about other matters, including—as we felt surer of each other—having a baby. I played bold, but the idea frightened me beyond words, for I thought of myself, socially and in relation to my family, as the last of a line rather than the progenitor of a new one, but this I couldn't say to Pauline for fear that she would misunderstand . . . We talked too about Deelie, whom we both enjoyed, Pauline somewhat more than I. Which was unusual, because Deelie's poise and self-assurance were qualities that seldom endear one woman to another. But Pauline knew that Deelie could never pose any threat to her. Not with me. The whole business of sizing up other women as sexual possibilities simply wasn't occurring to me at that time. In consequence I could be, and often was, more objective about girls than Pauline. Deelie was a surprisingly good mimic, with an eye for little surface mannerisms. She could for example do a sharp take-off of Peerless Willie coming to a party with a new girl on his arm. And yet she didn't really understand, or care, why Willie had to have so many different girls, or what kind of person he was beneath the boulevardier manner. That was what made me a little uncomfortable.

During the spring she did catch on as understudy to an ingénue, but we had barely prayed for the ingénue to develop laryngitis when the show folded. By June, Deelie had taken a leave from her gallery job in order to go into summer stock up on the Cape. Barney had a couple of weeks' vacation due him, and was going to take two more weeks unpaid in order to be with Deelie at Provincetown.

Pauline and I couldn't afford to go away, nor were we entitled to substantial vacations, and the summer was hot—but in New York you expect that, and anyway we didn't care. After supper we'd play tennis at the private courts (gone now too) around the corner on Henry Street, and week ends we fought our way out to Brighton for a romp in the surf and a few square feet of hot sand. There we would lie, taking turns using each other for a pillow, and daydreaming of the future.

I had to begin thinking, no matter how reluctantly, of what would follow the Census Bureau, not only because Pauline was getting serious about a baby, but also because I had been brought up to consider it irresponsible, if not downright immoral, to have fun at what you did for a living (I think Barney had this streak in him too). Well, we battled around crazy schemes of sailing for a South American pampas and raising our unconceived son as a Latin cowboy, or settling in Thailand simply because it looked good on the exquisite cards that a Siamese classmate sent me from its canal-veined capital. If I had to give up my fun and make money, I didn't want—for obscure reasons—to do it in New York.

As the summer weeks drifted by, we saw more of Dante Brunini. Barney was away, so was Peerless Willie, and increasingly Dante attached himself to us, although we weren't quite sure why.

Dante loved to talk about himself, like most actors, but he did it very engagingly. He wasn't at all bitter—I know I would have been—at having been turned down by Yale Drama School when he tried to enroll with a bum leg. He had interrupted his acting studies to go into the navy, but was back within seventeen months, after a falling sling caught him in the hold of a navy cargo ship in Naples harbor and smashed his hip, leaving one leg shorter than the other. He betook himself to Stella Adler and to a neighborhood theatre in his own back yard, between Little Italy and Chinatown. Short leg aside, he had the equipment of a matinee idol: self-confidence coupled with an easy peasant masculinity; a compact, vigorous frame; and a classical head, capped with tight wiry curls. All he needed was brains.

But he was smart enough to see that the Census Bureau job would free him, if he arranged his time right, for auditions or rehearsals. He lived at home on Thompson Street with the old folks. "I've got time, kids," he'd say in the rich baritone from which he had carefully filtered the New York accent. "When I make it I'll move uptown. Right now I need money in my jeans." Apparently the money went on clothes. He was the sharpest man in the Federal Building, and the only one of our crowd who knew enough to wear a knit tie with a plaid shirt.

It was Dante who insisted that we all come on over to his old neighborhood for the Festival of San Gennaro. Summer was just ending, Barney was getting ready to sign up for an evening course at Columbia, Deelie had gone back to the gallery, Peerless Willie was actually engaged, and this was to be a big blow-out.

I don't remember us as individuals particularly, but I know we filled the sidewalk on Houston Street, arms linked and singing "O Sole Mio." I think it was the last evening all of us were together in one group.

It was a glorious evening. The air was mild, yet suffused with the expectant almost theatrical hush that precedes the change of seasons. At the very beginning of the fiesta, bulbs were draped across Mulberry Street, from one side to the other, like half-raised curtains. Thereafter, at short intervals and receding into the twilight for perhaps a dozen blocks, glowing clusters of bulbs illuminated the carless street and served as a brilliant archway for the throng that pressed, laughing, from curb to curb as darkness descended above.

It was as noisy as Naples, as buoyant as Bordighera. The sidewalks were banked with stands, some canopied, some open to the night air, many displaying food, a few, toys and novelties, and others games of chance with decanters of rye and cellophane-wrapped mama dolls as prizes.

"Bellyache, here I come!" Barney elbowed his way to a three-foot-deep vat at the gutter's edge. The vat rested on a red-hot charcoal grate; oil bubbled and then sizzled in it as the shirt-sleeved boy who tended it dropped in little puffballs of raw dough and fished out those which floated up, swollen and crisp. Barney bought a sackful, sprinkled with powdered sugar, and we moved on, already loaded down with pistachio nuts and nougat bars, to the clam bar where Peerless Willie was squirting lemon juice over a plate of newly opened clams while his bride-to-be solicitously tucked a paper napkin into his collar.

"Those are for me," Barney announced, his mouth still stuck with pastry. "Clams! If I'd known, I wouldn't have bought this stuff. Here," he turned on Deelie, "you take these things while I get outside some clams."

"I can't bear to watch."

"Me either," Pauline said. "It makes everything come up inside me." They took arms and pressed on through the crowd.

Dante threw back his head and laughed, showing his fine white teeth. "Man, we haven't even started yet." He gestured forward with his thumb.

Just ahead, clouds of smoke billowed into the night air, obscuring the stand from which they arose. Skewers of beef and pork tripe were burning ferociously, spitting and sizzling at the heart of the smoke as white-aproned ladies labored to stuff them into foot-long hero sandwiches with tomatoes and onions and green peppers. Navel-high kids darted in and out, faces sticky with the red remnants of apple suckers, threatening us with paper snakes on sticks and wooden clapper noisemakers. There were kiddy rides for them, little city-size merry-go-rounds mounted on the backs of trucks, and in an empty lot a brilliantly lit Ferris wheel, slowly revolving in the September sky and then stopping so that the couples dangling in the boxes at the top of the swaying circle could shriek and plead to be lowered. Pop music burst from a parked sound truck, fighting with the older tinnier noises of the merry-go-round. The high-school kids moved like mercury, joining and breaking, snapping their fingers and singing as they danced, surging from street to sidewalk and back again.

By shoving and calling to each other, we managed to foregather on the corner of Broome Street—I think there were seven of us—and we had no sooner formed our own circle, exchanging swallows of scungilli, spumone, anguilla, wine from wicker bottles, and God knows what else, than we were squashed together, to one side, to permit a sacred procession, bearing the holy ikons, to pass on its way to the church. The air was alive with burning and chanting and the cries of children and the high yipping of running mongrel dogs. Flames from the braziers, followed by showers of sparks, shot into the sky and the air was thick with the smell of burning meat and frying dough as we all tumbled hand in hand after the procession.

"I should have brought Dottie," Dante yelled in my ear. "She would have enjoyed it."

"Dottie?" Pauline broke her stride. It was the first time we'd ever heard him mention a girl's name. "Who's she?"

"Dottie," Dante repeated a little impatiently. "You know, my wife. Maybe I'll take her another night."

"What are you talking about?" I demanded. "You never said you had a wife."

We had reached the face of the church, garlanded with twelve-foot-high masses of flowers, white, green, and red, in the shape of a heart. As we stared, the faithful fought to push dollar bills into the hearts of the flowers, from which they protruded like crisp speckled leaves. It was a sight to carry with you forever, those struggling hands beseeching for love and forgiveness with the bills.

Willie and his fiancée were ahead of us, gaping in fascination at the lilies and the carnations, the leaves and the money. I was sure that they had not heard Dante. But I was not so sure about big-eared Barney and Deelie, who was hanging on his arm, a little tired now but stunned by the scene. What struck me was that if they had—and it seemed to me that they must have—neither of them seemed nearly as surprised as Pauline and I. Was I simply naïve?

"It's no secret," Dante replied to me, stepping on a cigarette end, his head lowered. Then he looked at me. "She's old-fashioned, the European type. She'd rather stay home with my mother and mind the baby."

"Baby?"

Now I was sure of it. Deelie had overheard it all. She paused before us, not bothering to conceal the fact that she was listening—no, more than listening, attending to him as though she had never before really seen him —not in surprise but in fascination, her head cocked to one side, appraising.

"We've got a four-month-old daughter. I married Dottie in the old country, I met her in Naples. She doesn't know much English yet. That's another reason she's bashful. You mean I never told you?"

I said something, but my reply must have been drowned out in the sudden burst of noise from a bandstand down the block. A group of seven men, some in oddments of uniform—the trumpeter with a braided cap and jacket, a fiddler with striped trousers of the same blue—and the rest in mufti, had gone to work, without tuning up, on "Come Back to Sorrento." As all of us stood gazing up at the musicians in the drifting garbage of beer cans, slimy stubs of mustard-smeared frankfurters, oozing tortoni cups, blackened bits of popcorn, burst paper bags and candy wrappers, a chesty little man with a pomaded pompadour and a determined scowl came forward and began to sing. With left hand, all but the thumb, jammed into his jacket pocket, and right arm extended to implore the heavens, he bellowed his ardent plea. The microphone before his lips squealed in protest.

Barney leaned over to me, his eyes gleaming. "Break down, sourpuss. Admit you're having fun, you retired world-saver."

"Wait a minute," I replied, half-laughing, half-annoyed. "You were the one, just the other—" But then I felt Pauline pulling ever so slightly at my arm, and I stopped. She was more sensitive than I. Barney was happy, and there was no sense in my spoiling things.

After two ballads we moved on in the wake of Willie and his fiancée. Suddenly I realized that the street was coming alive, for blocks, with the same noise from dozens of portable radios, some sitting on the curb, some wobbling on plank counters and plugged into the sockets of the haphazard overhead wiring, some perched on the window sills of the tenements that went up story after story into the night. They were all tuned to the broadcast of the Graziano-Zale fight.

I don't remember which of their three fights it was—it doesn't make any difference, they were all good—but the whole neighborhood was for Rocky Graziano, the crowds shoving good-naturedly the width of the street, the busy women cooking and the men in their undershirts deep-frying, the kids running loose, the old folks leaning out the windows. Tony Zale was well liked, but Rocky was their boy. We followed the mounting roar from radio to radio, stand to stand, block to block.

The tension was infectious, particularly for Dante. Cutting in front of us in the littered street, he began to bob and weave before Barney, his trousers tangled with red and purple streamers.

"Come on, boy," he challenged, "you be Tony, I'll be Rocky."

Barney was a little embarrassed. He was still gay, but not quite sure of what he ought to do. He jabbed out tentatively, defensively, with a stiff left arm. "Don't pick on me," he said. "I never had a lesson in my life."

"I'll give you some lessons, Tony!" Dante cried, dancing forward. "Watch for my counter punch!"

"Let him have it, Rock!" A gang of kids, bored with each other, had already ringed Dante and Barney and the rest of us, and made our progress more difficult. "Give him the old one-two!"

Encouraged by the sudden support of new fans, Dante squirmed up and down, trying to move in rhythm to the announcer's shrill recital of Graziano's lefts and rights to Zale's head and body. But his game leg was giving him trouble, although he tried to ignore it. Barney, sensing this, could not proclaim its obviousness by refusing to horse around with Dante. So he continued to respond with a halfhearted flailing of his long thin arms. Dante stumbled, perhaps because the kids, yelling encouragement, were now so close at his back, and fell into the path of one of Barney's sweeping gestures. The open hand caught him across the side of the cheek, reddening it, and seemed momentarily to make him really angry. Ducking low, he bored in fast, his weight on his good left leg, and threw his clenched left fist full force at Barney's belly.

"Hey!" I shouted, but too late, and besides it was already over.

Barney stood gasping for breath, astonished and speechless with pain and surprise. Dante was sucking the blood from his knuckles which he had bruised against Barney's belt buckle. "Sorry, old bean," he said, pummeling Barney lightly, carefully, on the back with his right hand. "Got carried away by the drama of it. Didn't hurt you, did I?"

It took Barney a while to get his breath back. The rest of us stood around foolishly, making foolish talk, lighting cigarettes, making plans to go home. At last he said, "You play too hard. But I'll survive."

It was three days before I saw Barney again. We met in the bar of the old Murray Hill Hotel, soon to be torn down. I had been down on the Lower East Side, hunting for an old lady in a tenement off Avenue C. When I got to the building, I was sure they'd made a mistake in the office. The whole block was being demolished, and everything had been leveled on either side of the tenement, right down to some rubble on the ground so that as you approached the building you could see the scars of the walls that were no longer there. It reminded me of a bombed-out London block.

Almost all the flats inside were empty, padlocked or boarded up. In fact there was a condemned sign in the front hall. The hallway toilets, one to a floor, reeked of lye and urine. Two or three of the tenants still remained, probably because the city hadn't yet found rooms for them. One of them turned out to be my quarry, a squat, somber, dignified old woman in carpet slippers and an immaculate housedress, on the third floor rear. She was quite alone.

There had been a son and daughter, but she had survived them both. Now she was on welfare, holed up in an old kitchen, seated at the table in the gloom with the teakettle bubbling away on the chipped old stove. I felt as though I were in a place that was going to last forever. I had some difficulty with the interview, since she knew little English, and I could hardly understand her Yiddish. But it didn't seem to make much difference, we took our time, she shuffled back and forth across the kitchen, getting her glasses, steeping the tea, showing me her second papers.

It was strange how, despite the closeness of the atmosphere in the antiquated, overheated flat, and the homeliness of the old lady, I had been reluctant to leave. I was mulling this over as I arrived at the Murray Hill bar, which was a dark splendid old place, with much mahogany paneling and elderly, well-nourished gentlemen chatting in quiet well-modulated voices. It made me feel substantial and of some importance to drink there; I can't say the same for those Manhattan bars which feature (Nitely) a young lady playing an electric organ and cater to amorous couples indulging in public foreplay.

Barney looked abstracted. I wondered, as I joined him and gave my order, whether he was still brooding over Dante Bruinini.

"Say," I said, "wasn't that whole business with Dante crazy the other night? And that bit about his having a wife and kid . . ."

Barney hardly seemed to have heard me. "You want to know something? I've been locked out of my job."

"Locked out?" I stared at him. "What does that mean?"

"I went in yesterday and found my desk locked. I thought it was a practical joke. The office manager said he didn't know a thing about it, so I went in to see McKenna, the project leader. You know, my boss."

My stomach felt queer. "Go on, go ahead."

"Mac was sorry and all that, but word had come through. No more access to classified material. Everything we work on is classified, for God's sake."

"Does that mean you're fired?"

"When I asked that question Mac began to sweat. He babbled about my valuable services to the lab. He said they have no intention of severing me. Sounds like decapitation, severing."

"Still, as long as they don't decapitate."

"But they have. I'm off the payroll until I clear it up. What it comes down to is, they got the word to dump me. They just don't want me to blame them for it."

"But why? Who gave them the word?"

"They don't say. Maybe the navy. I've got a date tomorrow with some commander down on Church Street."

"Maybe he'll clear it up."

Barney laughed briefly. "You were the one that used to say I was naïve. Even if I insist it's all a mistake, did you ever catch an officer and a gentleman admitting a mistake?"

"But if you can prove it—"

"What in hell is there to prove? Or disprove? That I've been sleeping with Deelie? That ought to give me ten merit points—her old man belongs to Hasty Pudding and Racquet and Squash and was a charter member of America First." Barney started to bite his nails.

"Here, eat peanuts instead." I pushed the bowl at him. "Maybe it's your cousins in Russia, the engineers."

"But I don't know them from the Smith Brothers. Even poor Mama, who's been writing all these years to Odessa, never gets an answer nowadays."

"What was okay all these years isn't okay any more. In case you hadn't heard, our glorious ally . . ." A thought struck me. I grasped him by the arm. "Wait. Maybe it's me."

Barney did not look surprised. He didn't look at me, either. He pushed a half-peanut jaggedly across the bar. With his head down he replied, "I thought of that too."

"In that case it's simple."

"Sure, I'll tell the commander that I never heard of you. Or that when you asked me to pass out leaflets in college, I thought they were ads for a beauty parlor."

"I'll go with you. I'll tell them I could never get you interested in politics. Which is the truth. And that—"

"No good. You can't go around confessing to something you haven't been accused of. My dear fellow, they'll say, we didn't have you in mind at all. Then what?"

"I suppose you're right."

"What's more, you'd only get yourself in hot water. You're working for the government, remember? It isn't much of a job, but why lose it? Besides, it wouldn't look good on your record."

"They wouldn't—" I started to say, Fire me, and then I thought, why wouldn't they? Of course they would. And chasms opened before me.

This was just before the great inquisitions. We had had no experience with anything like it; we had nothing to go by, not even the knowledge that there were others in the same trouble.

"What will you do?" I asked.

"See if the navy will tell me what they've got against me. If I can square it I'll dig up another job before they draft me. I'll never go back to McKenna and those bastards again, that's for sure."

I started casting around in my mind for something with which to distract Barney. It occurred to me that he might be entertained by the odd hour I had just spent with the old lady down on the Lower East Side, so I told him about it.

He listened politely, no more, and I was about to wind it up and try something else when he lifted his hand.

"Wait. What did you say her name was?"

"Marya something or other."

"We used to have a Cousin Marya in our family. You don't suppose
. . .Was there a daughter named Thelma?"

"There was a daughter, but I don't know the name. Anyway she's
dead."

"I bet she's my mother's cousin." Barney gazed at me speculatively.
"What a funny world. I would have thought she was dead and gone long
ago."

"Who was dead and gone?"

It was Deelie. She and Pauline had slipped up behind us without our
becoming aware of them. I had to recapitulate the whole story for them.

"How quaint!" Deelie cried. "Imagine it, the poor old soul!"

She drew from me all the details of my interview with Cousin Marya,
the lonely survivor of a condemned building: the empty flats, the strangely
echoing stairs, the half-deaf old lady, half-crippled by lumbago and
sciatica, insisting on serving me a glass of tea and rye bread with *povidl*
while I confused her with my questions.

"Rye bread with what?"

"It's a kind of plum jam."

"Oh Barney," she pleaded, "Let's go see her."

"Nuts to that. I don't even know that she's the same one. And even
if she was, then what? I wouldn't know her, she wouldn't know me."

"But—"

"Anyway, if she was related to my family, somebody would have gotten
in touch, wouldn't they? Let's forget it."

So it ended. But it was strange, how I continued to worry about
Cousin Marya as though she were some connection of mine rather than
a possible one of Barney's. I would have felt a little uneasy about her
being shown off to Deelie, like something in a cage, and yet I was
bothered that he hadn't taken the trouble to make sure. It wasn't that
Barney was insensitive, but he was inclined to be thoughtless. At last,
about a week later, I jammed my briefcase under my arm and went to
see the old woman.

Things had not been good during that week. Barney was of course quite
right about the navy. The commander referred him to naval intelligence,
which assured him blandly that it had never so much as heard of him, and
suggested army intelligence. It took the better part of the week for him

to find someone to talk to there, and the results were hardly different. They were kind enough to suggest that he check with the FBI. Barney discovered that it was easier to have the FBI investigate you than to investigate them. When they learned that he had come not to answer questions, but to ask them, their hospitality evaporated. Two appointments had been fruitless, and though he had still to see the area director, Barney's sardonic smile was already growing strained and his manner stiff. It was almost as though he had indeed been persuaded that there was something wrong with him that he hadn't been aware of before.

Meanwhile, at my office, Herman Appleman had quit to go into business. His G.I. loan had come through. And my other working buddy, Dante Brunini, greeted me more formally each time we met, as though I was the one he had punched in the belly. It bothered me a bit, and I discussed it with Pauline. She thought he might be upset at the business about his wife and baby, but I couldn't see that. What difference did it make to me?

I was still thinking of these matters when I headed for the East Side to see Barney's Cousin Marya. Maybe they even impelled me to go where I had no excuse to be and where I hadn't been invited. But I needn't have worried on that score, at least. When the old lady shot the bolt and peered through the partly opened door on the chain, her suspicious frown faded and she fumbled the chain free.

"Come in," she greeted me. "Come, come. Nobody ever comes any more except the welfare lady."

She shuffled back into the kitchen in her carpet slippers, the heels folded flat under heavy feet and her cotton lisle stockings wrinkling about her swollen ankles. I made as if to wipe my feet at the door, but there was no need. The linoleum—its pattern worn through at the stove and around the porcelain table—was all but covered with spread-out pages of the *Jewish Morning Journal.*

"Sit by the table, you can ask the questions."

I sat opposite her and looked into her heavy-featured face, the cheeks and brow scored with a network of lines as fine as cobwebs. She had a massive, mannish nose with a wart on one wing, a set of imperfectly fitted teeth, and kind, kind eyes which redeemed everything. They forgave me for intruding, they invited me to tell everything, they promised to try hard to understand.

I cleared my throat. "I didn't come for questions. Not for three weeks yet. They're not due for three weeks yet, you understand?"

"So you came anyway. Why not?"

"I came . . ." I hesitated. "Do you know a Barney Meltzer? Your cousin's son?"

"My cousin Sadie's a boy? You know him? Bernie Miltz?"

"If it's the same one."

"Why it shouldn't be? You know how long it is I didn't see him? I got the announcement from his Bar Mitzvah maybe ten years ago. But I don't remember, tsu did I send a present, tsu didn't I." She smiled shyly. "He came to the door when he graduated high school, I didn't recanize him. A giant. A beauty, like a policeman, big, handsome. What's a matter, Bernie, I said, you didn't come by me sooner? Now I don't know, will he come again."

I was embarrassed. And confused too—we were probably talking about two different people. "Well, like all of us, he's got trouble. *Tsurros.* With his job, you know, brain-work."

She nodded knowingly. "So how's by you, with the government?"

We chatted desultorily after that. I felt a vast sense of ease and relaxation with the old lady once we got away from such topics as Barney. My own tensions seemed to find release in her kitchen as nowhere else. Perhaps that was why, after I had left and gone about my business, I decided not to mention it to Pauline. My first meeting with Marya had aroused more curiosity in Deelie, it was true, than in Pauline, who was used to my encounters. But how could I explain to Pauline, particularly when I couldn't even explain it properly to myself, this second visit, which had no excuse at all? So I didn't mention to Pauline a meeting apparently trivial, but yet of a significance that I could not quite fathom.

For a while I persuaded myself that I had stopped by first to find out whether Barney was indeed related to Marya, and thereafter because her flat was convenient for a breather and a glass of tea. Only gradually did I admit to myself that it made no real difference to me whether or not she was Barney's relative, that I had no other calls within a radius of eight blocks of her blasted and devastated neighborhood, and that it was an effort to arrive at that lonely tottering tenement surrounded by rubble, and to climb the moldy and odorous three flights of decaying stairs to the serene sanctuary of her changeless apartment.

For a while I was afraid that I was imposing on her privacy, so I took to bringing along small presents: a net sack of oranges, a tin of Swee-Touch-Nee Tea, a bag of Bialystoker rolls, things that I thought she could use. And it was always with an indescribable sense of relief that I heard her shuffling to the door in response to the rap-rap-rap code signal of my knock: "Who's dere? Is you?"

We became friends. As the fortunes of my other friends turned, and the face of the city closed and hardened for us, I looked forward more eagerly to my visits with Marya. Barney had had no luck with the FBI. In desperation, he was commuting to Washington, hoping to find somewhere in the blank impersonal corridors of the federal investigative agencies an answer to his dilemma before it would be too late. He stayed three days, he came back, he went out to Jersey to quiz McKenna again, he explained the unexplainable to his draft board, he went to Washington. There was little we could do to help. Deelie was concerned, but her mother in Greenwich had developed an acute liver ailment (probably cirrhosis, I thought unkindly, from too many martinis) which kept Deelie running back and forth too.

But when I went to see Marya, I didn't talk to her about any of this, although it was preying on my mind. I think all I wanted was the assurance of her solidity and permanence in those rooms in which she had spent so many rooted years. As long as she was there I could not be soured on the city, with its grinding drive for money and place, or frightened by the rank growth of ambition among my friends, whom I had thought to be as happy and careless as Pauline and I, but who were learning a vocabulary —"in the know," "lunch dates," "capital gains"—that was new in our lives.

I could never explain to Pauline, who was hurt by my stubborn resistance to being bored every Friday night at her parents', that I was the one who had found a relative in Cousin Marya. That she had been teaching me a game called *sechs und sechsig,* which we played with some matchstick pegs, a pad, and a greasy, rubbed, and creased pack of cards. That I enjoyed watching her ringless hands, of which she was very vain (with good reason, they were her best feature), patting the cards together and dealing them out deliberately, her heavy lips, shadowed with white hairs, moving silently, counting, as she dealt. That, although I was crudely, even vocally grateful for my mother-in-law's weak heart, which prevented her from coming to Brooklyn to visit us, I even enjoyed sitting in silence with Marya over a glass of tea, watching her fingers drumming endlessly, patiently, on the stained tablecloth as she marked the measured passage of time in my company.

One afternoon late in the winter I ventured to try to explain to Marya some of the things that were troubling me, not specifically—what could she understand of making contacts or getting in on the ground floor?— but in a general way, as one would tell one's grandmother of a disappointment in love. She covered my hand with hers as she had never done before, so that I could feel the warmth flowing from her fingers—wrinkled somewhat at the tips from many years of immersion in soapy water, but meticulously trimmed and still shapely—to mine; and she murmured something in Yiddish that I didn't quite understand, but that seemed to me to mean, "As long as I'm here, you've got where to spill out your heart."

After I had said goodbye to her, I found that I wanted to walk, so that I could think about myself and Pauline, Barney and Deelie (who, it appeared to me, was not cherishing Barney at this hard time of his life as she should have). Was it my imagination that she seemed to be moving away from him, retreating, as the fissure deepened at his feet? Was she not only bothered, but bored by his trouble? Was I being unfair, or smugly parading my own innocence, to feel that Deelie was simply out in front of us all, but was not traveling in a direction essentially different from that taken by our other friends?

I walked for miles. Finally I emerged from the Lower Manhattan jungle at City Hall and mounted the steps to the promenade of the Brooklyn Bridge. While I crossed in the dusty gloaming, only half aware of the city, the harbor, the Statue all winking on behind the delicate fretwork of Roebling's dream, I made up my mind to tell Pauline all about my meetings these last weeks with Marya, and to ask her whether we ought to talk to Deelie about Barney.

But how idle it is to attempt to arrange the future! Especially when what you plan for is shifting a burden from your own shoulders to someone else's. Thinking that I would be the first one home, I stopped at the liquor store to buy a ninety-seven-cent bottle of chianti. We would have a quiet glass of wine while we relaxed and talked, and then we would go on out to dinner.

When I opened our door there was a flickering light under the sill, and soft music playing. Surprised and uneasy, I paused at the threshold, the wrapped bottle dangling from my hand. The apartment had been cleaned, and candles glowed on top of the bookcase. There were six fresh-cut roses in the glass vase I had bought on Third Avenue. I smelled chicken cooking. Then as I stepped forward the door swung to behind me and Pauline was upon me, her arms around my neck and her lips on mine.

I held her off and looked. She was as freshly made up as the apartment. She had tied back her hair and was wearing a new pair of slacks and an Italian embroidered blouse.

"It's not my birthday, is it?" I asked.

She shook her head. "I just thought it would be nice, for a change . . . We don't want to get into a rut, do we?"

"Never." I hung up my coat and reached farther back into the clothes closet, where we kept our small stock of kitchen utensils, for the corkscrew. "But you must have gotten home very early."

"I took the afternoon off. Oh, I can't hide it, I can't keep anything back! I was going to wait until we ate, and then break it to you slowly. I'm going to have a baby. *We're* going to have a baby."

I stared at her dumbly. She looked the same as always. Fresher, yes, excited, but not changed. But I must have looked different, because Pauline's eyes filled with tears.

"You're not angry, are you?"

Then I found my voice. "My darling, I was just so surprised. Now that it's real—it is real, isn't it?"

We fell together onto the rickety studio couch that Pauline had tried so bravely to smarten up with a piece of fabric. Pauline made herself small in my arms. "I went to see the doctor after lunch. Then I didn't go back to work. Don't you think we ought to celebrate a little? It's only five or six months earlier than we'd planned on."

"Yes, that's so." It was so. When you look back on it—or when you're the woman in the case—it's such a small thing, six months. But the moment of impact, when you're totally unready, is as thudding and heart-stopping as the moment when the doctor comes toward you from the operating room. The saliva dries in your mouth as you struggle to understand that nothing will ever be the same.

As our reveries spun out, they overshadowed my earlier need to reveal my meetings with Marya and what I in my turn had been trying to come to terms with during the afternoon. How could I inflict that on Pauline now? I would have to make up my own mind, alone, what to do about Barney—although during the course of the evening, as we drank and whispered and gnawed on little pieces of chicken, I came to feel that just possibly there was very little I could do, any more than I could have held Pauline back from motherhood when some inner certainty urged her that the time was ripe. Maybe, I thought, maturity lay in the discovery of my own limitations.

Late in the evening, before we moved to the bed in our stockinged feet, arms twined each around the other's waist, I took it upon myself to say what Pauline was too considerate of my confused feelings to utter aloud.

"This is no place for a baby. No kitchen. No room to mix a formula, change a diaper, rinse bottles—except the bathroom sink."

"I guess that's so." Pauline knew that it was. She knew too how much harder it was for me than for her, at that moment, to turn from the past toward an incalculable future. So with infinite tenderness she added, "But let's not be cold about this place. I've been happy here, alone with you. Have you been? You have, haven't you?"

I nodded, my face against her throat. Once again I found it impossible to speak, perhaps because now I was close to tears, perhaps because she was mothering me just when I should have been reassuring her. We had eaten and turned off the lights, and by the uncertain flicker of the one candle that still guttered on our teetering bookcase, and the yellow ray that splayed out around the cracked dial of our portable radio, we could just discern each other's features, and our surroundings—the secondhand and second-rate objects with which we had hopefully furnished our two small rooms. Outside the window, the night breeze rattled the dead leaves on the lonely tree that rose defiantly for two stories from the shabby garden in the courtyard below.

All evening the radio had been playing. Now, as we remained still, listening to the voice of the rising wind and the beating of our hearts, the WQXR announcer's deadly familiar voice broke in on us: "Next we are to hear 'Nights in the Gardens of Spain,' by Manuel de Falla."

Pauline reached out to turn it off. "We don't need it. We've had our own nights in the gardens of Brooklyn, for a whole year." She touched my lips with her fingers. "I'll never forget this room. Or these nights. We had fun all over New York, but the heart of it was here. After all, it was on a night like this, with the window open and the birds fluttering in the garden, that we made our baby . . ."

Next time we saw him, Barney had gotten another job, at a small place in the Bronx. For one thing, his money was running out. He had engaged a lawyer, and was still running down to Washington on his hopeless quest for derogatory information about himself. For another, he had to hold off his draft board, at least until they quit reaching for men in his age bracket, if not until the draft act expired. What could I say to him?

Besides, I was retreating into my own troubles. Not, I prefer to think, out of selfishness, but because that was the trend of the times, of our age, of what the city slowly pressed us to do. I had to find a place for the three of us, with a real kitchen and bath, and I didn't have forever in which to do it. In New York that year it was all but impossible; it was totally impossible on our money.

So one thing brought another in its wake. And up in the Bronx, the Friedes, not yet aware that they were going to become grandparents (I had pleaded with Pauline for an extension while I coped with the problems of expectant fatherhood, knowing that her mother would be hurt beyond words if the secret was kept from her too long), were already sending out feelers, like lonely polar explorers tapping out radio messages. Their boy would be graduating from high school soon. They had high hopes for him. If only he could get a boost from his sister and brother-in-law . . . I hadn't asked for the paper bags of jelly cookies made by Mrs. Friede's loving hands, any more than I had asked for the bills that she wadded into her daughter's purse during our Friday evening visits. Neither had I foreseen that I would be expected to change my life so that my brother-in-law could go to college.

One night Barney came over to play the fiddle with me. We weren't doing that as often as we used to. "We may not be doing it at all in the future. Who knows?" he demanded gloomily.

I tightened my bow and rubbed resin. "If you want to look at it another way," I said, "we're lucky we've had this year. It's been pure gravy. Now comes Real Life."

"Some life. If it wasn't for Cordelia—well, you know what I mean. I got fired again today."

I put down my fiddle. "Again?"

"Are you surprised? All the work is classified, no matter where I go. It may take a day, it may take three weeks, but as soon as the word comes through, out I go. With regrets."

"Barney, go back to school. You ought to be teaching. The longer you put off your Ph.D. the harder it'll be."

"You bore me, man. Don't make me bore you. My draft board won't let me, it's the middle of the year anyway, I haven't got the money to do it on my own, I can't get a teaching fellowship with all these jobs shot out from under me . . . Come on," he wound up irritably, "let's play."

I felt there was more to it than that, but for the first time in our friendship there were things we couldn't talk about. I hadn't been able to tell Deelie (I never saw her alone) that Barney desperately needed help to break out of his trap. I couldn't explain to Barney my conviction that we were moving, all of us, to a point of crisis. Did our lives have to be compressed into narrower confines, bounded by the twin measurements of ambition and fear?

Daily my confidence shrank. On the streets the girls' dresses grew longer as they scurried, like so many mindless mice, to let out their hems in accordance with the dictates of Dior. In the bars, the elevators, the Federal Building where I used to chew the fat with Dante Brunini (he never seemed to turn up any more when I was there), the men's faces grew longer as they took the bit between their clenching teeth and bent their necks to the supposedly necessary burdens of metropolitan manhood.

I rang doorbells in search of an apartment, the way I had as a newly fledged civilian. But now nobody was interested in what I was, or in my hopes and dreams. Nobody had any apartments either. That is, nobody except a ferret-faced couple who wanted two thousand dollars for the wicker porch furniture they had furtively imported in the dead of night.

The decorating DeFees, however, had turned up both an apartment and key money to buy their way into it. When they had finished stripping walls down to the bare brick, rewiring, and installing new floors and false ceilings, they threw a big party to celebrate—and also to announce discreetly their going into joint business. It was perfectly plain to Pauline and me, when we arrived and pressed their shiny buzzer, that the DeFees were scrambling into a milieu far removed from the likes of us, in terms of both décor and guests.

We were barely out of our coats when Eleanor DeFee took us on an escorted tour. All too obviously she was bucking for a photo spread of their careful apartment in *House Beautiful* ("Two Careers, Two Lives, One Charming Home"). It was all gracious and elegant, from the black and gold inlaid tiles of the foyer to the Somali masks set into the living room walls in cunningly lit shadow boxes, and the imported terrazzo in cool seaweed around the lavabo. There was even a French coffee grinder on the kitchen cabinet beside the Italian espresso machine.

As for the guests, they seemed to me to fall into two groups, mingling for two distinct purposes: our old friends, there to stare and to measure their own ambitions against the DeFees' acquisitions; and a new crowd, invited because they could be of use to the DeFees and their pals in the future. I was separated from Pauline (public policy at these gatherings) and unloaded by Eleanor DeFee at the side of a dean's wife, who was sitting straight up in an Eames chair, smiling fixedly at nothing. I lit her cigarette (her first, judging from the way she manipulated it) and we began to talk at each other, desperately, about the charming apartment and the imaginative décor. Just as things were petering out, we hit on the clever expedient of chatting about our spouses.

I peered through the growing crowd of overdressed and overcautious people, all rotating slowly, delicately, through the film of smoke and talk, balancing cigarettes and glasses as though they glided on eggs, instead of taupe broadloom, or feared to disturb the invalid in the bedroom beyond. Finally I spotted Pauline at the modular bookcase, deep in discourse with my cousin Zack, of all people.

"That's her," I said, in a sudden access of honest pride. "That's my wife, the little one. The beauty."

"Aren't you a lucky fellow! Now let's see, where's Fred—oh yes, right there at the fireplace. You see, the distinguished-looking man? I think it's wonderful for him to get out with younger people. He finds them so stimulating."

The dean was being stimulated by none other than Peerless Willie, who was urging his own pipe tobacco mixture on the older man. He was also urging himself. Before my eyes he was changing from Peerless Willie to

Bill, he was laughing less, he was using his fiancée at his side as further proof of his stability, he was adopting chin-stroking and agreeable politenesses. It might take him a dozen years, but he would make Chairman of the Department, of that I was sure.

I was rescued from the dean's wife (and she from me) by Barney, along with the cleanest-cut Negro I'd ever seen.

"Thank God," I said to him, after he'd drawn me aside. "What a drag."

"Old boy," he demanded solicitously, "are you shy with new faces?"

"It isn't the new ones, it's the careful ones, so anxious to say the right things about Sartre, Henry Wallace, Chaplin, Le Corbusier, Stravinsky."

The Negro laughed, but only to be polite, because he was one of the careful faces—scrubbed, handsome, polite, and so refined that he made me feel like a boor and a yokel. Barney introduced him as a pianist who was working as accompanist to a famous Negro singer. The singer was thinking of having her apartment redone by the DeFees; in consequence—or in anticipation—they were courting this fellow, who was so starched that his arm creaked every time he extended it with his monogrammed butane lighter. Fortunately he spotted bigger game and was shortly sniffing their spoor, not forgetting, however, to take courteous leave of us.

"Why so sour?" Barney asked. "What's wrong?"

"Nothing is wrong. Everything is so right that it's deadly, from their copy of *Verve* at the careless angle on the coffee table to their bamboo and glass cups. That piano player goes with the cups—the whole crowd does." I poked him with my elbow. "Let's go talk to Pauline and Zack."

We hadn't seen Zack in some time. He looked Barney up and down. "Well," he asked, "where's Deelie?"

"She told me she'd be along later." Barney gnawed at his lip. "So she said, anyway . . . How's the book going, Zack?"

I don't know whether Barney had simply wanted to change the subject or to embarrass Zack. In any case, Zack's answer stunned me.

"I'm packing it in for now, kid. Going home, day after tomorrow, to Syracuse, before the money runs out. My sister's husband has offered me a hell of a good job in his ad agency, too good to turn down. I'll get back to the book after I'm in the swing of the job."

I stared at my cousin. He looked me in the eye without flinching, my only near relative, who had told his family to go blow so he could live in a crummy sailors' rooming house in Chelsea and work undisturbed on his novel.

"Well," he said, "guess I'll go circulate."

We all watched him move off through the crowd, glass gripped in his hand, confident but wary, much as he must have glided, the beady-eyed rifleman, through the New Guinea jungle.

I said, "Another one bites the dust."

"Don't hate everybody," Pauline said to me quietly, "just because they're dying to make out and you're not."

"Pardon me," said a pretty brunette in a tight black dress, who had been introduced to us earlier as some connection or employee of Milton Berle's, "do you know that couple? The man looks so familiar . . ."

I looked out at the foyer. There, just inside the door, arm in arm, stood Dante and Cordelia. They had been walking in the rain, their faces were damp and flushed, Dante's coat collar was turned up dramatically, his curly black hair glittered with raindrops. He was smiling expectantly, showing his fine teeth and his complacent pride in having brought a belle to the party. He hid nothing, it was hardly necessary; but then neither did Deelie. Each had dashed greedily to grasp for something momentarily exciting—and useful.

At my side Barney uttered a grunt that ended in a moan as he broke away from us and made for the bedroom. Before I could think of what to do or say, or even fully understand, Barney was in the foyer and plunging for the door with his coat over his arm, his face white, ignoring the couple who were making their way into the throng of ambitious decorators and editors and young academics on the make. The door slammed behind him and he was gone.

"I'm going after him."

"No." Pauline shook her head. "Leave him alone."

"I can't stay here any more. I don't want any part of it."

"We'll go in a few minutes. But let's not give anybody any satisfaction."

We did it Pauline's way. After a while we said our good nights and slipped away unnoticed. We said nothing to each other all the way home (except for neutral remarks on the subway platform: "Do you want a *Times?*" "No, thanks.") until, at our very door, Pauline put her hand on mine.

"He'll be back."

"It won't be any good. It's all over."

I lay all night thinking about Barney, and about those two who had betrayed him. And us, I wondered, what about us?

When I got to Manhattan the next morning, instead of going to work I took the Grand Street bus on over to the East Side. I hastened down the bleak street with the bitter wind whipping stained sheets of newsprint about my legs.

Marya's building, that great rotting corpse, was more ghastly than ever in its loneliness now that foundations were actually being dug around it for the new projects. Gloved workmen were hauling away the debris of the toppled structure next door. I mounted the three flights to her flat, past walls which stank of wet and rotting plaster, on floors which had heaved from the wrecker's ball swung against the groaning neighboring beams.

She was gone. I stared at the padlock on her door, shook it, pounded senselessly in a frozen rage on the panel. The building was quite empty. Where had they taken her? I sat down on the steps in the cold, the dirt, and the echoing quiet, and tried to think. No one knew I knew her. She didn't even know my last name, or care. We were torn apart as effectively as though she had indeed died.

And if I could find her? What difference would it make, what good would it do for me to come upon her homeless in a Home, or bewildered in a project apartment with thermostat and engineered kitchen?

I got up and blew my nose and brushed myself off and walked out of the tenement without once looking back. In my mind it was already pulled down.

When I got home to Brooklyn I set to work at once on my census reports. When Pauline arrived I told her that I was up to date and prepared in good conscience to quit. And prepared too to leave the dingy inadequate apartment where we had spent all our nights, our nostrils filled with the nocturnal scents of real and dreamed-of gardens. And to leave the city, where I had found my love and been so happy—and where I could never be happy again.

When I first went to the suburbs in search of a place where we could rent a small house, raise a baby, and go into business, Barney gave me a skeptical farewell. "You'll be back soon. One winter on the moors, and you'll head back for civilization."

He was wrong. But since he was New York born and bred, he had never quite understood how passionately I had needed New York, nor how abruptly that need had been quenched.

I got a G.I. loan—it was Herman Appleman who put the idea in my head—to start a music and record shop. I did well not because I am a brilliant businessman, but because LP's came out, and I rode the wave of the culture boom. Who could go wrong? I had Pauline to help, too. Her brother came in with me after we saw him through college and he put in his time in Korea. With him in the shop, and a woman at home to watch the kids, Pauline and I are free of an evening to go to New York.

Every so often we get together with Barney and his wife. They own a very substantial house on Avenue J, with a two-car garage and a big lawn, for Brooklyn. We don't find a lot to talk about. I had made the mistake of nagging at Barney, in those early months of his misery and loneliness, to get out of industry and back to graduate school. At last, after even the draft had finally blown over his head, he turned on me and cried angrily, "Would you ask a thirty-year-old arthritic to go into training for the Davis Cup matches? Why don't you lay off?"

I think too that Barney was aggrieved at me for a while for having introduced Dante Brunini to our crowd. Certainly it was after he found out about Cordelia and Dante that he said to me, apparently apropos of nothing in particular, "It's always bad to mix your business life and your social life."

That shook me. "But that's why we were happy in New York for a while. Everything was of a piece—work, play . . ."

"Life doesn't work out that way."

It hurt to hear him say that. But I knew then that we were going to have to go our separate ways. At least I had my music. Barney had neither his music nor his math.

Sometimes we still make a foursome of it and meet at the theatre or at Town Hall, but Barney is not very good company. He is not just balding, he is embittered. His wife seems pleasant enough, so are their children, and he has done well—even better than I—as an executive in a toilet supply service owned by a wealthy brother-in-law. Always the brothers-in-law! But he is disappointed in himself in a way that makes me want to turn away and go.

I don't think it was just Deelie. Surely Barney would have gotten over her sooner or later, Dante or no, because she doesn't seem to wear well. After Dante she married twice, unsuccessfully; first a producer and then a vague European man of the world. From time to time I heard of her, a little high at art show openings and quite striking at first nights; once I bumped into her at a lavish impersonal cocktail party given by a record company to greet the arrival of stereo—she barely knew me.

She never did become an actress—the last I heard she was promoting the talents of a welder of fifteen-foot-high towers of crankcases and pistons —but Dante Brunini stuck at it. He has had some luck on TV as Dan Bruno. He wears a built-up shoe and is better looking than ever, and I read an item in the *Times* recently about his signing for a supporting role in a Tennessee Williams play. I still don't like him, and I can imagine what he has done to get ahead.

I suppose that is what bothered me most about New York, aside from the actual fate of all of us. Whom you had to sleep with, be nice to, eat lunch with, in order to stay in the race, struggling blindly for unknown ends. I could never be happy in a city where drink and food, and friendship itself (as impermanent as the buildings), became a part of the whole grinding success mechanism. Nor could I be happy in the place where I truly learned, as I had only begun to in the army, what sin and sellout meant. After I understood what compromises would be expected of me —demanded of me—I had to leave.

I know the streets still, I know the stops on the GG Local as few New Yorkers do, I know where the best chances are for finding parking space. I know where to buy button coverings and Pakistani food. But the magic and the mystery of the city are gone. Now it is just a place, no worse, for those want to look at it that way, than the placid and self-satisfied town where I live. Yet it persists, an indelible part of my young manhood. And like everything else I endured in those passionate years, it will remain until the end of my days embedded in the very core of my being, an internal capital, aflame with romance and infected with disillusion.

A GLANCE IN THE MIRROR

Waiting for the doors of the high school to open and his daughter to come running out, Roy Farrow was thinking about how stealthily spring had crept up on him. He had taken the usual precautions with the change of season—put his overcoat and tweeds in storage, brought the car in for tune up and overhaul—and he had even noticed, as he drove alone, not stopping for hitchhikers, across New York State, Pennsylvania, and Ohio, that he could keep the windows down and that beyond the curbs in town after town the forsythias were turning to gold and the daffodils were blowing open, yellow and wet with spring rain on the lawns of all the old houses that drifted back away from him as he sped on to the place where he had been born forty years before.

But now that he was here he really felt it in his heart, which was where you really should feel spring if you were to know it at all. Lazily slouched like this in the open convertible with the warm wind in his hair and the strengthening sun on his hands lax across the steering wheel, he was uncertain whether the quickening in his chest could be charged to the weather, to his return to his birthplace, or to the fact that in a moment he would be seeing his only child for the first time in twelve years. Indeed, it might have been the intoxicating fragrance of the early spring breeze bellying through the riverward windows of his Manhattan apartment that had first filled him with an unease verging on disgust when he turned to observe Minerva, half-drunk in broad daylight at the piano, and drove him to consider how he might repossess himself by screwing up his courage to return home at last and identify himself to his daughter.

A quarter of a century earlier, at this very time of year, he had been jogging along the cinder track that girdled the cathedral-spired school, desperately trying to earn his letter; and for an instant now he was shaken with a comical yearning to re-experience that boyish agony, even if he had to turn up the cuffs of his doeskin slacks and trot his heart out just once more on the hot, half-forgotten cinders; but in five minutes the doors would open, and beyond all this spring craziness was a painful desire to watch his daughter unobserved for a moment or two before he should walk up to her and take her by the hand.

He knew that he would recognize Kate at once from the snapshots that her mother sent him in response to the requests that sometimes accompanied his checks. Even without the pictures in his wallet, he would know her from a thousand other girls of her age, because of his ineradicable memory of how she had looked and felt as a three-year-old when he had hugged her goodbye, or maybe simply because of the special affinity of fathers for daughters, even for the daughters they left behind and came home to only after it was too late.

But then he thought: Suppose she doesn't recognize me? What would he do if she were to stare at him blankly when he called out her name, and then turn away, as her mother must have taught her to do when strange men offered her candy or automobile rides? Roy wrenched about convulsively on the leather seat. Now he would probably have to pay the price for not having behaved sensibly, written ahead to Lisa that he was coming and then waited prudently at her house for Kate to come home from school. As he twisted about he caught a glimpse of his angry and ashamed face in the rearview mirror.

He pulled down the mirror for a better look at himself in this final moment and stared coldly at the empty stranger's face. Bland and unlined, it had an aura of perennial youth that had been commercially useful in his trade but now struck him as almost hideous for a man of forty; and besides he knew, as few others did, that when he put on his reading glasses the pastiness of his complexion was accentuated and the large pores of his nose became perfectly noticeable. Beyond his broad pale forehead his platinum hair lay flat against his scalp like a smooth shining cap, just as it had done fifteen years before—no one but Minerva and his barber knew just how sparse it was getting. In five or six years he would be quite bald; already he could hear the wheedling words that his manager would use when he persuaded him to wear a hairpiece.

As he poked the mirror back into place, the school doors banged open and the walk before him became alive. First were the boys, cavorting, sniggering, elbowing, tossing balls back and forth, shouting. Then came the girls, moving more sedately than he would have thought possible, ruminant and bovine, and all wearing what looked like outlandish castoff skirts of their mothers, voluminous and puffed out fore and aft, above the thick shapeless white wool socks folded double over their ankles. But there were so many of them!

Roy was suddenly panicked. Supposing he were to miss her? He would have to drive to Lisa's and hang around, like a rent collector or a man come to fix the faucet, in that house he had been dreading to visit. He jumped out and made his way through the pack of yelling boys to the girls strolling with linked hands and schoolbooks cradled in their arms like babies. Where was she?

When he heard someone calling, "Father! Father!" in a high clear voice, he could not at first believe that it was meant for him. He was taken by the arm, then, and half turned around by a tall thin girl who came up to his eyes. "Don't you recognize me? I'm Kate!"

He felt himself flushing. He had to speak loudly to make himself heard. "I didn't think *you'd* recognize *me* . . . Say, can't we get out of here?"

But it was too late already. He and Kate were surrounded by a growing circle of boys and girls who shoved at each other with happy ferocity, poking pencils at him for his autograph and chanting his name as though it were an incantation; he had to strain his ears to hear Kate, who clung fiercely to his arm, her eyes burning with pride and devotion. "You're so modest! *Anybody* would recognize you, even if you weren't their father! And I'm so glad you're here! I knew it, I always knew you'd come!"

Yes, she was glad—but was this what he had wanted? With their arms twined awkwardly around each other's shoulders, they moved slowly away from the school and down to his sloping convertible, which looked out of place and affected here. More students had gathered admiringly around the car and were waiting to be introduced by Kate. For one self-hating moment he wondered whether this cheap and easy hero worship had been his real reason for coming unannounced to pick up his daughter. And even if he hadn't, why else was *Kate* so delighted to see the father who hadn't even bothered to visit her in a dozen years?

At the curb some of the noisy crowd fell back to make way for a tall stout man who came forward with his arm outstretched and a hearty smile on his florid face. "This is Mr. Klass," Kate said. "He's our vice principal."

"Delighted to meet you at last, Mr. Farrow." He squeezed Roy's hand fiercely. He was as bulky and self-assured as a football coach. "It's always a pleasure to greet an outstanding alumnus. May I ask if you expect to be in town long? We'd be honored to have you address our assembly next Wednesday morning."

"That's very kind of you. But I'm just here for a very short visit with my daughter. I'm sure you understand."

The vice principal was swallowed up in the press of his students before he could reply. Roy opened the door for Kate and then slipped behind the wheel himself. "Why don't we meet your gang someplace?" he asked.

She said a little timidly, "Would you mind going to the ice cream parlor? That's where everybody hangs out."

It was only four blocks away. Kate's hair, as fine as her mother's, was blowing against his face, and as he reached down to shift into high his hand brushed her thigh, thin and not yet fully developed; but he could not see her face without squinting out of the corner of his eye, and indeed he was beginning to wonder if he would be able to look at her directly at all during the afternoon.

But when they were settled in a booth at the soda parlor, Roy found himself seated near the wall across from his daughter, with only two of her friends to keep them company. He glanced at the record selector at his elbow; four of the fifteen records listed were his. Guiltily he turned back to the glowing face of his daughter, as one of the girls leaned across him to insert a nickel.

"You don't have to pick one of mine just because I'm here, Sally," he said to the girl.

"What do you mean?" she said gruffly. "Roy Farrow and the Music of Tomorrow? We hardly ever play anything else, except for singers. You're our favorite."

Kate added excitedly, "She's not just saying that because you're my father, either. Even our music appreciation teacher had to admit that your band plays wonderful arrangements and that people are starting to play string instruments again on account of you."

"But you don't play a string instrument, do you?"

"Didn't Mother write you? I'm taking the cello from Mr. Poggi. I know you don't use cellos in your orchestra, but ever since I heard Gregor Piatigorsky play the Dvořák Cello Concerto I've been crazy about it." She went on, somewhat defensively, "Some of the kids think it's not graceful for a girl."

"That's silly." He had to speak loudly, over his own music—it was "Atomic Cloud." That it was unbalanced in the rhythm section he had suspected before this; but why hadn't he realized that the whole idea of it was pretentious and phony? "When people say things like that, it's generally because they're envious."

"They've got reason to be envious of *me.*"

For one horrible moment he was sure that his daughter was being sarcastic. But he looked into her sparkling eyes, smiling gratefully and frankly above her ice cream soda, and he was ashamed. So she was proud of him. Well, when you were fifteen it was easier to be proud of someone you didn't know than of someone you knew.

But how could he get to know her here, any more than in his apartment on Seventy-sixth Street, or in the recording studio, or in any of the hotels where he worked? All that he could learn here, as he chatted pleasantly with her friends about his band, about what *Down Beat* had said, about what they liked to hear best, was her facial expression and her public manner. He liked her thinness, her wide eyes, her tension; and behind the school-girl flutter he could sense already a coolness, a self-possession that could only grow stronger as she matured. "It must be a little sleepy here after all the excitement you've been used to," she said, smiling, and it seemed to him that if he had waited another year, or perhaps two, before seeing her, she would have been not merely smiling, but mocking.

Since it was impossible to get any closer to her, Roy resolved to be simply amiable. The afternoon passed pleasantly, and when he had paid the waitress for all of Kate's crowd, she turned to him and said, "You were a peach."

Startled, he turned sideways and stared at her. "Kate . . . What do you mean?"

"All the kids thought you were swell, not stuck-up or acting like a famous person or even like a father. I could tell."

He took her firmly by her thin elbow and led her out to the car, waving his goodbyes to her friends who still remained in the soda parlor.

Now, he thought, we are alone. They settled down in the car and drove off slowly.

"I guess . . ." she hesitated, ". . . you know the way to the house."

"I certainly do," he replied, a shade too grimly.

"Father."

It still made him shiver to hear the word. "Yes."

"Why did you wait so long to come back?"

Was it the uninhibited tactlessness of children that was so endearing, so ruthless that it became a kind of tactfulness of which adults were incapable—or was it simply that he would have expected, instead of this question, the more brutal query: *Why did you come back at all? Why did you come back now?*

"When I first left . . ." he hesitated, stopped, and then began again, "At the time your mother and I were divorced, we were very angry at each other. We—hated each other. It lasted for quite a long time, with me anyway. Then of course there was the war, and I was in England. And after that I was very busy getting re-established."

"But in the last few years—"

Roy did not look at her. "By that time it seemed wiser to stay away and let you and your mother continue with your own lives. I *am* a stranger, you know, even if we do write to each other. And besides," he concluded lightly, "maybe I was a little afraid to come back."

"That's funny. That's what Mother said once, but when I asked her what she meant . . . she said she was just being unfair, and she really didn't mean it."

Oh, she meant it, all right, he thought bitterly. For an instant he could taste the old hatred on his tongue, rank and salty as his own sweat. You could forget hatred, thank God, just as you forgot pain and grief and even ecstasy; but suddenly you could get a flash of the old memory, like an anginal cramp bringing you stabbingly face to face with eternity. Christ, how he had hated her! Within two years after their marriage, she had repudiated everything he had naïvely thought that they both believed in, she had mocked at his dreams of becoming a composer, she had whined and wheedled at him for things that he did not want or even know how to provide. And how she must have hated him! Ambitious and determined, it must have galled her to see her friends go off to New York, to Chicago, to Hollywood, to *go,* even if they did not become rich or famous, while she rotted away in the town where she had been brought up, in the very house where she had been born—and simply because her husband was content to give piano lessons at a dollar an hour and daydream at home of writing the kind of music he had studied with her at the conservatory, when she knew in her heart and soul that he could never do it and would only succeed in reducing her prospect to an endless vista of small-town drudgery.

Was that what had been in the back of his mind when he decided to drive out to visit Kate? Was he really so mean that he had only wanted to rub it in, to park his white Jaguar in front of Lisa's house, to cross his legs in her parlor and display his seven-dollar argyles and sixty-dollar shoes to her burningly envious gaze?

He said to his daughter, "I've been very lonesome, Kate. This seemed like a good time for me to come out and get to know you," and even as he was speaking he knew that he was being something less than completely honest. "If I *was* afraid, it was only of how you'd feel about seeing me." He added winningly, "You know what I mean."

"Yes, I do." She spoke gravely, staring down at her hands that lay folded in her lap. "But you shouldn't ever have worried about that. I knew how it was with you and Mother, and that you've had your own life to lead."

"You don't think I've been selfish."

"Oh no!"

It was strange how you could go on, always believing you were better than people thought you were, reassuring yourself, protecting yourself against the smirks of the columnists and the gibes of the envious by reminding yourself of your secret kindliness and measuring your own sensitivity against the callousness of others; then suddenly it was turned topsy-turvy when a girl, your own daughter, told you that you were better then you were, or seemed to be, and you knew in your own heart that she was wrong.

What was right? What was fair? Was it better to stay away—or to go away, now that he was here—and leave Kate with her childish illusions untarnished—or should he assume the responsibilities of a father even to the point of trying to open her eyes to the truth about him? No one could answer such a question for you, not your agent or your manager or your current girl friend or your best drinking pal.

He tightened his lips and turned into the block of elm-shaded bungalows where fathers were walking home to dinner down the cracked old concrete sidewalks and their children were coasting slowly alongside them on box scooters; they turned their heads to stare at his car as he brought it to a stop in front of Lisa's house.

"I'll just drop you here, Kate," he said. "You can tell your mother that I'll come by after dinner, if she won't mind."

Kate stopped dead, her hand frozen on the door handle. He was not sure in that instant whether she was bewildered or angry. Her eyebrows came together in a frown and she said in a pained voice, "Do you mean you don't want to see her at all? Do you want her to be away when you come back, is that it?"

"No, no," he replied agitatedly, "it's just that it's almost suppertime and I don't—" but he had to stop because it was obvious that the only way he could prove to her that her father was not a coward after all was to walk up the weathered grey wooden steps of the porch with her and spin the rusting iron bell in the middle of the front door. "Come on," he said gruffly, "let's go."

But of course Kate would not let him stand formally on the porch of her house, waiting for her mother to answer the bell. Roy had time only to notice that the house needed painting and that the metal glider, still standing where it had a dozen years ago, was mottled with rust spots, before he was pulled into the dim front hall and then into the parlor, with Kate shouting, "Mother, Mother, see who I brought home with me!"

Lisa came out from the kitchen, wiping her hands on her apron. The light was behind her as she advanced, and his first thought was that she had not put on any weight at all. Her figure was slim and fine, just as it had been when they were first married; but then she turned her head in response to a kitchen noise, cocking it a little, like a pretty canary in a cage, just as she used to do when he played something for her that he had just composed, and he saw that she was middle-aged.

Although he had been creating mental images of what Lisa would look like for some time now, her actual appearance was a revelation to him— while she, who was utterly unprepared for this occasion, looked at him almost serenely now, her shock betrayed only by a quick intake of breath and by a widening and darkening of her pupils that became apparent as she moved toward him through the twilit dining room and the waning light struck her face.

Her nose seemed sharper than he remembered, and as her nostrils dilated and her chest rose in a shuddering sigh, two grooves that he did not remember appeared on either side of her nose and mouth; her neck, that had been arched and swanlike in her girlhood, was beginning to sag under her chin. Roy felt sick with anguish and pity, both for Lisa and for himself—he was staring, he knew, at the wreckage of his youth—and yet it seemed to him that, simply because she carried the stigmata more obviously, she bore the encroachments of approaching middle age more gracefully than he.

"Hello, Roy," she said. "This is quite a surprise. How are you?"

"Just fine. You're looking very well, Lisa." He was tempted to add, *You're starting to look like the librarians and the schoolteachers and the spinsters that you used to point out in such terror when you pleaded with me to get some gumption and get you out of this town;* but there was no bitterness in her face now, and if the resignation that he saw in it was like what she had seen in the faces of older townswomen when she was a girl, it could only be wanton cruelty to point it out to her.

"You'll stay for dinner."

"Oh no, I'll drop back later. I picked Katie up at school and we spent the afternoon together, so I drove her home. But I wouldn't dream of popping in on you like this at suppertime."

"Nonsense. You don't have to be formal. We're having chicken—I can always fish out an extra wing for you."

They sat in the kitchen—Roy would have preferred the somewhat less chummy formality of the dining room, if only because the dimensions of the round oak table would have kept him further away from Lisa—and chatted about Kate: her ice skating, her cello instructor, her girl friends, her school marks, the clothing that she was outgrowing. And all through the meal, even afterward, while Kate washed, he wiped, and Lisa put things away, he waited tensely for the questions about himself that would betray her real feelings, the emotions she had never dared to reveal in all her years of businesslike letters.

When they had finished with the last of the dessert dishes (the meal had been substantial and filling, if not particularly tasty, and when he complimented Lisa on it she had smiled, a little grimly, he thought), Lisa glanced about vaguely, rubbed her hands on her apron with seeming nervousness as she folded it and put it down, and said, "Roy . . ."

He tensed and closed the lighter that he had been about to touch to his cigarette. "Yes?"

"I don't think we've had the chance to write you that Kate has been accepted as a junior counselor at the YW camp, you know, out on the lakeshore. Isn't that fine?"

Kate was standing in the doorway, looking at him eagerly. "Say," he said, "that's perfectly swell. Have you got your lifesaving certificate, Katie?"

"They wouldn't have taken me otherwise. I wrote you last year when I got it, don't you remember?"

"It comes back to me now."

"Your father has more on his mind than your lifesaving tests, Katie."

Roy glanced sharply at Lisa as they walked into the parlor, but her face was perfectly serene. She means it, he thought to himself in wonder, she really means it.

Seated in the parlor on the same sofa on which he had once held his wife on his knees, he leaned back and gazed first at the framed portraits of her long-dead parents staring mildly and eternally back at him from the mantelpiece, and then at Lisa herself, curled up on the slipcovered wing chair across the room from him with her feet tucked beneath her. She looked back at him equably, passed her hand over her hair, and reached for the knitting bag which lay beside her on the rug.

"Kate," she said, "you ought to go upstairs and get cleaned up. It's almost time for your club meeting."

"Oh Mother! Not tonight!" Kate had flung herself down on the floor at his feet and leaned back against the couch with her head just under his hand. "This is a special occasion. I don't want to go any place while Father is here."

Roy ran his fingertips lightly over her pale hair. "I'd rather you stayed home too, Kate. But your mother and I might have a few things to talk over alone together." Her head stirred restlessly under his hand.

Lisa too shifted about uncomfortably; it was almost as if she hadn't expected, or wanted, to be alone with him. But she said, "It's up to you if you want to skip the meeting. But you have to do your homework anyway. Go up to your room and do your Latin and your geometry while your father and I talk, and you can come down as soon as you've finished."

"All . . . right . . ." Kate arose lingeringly and drifted from the room, waving farewell at the foot of the stairs. "I'll be down soon, Father."

The silence, after she had gone upstairs, was unpleasantly heavy—for both of them, it seemed, since they both began to talk at once.

Lisa said, "Kate doesn't often—"

And he said, "It seemed to me—"

Lisa laughed. "I'm sorry. Go ahead."

Was she determined to speak of nothing but Kate? He couldn't let her get away with it, even if Kate was the obvious reason for his being here. He was oppressed suddenly by a peculiar sense of frustration, as if he had gotten here only to find that his daughter had already gone away on vacation.

"I suppose it all seems pretty ironical to you," he said.

"What does, Roy?" she asked calmly.

"Why . . . my coming out like this . . . fancy car, fancy clothes, after all these years. It's just what you always wanted for me."

"Of course I did."

There was neither bitterness nor resentment in her voice; yet perhaps she was giving him the needle in a peculiarly subtle way, against which he had no defense.

"It's what you always wanted for yourself too," he went on stubbornly.

At last her smile seemed to turn a little sour. "Not always," she corrected him. "Only when you knew me. I mean, when we were married."

He looked at her incredulously. "And after I left, you changed?"

"Not exactly. But my life became all Kate, a hundred per cent. Then when time went by I sort of resigned myself to staying here. I knew you weren't having such an easy time of it either, so I really didn't hate you. And besides, I knew the day would come when you'd really make it." She added firmly, "That I always knew."

He leaned forward and said, with a kind of feeble desperation, "But Lisa, you *knew* how I hated the idea. You *knew* what I actually wanted out of life."

Her smile became almost malicious. She glanced down at her knitting. "But then you changed, too, didn't you, after you left? You must have.

And I knew you would, because sooner or later you'd have to realize what was right for you. I always told you, you had the voice for it, and the figure, and you had the personality too. And now when I turn on the TV and watch you every Saturday, it's just as though all of those old dreams have come true."

Dreams come true . . . Good God, he thought, she can be cruel . . . or does she listen to soap operas all day, while she reads about me in the gossip columns and waits to see me at night on the screen? He got to his feet angrily, and in his clumsiness almost knocked over the floor lamp at his elbow.

"What is it, Roy?" Lisa asked. "Is something wrong?"

"Don't you remember the fights at all any more? Don't you remember how I used to swear that I'd never get caught in the success trap?"

"You were young then. We both were. But every time I hear you on the radio, or see you on TV, I know that I was justified in predicting what I did." She hesitated. "I'm very proud of you, Roy, even though we couldn't stick it out together. Kate is too—you can see that without my telling you. In fact the whole community is. People stop me on the street."

There came to his mind then, as he stood nervously picking at the fringe of the lamp, a conversation he had had not long ago with Minerva, with whom he had been living off and on ever since the war. "You don't even understand," she had said, "why that poor woman still keeps your name." "No," he had muttered, "unless it's to get even with me in some way." "Nonsense. It makes her a big shot in town, that's all. She probably still thinks you're wonderful." She smiled crookedly. "Just like I do."

He said in a choked voice, "You don't dislike me then, Lisa. You don't hold anything against me?"

She shook her head slowly. "Not any more. I used to, but not any more. Things worked out the way they had to. I'm glad for you, too."

"Thank you." It was impossible now to tell her any of the things he had been burning to: to throw up his success to her, to say, I hate it just as I told you I would, it's phony and I'm a failure and I hope you're satisfied, I did what you wanted and now I have to worry about my hair and my arranger and my singer's sex life and my doctored state income tax returns. Certainly he did not dare to tell her that in the dark moments of the night he despised himself and his white Jaguar, and shrank with terror from the thought of what lay in wait when his temporary popularity had run its course. It was too late, it was far too late for him ever to accomplish any of the things he had dreamed of doing ten and fifteen years earlier, and all he could look forward to was cushioning the bruising impact of this desolate realization with as much material comfort and financial security as he could finagle.

"I read in the paper," Lisa said shyly, "that you're making a movie."

"Yes," he murmured, "they're going to shoot it in New York, mostly." In all honesty he would have added—if it had not been for the light in her eyes—that he would not clear a dime on the picture after paying off the band and his back taxes and that his only reason for engaging in the idiocies that the script called for was to keep his name before the adolescents who went to the movies. He looked up at her from the lamp fringe that he had been twirling around his finger and said lightly, "It should be fun."

"I'll bet. We'll be watching for it—you have no idea how much your career means to us in this town."

She was nourished by it, and Katie was too—that was what she was trying to say. Who was he to deprive her? He put his hand to the knot of the Sulka tie that Minerva had given him and said, "The movie may not be in the can until fall or winter. I don't suppose you know that the boys and I are booked into the Palladium in London next month."

"London!" Her eyes widened.

"As soon as the agency gets a summer replacement for the TV show. So that—" he stopped at the sound of Kate's footsteps. She walked swiftly to his side and turned to face her mother.

"I did my Latin, it was easy, and I can do my geometry during study period tomorrow. Can't I stay here with Father now?"

"I was just telling your mother," Roy said, slipping his arm around her waist, "that I'm going to have to leave for London very soon. We've got an engagement there."

"How are you going to go? Are you going by jet?"

He laughed. "Oh, sure. I wouldn't want to disappoint you. And I'll send you a cashmere cardigan sweater. Would you like that?"

Her eyes were like her mother's. Glowing brilliantly, they seemed to be pleading with him never to falter, never to allow his dream image to become tarnished. He released his hold on her waist and stepped back so as to be able to look at Kate and her mother at once. They gazed back at him with that same compound of arrogant possession and humble abasement that he had seen so often in the eyes of his adolescent audiences. Was he playing up to that look now because he had become so completely an article of commerce that he was incapable of any other response? What else could he do but respond with a false and hearty smile?

"If I manage to get to Paris," he heard himself saying with great calmness, "even if it's only for a day, I'll get you both some perfume. I think I know what kinds you like."

"Now, Roy," Lisa said, "don't go spoiling Kate."

"Tell you what. You keep tabs on her and let me know if she really deserves it. Okay?" He winked at Kate. "And now I have to be getting along."

"Why don't you stay here, Father? We've got a spare room."

Lisa arose and dropped her knitting behind her in the chair. "If your father prefers, honey, he can come back first thing in the morning and have breakfast with us."

Roy found himself biting at the nail of his little finger. "I'm afraid I haven't made myself clear. You see, I really won't be able to come back in the morning, or to see you again for quite a while."

The two stared at him in consternation. For one terrible second he thought that one of them—it might be either, the way they both gazed at him with their soft mouths slightly open—would accuse him of running away, just as Kate had suspected him of cowardice when he had brought her home.

He heard himself saying, swiftly but smoothly, "I simply have to be in Chicago and Cleveland before I get back to New York for my show. As it is, I'm going to have to drive all night." It was a poor lie, but as the hurt faded from their eyes and was replaced by awe and pride, he went on, "I purposely went out of my way to stop here—figured I've been feeling guilty long enough about not seeing you. Besides, I wanted to ask you, Lisa, if you'd give Kate permission to come and visit me later this summer—after I get back from England, that is."

He couldn't even remember now, looking into his daughter's glowing eyes in the moment before she flung herself on him and began to hug him, whether he had intended to ask this of Lisa before he got here. But, smiling at her over the top of Kate's head, he had the impression that she was pleased, almost as pleased as her daughter, but that she would not let her go to New York alone. Next year, perhaps.

The good byes were a little prolonged. Kate and Lisa walked him out to the car (it struck him as fortunate that they had no way of telling from the car or from his one valise how long he had intended to stay) and stood at the curb with their arms around each other in the moonlight, like a couple of school-girls. In the hushed spring moment of rural silence before he gunned the roaring motor and flipped the gearshift into first, it was borne upon Roy that his former wife and his daughter were clinging to each other protectively, shielding each other from the desolation of his departure, perhaps, or merely from what the incalculable future could bring them, as today it had brought them this unforeseen visit. They would talk about the visit for a long while, probably, but in the end there would be other things, more important things, from which to protect each other.

Then he was off, floating like a moth through the green and black avenues of the town in which he had been born, passing the hospital where he had had his tonsils out and where his wife, after severe travail, had been delivered of his daughter, and he wondered fleetingly whether either of them would ever accuse him—not to his face, but to each other —of having come only to preen himself for one pathetic hour. It was not likely; they lived a little too meanly, though, all things considered; I will have to ask Archie, he thought, if I can't hike Lisa's checks just a little. When he reached the state highway heading east, his foot came down lightly and the automobile leaped forward easily at seventy miles an hour. He leaned back snugly in the bucket seat that cradled him as the tires sang beneath him, and while he listened to the song of the humming rubber in the dark of the night, he began to compose in his mind for Minerva (who was bound to consider the episode as faintly ridiculous) a defense of what he had done, of what he had not done—as if in the end there could ever be any defense of what you had made of your life.

A QUESTION OF LONELINESS

The Hamlins had gotten into the habit of telling each other that their main problem was one of money. Throughout the first year of their marriage they had enjoyed a double income, but when Alice became pregnant there was only Paul's salary, which wasn't enough to enable them to hire help after Alice's return from the hospital. The pregnancy had been an unadmitted accident, and in the exhausting weeks that followed the childbirth Paul was driven to the suspicion that it was not so much the lack of money that was making their lives miserable, despite the fact that finances had become their chief topic of conversation, as it was Alice's inability to cope with her new responsibilities.

She had taken to concealing her weariness and anxiety from outsiders with an over-effusive display of affection for little Barby, which worried Paul at least as much as the lassitude and disorderliness that served only to remind him constantly of his deficiencies as a wage-earner. Alice's excessive pride was accepted by the aunts and cousins who came to examine the new member of the family as proof of her devotion to her child, but acquaintances who called were obviously annoyed. One evening after a classmate of Paul's had dropped in with his wife for a brief visit, the Hamlins stood at their door and listened to the fading voices of their guests as they descended the stairs. The woman was saying, "You'd think she was the first girl in the world who ever had a baby!"

Alice burst into tears. She was trembling with tiredness, and Paul knew by now that she would probably have cried even if she hadn't overheard the remark, but the least he could do was to assure her that it had been prompted by spiteful envy. Just as he began to speak, the baby let out a cry. It was only a little cry, but even as Paul felt his wife's back stiffen under his outspread hands he knew that it was the inevitable forerunner of another difficult night.

Ever since the birth of the baby their life together had been a series of difficult nights. All the gaiety of the early days while they were getting to know each other—sightseeing, playgoing, hunting for a little Village apartment and then furnishing it—seemed to have disappeared so quickly with the baby's earliest whimpers that Paul began to believe he had discounted too quickly the earlier indications that Alice felt herself too good for this world. Just as she had complained before that her stenographer's job in the shipping agency where he worked was beneath her intellectual capacities and threw her into the company of her inferiors, so now she seemed to take as a personal affront the croupiness and poor sleeping habits of her baby.

"I wasn't made for this!" Alice burst out one evening, flinging a soiled diaper into the toilet bowl.

Paul looked up from the sink where he was rinsing his nylon shirt. "For what?"

"For what? For what?" she mimicked angrily. "I studied psychology in college. I trained my mind. I prepared for something better than a dingy apartment and smelly diapers."

"Would you like to go back to work?"

"That's what you think, isn't it—that I want to run away from my baby!"

Paul knew that even the most mollifying answer would upset Alice even more. "Postpartum melancholia," the Health Insurance Plan doctor had cheerily explained to Paul. He had consulted the doctor about Alice's depression immediately after the childbirth, for she had turned her face to the wall each time he came to visit her, but the doctor had been irritatingly nonchalant. "Give her lots of love and kisses. She needs affection."

Alice had needed affection, but she also needed the things that money could buy. The doctor could not have been expected to foresee that Alice would grow thin and querulous, that the baby would be cranky and a nuisance to carry up and down three steep flights of stairs, that the super would make nasty remarks about the baby carriage in the stairwell, or that they would be horribly lonely, unable to afford to go out, and with nobody to keep them company during the long evenings but the crying baby and the radio that Alice had come to hate because it reminded her of both the outside world and her own remoteness from it.

Neither of them really knew many people in New York City. After the relatives and office acquaintances had paid their duty calls, no one came but the diaper-service man and the delivery boy from the drugstore.

"Not that I blame anybody," Alice said bitterly. "Who would want to come here, when we can't even afford to offer them a drink, and the baby is liable to wake up any minute?"

"It's inevitable that we should have less and less in common with the people we used to know."

"What kind of an answer is that? Am I supposed to wait until Barby is in school to have a normal life? At least you get out to work—how would you like to be locked up in this jail?"

Paul decided to take matters into his own hands. From his small allowance he saved painfully and secretly until there was enough for two good tickets to a popular Broadway play. Then he jotted down the telephone number of a baby-sitter service that advertised in *The Villager,* and came to Alice with the news that they were going out.

"To a party?" she asked suspiciously.

"No." He smiled encouragingly.

"To visit people? Because if you think I'll do that, you're crazy. I won't chase people who never came around or offered to help."

Then he told her, and Alice threw her arms around his neck. Her warm response was in sharp and uncomfortable contrast to her usual behavior, but Paul knew that she had read the reviews of the play in the *Times* and the *New Yorker,* and the very bitterness with which she had envied the fortunate few who could go to plays as they chose now intensified her almost childish happiness. Suddenly she drew back.

"How can we possibly leave Barby?" The tone in which she asked the question was sufficient evidence to Paul that she wanted only to be reassured.

"We have to, Alice. It's important for all of us."

"If only we—" Alice bit her lip, her face betraying a guilty confusion that completed the unfinished sentence for her. She began again, speaking with such a transparent attempt at casual honesty that Paul was amused and touched. "I wonder if it will be fair to the sitter? You know Barby is going to wake up."

"That's a sitter's hazard, like cave-ins for coal miners."

They both laughed, and everything was all right for a moment. But then the baby awoke, dirty and screaming, and Alice pulled away from him with a jerk, her face contorted. They did not speak to each other again until their child was quiet.

It was only when Paul called the baby-sitter service that they stopped avoiding each other's eyes. It seemed the most wonderful good fortune that when the doorbell rang they were bathed, shaved, powdered, and the baby was sound asleep. Paul opened the door. A dumpy, heavily breathing old lady came waddling into the room.

"Well!" she panted cheerfully. "Fleischer's the name. If they'd told me it was three flights up, I wouldn't be here. Not with my weak heart."

"Won't you sit down?" Alice asked.

The old lady was unusually homely, with spreading nostrils, a hairy chin, and an ungainly body set on swollen legs. Instead of responding directly to Alice's invitation she said bluntly, "Where's baby?"

"In there." Paul nodded at their small dark bedroom. "But she's asleep now."

"Bless her little heart. Where's the radio? Ah, I see it, in the bookcase. Very clever! No television, I suppose. Well, that's the way things are." She sighed, but whether in pity for herself or for the Hamlins was not clear. "You can leave now—I'll find everything if baby should wake up."

"Her name is Barby," Alice said tensely.

The old lady let out a surprising cackle. "You two look like you were expecting a bobby-soxer. Don't worry, I've had 'em and I've raised 'em. That's more than the bobby-soxers can say, isn't it? Now go on, have a nice time." She bullied them through the open door and snapped it smartly to behind them.

On the way to the subway station Paul said thoughtfully, "She read my mind all right. A baby sitter should come in with schoolbooks, not with arthritis, isn't it so?"

"Paul, I'm afraid. Do you think we should have—"

"If she's good enough for her own grandchildren she ought to be good enough for Barby. We'll phone after the first act, to check."

It was only a two-act play, however; and after the long first act the balcony and mezzanine were so crowded that they had barely reached the head of the line at the telephone booth when the buzzer sounded for the final act.

"The hell with it." Paul took his wife by the arm. "Come on, we'll miss the curtain."

"I must talk to Mrs. Fleischer first."

"If she tells you Barby woke up, will you rush home?"

"That's not the point." But Alice grew irresolute, and Paul tightened his grip on her arm.

"We'll call as soon as the play is over. I promise."

"Well . . ."

"Come on."

When the play had ended, they found the telephone booth standing hospitably empty. Paul dropped a dime in the machine and dialed their number. "I'll tell her we'll be home in about an hour, after we've stopped in someplace for a drink. . . . Say, that's funny."

"What's funny?"

"No answer."

"You must have dialed the wrong number."

He hung up and dialed again. He listened to the steady ringing. It rang and rang, stupidly and incessantly, until Paul found himself cursing the telephone as venomously as if it were a dog or a relative.

"Are you going to sit there forever?"

Paul looked up blankly. Alice's pleasant brown eyes were dilated with fear and hate. She said in a trembling voice, "I'm going home. You do what you want."

Hastening after her, Paul could not keep from making mental calculations even as he ran, balancing the cost of the taxi against two drinks and another hour for Mrs. Fleischer. It would be cheaper at that, he thought as he raised his arm and flagged down a cab. He tried to help Alice, but when she brushed past him he said, "Listen, there could be a dozen reasons why she didn't answer."

Alice, sitting in the far corner with her hands pressed together, did not reply or even turn her head towards him.

"Supposing she was in the bathroom. Supposing she was busy with Barby and couldn't leave her to pick up the phone."

Alice said nothing.

"She might even be deaf."

"Leave me alone."

When the taxi reached their corner Paul began to figure out the tip. By the time he had gotten his change Alice was inside the house. He took the steps two at a time, caught up with her at the second floor, passed her on the landing, and opened the door of their apartment with Alice just behind him.

All the lights were on and soft dance music was coming from the radio. At the far end of the room Mrs. Fleischer sat motionless with the baby in her arms. His first thought was that both Mrs. Fleischer and his baby were dead.

As he advanced into the living room, unable to speak, his throat constricted and his heart suddenly pounding, Paul saw his daughter lurch awkwardly in the old lady's arms and belch softly. Mrs. Fleischer was staring at him unblinkingly, her head forward and her mouth a little ajar. He could go no further. In the silence he could feel, he could almost hear a blood vessel thudding in his neck like a muffled drum. While he stood transfixed Alice pushed past him and ran forward across the room.

She picked up the baby and removed a half-empty bottle that was wedged between the old lady's arm and her body. When she turned with the sleeping baby in her arms her eyes were glittering, but she was so calm that Paul was suddenly conscious, to his intense shame, of his own convulsive shivering. "I'm putting Barby to bed. She seems all right. You'll have to call the police. Tell them to bring a stretcher."

He started to reply, but his voice was only a croak, and he was almost relieved to see Alice hurry directly into the bedroom with the baby. He was alone with Mrs. Fleischer. He took a step toward the telephone and then turned for one final glance at her. She seemed to be hardening before his eyes into a rigid waxed figure, a strange and ugly statue invested with a new dignity, at once pathetic and accusing.

Paul could not bring himself to make the gestures that would assert his human connection with the old lady, to touch her forehead, her eyelids, her wrists. He turned away blindly and picked up the telephone.

Perhaps the most unusual thing about the rest of the night was that the baby did not wake up once, not even when the apartment was crowded with policemen, stretcher-bearers, and the interne who pronounced Mrs. Fleischer dead. People were constantly at the telephone, with calls to the baby-sitter service and then to Mrs. Fleischer's relatives, a nephew and niece in the Bronx.

After she had been taken away—an arduous and noisy job that shook the hallway—the girls next door, whom the Hamlins had never met before, and the couple below, whom they thought of guiltily every time the baby awoke screaming during the night, came in to express their sympathy. The girls next door brought in a pot of fresh coffee and did their best, with the aid of the people from the second floor, to distract Alice and Paul from the sickening memory that pervaded their apartment like a strange and lingering odor.

Alice was remarkable throughout the night. She was much more helpful to the police than Paul, who was sure that the contrast between her self-possession and his uncontrollable trembling must be obvious to everyone. He was grateful when the neighbors finally said good night at three in the morning, but Alice seemed genuinely sorry to see them leave, not from the fear of being alone, but rather because even in these tragic circumstances she had really enjoyed playing hostess to people whom she had never had the opportunity to meet before.

When they were alone together at last, there seemed to be nothing for them to say to each other. They undressed wearily in the darkness of the narrow bedroom in order not to disturb the baby. In bed side by side, they listened to each other's deep and slow breathing, and when Paul could no longer bear the silence or his wife's open, staring eyes, he turned on his side to take her into his arms.

But she lay as stiff and cold as Mrs. Fleischer, and when he began in terror to whisper desperate words into her ear, she opened her lips and ground her teeth so that he had to stop to hear what it was that she was saying.

"Murderer," she whispered. "Murderer, murderer, murderer."

A CHANCE ENCOUNTER

I couldn't expect you to know anything about that kind of poverty," the doctor said to me. "Consider yourself lucky. The man never would have called me, he never could have called any doctor, if it hadn't been that the city welfare allowed me a buck for every house visited in those days. I used to count on those dollar bills for gas for my Chevvy, even though it was nine for a buck then and they threw in premiums to boot and had three college students wiping your windshield while the tank was being filled."

"But the call," I started to say.

"I'm coming to that," he replied so sharply that the ash flew like a breaking thundercloud from his clenched cigar and scattered among the horizontal pleats of his vest. He brushed his hand impatiently over his old paunch and continued, "I'm setting the scene for you. How else could you visualize it?

"The hallway was bitterly cold, with water leaking through the cracks in the plaster and curling down the walls like sweat leaking down your back. It wasn't cold enough though to kill the smell of rat droppings and broken bags of garbage, of damp spots where kids had peed and of lard bubbling in pots behind the closed doors.

"I climbed three flights to earn my dollar, with the satchel getting heavier every step of the way, but I didn't even give it a thought, partly because it was my job and I was used to it, and mostly because on my mind all the while was the man who must have gone down those three flights and then over to the drugstore and probably borrowed a nickel to call me and say his wife looked to be pretty bad off and what should he do, and then climbed back up the three flights and stood there next to the moribund woman, waiting for me. For me, of all people.

"They didn't bother—they still don't, except in the new housing-project slums—with name plates or even with numbers. Either you knew where you were going or you took your chances, and I made one wrong try before I found the man who had called me. At that I figured I'd made another bum guess when I rang his bell and pushed open the unlocked door, because the room was bare. It had two orange crates standing in the far corner, a midget radio plugged into the baseboard and sitting on the bare floor, and that was all, period. The walls were caving in, there were places where even the lath was chewed away behind the plaster, chewed away by you know what, and here and there you could see a stud sticking out like the backbone of a cadaver that this fellow had done his best to conceal decently with Hoot Gibson and Loretta Young and Richard Dix posters that he must have mooched from the local movie palace, and also with old calendars that he probably got from a garage after he was lucky enough to put in a day's work flat on his back on the cold concrete draining crankcases. They were ugly—the calendars, I mean—and the naked girls on them were scrawled over with phone numbers, but they helped to keep out the cold and conceal the decay."

"You said there was a radio."

"That was what made me realize the flat wasn't empty. Even though it probably wasn't working, even though the electricity was probably shut off anyway all through the building, I figured that nobody was going to move out and leave behind two or three dollars' worth of tubes and wires. And besides—" the doctor's moon face wrinkled up in what I took to be a grin, "—I heard voices."

"Like Joan of Arc?"

"Real voices. Two men were talking very quietly in the kitchen, and as soon as I heard them I realized that the doorbell didn't work either, and they hadn't heard me come in. But when I walked across that floor they heard me all right, and the man that had called me came out to greet me.

"He was as black as they come. He reminded me of the Assyrian kings you see in the museums, with his beaked, flaring nose, and his forehead sloping steeply back to the curls, and an air of dignity dangerously quick to outrage. But he had a smile of such sweetness that I was ashamed for taking him to be one of those snobs who look down on white men, and I could tell simply by the way he stood there that he wasn't ashamed at having to watch the finance company take back the furniture, or at having to pawn all his other possessions so that there was nothing in the world any more that he could call his own but the stuff in the kitchen and the two orange crates and the radio on the floor and the bed on which his wife was dying. And the clothes on his back.

"I looked down from his royal face to his splayed feet, that were covered after a fashion with torn ankle-high sneakers which gave him room for his bunions but must have been pretty miserable for walking through slush. The army pants he had on didn't meet the tops of his sneakers, and there was an inch of black shinbone sticking out. He didn't wear a shirt, just two sweaters one on top of the other—a black one underneath, and a khaki-colored one with a kind of collar on it on the outside.

"I was about to follow him into the bedroom when something, a noise or maybe just a feeling, made me look into the kitchen. A white man like me, of about my age and size and disposition, maybe a little older and fatter and sloppier and sallower, was snapping shut a satchel on the lonesome kitchen table in the middle of a mess of sliced bread wrappings, opened-up tin cans, and dirty dishes. He raised his head and took one nervous look, like an alley cat glancing up at the toe of your shoe and calculating whether you'll smash his ribs in if he doesn't make tracks, and when he saw me standing there with my satchel his face caved in just as though I'd walloped him in the belly. I couldn't help it, I felt my face turn red as if I'd discovered that I'd been walking around with my fly open."

The doctor pinched his butt in the glass ash try that lay between us on the table and looked up expectantly as he ground the cigar out between his thumb and forefinger, but I waited silently for him to go on.

After a pause he said, "It isn't funny, when someone is crushed just because he looks up and sees you. Who feels guiltier, the one who is looking or the one who is being looked at? That's a question for the philosophers. I had the feeling that he recognized me and I recognized him as a colleague, you see, maybe on account of the old-fashioned satchel on the table, maybe simply because there was something about him, God knows what, that nagged at my memory. I admit it, my memory is poor, I'm no good at names, and I was sure I hadn't seen him in ten years. Probably I wouldn't have been so embarrassed and my mind would have functioned a little faster if it hadn't been for that trapped, desperate look he gave me, like a boy caught in the bathroom by his old man, before he ducked his head, but as it was all I could think of was how shameful it was that the nice comfortable middle-class professional front that some of us doctors love even more than our incomes had to be torn away here, so that we stood shivering in a cold-water flat, glaring at each other in our nakedness and hating ourselves for having to scrabble over a lousy dollar that the city would pay out for our helping an old colored woman to die gracefully.

"Or so I thought. But as soon as I said, 'I'm sorry, Doctor, I didn't realize there was somebody on the case already,' he muttered something so low that I couldn't even make out the tone of his voice, much less what he was trying to say, and he slipped past me fast with his head still down and scrambled through the open door with the heavy satchel bumping against his legs and his hat jammed cockeyed on his head. I didn't try to stop him.

"Right then I didn't even have a chance to think about him, because the old lady was waiting for me. She was pleased at my being there, which was enough to make the trip worthwhile, even though she couldn't really make me out and could barely hear me when I bent over the bed. There wasn't much I could do for her beyond making her more comfortable, but I did think she should go to the hospital and not be allowed to die in this place without any heat or anybody to give her medication but her husband."

The doctor blinked his baby-blue eyes three times in rapid succession, almost as if he were attempting to signal me some message that could not be conveyed with mere words. "Her husband and I went into the kitchen so she couldn't hear us, and I told him that I thought she'd be better off in the hospital.

" 'I know that,' he said, 'and I thank you. But even at the end I'm selfish, and I keep thinking of myself. How much can I be with her in the hospital? How can I stay here all alone?'

"I didn't answer him. I let him think about it while I made out a prescription and finally he said, just the way I knew he would, 'You're right, Doctor. I leave it in your hands. What should I do?'

" 'I'll call the hospital from the drugstore,' I told him, 'and get her admitted. It may take a day. You can stay with her and ride with her in the ambulance when it shows up.' And then I said, because I wanted to change the subject and because it was starting to eat at me all over again, 'I was surprised to find another doctor here when I first came in.'

"He looked at me as if I was out of my mind. His face was shiny with grief and terror, and his eyeballs on either side of that jutting beak of a nose were as yellow as nicotine. For a moment it occurred to me that he was trying to bluff me by playing stupid—which made me feel that he couldn't have much respect for *my* brains. It made me doubly sore when he didn't even answer me.

" 'You know what I'm talking about,' I said. 'You were standing in the kitchen with him when I came in.'

" 'Him?' He was amused and relieved. 'He's no doctor.'

"It was remarkable. As soon as I heard the words, *He's no doctor,* it all fell into place, and I remembered everything at once about the man in the kitchen, his name, his background, everything."

"So you were wrong about him," I said.

The doctor shook his head. "On the contrary. How could I be wrong? It was only my memory that had been protecting me from the truth, like a well-intentioned relative. The man's name was Stamler, I knew the kind of practice he had, where his office had been—although I'd never really met him except once or twice in the hospital corridor or at a medical society meeting—and I knew, the way you get to know those things, that he was going in for shady stuff."

"When was this?"

"It must have been six or eight years before the meeting that I'm telling you about. I think it was women, but it might have been horses or bad investments or the desire to play God, or simply a rotten childhood and a rotten upbringing. I'm always leery of assigning an ultimate cause to a man's behavior, especially when it's eccentric or criminal. Whatever was behind it, Stamler began to go in for abortions. A girl died, and when they caught up with him he had another one screaming on the table, so that the smartest lawyer in the world wouldn't have been able to get him off, or to keep him from being ruined—which he was, because he lost his license and got sent up the river, and I heard that an aunt and a cousin who were his closest relatives and who were stuck with the same name and had probably been living off him anyway, picked up and left town after he was convicted. That was the last I saw of Stamler, or heard of him, until we met in the kitchen.

"All the time I was thinking this—a matter of seconds, I suppose—the man was standing there showing me what teeth he had left, smiling not insolently or cruelly, but sympathetically, the way people do when you've pulled a hell of a boner. For all I know he might have been talking the whole time I was thinking about Stamler, but I didn't hear a word until he began to tell me what Stamler had been doing in his kitchen.

" 'He's a character,' he said. 'Everybody in the building knows him.'

" 'Why?'

" 'He keeps that old bag crammed full of shirts. I don't know where he gets them, whether his wife makes them or he steals them or what, but he sells them for fifty-nine cents apiece, two for a dollar, first quality white shirts.' I think he kept on talking because *he* was sorry for *me* and wanted to give me a chance to get the shocked expression off my face, and maybe partly because he just humanly wanted to keep me there as long as he could. He said wistfully, "They're nice shirts, all right. I told him I'd buy a couple if I only had the money, but I just haven't. Anyway, he's no doctor.'

"Two for a dollar, I thought, and I asked, 'Has he been around long?'

"The man shrugged. He said, 'Long enough for everybody around here to know him. They call him the white shirt man.'

"So if you want you can say I was wrong about Stamler, as wrong as a man can possibly be. But I'm not so sure, and I can only tell you that it's a thousand times harder to predict what a man will say or do in an extreme circumstance than it is to diagnose what's wrong with his insides from the cast of his eye or the twitch of his hand. If you want to claim that he was subconsciously driven to pull the whole thing—profession, what there was of his reputation, and all—down around his ears, the years in prison should have done it, shouldn't they? He shouldn't have felt the need, should he, to return to the place from which his relatives had sneaked away so quietly that nobody saw them go, to the city where eventually somebody who had known him in his earlier incarnation was bound to find him hawking shirts in a Negro slum?

"Nobody can ever convince me, not after we looked into each other's eyes in that awful moment, that he wanted—even subconsciously—to be discovered with his old satchel stuffed with shirts, a physician turned peddler to people who laughed when they talked about him."

"Then why?"

"How do I know? Maybe when they let him out of the can he crawled back to his home town like a wounded animal that instinctively drags itself back to its lair even though it knows that the old stream is poisoned and that it will be ostracized by the other animals who bear different kinds of scars. Anyway that's what I was thinking of while I stood there talking to my patient's husband, who was shriveling up inside his two sweaters because he couldn't press a bill into my hand as we parted. And then the worst thought of all occurred to me—maybe you've already thought of it."

"No," I said, "I don't know what you mean."

The doctor shifted his heavy shoulders and pulled a fresh cigar from his breast pocket. "It suddenly struck me," he said wearily, "that they might both have felt I was making fun of them."

"I don't understand."

"As far as he was concerned, it was preposterous that anyone should take the white shirt man for a doctor. And when I persisted in making a point of it, what else could he think but that I was trying to ridicule him in the worst possible way, that I was poking at the sorest spot of all? He couldn't afford to put a shirt on his back, and here I was needling him about calling two doctors."

"But you don't really know he thought that."

"Not any more than I know what Stamler thought, but don't you see that as soon as he saw me staring at him he must have figured that I knew what he was doing? And as soon as I started to apologize he must have figured, remembering the kind of clown I am, that I was warming up to tease him in the most heartless and vicious way. Why else did he duck his head down and scuttle out without saying a word, without so much as answering me?"

"He was embarrassed. He was afraid he'd have to explain to you what he was doing there."

"Maybe. I'm not sure. Even if that was so, I leave it to you to imagine what agony that first instant of recognition must have been for him."

"That wasn't your fault. There was a dying woman—"

"Whose final suffering he could have eased as well as any doctor, even though the last woman he'd treated had died in agony under his hands?

No, even if he didn't think I'd been mocking him, I had to face it— Stamler was going through hell because he'd seen me, or because I'd seen him.

"I had to try to find him, and I had to get away from the man who was shivering in his sweaters. He was so decent about my breaking loose and heading for the door, he must have figured I was trying to spare him the necessity of thanking me, or maybe he was smart enough to understand that I still had the white shirt man on my mind.

"I went down the stairs fast, wondering whether Stamler mightn't just be hiding behind one of the doors that I passed, but I didn't see or hear any sign of him. For that matter I went all the way to the corner drugstore which was a kind of monument to the depression in its own way, with its windows displaying flyspecked before-and-after posters of patent medicines for skin diseases and its long row of empty soda fountain stools that nobody could afford to sit on; and I didn't see Stamler, either on the street or in the lonely drugstore."

"You never saw him again, did you?"

"I hate to disappoint you, but I never did. I'll tell you what I did, though." He stopped, coughed an old man's dry cough, lit the fresh cigar which he had been toying with, and drew on it slowly.

I said a little impatiently, "You asked the druggist about him."

"That would have been pointless. I remember him well—he was a sad-eyed Russian Jew with untrimmed moustaches and a look of absent-minded misery about him as though all he was worrying about was how to pay the rent on the store and turn up a miracle that would send his son to medical school. I put a dollar bill in an envelope—an advance against the check the city would send me for my call—and asked the druggist to give it to the man when he came in to pick up the prescription."

"What for?"

"What for? So he could buy a couple shirts from Stamler. I knew Stamler would be back as soon as the woman was shipped off to the hospital and he was reasonably sure he wouldn't bump into me again." He stopped and then added belligerently, "Why shouldn't I have helped him to make a sale?"

I stared at him. "What made you think the man would spend the dollar on shirts? Why not on booze, or groceries, or cigarettes?"

"Because he had to have a shirt to wear to his wife's funeral. He wasn't the kind of person to wear a sweater when he stood at her grave, not if he could help it. I think he understood what the dollar was for." The doctor arose abruptly, scattering ashes once again on his vest. "Come on, let's go. Fortunately someone is waiting for me. Do you know what was waiting for the man when I ran away from him? Death, that's all. And what do you suppose was waiting for Stamler when he ran away from me? Nothing. Not even death. Nobody. Nothing at all. Come, are you ready?"

A HANDFUL OF BALL-POINTS,
A HEARTFUL OF LOVE

N obody is going to believe me. If you want to laugh, laugh. I'm used to it. If you want to cry, cry. As long as you don't blame me— for that I don't need any help.

I had a twelve o'clock lunch date at the Times Square Automat with a salesman named Jack Storer, with whom I sometimes do a little business.

This was a real scorcher of a July day, a Friday, I remember. The streets were melting, the men were carrying their suit coats, the women were hanging out of their summer dresses, their kids were whining. Only the custard salesmen were making out, and the one thing that made it beara-ble for me was the knowledge that at least my family was cool up in the mountains. I dragged myself into the Automat and I could hardly believe my eyes. There was an empty table for two right near the front, next to the stairway. Jack and I have got a standing joke that when we're going to eat at the Automat we should call up first and make a reservation.

I grabbed it quick, parked myself facing the street, and threw my briefcase onto the other chair to save it for Jack. After I had a long drink of ice water, I hauled out of the briefcase a bunch of ball-point pens that I was planning on showing to Jack. They were four-color jobs engraved with mottoes that glowed in the dark—a nice novelty item that Jack could move in quantity. I was spreading them out before me so he could see the color selection when my eye happened to catch that of an elderly man who was carrying a tray with a slice of berry pie and a cup of light coffee on it. It was one of those mutual glances where two strangers seem to see right inside each other in an instant, as though they are really old friends. The old man was shaved to within an inch of his life, but his hair was cut by hand and he was dressed shabby, almost like a panhandler. I figured, probably he was living on a small pension and picking up a couple extra bucks as a messenger boy.

He was a little flustered by my sizing him up the way I did, and he must have decided that at one time or another he had delivered me a bag of sandwiches or a roll of blueprints, because he turned on a small smile and a faint nod. It was such a tiny nod that he could have denied its existence if I had frozen up. But I didn't. What happened instead was that this business of acknowledging me made him lose his stride, so that when he hit the bottom step of the stairway he wavered uncertainly and the tray tipped in his hands. Another guy coming down the stairs jostled him at the shoulder, and that did it.

The pie and the coffee went skating across the black shiny tray and hit the marble steps, slosh, smack. I knew in that very instant, even before the Puerto Rican bus boy came along with his mop to clean up the mess of berry jam, pie crust, and coffee, that the old man had just lost his lunch and was going to have to go hungry until suppertime. Sure enough, he stood there for a moment with a weak sickly grin on his face, then instead of heading back for the Pies and Desserts section he made straight for the door and went out into the street.

I sat paralyzed for a second. Then I was after him, grabbing my brief-case and ball-points as I went. I didn't have any idea what I'd do. In fact, I doubt if I'd have had the nerve to walk up to the old-timer and ask if I could get him some lunch, not with him wearing that smile. But I figured at least I could take off after him and see where he was going.

It was no use. He was swallowed up in the sticky crowd flowing slug-gishly up and down Broadway. What was worse, when I barged out of that freezing restaurant into the ninety-one degrees of high noon, the sun struck down at me out of the sky and the heat rose up at me off the suffering sidewalk, and I thought I'd keel over right on the spot. I leaned back against the wall of the building to try to catch a breath of air, with the ice water bubbling in my belly, and I dropped the briefcase to the ground so I could get my dark glasses out of my breast pocket and onto my nose before I was blinded. I did manage to take off my Panama, because I wanted to wipe the sweat off what's left of my hair, but I just didn't seem to have enough strength left to get rid of the ball-points and haul out a handkerchief. The last thing I can remember was thinking that our table was gone and the hell with it, we'd have to eat someplace else, it was Jack's fault for coming late. Then I guess I passed out, hat in one hand, ball-points in the other. I suppose the only reason I didn't hit the sidewalk was that my shoulders were wedged against the brick and my feet were squeezed against the briefcase.

When I came to, I felt like I was wrestling the world, and I had a really stinking headache. Actually Jack Storer was shaking my arm to snap me out of it, and I was trying to throw him off. And part of the reason for the headache was that he had taken off my sunglasses to make sure it was me, and that blazing sudden light was burning hell out of my eyelids. I managed to blink my eyes open, and I saw his face, worried and scared, and behind him some nosy passers-by, mostly out-of-towners and tourists. The ordinary New Yorkers were ignoring us, thank God, as usual.

"Lay off, Jack, will you?" I said, exasperated. "You'll pull my arm out of the socket. It's not me that was late, it's you."

He was so relieved that he didn't start to laugh right away, not until he had helped me pull myself together—I was still groggy—and stuff those damn ball-points into my briefcase. But then I mopped off my thin hair and went to put on my Panama (it's a wonder I didn't get sunstroke, or maybe I did have a touch of it already) and it was full of money, for God's sake.

I stood there like one of those nuts you see on Broadway sometimes, talking to themselves, muttering, waving their arms. Absolutely confused. Jack started to laugh like a maniac.

"Come on," he choked. "Count it, count it!"

So I put down the briefcase once more—we were standing near a theater marquee, with the dead air from the cooling unit blasting out at us and the woman at the ticket counter staring out at us like a death's head—and dug my hand into my upside-down hat. There were half a dozen bills inside, all singles, and a solid fistful of coins—a few pennies, but mostly silver. I handed Jack the paper money and added up the coins.

"Comes to thirteen-seventy-three," I said finally, "counting what you got there. But I don't get it. What . . . ?"

"They thought you were a panhandler." I thought Jack was going to bust, he was laughing so hard the tears came to those piggy little eyes. "That's the greatest haul I ever heard of for standing fifteen minutes with dark glasses and a bunch of pencils."

"What do you mean, fifteen minutes?" I looked at my watch. It was twenty after one. "An hour and fifteen minutes is more like it. I must have been there easy that long. We made it for twelve o'clock and I was there twelve o'clock."

"Twelve o'clock? We made it for one." He saw I was starting to burn, so he said quickly, "I must have misunderstood. Honest, I'm sorry. Listen, if you've still got an hour, let's go spend some of that loot on a nice crisp Caesar salad in a nice quiet restaurant."

I was feeling a little better, and I thought to myself, I might as well buy him lunch, maybe we can still do some business.

But when we were finally sitting down in a dark booth, I found that what I wanted most from Jack was that he should promise me not to tell anybody about what had happened.

"Supposing it gets around," I said, "to people I know in my line of business. They'll think I'm sick in the head."

"Oh, I don't know," Jack laughed some more, "they might have more respect than ever for an operator that can go out and pick up that kind of change on his lunch hour. What do you say to the fruit salad with iced coffee? Let's stay healthy."

I finally got Jack to promise, for what it was worth, and we even made a deal on the ball-points (although I might as well add that he pushed me a little hard), but all day long it kept nagging at me. Not just that it should be kept a secret, but what I ought to do about it to make it good, to square it, or whatever.

I knocked off early, around four, went up to One-hundred-and-eighty-fourth Street and got my car out of the garage, and all the way up to Ellenville I turned it around in my mind. At last I decided, I'll talk it over with Bernice, maybe she'll have some suggestions.

That turned out to be not such a hot idea either. By the time I got to the bungalow the kids were overtired from day camp and waiting up, and they didn't feel like holding still while I sat down to a late supper with their mother. Then after we got them tucked in and Bernice took the pincurls out of her hair that she washed and set every Friday in honor of

my arrival, she was raring to go down to the casino and show us off to all
the other couples who were starting to celebrate the week end.

"Wait a second, Bern," I said, and while she was wriggling into her slip
I told her the whole story. I included what I had never gotten around to
telling Jack Storer, the business about the old-timer who slipped and
dropped his berry pie and coffee.

"I don't see what it's got to do," she said, after I had finished. "I mean,
the old man dropping the pie and you picking up all that money. What's
one thing got to do with the other?"

I did wrong, I wanted to say, but the words stuck in my throat. Saying
that wouldn't have made the whole story sound any the less cracked. On
the contrary. But Bernice is far from a dope, after all, she's a college
woman. Naturally she laughed at the idea of me snoring out on the street
and strangers throwing money into my fifteen-dollar Dobbs. Who
wouldn't laugh? But she saw that I was serious, and that it was getting
under my skin. She took my arm going down the hill to the casino, so she
shouldn't trip in her satin pumps with the high glass heels, and she tried
to comfort me.

"I tell you what," she said. "You got it into your head that the thirteen
dollars and seventy-three cents is blood money, don't you? I mean, because you weren't entitled to it."

"Something like that."

"So get rid of it tonight. Spend it on something useless, down at the
casino, like mah-jongg or bingo, then you won't have it on your mind."

Well, I did that anyway, like always when I get up to the mountains
for the week end. What good did it do? I only felt like I was spending
my own thirteen dollars and seventy-three cents. Came two A.M., when
I hung my pants over the chair and took out my wallet, I felt I still had
their money in it. I could buy guys like Jack all the lunches in the world,
I could blow all the money I had in games on week ends, I would still have
money that didn't belong to me.

I turned it over in my mind all Saturday and Sunday. I thought, maybe
I should give it to charity, but there again it would be the same problem,
I would only be giving away my own money, nobody else's. And it wasn't
charity gave it to me in the first place, it was people that could afford to
do it because it made them feel a little better.

Maybe that was what gave me my brainstorm. Monday morning, a quarter to five, I dragged myself out of bed and crawled into the car. I must have been halfway to New York on Route 17 when it hit me, what I ought to do.

I couldn't wait to get through the morning. Came half past eleven, I got our bookkeeper to give me twenty singles for two tens. Then I took a bus up to Duffy Square and got out. I started on the corner just north of the Automat, not an arm's length from a guy with a driver's hat who was shilling for the sightseeing bus lines. At first I was a little scared, after all I never did anything like it before, but as soon as I had the bills in my hand it went like cream cheese.

I honestly don't remember, did I say anything, didn't I say anything, but I'll never forget how good it felt those first couple minutes, handing out the money. I just held it in my left hand, and peeled off singles and handed them to people coming toward me. Some of them shook their heads No and kept on walking, refused to take the money; others took without even looking to see what it was. Both kinds, those that took and those that didn't, must have thought they were handbills.

But inside of two or three minutes they got the message. The wise guys and the rubbernecks both started crowding in on me. By the time I had given out maybe a dozen singles, I was trapped in the middle of a clawing, shoving, laughing, yelling mob. My head was buzzing, my hat fell off, I had to hold my hands high, they were jumping for the dough.

"Why don't you just throw it, Mac!" somebody yelled.

That sounded like a good idea, so I opened my fists and let fly, sending the money floating like candy wrappers through the hot smelly sticky air.

Then everybody was screaming and grabbing at once and I felt my suit coat giving way at the armpits as they tore at me. A cop was banging his way through the mob, jabbing and rapping with his club—it was the first time in my life outside the newsreels that I actually saw a cop using a billy —and when he finally reached me he linked his arm with mine and cleared us a path through the screaming faces.

"You going to come quietly?" he asked, when we were loose.

"Come where?"

"I'm going to book you for disturbing the peace."

What was I going to do, give him an argument there in the hot sun on the broiling sidewalk while he mopped his face and took out his book? I wanted to ask, What kind of a world is this, where it's okay if you take money, but if you give money you get arrested? I've always been afraid of cops, I admit it, so I kept my mouth shut.

I did have to do some talking before the day was over, though. Otherwise they would have sent me to Bellevue for observation. What I did was, I told the magistrate I'd had a couple of drinks and the sun hit me and I tried to be a big shot, and I was sorry as hell about the whole thing, and I'd take what was coming to me, and it wouldn't happen again.

So I paid my fine and walked out a free man, thank God. The only thing I left out when I sweet-talked the magistrate was that it wasn't now that the sun had hit me, and it wasn't now that I had acted like a damn fool. It was that first time, that Friday noon, when the old man lost his lunch on account of me. Even though I feel sure now that I did my best to pay it back, that's something I can't seem to make clear to anybody, even though I keep trying and trying and trying.

THE LETTERS

The first week out of Brisbane was a throbbing nightmare. The tanker rode easily enough in the long slow swells of the South Pacific, but Philip Stolz, the radio operator, was slow in recovering from a prolonged bout of alcohol and sex in which he had indulged at Lennons Hotel.

The ship had sailed somewhat early. They were already casting off, the first mate hanging over the bow and the old man standing on the bridge cursing at him, when Philip arrived at the pier in a taxi. His armpits were not yet dry, his uniform was wrinkled, stained, and ill-smelling, his hair was matted under the no longer clean summer white hat, and his parched lips, on which he could feel some flakes of the girl's cosmetics, still tasted of her sleep- and brandy-swollen kisses. But as soon as he had stripped off his soiled blue jacket and rolled up the grimy cuffs of his white shirt he had to mount to the bridge, sore, damp, and sleepy, and see that the antennas were properly rigged, with the sun beating down mercilessly on his strained eyeballs; and then, covered with grease and his head ringing like a gong, he had to go into the radio shack and test the equipment. When he finally finished he tore off his clothes, fell on his bunk, and slept through dinner and the slow journey out of Brisbane harbor, awaking only in the middle of the night, the ship already at sea, and time for him to go on watch.

It was like that for the first week. The physical effects of the thirty-six hours he had spent locked in the hotel room with the tart wore off after a few cold showers and a few glasses of orange juice, except for a trembling at the knees when he made the long walk aft along the catwalk to the saloon at mealtime, and a dead sensation in the pit of his stomach when he raised his head from his plate and looked at the greasy mouths of the intent diners in the saloon. But the other effects of Philip's private little orgy were far more persistent. Over and over he reviewed the details of the wild hours he had passed with the abandoned girl: at the most inopportune moments—when he was busy trying to raise Honolulu by short wave, when he stood under a cold shower with the tropical sun beating in through the open porthole, when he lay on his bunk slimed with sweat trying to read a paper-bound book of short stories—he smelled the girl's fevered flesh, or recalled her breasts swinging frantically above his face as she crouched over his recumbent frame, or felt the bedsheets grating under his fingertips, or saw the brandy bottles rolling about, tangled in her torn stockings, on the speckled carpet.

Probably his most painful memory was the shameful recollection of the way he had whipped up his flagging appetites with the aid of the brandy and the violent and cunning connivance of the fantastically insatiable girl. He had regarded the episode at first as a duty he owed to his body, and then, while the febrile hours slid by in the half-darkened room, as something that had to run its predestined course, like a long and useless life. How his wife (when he wanted to be funny, he occasionally referred to her as "my current wife") would have wrinkled her nose in disgust! It was not the idea that he had been unfaithful to her that galled Phil—he had been going to sea too long for that—but the certainty of the scorn with which she would greet his depraved conduct, seated at her metal desk in the insurance company offices in Hartford. Phil recognized the fact that he was no longer very fond of his wife, and that his prolonged absences had made her less interesting to him, but he was as vulnerable as ever to her intimations of superiority, made on the basis of her regular attendance at concerts, her regular reading of advanced periodicals, and her association with what she liked to call "thoughtful" people. It was difficult to justify his mode of existence when his wife asserted that he enjoyed living with seamen because they were his intellectual inferiors, or that he continued to go to sea because it gave him an excuse to keep from "really doing anything." And now this . . .

The sun and the sea did their marvelous recuperative work. Sitting on the boat deck with his desk chair tilted against a bulkhead, full in the sun, Phil gazed through his dark glasses at the dully shining endless water stretching monotonously through space to the horizon. After a few days, he could step from the dark sweaty loneliness of the radio shack directly into the tropical sun, feeling with a hard delight the burning heat of the deck plates on his thin sneakers; easing himself slowly into the chair, his bare flesh crying out against the white sun, he could really open *Tour to the Hebrides* and give himself over to it and to the sun, without having to stare fixedly, like an angry victim of tuberculosis, at the impersonal spectacle of nature surrounding him on all sides. And eventually, he could even begin to look about the ship itself and note the little changes that had taken place around him.

There were, for example, several men aboard the tanker who had not been there on the trip out from Panama. Two of these passengers who had boarded the ship in Brisbane ate in the saloon, although Phil did not see them there very often, since he usually got there almost at the end of the serving period, ate quickly, and left without stopping for a cigarette. One of them, who was obviously not a seafaring man, was a genuine puzzle: what was this fat middle-aged man, self-consciously dressed in creased khakis, doing on a slow-moving tanker that rarely carried passengers? But when he finally accosted Phil one morning by the Number Two lifeboat, he turned out to be such an uninteresting fat man that Phil could not even bring himself to find out what he was doing aboard ship.

"You're the radio operator, aren't you?"

"That's right."

"How do you keep from going nuts? Always the same, day in and day out, week in and week out. You can't even see a movie. No variety, not a bit of variety."

"I like it." It was of course impossible to explain to the passenger that he had named precisely the things about sailing on the flat Pacific that Phil liked best. He picked up his book and began to read rudely, dismissing the man with the lowering of his eyelids.

The other passenger was something else. The first time that Phil really saw him he was jumping up and down on the catwalk. Phil felt the vibrations, perhaps; at any rate, he looked up, blinking away from Boswell, and saw a tall, excessively thin young man, wearing only (like himself) shorts and sneakers, skipping rope along the catwalk, his thin hairy arms flashing through the sunny air as he vaulted up and down, moving erratically astern along the steel walk like some great eccentric spider. Despite these unusual actions he looked as though he was somehow at home on a ship; but Phil took an immediate dislike to him. This leaping about with a piece of clothesline seemed an overly familiar action for one who was aboard on sufferance, so to speak, and was not integrally concerned with the movement of the vessel on which he jumped. The passenger's skin was extraordinarily white, gleaming flatly like the belly of a leaping fish suddenly exposed to the sun; if he was a seafaring man, it was strange that here in the South Seas there should be no trace of sun on his long thin body.

If there was anything mystical about this swift dislike, it was strengthened early that evening when Henson, the third mate, and the only man aboard ship whose company Phil enjoyed, said to him, "Come into my stable, Phil. Eight days out and you haven't even shown your face yet."

"All right," Phil said. "In a few minutes."

There were three men in Henson's cabin when Phil walked in: Henson himself, Caputo, the steward, and the tall passenger who had been skipping rope along the catwalk during the afternoon. Although the door was open wide and the porthole glass was hooked back against the overhead, there was little air in the room. All three men were smoking, and each one held a bottle of Panamanian beer; and since Henson slouched in his armchair, Caputo lay across the bunk, and the stranger sat on the settee, the room appeared unpleasantly crowded. Phil began to regret the sociable impulse that had drawn him down here, especially when he observed that all of the men were dressed only in shorts and slippers. Their skin was slick with a fine film of tropic sweat, and the cabin seemed to be filled with their heavy naked legs.

Henson handed Phil a bottle of beer and said, "I don't think you've met Bradley Holliday, Phil. Holliday, this is our radio man, Phil Stolz."

They shook hands.

"Holliday's an engineer." Henson's round old face smiled blandly, his eyes roving, joke-making, behind old-fashioned steel-rimmed glasses. "But we let him up forward because he's got some new records. We're a very democratic ship."

Phil seated himself next to Holliday, who smiled pleasantly at him and offered a cigarette. "Smoke, Sparks?"

"Thanks."

Holliday was losing his hair. His face was long, smiling, and polite; the balding skull gave his head just the needed touch of elegance, like a boutonniere. For without the gently receding hairline that made him look properly twenty-eight or thirty, there would have been something vulgar, something falsely genteel and cultivated, in his young American college man's expression. He gets away with it, Phil thought, looking down at the Rachmaninoff album that Holliday held across his bony knees.

He in his turn glanced down at the bright yellow dustjacket of Phil's book and murmured, "I see you're a lover of fine books."

"I like to read." Philip hated the man, he was sure of it now, but he could not get up and leave, if only because Henson would be embarrassed.

"I don't care much for travel books," Holliday said. "I prefer poetry, like Carl Sandburg." He smiled around the cabin. "I'm a West Coast sailor myself, but Sandburg made me *feel* just what Chicago is like."

One poem, Phil said to himself, one poem in a stray anthology has made him an intellectual. The man's very name was an affront; Bradley Holliday indeed . . . it sounded like the hero in one of the *American Boy* stories that Phil had read every month in an agony of excitement and envy when he was thirteen: Brad Holliday, madcap leader of Dormitory B, Brad Holliday, ace goalie of Percival Prep, Bradley Holliday, bronzed lifeguard at Bide-A-While Summer Camp . . .

Watching Holliday as he slipped the first record out of the album with long graceful fingers and placed it on the hand-winding victrola, Phil realized, in one of those sudden painful bursts of insight that bring one face to face with the condition of one's life, that if the man's name only betrayed a Jewish or a European origin one would feel compelled by one's sense of fairness not to condemn him without searching for the neurotic roots of his slippery and false manner; but a Bradley Holliday had to be held accountable for every overt expression of his essential vulgarity. Philip felt his spirit withdrawing from the room, leaving only his gross body seated next to Holliday, as the passenger tested the needle with his forefinger and said, "I hope you men enjoy this. I prefer Victor Herbert myself, but my girl is very fond of Rachmaninoff, so I bought her this album in Calcutta. After all, if you only have a limited number of records, this will be a change." He finished his beer and chuckled, "It's a long voyage home, as Eugene O'Neill once said."

Phil sat quietly through the recording, which happened to be excellent; the beer was not cold but cool, the ship pulsated quietly beneath the scratching needle, and when a touch of a breeze slipped in through the open porthole he could smell Holliday's pungent shaving lotion. At one point—Holliday was changing a record and saying something about the value of great music as a solace for lonely seamen—Henson's round and wrinkled eyelid drooped slowly behind the steel-rimmed eyeglasses in an exaggerated wink. The gesture was almost enough to establish a community of dislike, and Phil relaxed a little on the settee.

The final notes of the Rachmaninoff concerto were still floating heedlessly out to sea on the tropical evening air as Henson heaved himself out of his chair and pulled on a pair of khaki trousers. "Almost eight," he said. "I'm due on the bridge. But stay," he gestured hospitably, "stay right where you are. I never lock my valuables."

Philip arose. "I want to get a few hours' sleep before I go on watch."

Holliday glanced at him curiously. "Don't you keep a day watch?"

"I prefer to split the hours. I enjoy the quiet at night, and the reception is usually better."

"I wonder . . ." Holliday looked down uncertainly at the book that Phil held in his hand, apparently unable to formulate a transitional statement that would smoothly bridge the gap between his feelings and his expectations. "Do you think it would be all right . . ." Once again he hesitated, and at that instant, that moment of honest uncertainty, his real charm, natural and unforced, shone through his false exterior. It seemed to Philip that whereas all too many people were cloying and overconfidential when their guard was down, men like Holliday could only be more likeable in their moments of revelatory weakness. He smiled encouragingly, and Holliday destroyed everything by saying, "I don't often get the chance to talk with a man who enjoys good reading. You're a college graduate, aren't you?"

How false he rang after his little moment of sincerity! Philip replied coldly, "I had two years at Tufts once."

"Would it be all right if I came up to the shack some time, just to shoot the breeze for a while?"

"The old man doesn't want visitors in the shack, especially during watchkeeping hours. The best time to stop in is during my night watch, when he's asleep." Why didn't he lie? He could have insisted that no one ever entered the radio shack. Holliday's very irresoluteness, his sudden uncertainty, had wrung from him this grudging invitation.

Holliday was once again in command of the situation. "That's very white of you, Sparks. I'll drop up real soon, and we'll have a good long talk. I'm sure we'll find that we have a lot in common."

Thus dismissed, Phil retreated in some confusion, tripping over the mat in Henson's doorway as he stepped out to the passageway.

Shortly after Philip went on watch that evening the third mate stepped into the shack on his way down from the wheelhouse. "I'm going to examine the night lunch," he said. "Can I bring you a sandwich?"

Phil shook his head. "No. What's the story on the passenger?"

Henson smiled slowly. "Holliday? You don't like him, do you?"

"Not much. He's a phony, Henson."

"I wouldn't put it that strongly. There's some good in the worst—"

"He skips rope."

Henson laughed. "Christ, Phil, if you're looking for gossip . . . He's been passing himself off on the black gang as a First Assistant Engineer—he even hinted that he sailed Chief during the war. But I've seen his license, you know. The man's only a Third Assistant."

"That's typical." Phil looked up angrily. "Isn't it typical, Henson?"

"You're pretty hard on him. I think Holliday is a likeable fellow, with more on the ball than the average engineer. I've seen more of him than you have this past week, and I find him good company. If I had his trouble, I doubt if I'd be so even-tempered and cheerful."

"What's his trouble?"

"He's got syphilis."

"Are you sure?"

Henson waved his hand tiredly through the hot breathless air. As he reached up to remove his steel-rimmed glasses he blinked; without the glasses he looked old and worn. Philip felt ashamed, looking at him like this.

"You know that fat passenger?"

"Yes."

"He's a company doctor going home on leave. He's been treating Holliday, trying to keep things under control until we dump him at Pearl, or Pedro. That's why we couldn't sign Holliday on as a workaway back in Brisbane. He isn't fit to stand a watch, so the company decided to give him a break and a free ride home. After all, he's been riding their tankers for a good many years. And Phil . . ."

"Yes?"

"If the company can afford to be charitable, why can't you? Sometimes you tend to judge people as though they were on trial. I'm not complaining about that," he added hastily, warding off Philip's protestations with his outspread hand. "That's your privilege. But can't you take into account the troubles that people have had when you pass judgment on them? Suppose that Holliday talked this way about you—wouldn't you want him to make an effort to understand you before he shot off his mouth?"

"I don't—" Phil checked himself. Suddenly he saw Holliday as he had been that afternoon, his thin, sick body clothed only in khaki shorts, cavorting about on the catwalk, trying to *build himself up,* trying to *soak up sunshine.* "What about his girl? The one he brought the Rack-maninoff records for?"

"Are you being cruel?"

Phil flushed. "No. I'm curious."

"And I'm a cynic." Henson lifted his shoulder wearily. He moved slowly to the door. "For all I know, she gave him the chancre as a going-away present, before he left home . . ."

Phil sat until four o'clock in the morning in his iron and concrete room, listening to the throbbing heartbeat of the ship, choked and muffled as though it were slowly strangling in the warm Pacific, and listening occasionally to the plaintive chirping of other ships far away, which sounded as though they had settled only momentarily, like some strange and frightened birds, on the bosom of the southern sea. Conscientiously he noted what they had to say in his log, but their weak cries were no different on this white and star-filled night from what they had been or would be on any other such night. The peace and terror of the world, a thousand miles from the nearest thrust of rock, were such that it was almost an impiety to listen to other voices when one floated godlike and alone.

But *What do you do with all your time?* his wife had to ask him when they lay in bed. "Some men paint watercolors of the sea, Joseph Conrad even wrote great novels about it, but you don't even seem to be able to keep up with your reading." *Keep up,* indeed. How could one possibly explain that he floated alone, like this, in order that it should not be demanded of him that he keep up? If the noblest human achievements could not compete with the annihilating force of the marine sun and moon on one's lowered eyelids, why should one even attempt to struggle against a surrender to the timeless bronze days and the white silent nights?

He no longer maintained the pretense of holding a book before him on the desk while he sat half-listening to the little voices of the distant ships. It was in these hours that he knew his own life and its ugliness as no artist could possibly reveal it to him, simply by extending his palm (which had participated in the countless brutalities he had committed in common with all the rest of humanity) and feeling, along its coarse surface, the velvety breath of this pure and unpeopled night. Shortly before dawn he could rouse himself and type *Off Watch on 500 KC,* leaving the swivel chair and the radio which committed him to the reactionary necessity of facing in the direction from which he had come.

He customarily slept out on deck, on an army cot which he had borrowed from the sick bay. Tonight he lowered himself quietly to the cot, slipped off his sneakers, loosened his shorts, and stretched himself out at full length beneath the white and blue brilliance of the stars. There, on the slowly rocking sliver of cooling metal, his eyes bathed in an effulgence so brilliant that he had finally to blot it from his vision, Phil felt the very essence of his being stirring itself slowly, uncoiling and rising to the very heights for which it had striven unsuccessfully for thirty years . . .

The next day Holliday did not present himself on deck with his skipping rope, and Philip felt obscurely grateful, as though there had been some unspoken understanding between them in the final moments of their meeting in Henson's cabin the night before, as though Holliday had agreed: if you won't hate me any more, Sparks, I won't exercise in public any more.

They did not, in fact, meet at all during the day, and Phil went about his marvelously monotonous routine: breakfast with the captain and his sullen Swedish jokes about things that had probably not happened aboard a windjammer in 1911; shaving before the unrevealing mirror, the disc of the sun once again driving heat before it like a searing knife through the portholes; inspection of the massive batteries oozing sulphuric acid; the specially cold water of the shower stall dripping continuously behind all the other noises on this deck; the colorless hot iron of the ship itself as he made his way aft once again to the saloon where the engineers and deck officers, their chins sweating, fattened themselves on hot food and loud lying memories of their nights in Noumea and Brisbane.

This same, same routine, hour following hour like the endless plash-plash of blue water slapping the plates of the ship, was as soothing to Phil as a compress laid across his dry burning eyes. While he sat and baked, Boswell hanging laxly from his sweating hand, he could watch the first mate standing at the clothesline on deck below him, tying up his dripping white socks and shorts; he could watch the arc of the sky, curving like a concave plate-glass window to meet the pale shining body of the sea. The sun, suspended behind the arching sky as though it hung in a clear curved window, sparkled coolly as always on the wetly glistening sea; but against his bare wet brown flesh it felt as though it were being focused through a burning glass. He squirmed about in a slow agony of pleasure, observing his skin browning through the dark glasses while rancor oozed like sweat out of his pores. Yes, while he broiled in the equatorial blaze, shifting now and again to match the slow swing of the day, he grew certain that every mean deed—the rotten fornications, the small hatreds and puny envies, the inconsequential and fruitless marriages—all were being baked out of his interior being; if he were ever again to touch land, he would return to combat renewed and whole.

By evening the recuperative process had advanced so far that Phil could regard even Bradley Holliday with a kind of benevolent neutrality. He awoke from an evening's slumber in time for a cold shower and a beef sandwich; it was midnight and time for him once again to go on watch.

And once again he sat facing Australia, facing the slate-grey radio panels with their eye-like dials that kept him, literally, in touch with the other little vessels sliding along the surface of the southern sea—an island, two islands, three islands away. *Wiper age 39, cramps lower rt. qdrt., pse adv med. . . .* The plaintive little calls of the distant ships, flutey and disembodied in the rich velvet-black air, served only to lull him further away from the reality of their thread-connected world.

It was with some surprise, therefore, that Phil looked up from the deep green of his desk, and saw Bradley Holliday standing in the doorway. He must have made some slight gesture in order to attract Phil's attention, perhaps he merely coughed; in any event, he was carrying a tall bottle of Bols gin with two glasses, a leather case the size of a notebook, and a bulky folder wrapped in manila paper.

"I'm not intruding, am I?" Holliday looked serious, and even—aided by his impressive paraphernalia—purposeful. "You suggested—"

"Come in. Take my sneakers off the chair and sit down."

"Thanks." Holliday did as he was told, then held the gin bottle critically up to the light. "You don't have any scruples about drinking on watch, do you, Sparks?"

"This is a free and easy ship."

"So I've noticed. I go up on the bridge every afternoon to chew the fat with the second mate, and the old man hasn't kicked me down below yet. That's remarkable in itself."

"I suppose so."

"You've got a good feeding ship too—the steward is an all right guy. As a matter of fact, I persuaded him to give me—" he unbuttoned his khaki shirt and drew forth a bottle of Australian lemon juice, "—a quart of this stuff from the freezer. Makes the gin more palatable, you know. Say when."

Phil indicated the correct level with his forefinger as Holliday decanted the bottle, then placed it on the desk before the little set of radio manuals and Penguin books and leaned back gingerly in his chair as though he were still unsure of his welcome.

"But no matter how good . . ." He stopped, moistened his lips, and then said determinedly, "It really doesn't matter whether you're on a happy ship or not if you have a serious problem. There's something about being at sea that cuts you off psychologically from the ordinary solutions. If you come up against something that you can't find an answer for by yourself, then you're stuck. You're really stuck."

Philip looked at him in surprise.

"It doesn't make any difference what the size of the crew is either, whether it's forty-five, or fifty, or a hundred and fifty. The point is that

although they're your shipmates, they're still not the people you'd volun-
tarily choose for friends. It's sheer luck if you find just one person you can
talk to. That's why I've come up here tonight."

The earphones which Phil wore looped around his throat like a primitive necklace seemed to have grown suddenly both heavy and loud; would
Holliday feel that it was rude of him to go on wearing them? He lowered
their volume and suspended them from one of the knobs of the short-wave
receiver where they swung like a gift offering, squawking faintly. If Holliday wanted to, he could accept the gesture as an invitation to proceed.

"Frankly," Holliday said warmly, "I felt that you were the kind of
person I could talk to. Perhaps it sounds silly, but I believe that college
men and people who like good books in general are usually more understanding than uncultured people. I studied engineering at U.C.L.A. for
a while, until my dad's money ran out, and I appreciate the difference
between people who are *simpatico,* like yourself, from having really made
an effort to appreciate the finer things, and people who simply don't care."

Philip was paralyzed into silence by the presumptuousness of this nonsense; it was a marvel how smoothly the passenger seemed to maneuver
in this No Man's Land between sincerity and insincerity. And yet . . . and
yet . . . Philip was forced to admit to himself that an appeal to his superior
sensibility was gratifying, flattering, no matter how or by whom it was
uttered. Although he had raised his hand protestingly during Holliday's
brief oration, he dropped it as the statement was brought to a close and
Holliday handed him a glass. "Here's looking at you, Sparks."

Phil gulped at the concoction, glancing uneasily over the rim of the
glass at his drinking companion. Would he begin by being a little reticent,
simply because his conception of the cultivated young man included a
modicum of reserve as standard equipment? Phil set down his glass as
Holliday unwrapped the manila bundle and straightened the leather case.

"I've been having a bit of trouble with my girl," Holliday said, in a more
casual tone. "You know how it is when you're out on one of these Pacific
runs. There's so much time to think things over that you don't take
anything for granted. Are you married, Sparks?"

Phil nodded, but did not volunteer any information. It was one thing
for this man to walk into the room with his personal troubles in his
pocket, ready to be uncorked and poured like gin; but there was no
reason for Phil himself to counter with Natalie, as though the calculated

wifely hypocrisy which he suffered from her could somehow cancel out Holliday's difficulties.

"Then you'll see my problem that much more clearly." He unfolded the leather case and stood it on end, like an open book, facing Phil. It contained a Kodachrome photograph of a girl who smiled directly out of the picture at him. "This is Phyllis. I thought I'd set the scene for you a little, so to speak, if I brought her picture along so you could see what she looks like. Attractive, isn't she?"

The picture, embossed with the label of a prominent Hollywood photographer, was of a girl in her twenties, no longer flushed with youth, but still fresh and piquant. Her Norse cheekbones were thrown into relief by her smile, which was not the cajoled grimace of an ordinary portrait. There was a wistfulness in the slight arch of her back-flung neck and in the pouting curve of her full parted lips that was reminiscent of the wholehearted tenderness possessed by a few girls whom Phil had known. Only her hair was uninteresting; it was set in conventional curls as though she dared not make one gesture that would set her apart from all the other girls of her world, as though finally she had to cling, to capitulate in this little way to its demands.

Everything that the photograph revealed about this girl, yes, even her hair, was infinitely touching to Phil, and he paid her the tribute of saying to the man who claimed her, "She's really lovely."

"Isn't she?" Bradley Holliday smiled gratefully. "She's just that good in bed too. Sensational." His smile broadened but did not become vulgar. "I know I can speak frankly to you, Sparks. A lot of sailors would blow their corks if I said anything like that to them. Once you sleep with a girl you're not supposed to have any respect for her, unless she's your wife; and then you can't ever mention the fact that you lay her. The whole world is divided into the whores that you bang and the women you love. Some of these smart apples brag to me—they actually brag!—that they've never seen their wives with their clothes off. With people like that it's useless to talk.

"But my problem is a little more complicated than anything those sailors ever encountered. For one thing, Phyllis is after me to marry her and I'm damned if I know what to do. Sometimes I think, go ahead, marry her. One of these days you may hit the beach and find her married to someone else. And then I say to myself, why look for trouble? She's got a nice apartment and a comfortable bed. Everything is fine as long as I come and go when I please. How do I know what will happen after we get married? Supposing I discover that we're not compatible after all?"

It was really absurd. Philip had posed the same unreal questions to himself when he married Grace, and again when he met Natalie, and he had been unable to answer them sensibly. How then could he answer them now, when they were asked by a man who was not even aware of the meaning of the words that he used?

But apparently Holliday did not expect an answer. "I took the liberty," he said quietly, as he opened the manila folder and drew forth a packet tied with string, "of bringing along Phyl's letters, the ones she's written me since I left on the last voyage. If I may—"

"Whose letters?"

"Phyl." Holliday inclined his head toward the picture. "My fiancée."

"You startled me. That's my name too, you know."

"Oh, is it? I'm afraid I didn't catch it when we were introduced. What did you say your last name was?"

"Stolz." Phil hesitated for an instant. "That means 'proud' or 'pride' in German," he added, and hated himself as soon as the words were out. What a horror, he thought agitatedly, what a lurking horror to know that the hateful need of "justifying" one's very name lay always hidden in ambush, like an ugly beast, ready to leap forth snarling whenever identification was demanded.

Holliday did not seem to notice Philip's perturbation. He turned over the tied bundle of letters with curious caution, as though he were examining a stack of new banknotes. "Would it be too much of an imposition—" he glanced up warily, as if to say *We* know that I'm not worried about it being an imposition, "—if I were to read some of Phyl's letters to you now?"

But if he had come to the radio room simply to read the letters, why did he bother to ask permission? Was it possible that he was troubled by pangs of conscience, that he desired simple masculine approval for what might otherwise be considered a betrayal of confidence?

Phil said, "I'm perfectly willing to listen. But do you think—"

"Oh, I know!" Holliday cried, almost gaily. "You're afraid that Phyl might be offended. But she's not that type, not at all. In fact, I think she'd be rather pleased about my reading some passages to you. You'll see what

I mean; some of her letters sound as though she'd written them for an audience, instead of just for me."

Phil studied the girl's photograph. It was possible, wasn't it, that Holliday was right, that this girl, with her determined brows and her smiling but fervent eyes, was fully capable of a public utterance of her feelings. . . . Or was he being swayed, as Phyllis very likely had been, by Holliday's insolent charm?

Holliday clinched it by saying calmly, "Phyllis works for an advertising agency. Unfortunately, she takes it seriously, so . . ." His shrug was both worldly and cynical.

Phil felt baffled and powerless. Even if he too were to shrug in reply, the graceless motion of his shoulders could hardly compete with Holliday's eloquent gesture. But before the silence could become awkward, Holliday had snapped the string and begun to read the topmost letter.

"Darling Brad, just a few hours since you've left—this was last May—*and yet everything seems different. Isn't it odd how you can go on doing the same things, and yet feel that all meaning has been sucked out of them, merely by virtue of one person's departure from your life? The egg that was so juicy and tempting suddenly becomes an Easter egg, gaily colored still, but hollow and empty on the inside . . ."*

So this was the prose that she had polished for Holliday and his chance acquaintances. Phil looked at the girl's picture with compassion and contempt. If she had entrusted her private dreams to Holliday, she had no one to blame but herself for what became of them.

". . . of course, I can hear you saying, isn't it foolish of her to sit down and write to me when I've just left, and she hasn't any news for me? But, darling, I only want to tell you that suddenly I understand how it is that there won't be any news, not any at all, until you come back. The job isn't going to have any flavor, even the apartment that I've been so proud of because you've been so comfortable here . . ."

Phil knew now that he was going to have to listen to the entire series of letters. He reached for the bottle and poured two more drinks. It was the first liquor he had tasted since the final night with the girl at Lennons Hotel, but it aroused only pictorial memories of that scene as it trickled warmly down his throat. This was going to be one of those occasions when he would remain sober, seeing everything with a cold and painful clarity, no matter how much he drank. Holliday, already absorbed in presenting the evidence of his manhood, gulped absently at the gin, drew forth another letter, and cleared his throat.

"*Darling Brad,*" he read, "*here goes another letter off into space. I sometimes think that the worst thing about separation is this hollow routine of sending off a whole series of letters before I can even hope for a single answer. But then that's not your fault, is it? If I had been shrewd and calculating I would have tied in with a junior executive type who would be here for dinner every evening at six-thirty sharp, instead of with a sea-going engineer. Perhaps things will be different when you return from this voyage . . .* dot, dot, dot," Holliday said. "She puts three dots here, after voyage. That's a little habit of hers."

Phil nodded ambiguously. Was it really possible that with hardly anything more to go on than three dots (and God alone knew what they signified to Holliday) he could begin to construct for himself a portrait of the girl, not contradicting, but only paralleling the portrait that stood before him on the desk?

"*. . . so that by the time I got home I was really too worn out to curl up on the studio couch with a box of stationery and write you all about the concert, as I really wanted to. Anyway, Serkin was simply magnificent, at the top of his form, and I wanted to cry—I would have cried—during that wrenching, indescribable slow movement, if only it had been you sitting next to me instead of Doris.* That's the girl she shares the apartment with. *But I couldn't very well hold Doris's hand, could I, dear? . . . the result is that I'm stealing company time to write to you, and even, as you can see only too plainly, company paper. The folder that I'm supposed to be working up on California lettuce just doesn't seem particularly intriguing to me now, especially when I think of you making for those sloe-eyed Oriental maidens. Tell me, Brad, are they really sloe-eyed?*" Holliday paused and cocked an eye at Phil. "She's being eu-pha-mistic, you know," he explained.

Phil did not answer. The badly pronounced interpolation was doubly offensive; he was just beginning to feel like an omniscient author who is presented the facts of the case by a nervous shipboard acquaintance. This pleasurable certainty that he was being given a series of facts, some essential and some peripheral, whose significance as fiction he would determine for himself at his leisure, was badly shaken by the engineer's self-interruption. In a sense it recalled him to a gross reality that had been gratefully diminishing during the reading of the first few letters. He looked up from the scratch pad (on which he had been abstractedly jotting the weather report of a distant freighter as it cheeped from the earphones before him, high above Holliday's voice), intending to say "Please go on reading," or something of the sort, but en route to Holliday his eyes met the girl's, smiling warningly at him from the picture frame, and suddenly he understood that he and Phyllis had become friends. Was she as much of a friend as an author's newly developing character? More, perhaps, for with any luck at all he would now learn from her own pen, aided by his own retrospective surmises, those things which an author is never quite able to construct; and as he moved towards an identification so absolute that it emboldened him to forecast the entire course of the correspondence, he was gladdened by a sense of his own power and insight surely surpassing, he thought, even the vision of a skilled and inventive writer. He leaned forward eagerly to hear the ardent beginning of a new series of letters.

Holliday smoothed the sheets over his bare hairy knees. "*My own darling,*" he read, with an odd kind of detached fervor, like an actor reading for an audition, "*it's a week today that you're gone, a week torn out of my life, as useless and meaningless as the seven empty sheets of the calendar that I crumple up and throw away. It's just impossible to write you a chatty letter about Doris or the new slip covers or what the supervisor said to me yesterday or those brutal cramps that started up this morning. I can't, Bradley, because I am sick from thinking about you and about how I love your slow, hard smile and the way you smoke in bed with your arms clasped behind your head and the cigarette dangling down towards your chest and the smoke curling over your face . . .*"

Philip felt himself flushing. But Holliday, pausing only to replenish his glass, continued to read in an impersonal monotone, his voice gradually thickening as the gin slurred down his throat.

"*. . . one thing I can't discuss with Doris, even tho' she sleeps in the next room and is closer to me than anyone in the world but you. Precisely because she's always slept alone, how could she know anything of that sickening loneliness on a Sunday morning in May? No one else could know the way it was when you and I lay here watching the sun sneak through the long window and crawl across the foot of the bed, while E. Power Biggs blasted away majestically at the organ all the way across the country, and*

we sipped coffee and listened to Bach and got ready to make love . . ."
Holliday flipped open his Zippo lighter with a metallic snap and lighted
a fresh cigarette, then went on: ". . . *that dreadful thrashing about, which
is at bottom I suppose the fear that everything is lost and irrevocably in the
past. And then . . . la recherche du temps—*" He pronounced the word
temps as though it were *Thames.*

Philip broke in furiously, "You're pronouncing it wrong!"

"That's possible." Holliday nodded equably. "My French is pretty poor
—although I've never had any trouble making myself understood by the
babes in Marseilles. It's different with Phyl. She takes it as a personal
affront every time I mispronounce a word."

It was fantastic. By admitting his inadequacy, Holliday succeeded in
representing himself as a simple, straightforward fellow; while Phyllis
became, to just that extent, the snob and the fake. But was that completely false? Wasn't Phyllis being driven by anxiety and ambition to the
kind of extreme attitudes that would entitle her lover to smile patroniz-
ingly, secure in the knowledge that he was by comparison more unassum-
ing and more honest?

Holliday however could not rest content with having planted these
seeds of doubt in his listener's mind; he had to add, "Phyl claims that she
prefers French movies to Hollywood movies. I think it's just an affecta-
tion. We have to sit through all those arty movies instead of being able
to see a decent show, just so she can discuss them afterwards with her
intellectual friends. Let me read on a bit—you'll see what I mean."

As Holliday read on, the all too familiar words, *anguish, love, the
hideous power of loneliness, the memory of you lying beside me in the dark,*
falling dully from his lips like tarnished stones, Phil asked himself: Why
did I become angry? Why should I care how he pronounces her words?

The answer lay not so much in Holliday as it did in the girl, and in
Philip's own attitude towards her. It was no longer possible for him to
maintain the pose of the detached author, to listen to these revelations
with the keen hopefulness of one who would hasten to note his impres-
sions in his journal upon the conclusion of the reading. For he knew the
girl too well already, and any further display of the literary efforts and the
borrowed French phrases with which she exposed herself to this coarse
man reflected less on Holliday than it did on her, or even on Phil himself.

Something very strange was happening. It wasn't even necessary for him to regard her taut cheekbones, or her serious and sensuous mouth, in order to visualize her in any number of "honest" poses: listening to a Horowitz recording, semi-recumbent on a studio couch in her stockinged feet, her paired shoes standing neatly on the rug; leaning forward in a hard undertaker's chair at a protest meeting for Spain, or Czechoslovakia, or Greece, or Palestine, her chin cupped firmly in her large white hand and her hair tied back behind her ears; lounging in an armchair with him, running her fingers easily through his hair and teasing him with a little private dirty joke about the similarity of their names, her legs lying fluidly athwart his lap while he plucked at the nylon hose, feeling the close grain of her neatly shaved shins under his thumb, and thinking cloudily of how it would be when he moved his hands upwards under her clothing to undefended smoother places. He shuddered . . .

Meanwhile Holliday was reading: ". . . *as though I could burst when the crescendo swells through the room. Brahms appeals to the adolescent in me, my darling, just as Thomas Wolfe would appeal to the adolescent in you.*" Holliday flicked at the letter with his long index finger. "Phyl thinks there's something of me in Wolfe. Or vice versa. She's a great one for literary allusions—is that the expression? Here, for example, she says: *"I must quote you a few lines from Jean Stafford's lovely first novel, which I am belatedly reading. Miss Pride, a crusty old spinster, like me, is . . ."*

Phil looked at him in horror. You son of a bitch, he thought, you're reading my mail. Who do you think would write you letters like that? How dare you open my mail? Why, even Natalie had written to him like this before the game had palled on her. He could have predicted, if Holliday had asked him, that presently Phyllis's pride and frustration would fuse into an irritated analysis of what she now began to call "our relationship."

"Our relationship," Holliday read stolidly (if they only knew, Phil thought, how I despise those stale words!), *"can only be understood when we're separated. Because it's true, isn't it, my dear, that our mutual sexual attraction blurs the edges of all the sharp and strong reasons for our remaining separated? Any rational attempt to explain what we mean to each other has to start from the premise that . . ."*

As Holliday droned on, Phil felt himself shrinking down into his chair, embarrassed for Phyl by what she was saying to him, the way she was saying it, and the intermediary who was intercepting her letters to him. Ah, Phyl, Phyl, he thought, everything you're going to tell me has been told to me before; why must you persist in spelling it out, why must you delude yourself into believing that you are saying something profound or acute, or even especially intelligent? He looked at her picture again. She still looked as bright and as pretty, in her wistful and touching way, as she had when Bradley Holliday had first placed the photo on the desk; but now Phil sensed another quality in her taut and sharp-boned face that he had not seen before when he looked into her full piquant smile: it was a special kind of ambition, the ambition to achieve sexual dominance and psychic mastery peculiar to educated American women. But your aggressive ambition, my love, he said silently to the photograph, is really nothing more than fear. You can disguise it with tough secondhand phrases about —he heard Holliday mouthing the words—*personality differences* and *clashes of interest* and *areas of incompatibility*, but behind this tangled shrubbery of pseudo-technical jargon there lies still the cold sweating body of fear. And that's why, in the end, after you have bravely attempted to talk away the salty terror, the awful certainty that the final decision: to quit or not to quit? lies not in your hands, but in mine, then you will capitulate. Yes, you will capitulate. Because you know what it means, you and all the other girls like you that I have known so well, to be past twenty-five and to feel in the very marrow of your bones that there will no longer be an infinite number of Philip Stolzes, or even Bradley Hollidays, for you to meet, with a shivery foretaste of excitement, at a party, on a bus, or even in your imagination. It is this knowledge that breeds the bitter rebellion, and yet also enforces the ultimate capitulation. I know, Phyl, he told the picture, because it was my profile that graced the other side of the coin in the bedroom in Brisbane; heads or tails, we all proceed, protest though we may, to be melted down together in the same final furnace.

Holliday was drinking from the bottle now. He wiped his lips carefully with a clean white handkerchief and said shrewdly, "You know where she gets this analytical business—it's her job. That advertising agency pays her sixty bucks a week for what they call market research. Women are all the same, aren't they? Instead of forgetting about the job when she gets home, she has to sit down and write up a report on the status of her love-life." He stared cunningly at the photograph. "You don't fool me, baby. I don't impress as easily as you think, not even when I'm all alone in the middle of no-place, and sick, and—" Turning back to Phil, he said lightly, "She doesn't pull any of that stuff when we're alone together. She may indulge herself in public, it's true, but never in the bedroom."

Well, wasn't it true of himself too? There was no reason for him to feel superior, no reason to hate this man who was so like himself, when he too had more than once been forced to recognize that what caused a girl's eyeballs to roll upwards, her toes to crisp, her fingers to scrape against his flesh, was something other than an intense satisfaction at the discovery of common intellectual interests.

"Watch how her mood changes now," Holliday said confidentially, like a mechanic explaining the workings of an engine. "This one is dated the twelfth of June, before she got my first batch of letters. *My very very dear Brad,* she says, *Still no word from you, and I begin to wonder if I shall ever open another one of your exotic envelopes. I feel obliged to tell you, prompted by the special kind of honesty that we have saved for each other, darling, that it might be better for us both if I were never to receive another letter from you.*"

"What a special kind of dishonesty!" Phil murmured aloud.

"What?"

"Nothing." He ducked his head, as if to listen to the earphones, and scrawled a few words on the pad before him. "Go ahead."

"*. . . another letter from you. There are two reasons for this feeling, which strengthens day by day. First is the very strong suspicion that we would both be too cowardly to ever bring things to an end face to face—perhaps if our love must end, it would be better for it to peter out in unwritten letters . . . And I must admit, darling, that the letters I have received from you during your previous absences have not been such to set me aflame with desire for you . . .*"

"I'm not that kind of a person." Surprisingly, the reading of these words had put Holliday a little on the defensive. He took another drink and coughed quietly, like an after-dinner speaker, preliminary to going on with his explanation. "I could never sit down and say all those things. It's a woman's place . . . Besides, how did I ever know if I'd be writing the truth? If I never really knew how I felt, how could I let go with a lot of romantic . . ."

Philip felt closer to his enemy than he had at any time since their first meeting. Phyl was forcing Holliday into the same kind of virtuous refusal to commit himself that Philip had always prided himself upon. This demonstration of honorable male solidarity was so unexpected that Phil did not now know quite how to react.

He listened with dismay as Phyl gave herself away in this series of letters written in the month of June, growing more vituperative as her desperation increased. How terrible that she could not find it in herself to maintain the minimal dignity of silence! But no, here aboard the tanker that slid along the surface of the black warm sea at three o'clock in the morning, Holliday, perceptibly drunk by now, went on relentlessly reading aloud from this serialized chronicle of guilt and shame.

"Was I a girlish fool to have expected that mere exposure to the books I liked, to the people whom I call my friends, to the music that is so important to me, would alter the ingrained attitude of vulgar mockery and lowbrow disdain that seems more important to you than any affection? . . . Shouldn't I have known, Bradley, from your first stilted, insincere letters, that you would fall asleep at a chamber music recital, and that on the way home you would attempt to justify yourself by impugning the sincerity of my appreciation of the music?"

Holliday looked up from the letter, his mouth twisted. "She doesn't mention how we made up when we got to her house that night. Funny, isn't it, the way they can forget the things that really count? Then she says, *Shouldn't I have known that you would seize the first opportunity to sneer at my dearest friend, the girl with whom I live, the girl whose hospitality you have accepted on so many occasions?* That's Doris Fleischman, her roommate. She's got a beak sharper than the bow of this ship."

Phil cringed. The hackles of terror rose tremblingly, his fingers suddenly began to drum senselessly against the green table, and he had to blink to clear the film from his eyeballs. All of the old taunting phrases came surging into his gullet like vomit. And Holliday was saying:

"All I said to Phyl was that Doris ought to get her nose bobbed if she really wanted a man. I wouldn't have said it to her face, Phyl knows that, and she didn't hear us, because she was out in the kitchen mixing drinks. Dor isn't a bad sort—for a Jew. She even baked some brownies once and mailed them out to me. But that's no reason to live with one, is it?"

So once again he was accepted into the community of Gentiles. What could be more humiliating than the knowledge that he was too cowardly to become enraged, that secretly he was pleased at what should have disgusted him. . . . Yes, he was pleased that this weak, sick, vulgar man, this personification of everything that he despised, had casually included him in his world; by its very nature, the compliment excluded even the possibility of his protesting. He lowered his head to the table, his forehead resting on his slowly sweating forearm, thinking that perhaps he might cry; but it was too long since he had indulged himself in the feminine pleasure, even the dry sobs of self-pity would not come, and he was forced to sit quietly with his face rubbed in his own sweat while his faithful antagonist read aloud from the pathetic diary of their mutual mistress.

". . . *seven of them, all at once! I was such a child, darling, I lined them up on the rug and plopped down on my stomach and fondled them, making sure that I would read them in the order in which you had written them. Such wonderful letters!*

"*Have I been terribly foolish, sweetheart? If I could have only one wish granted, I would wish with all my heart that the letters I have written you could disappear before they reached your hand. Did I really say that I couldn't possibly love anyone who didn't care for the Emperor Concerto? You're going to have to try very hard to forgive me for all the snobbish nonsense that I've been inflicting on you in these last few weeks. But pride feeds on loneliness, I guess. All I can promise you is that when you finally return to me I will know how to make you forget the cruel and stupid things I have been writing. I wouldn't care if you never wanted to go to another concert with me again, as long as you still wanted to be with me, Bradley. We have been so happy, and we will be happy again. I know it in my bones, just as I know that all of our superficial differences are not central to the one new person that both of us merge into when we are really alone together . . .*"

Above, on the night-wrapped bridge, the ship's bell tinkled seven times. It was half past three. This was the blackest hour of all. In another hour, perhaps two, dawn would come sneaking over the horizon like a sob. Holliday was still reciting the final chapter of the girl's capitulation; the ugly desperate lies knocked against Philip's ear with the flat finality of a radio announcer's description of doom. If only Holliday would accept her, how quickly Phyllis would prove that she meant what she said! How quickly the pot roasts and the babies would replace the anxious insistence upon an immediate acquaintance with the critically certified! You will put them off, Phyl, he thought tiredly, first the concerts, and then the plays, and at last the books. And in a few years you will content yourself with the intellectual luxury of a Saturday matinee while Bradley is out golfing —perhaps you will be able to slip off your shoes midway through the first act, to ease your swelling feet and your shriveling soul. . . .

He looked up from the green linoleum into Holliday's bleak eyes. The Bols was almost empty; in the sudden silence he could see, he could almost hear the last few ounces of gin stirring gently in the bottom of the bottle, quickened by the soft vibrations of the ship's engines.

Now was the time for confidences and revelations. In this final hour before dawn, Holliday doubtless expected to receive advice and sustenance that would enable him to adopt an unfaltering attitude toward Phyllis. But his hands trembled as he slid her picture carelessly in to the manila folder with all of her letters, so that her exquisite face, composite of all the best of Philip's girls, was pressed against her own truths and her own lies. Was there a light fragrance hanging in the air above the manila folder, a mild fresh scent emanating from the lonely letters of May, the bitter letters of June, the tear-drenched letters of July, that had outlasted the briny air in which they must have been handled so much?

Holliday, falsely casual, gathered together his liquor and his letters and rose to his feet. He wavered, belched, smiled an apology behind the back of his hand, but said nothing. Wasn't he going to ask any questions? Could he dare to believe that everything explained itself? You rotten coward, Phil muttered, staring malevolently at Holliday's naked bony feet that jutted from his sandals as they slapped across the room, you dirty rotten coward. Then he noticed that Holliday was still trembling involuntarily, as a tree moves when it is shaken by a slow steady soundless wind. It reminded Philip of something he had quite forgotten: Holliday's terrible sickness. Not even the fat doctor could know what it had already done to him. One thing however was certain; he wanted to be relieved of the moral responsibility of deciding in what way it would affect his future with Phyllis. Go ahead, ask me, Phil said to himself, ask me, you syphilitic bastard. I'll tell you what you ought to do.

But Holliday did not ask. Instead he walked quietly to the door and stopped there for a moment with one foot on the coaming, looking more like a gaunt drunken spider than ever, his lank shadow falling jaggedly across the high metal filing cabinet and the ten-gallon jug of distilled water. He smiled insolently and said, "I'd better hit the sack right away. I like to get up fairly early so that I can skip rope before the sun gets too high."

He was gone before Philip could open his mouth to reply. His conduct was as unexpected as it was unfathomable. Did he really believe that Philip was unaware of his illness, or did he mean to trade on Philip's knowledge of it, as a blind singer on a subway benefits from the guilty superiority of his seated listeners, so that he could wrench the final coins of pity from his own listener?

Philip jerked the typewriter towards him and typed out the entries in his log from the sweat-soaked jottings he had made while listening to the letters. When he had finished bringing himself up to the minute in this impersonal diary that no one would ever read aloud, he leaned back weakly, exhausted by the force of his hatred of Holliday and the realization of what it meant.

As he sat numbly watching the complex clock, with its slowly swinging silver second hand, and its hypnotic double circle of numbers that indicated both Greenwich Mean Time and Ship's Time (neither of which had any meaning for him now), Phil could smell the stale fumes of his visitor's gin. The room was too quiet. The subdued static that had sputtered softly throughout the reading of the letters was dying away to a whisper. One of his batteries had gone dead; he noted the fact in the log and signed his name as self-witness to his exit from this room. Then he dismounted the battery and connected a fresh one.

He stepped warily out on deck, staggering a little under the weight of the dead battery, which he now had to give a decent burial. Moving slowly along the boat deck past the captain's cabin, his eyes gradually strengthening in the pale glow of the masthead lights as the rest of his body weakened, the battery which he carried on his shoulder (like a young father stealthily bearing the coffin of his dead infant to a moonlit cemetery) growing heavier with each step, he came abreast of the chart room at last under the watchful stars and paused to catch his breath.

Then he noticed a figure standing on the bitts at the bow of the vessel. He was leaning over the side, apparently watching the phosphorescent fish fleeing in the white spume from the ship's cutting edge. He was not the bow lookout; he was not, in fact, a crew member at all. Who else but myself, thought Philip, would stand nervously peering ahead, towards America, at four o'clock in the morning, on this swaying, laggard vessel? The man straightened, flung something to leeward with the sweeping motion of a baseball pitcher, then bent over the gunwale once again. It was Bradley Holliday.

Rage rose like blood in Philip's throat. He hawked up a mouthful of Holliday's gin and lemon juice—it tasted sweet and thick, like blood—and spat it over the side. Holliday was probably so exultant over his betrayal of Phyllis that he could not go directly to sleep; now he looked forward, no doubt, to leaping up and down on the catwalk once again with a length of rope, exposing his rotting body to the sun and the sea and Philip's loathing gaze.

Philip lowered himself carefully and silently down from the boat deck on the iron-runged ladder. As he approached Holliday from the rear, stepping quietly in his sneakers, he saw the engineer pick up a bottle and stuff it with paper. Holliday was so intent upon his task, twisting sheets of paper and cramming them into the narrow neck of the bottle, that he would have been unaware of anyone's approach even if it had been less stealthy.

When Philip was only a few feet behind his quarry, he stopped and hefted the battery, high in the air. Held over his head in this way, like an offering, it seemed to have grown lighter; and yet, he reflected, how easily it could crush a man's skull! Standing this close, he could see the exact spot where it should land: a little bald area at the crown of Holliday's head, circled like a target by thin wet strands of hair. The blow would send Holliday and his letters to the bottom of the ocean. While Philip stood behind him and a little below him, gathering his moral strength to a focus, Holliday raised the gin bottle which he had stuffed with Phyllis's letters and flung it into the sea. At another time the gesture would have been outrageously melodramatic, but now, in the pearly grey morning just before dawn, alone at the wet clear bow of the tanker, it bore a stern logic of its own, terrible and final. Yet when Holliday proceeded to tear the girl's picture into long thin fluttering strips that took to the air almost of their own accord, like the colored rag-tails of a kite, Phil was moved to protest this abandoned act. He took a step forward.

Holliday whirled about and revealed his true face to Philip. Everything of the rake, the lady-killer, the poseur, was eaten away. His feet slid from the bitts to the deck. His eyes, spray-flecked and mad in the growing light, glared desolately at the dead battery that was suspended over his head, then moved across Philip's face until they encountered their mirror in Philip's eyes.

As they stood at the bow of the ship that swayed slowly towards their homeland, face to face in this final moment of recognition, they stared silently into each other's eyes, and the sun came slowly and silently crashing over the horizon of the southern sea.

YEAR OF GRACE

Burton Rettler had no intention of falling in love when he entered Vic's Pharmacy. There had been no warning of it while he downed his tuna sandwich, glancing occasionally from his horn-rimmed reflection in the steamy mirror beyond the Silexes and the tall aluminum urns to the slim girl making change at the window; but the moment he put his money into Victoria's cool hand and looked into her laughing eyes he knew that he was in trouble.

He asked why he had never seen her before—her voice was pitched somewhat lower than he would have expected; he asked for a magazine that he didn't want from a rack to the right of the cash register—her figure was so good that it made him nervous to watch her bending over; he asked for a date—her alacrity in accepting, and the gentle *way* she accepted, proved that she appreciated him for what she saw him to be, an intellectual and a man of honor. Four months later they were married.

Burton and Victoria were a levelheaded young couple. Both sets of parents—Victor Merz the college-town druggist and his lame wife, and Joe Rettler the windshield-wiper salesman and his rose-fancying wife—were pleased that their children had their feet on the ground. The marriage was a good bet from all points of view: Mr. and Mrs. Merz were delighted that Burton was both substantial and ambitious and that he would not be taking away their only child for at least another two years, or until he had finished his Ph.D. The Rettlers, especially after an initial period of uneasiness verging on bewilderment that their boy had decided to become a college professor, were agreed that the responsibilities of marriage would spur him on to a more realistic grappling with the demands of academic success; Burt himself, walking home alone late at night during those four months of premarital discovery, found his fear of being played the fool yielding to the delicious certainty that he was a very shrewd and lucky fellow. As for Victoria, she was simply in love with a cultivated man, as she had always known she would be.

Burt had been in Korea, and he was completing his studies in the language and culture of medieval Provence through the courtesy of the Federal Government. Victoria had just graduated in Psychology (The Abnormal Child), but was more than happy to go on clerking for her dad in order that her new husband might be free to complete his dissertation unhindered. Day by day they found that their tastes and aspirations dovetailed. Night by night they found that it was fun to be together, and to be married. Thanks to Victoria's realtor uncle, they rented a two-room apartment, which they furnished cautiously, little by little; they bought practical kitchen gadgets from the ads in the Sunday *Times* sports section; and for special occasions they gave each other long-playing records. By their first anniversary Burt was well into his dissertation, they had a Waring blender and two hundred and thirty-seven dollars in the bank, and Victoria was itching to have a baby.

This was a little alarming to Burton, who was becoming more and more concerned with his career as its outlines became progressively clearer to him. He could not exactly say to Victoria that motherhood would mean the loss of her job income, which in turn would mean delaying his degree for six months while he made up the difference and lost out on a possible appointment. Nor could he say that she would be a somewhat less gracious hostess to the head of his department and to the professor under whom he was writing his dissertation if she were constrained by a distended stomach or by an infant crying behind a screen in the corner of the living room. Nevertheless, he got the point across to Victoria, who was already dedicated to his advancement with a devotion that anticipated him in nearly every area, from typing and alphabetizing his bibliography to getting up cozy cocktail parties and intimate dinners for strategically placed faculty members; and she was willing to put off what she wanted until Burton had gotten what they both wanted.

Virtue and hard work were rewarded. Burton got his Ph.D., and what was more, an instructorship; Victoria was perhaps even happier than he, since she had been secretly apprehensive of leaving the town in which she had been born and lived all her life for another college town perhaps thousands of miles from her family. She had never said anything about it, but then as the months went by Burton too seemed to be acquiring the skill of reading her mind.

"You were really scared, weren't you," he said pleasantly one autumn evening, "at the idea of having to leave Mom and Pop Merz if I'd gotten an instructorship some place else."

"I've never traveled much, you know," she replied, suddenly shy. "I never lived away from home. You've been to Korea, and all."

"My home girl."

"Don't tease me."

"All right," he said seriously. "I'm applying for a Fulbright. I wouldn't do it if my chances didn't look good. A year in Provence, you wouldn't be afraid of that, would you, Vic?"

She had smiled. Of course, it seemed silly when you looked at it that way—to be afraid in this day and age to leave Mommy, afraid to cross the ocean, afraid to do what thousands were doing and millions were dying to do. There were two things that she might have said in reply: first, that it was hard to believe that she, Victoria Rettler, had earned a lady's life in Europe; and second, that the word for what she felt when she was actually faced with change was not fear but uneasiness. All it meant, she was reasonably sure, was that because of the way she had been brought up she greeted the prospect of any alteration not eagerly but with anxiety (or was that basically the way women were, the unadvanturous sex?); but that didn't mean that she was slack about going out and doing things when it became necessary—more efficiently, in fact, than someone like Burton himself. This wasn't something she could put into words, any more than Burton could say bluntly just why he wasn't ready to become a father, but this was what husbands and wives should be able, she thought, to understand about each other.

The opportunity to demonstrate her adaptability came very soon. Burton walked swiftly into the drugstore one morning, hatless and with his cheeks reddened by the winter wind, looking younger even than that first day when he had awkwardly requested a date. "It came," he said loudly, in a voice that almost cracked. "It came through, the Fulbright."

Victoria ran out from behind the counter. "I'm so proud! I'm so glad!" She hugged him hard. "Don't meet your class tonight, Burton. Let's go out and celebrate."

Burton's self-possession returned quickly. "We don't have to make a big thing out of it. But it *is* a feather in my cap, isn't it? What's more, it's a bargaining lever. When we get back I'll be able to start thinking in terms of promotion, and if necessary I'll be able to shop around." He added ebulliently, "Why, with that year's research under my belt—"

It was Victoria's turn to step back. She looked at her husband in puzzlement. "Aren't you excited about going there? About the trip and what you'll do and what the life will be like? You sound as though you're only calculating what the fellowship will buy after you get back."

Hurt and uncomfortable, Burton replied, "I was just trying to plan for us, that's all. In every family, someone has to do the. . . ." He caught himself up. "What the hell, this is no way to start our luckiest day. I'll take you down to Bauer's for beer and knockwurst after my class tonight. You know, I'll bet you lit into me just now because you're all tensed up about going to Europe. Aren't you?"

It was fun, getting ready—until they had to apply for their passports. "We'd better get separate passports." Burton said. "Costs ten bucks extra, but it's worth it. You never know—"

"But I'm not going to go wandering around Europe alone."

Burton looked at her in some bewilderment. "I'm just being practical. Suppose I have to go to Switzerland for a couple days, or—" He saw by the set of her jaw that he was getting nowhere. "What's the matter, my home girl," he said lightly. "Afraid I'm going to run away from you? It's no fun traveling without you. Honestly, I'd never . . ."

"All right, Burton."

So he applied for his passport, and she for hers, but somehow Victoria never seemed able to get downtown with her witnesses to complete the formalities. The time was growing short, and Burton held his temper, but finally he said rather brusquely, "Vicky, you can't travel very far without a passport."

"Beverly was supposed to meet me at the Federal Building, but she had a toothache."

"Last time it was supposed to be Aunt Helen, and she—"

"I'll get the damned thing, don't worry."

"It seems obvious that subconsciously you don't want to go. You're afraid, you don't want to leave Mom and Pop—"

"Stop psychoanalyzing me!" Victoria burst into tears.

She got the passport in time, just in time, hating herself for having cried about it. After that, everything was easy.

None of it had time to wear off, the initial shock, the unbelief, the buoyant spending of money for peculiar objects—passport cases, seasick pills, a travel iron—not when they kissed her mother and father goodbye at the station and boarded the train for New York, not even when they pushed their way through the crowds at the pier. But then at last everything was stowed away in their cabins (they were to sleep separately in Tourist Class, each with a bunk in a cabin for four) and they ran up on deck to bid farewell together to their native land. Seeing the enormous but fragile sky line through a blur of trembling hands and upflung scarves, seeing it fade like old lace in twilight almost before it could be believed, was like losing someone you knew you were on the point of falling in love with. Victoria felt herself crying like a fool; she unhooked her arm from her husband's and fled.

Burton found her, some moments later, lying on her bunk with a handkerchief pressed to her eyelids. He regarded her uneasily for a moment, then filled a glass with cold water from the carafe, squeezed down next to her, and offered her the glass.

She sat up soon, shook her hair, blew her nose, and drank the water which her husband was holding as if it were a bouquet. What made it more disconcerting was her sudden awareness that he was treating her like an invalid, or a neurotic. Not only didn't he share her emotion, he couldn't even understand it; behind his uncomfortable grin was an uncomfortable suspicion that he might as well steel himself to play nurse to her seasickness. *I'll be damned,* she said to herself, as she arose impatiently and took a brush to her hair; *nobody's going to take care of me.* She smiled courteously into the mirror at the smooth reflection of her husband, who stood behind her with his hands loosely at her waist, the Dramamine pills doubtless tucked away in his vest pocket, the worry of having to care for her instead of being taken care of by her reflected ever so faintly in a slight knitting of his brows.

"I'm fine now," she said. "Now that we're really on our way. . . . Let's go eat, I hear the bells. I signed up for first serving—you're always hungry so early, and they say that the sea air. . . ."

The voyage was a vacation. No, it was more than that. On their earlier vacations together, starting with their honeymoon at Lake Superior, Burton and Victoria had been engrossed in each other, and in their common dreams. Now they could—or at least Victoria could—become engrossed in other people. There were, it was true, many young couples more or less like themselves (they were the ones with whom Burton seemed to prefer to spend his time), but there were also people unlike any they had ever encountered before. Victoria found herself drinking at the little bar with a Fresno rug merchant bound for Amman and Damascus, playing shuffleboard with a scintillating blonde of uncertain age and occupation who was heading for a vacation (from what?) at Positano, defending the younger generation to elderly Italian peasant women who lay groaning in their deck chairs.

To Burton these people were amusing, although raffish and unprofitable. But he hesitated to complain to Victoria about her new acquaintances, if only because they apparently kept her in high spirits. He turned instead to those with whom he instinctively felt at home, and to preparations for his pending research, while Vic amused herself with the oddballs.

They disembarked, Tampax, foot warmers and reference books, at Cannes. The rug peddler, the blonde and all the elderly Italians stood at the rail smiling sadly and waving down at them as they bobbed off in the lighter toward Palm Beach and the white Greek yachts with their bowers of carnations and tanned ladies in shorts who sipped long smoky drinks and watched carelessly through binoculars as the launch bore them ashore.

Victoria turned to her husband and slipped her fingers into his free hand.

"Excited?" he asked. Several first-class passengers, smelling of brandy, French perfumes and fine cigars, turned and smiled at them.

"Yes." She added in a low voice, "But I'm scared now, too. That's worse."

Burton freed his arm and clasped her closely about the waist; but then he proceeded to say lightly, "This isn't an invasion barge, you know. Nobody's going to be shooting at us—they may even be glad to see our dollars."

As they were herded through customs and police and had their possessions loaded on a rickety old truck, Victoria's high-school French failed her utterly. It was simply up to Burton to get them out of there, to pay off the men who'd handled their baggage and to tell the driver where to take them. The unexpected effort hardly seemed beyond him—he was extraordinarily matter of fact about what could have been the first challenge of their new life—but the issuing of orders, the tiresome attention to detail, and the haggling infuriated him. By the time they were settled in the Citroën taxi his lips were quite white.

"Bastards," he said. "Trying to clip me just because I talk with an accent."

"Maybe," Victoria suggested somewhat timidly, "they overcharge everybody who lands here at Cannes. I mean, all the tourists must seem so rich, and look at those hotels. Maybe they just resent—"

"Haven't you heard about the French peasants? They bury their loot in the back yard." He laughed. "Don't worry about them—they can buy and sell us."

They were heading for a little village a bit inland from St. Tropez; a colleague of Burton's had spent a week there the summer before and had returned ecstatic, with colored slides of the cobbled, sun-dappled streets and stories of charming little villas for rent. Poring over a Hallweg map, Burton had decided that this would indeed be a cheap and cheerful headquarters for the year's Provençal research. It was not a hangout, although there was a congenial little foreign colony, and it was just too far from the sea to make it attractive to tourists. Carefully, Victoria had written ahead to their friend's inn with the aid of a Cassell's dictionary, requesting a reservation with full pension until they would be able to lease a suitable small villa.

The taxicab left the seacoast and began to mount, mount, mount, chugging furiously as though its innards were being put to the supreme test, and the driver leaning back hard against the seat cushions as though he were coaxing some recalcitrant beast. They emerged from the small, steep, sunless road, bordered on either hand by grimly shuttered stone houses, to the sudden dust-clouded heat of a high plateau ringed with small shops across whose doorways were suspended fish net or wooden-beaded hangings that reached to the ground and lay limply in the still, surly air. A greying old hound-dog that lay in the dust of the vacant village square lifted his jowls from the dirt as the cab approached, twitched his nostrils, and fell back asleep.

The taxi stammered to a stop at the far end of the square—the Place de Gaulle, it was called—before a red-awninged *bistro* with a potted oleander and four tables, all empty, all surrounded by spavined chairs rosy with rust, and all still bearing sticky wine glasses and empty Perrier bottles. *Chambres à louer,* said a sign painted on the masonry wall next to the wooden shingle announcing the *plat du jour* at 250 francs. There was no question—the cab driver leaned back even further and sighed with satisfaction, as though he had brought them up on his shoulders—this was the place.

Gingerly, they clambered down from the taxi and planted themselves in the dust. Already they were self-consciously aware that they were overdressed for this village, even in their plain summer clothing. But there was no one to see, only the drowsing dog. The cab driver began to unstrap their luggage from the roof, the old green *camionette* made it up the hill at last with its radiator singing like an old soprano and their belongings swaying sadly and shakily from side to side. Burton and Victoria stared with frightened surmise at the canting objects which were to help them make a home out of somebody's house, then glanced at each other and burst out laughing. Their laughter roused the square: a brandy-legged boy in a blue smock suddenly trotted out to stare, followed by a towheaded cowboy rolling a hoop with a baton, and small twin sisters with what looked like ballet slippers on their feet and their thumbs in their mouths. Shutters clattered not quite surreptitiously, an old lady shuffled out to the bench under an acacia tree near the taxi, squinting at them from under her straw hat, and finally a snaggle-toothed, smiling man clenching a curved calabash came out in straw slippers from the somnolent restaurant to greet them. They had arrived.

The early days in the village were a little like the sea voyage. With the same pleasurable feeling of unreality was an ambiance so unusual that it *had* to be felt as temporary, like crossing the ocean; and this temporariness was at once so exhilarating and so exhausting that a short trip to St.

Tropez to swim or buy a roll of linoleum was enough to send them scuffing home in their *espadrilles,* fit for nothing but an early bedtime.

They had found a little cliffside house that was almost exactly what they wanted, with a whitewashed bedroom and a study for Burton and a dazzling distant view of the Mediterranean.

There were no pressures, no schedules, nothing that had to be done that could not always wait another day. They were very happy in those early weeks. Victoria was unusually ardent, partly because Burton played the guide so well, helped her to learn shopping French and showed off his erudition both amicably and unostentatiously. They awakened early, no longer from necessity but out of a happy assurance that pleasant things were going to happen. Whenever they wanted they could start the day by hopping into their little *quat' chevaux* (the Rettlers and the Merzes had clubbed together to buy them the car) for an early swim at the chilly, placid beach, from which they always brought back a handful of finely striped pebbles simply to caress with the fingertips these little miracles of artistic perfection.

Then the house was quite fixed for their year's occupancy, and the weather began to turn a bit, and there was no longer any reason for Burton not to get on with his research. For a while Victoria accompanied him; but after a few weeks of prowling about musty churches, she began to tire of sitting and waiting in damp and gloomy pews, purse, paper and *Michelin* in hand, while Burton focused his flashlight and took notes. It was no better waiting out of doors or in the foyer of a museum or library while Burt pulled out catalogue cards or squinted over Provençal manuscripts and paintings of medieval tortures. For one thing, it made her uncomfortable to watch her husband in operation. He was not deliberately patronizing, or even impolite; but his American briskness, his obvious impatience to set about his work in preference to lingering, perhaps just over the weather, with someone who was for him not in authority but simply in attendance, marked him as an interloper, a special type of tourist to be tolerated out of common courtesy and nothing more. Besides he had a way of looking at *her* as he emerged, zipping up his briefcase, that seemed to say, *What, you still here?* and made her wish for a while that the things she had studied in college had some relevance to his special world.

Partly in self-defense, partly from boredom, Victoria began to look more carefully at the objects which absorbed her husband. Observed with any care, the religious paintings of southern France simply did not appear to her to be superior works of art. Of course she was no judge, she kept saying to herself, but even Burton's books acknowledged implicitly that the language, too, and the literature which had been created from it, were —with one or two extraordinary exceptions—far from the front rank of European culture. The suspicion gradually hardened into certainty that her husband was devoting his professional life to the exploration of what was at best a minor tributary in the broad stream of Western art. But why was he so immersed in a field that was of minimal interest even to cultured people?

The impulse was irresistible to attribute his ambition not to disinterested speculation, but to a shrewd calculation of his chances in a relatively uncrowded field. If only she could be convinced that Burton was mad about his work—how much more fun it would be to be married to a happy, dedicated crank!

If only he had more humility! A man had to set a reasonable value on his own work, not too much, not too little, if he wanted others to respect him. From her earliest childhood Victoria had read her father's trade journals, pored over the hieroglyphics in his fat volume of the *U.S. Pharmacopoeia*, studied the sentimentalized painting of the sturdy family druggist which had hung on their living room wall ever since she could remember; and she had grown up truly believing that he was a dedicated servant of humanity, a trusted adviser to bearded medicos who relied on his unerring hands to safely compound their crabbed Latin prescriptions. It had come as a painful disillusionment to discover that by far the greater portion of her daddy's income was from hamburger patties filled out with cereal, hot chocolate made with water instead of milk, girlie magazines and tabloid newspapers, and, in the biologicals department where she was not allowed to wait on customers, contraceptives for the students' Saturday nights. Without his knowing it, for she had tried hard to conceal it from him, Victor Merz had shrunk terribly in his daughter's estimation. There was nothing wrong in running a general store and luncheonette— not if you were frank about what you were doing.

Now the same thing was happening with Burton. Victoria found it difficult to conceal the consternation which overcame her when he would say, "Once this monograph appears in the *Journal*, I'll be a made man." Made for whom and for what? she wanted to ask, but dared not, feeling guilty for even allowing the questions to spring to her mind. After all, she was his wife, and she had committed herself. But how much easier it would be if only he would laugh, just once, about what he was doing! Or, barring that, if he would attempt, just once, to infect her with his own enthusiasm not for the academic goal (of which her promised share was comfort and babies), but for the studies themselves—even if a little simulation would be necessary. Instead, he took it for granted that she was content to be an auxiliary to his dogged task, established in his home like a motor installed in a sailing craft, to move him along when he was becalmed, to aid him in routine navigational problems of daily life, but otherwise to remain silent and passive and waiting.

"I don't think I'll go with you tomorrow, Burt," she said one evening, her fingers on the knob of the little radio. A fanfare was being played over and over while Paris-Inter waited for the Lamoureux concert to begin.

Burton looked up in some surprise from a book he was annotating. His heavy eyebrows came together in a frown over his sharply arched nose. "What will you do with yourself all day?"

Victoria laughed a little nervously. As she squirmed on the couch the announcers cut in, first French, then German, then Italian. She turned down the volume and said, "Oh, don't worry about me. I'll find plenty to keep me occupied right here in the village."

"Well, if you're sure. . . ."

He was relieved. It hurt her to acknowledge it, but obviously all that worried him was the minor fear that she might be at loose ends right here in the village, a lost little soul, unable to make her way through the streets unaided, alone and lonely with nothing to do but struggle with French cookbooks and French vegetables, twiddle the dials of the radio, and work weepily through the crossword puzzle in the Paris *Herald*.

She stayed home. In the hushed and glistening morning air she heard first the fish lady, with her little wooden cart and her scaly apron: *"Opay, opay, les belles sar-diiines!"* her voice rising excitedly on the penultimate syllable like the mating call of a beautiful bird; and then the egg-beater motor of her husband's *quat' chevaux* (she no longer thought of it as theirs, since he was afraid to let her drive it on these steep and narrow roads) churning into life beneath the church steeple at the highest part of town and then fading away down the hill.

Victoria went to the doorway and stood on the step with her arms folded, the morning sun striking her breast, awaiting the fish lady. They would have *dorade* that evening, with hand-whipped mayonnaise; and although the fish lady's prices were far higher than those of the fish stand in the *marché couvert*, Victoria was determined to try to make conversation with her, French or no. When she came, grunting behind the cart that thumped heavily over the cobbles, she opened her mouth to show all the gaps between her teeth and began picking up fish by their tails to display them in the morning light, the flies moving slowly out of the way as the shining fish swung through the air.

"Fresh caught," she seemed to be saying, "fine and fresh this morning."

Haltingly, Victoria began to talk to her. The woman was not particularly likeable, she was too shrewd and business-conscious for that, but she was willing to talk. After the fish there was necessarily a piece of ice to be bought for it from the truck that stopped mornings at the *bistro* on the Place de Gaulle. There Victoria met their former landlady, setting out leftovers for the dog, and while they were chatting (painfully, but chatting) Ellen Rumford came along. She was a desiccated but chirpy Englishwoman who sold bad pottery in a shop that reeked from the constant fumes of her Gauloises Bleues, and she insisted on buying Victoria a *café filtre*.

While they sat in the sunshine and waited for the coffee, bad as it was, to drip down into their little cups, they smoked and talked of England, Lake Superior and men; and when they were down to the dregs they walked companionably to the *tabac* for table matches and to the bakery for *baguettes* and the morning paper. There they met Françoise Roy, a tall, bony, grave alcoholic who had worked for de Gaulle in London during the Second World War and was (fortunately for Victoria) rather proud of her English. Françoise insisted on accompanying Victoria to the vegetable stall and then to the butcher's (to buy seven cents' worth of meat for the cat), where, when they pushed through the wooden-beaded hanging, they were greeted by the butcher's hoarse parrot, *"Bonjour, messieurs et 'dames!"*

They took their filets filled with the morning's purchases first to Victoria's and then to the tiny house of Françoise, who insisted upon Victoria's staying to lunch. When they came indoors from the terrace because the sun had dropped behind the cactuses they were astonished to see that it was nearly four o'clock.

"I must get home at once," Victoria said. "I have to clean up and get supper, or Burton'll think I've been off on a tear."

"Please bring him at Christmas for wine punch and to see my roses. They'll surely be in bloom then, and they're the finest in the village."

But Burton did not particularly want to meet any of Victoria's new friends. In the weeks that passed, as he arose every morning and left for Antibes or Grasse or Nice with his portfolio under his arm, and as he returned in the evening with the Paris *Herald* and a kiss for Victoria's cheek, she came to realize why he preferred to be unaccompanied on his daily expeditions. He was playing a game with himself—a game of never-left-home—and he was winning it. Yet he was "making the most" of his European year, dutifully filling out his three-by-five cards and filing them in his carefully labeled shoe boxes for future shipment home. These fetal lecture notes were the only evidence to Victoria that he had ever come so far, for he found the peasants either amusing or exasperating, the shopkeepers frigid or obsequious, the bureaucracy simply intolerable. He took his friends from among the Americans of his own generation, invariably on fellowships; occasionally he also brought home older countrymen who were paying their own way abroad—bankruptcy lawyers traveling around the world with their wives and sleeping until noon at the Carlton in Cannes because they knew of nothing better to do, pump manufacturers in Europe on business, successful second-generation Americans returning to show off the new Pontiac to the old folks.

Victoria was dutifully hospitable to these people; but they were so much like the people she had sold toothbrushes to in her father's drugstore that their shock at her village's open sewers and cobbled streets spotted with dog droppings was all too predictable. Besides, Burton refused to unbend to the new acquaintances that she herself had acquired. Ellen Rumford, Françoise and the others whom they in turn had introduced to Victoria —the Swedes, Danes, French, White Russians and exiled Yankees— neither toiled nor spun, and lived from binge to binge on remittances. To Burton's mind the only excuse his wife could have—and therefore *did* have—for associating with them was one of absolute desperation.

He came chugging up to the Place late one afternoon, parked near the sleeping hound, and stepped out of the car to be hailed by Victoria and Françoise, who were sitting in front of the *bistro* having a *pastis* with a reedy, sweatered young man who did sand pictures.

"Hi, Burton!" called the young man, who had his free, or drinkless, arm wrapped protectively around Victoria's chair. "Do come and have a drink with us."

It was all a little too cozy. Burton shook his head as he approached. "Got a headache," he replied. "I think I'll be better off if I just go home and lie down for a while before dinner."

"Young man," Françoise said pontifically, "you work too hard." Everybody laughed.

Burton realized that he was standing there too stiffly. He didn't care about the others at all, but as soon as Victoria had gotten up to join him, and almost before they were out of earshot, he said apologetically, "You poor kid. You must have been so lonely."

She loosened her arm from his grip. He said, "I thought you preferred staying home to going out with me, but if you're reduced to these extremities for companionship . . ."

Victoria looked at him consideringly. She replied at last, "We'll talk about it at home."

Burton opened their heavily barred door with a sigh. Then he was on his knees swearing incantations before the damnable little stove which barely kept them from freezing, and Victoria was lighting the fire under the *petits pois,* the *ratatouille,* and the coffee. All this time she was wondering to herself how to try to explain what was happening.

"I wasn't desperate, to be sitting out there with Françoise and that Scottish boy," she said, rubbing her palms dryly together over Burton's little fire and looking frankly into his reddened face. "I just thought I'd go for a little walk after I'd shelled the peas and gotten supper ready, so that I could watch the sunset from the Place. And I did." She paused. "I enjoyed it enormously, as I always do walking here. And then I bumped into Françoise and what's-his-name, Walter, and they asked me to join them for a drink. And I'm glad I did. We were having fun when you came along. I didn't seek them out because I was lonely. But I was happy to see them, not because I love them or am even especially fond of them, but simply because they were there, and obviously glad to see me, and laughing at something that they were willing to share with me—and it seemed like a very pleasant way to spend a half hour."

"Well, that's what I mean," Burton said reasonably, "only you put it a little differently. We were a little rash in coming here just on the word of Charlie Orne. Oh, it's quaint—he was right enough about that—and the sunsets are showy, but I didn't think enough about you, and about what you'd do for companionship. Sure you're thrown together with those people just because they're there, as you say, and it's my fault."

"But it's not your fault. I mean, I'm not unhappy." Victoria felt that her voice was rising dangerously. More calmly, she added, "I really do like it here. You're picking out one of the things I like about it, the different-ness of the people here—never mind that they may be worse people than the ones we know back home—and the way it's been so easy to see them or not, just as you please, without making dates, or having parties, or making a whole big thing out of your social life. It's something new for me, and I—"

"You've been a damn good sport," Burton broke in. The fire in the stove was drawing really well, and dinner was beginning to smell appetiz-ing. "I've got a little surprise for you. I've been putting off going to Grenoble because things have been going so well here, but now I've decided why don't we combine it with our trip to Paris? We'll stay in Grenoble long enough for me to do my work, a couple days, and then we'll drive on up to Paris for a fortnight or so. Like that?"

She did like it, all of it. The driving, the picknicking, the sightseeing; the frosted, forbidding Alps, the sunny checkerboard valleys, the rows of plane trees stretching out formally to infinity; this was what she had dreamed of, and even her husband became her lover once again in Paris. They stayed in a cheap hotel on the Left Bank, and every morning after coffee they would walk hand in hand up the Boulevard Raspail to stare at Rodin's statute of Balzac. They would squeeze each other, and it was lovely, all of it, even the raw damp and the hungry hunts for cheap restaurants and the half-dead leafless trees in the Luxembourg Gardens and the endless plays that they sat through half-asleep, dazed with rhetoric and drunk with fatigue.

But then one day in the Orangerie they met a distinguished colleague of Burton's, an older man serving as guest lecturer at the University of Bristol who had run over with his wife for a few days of shopping and picture-seeing. The wife, a most gracious silver-haired lady who did not look as if she had ever sold Luckies or Listerine in her father's drugstore, expressed her envy of this young couple for their good fortune in living in a warm, sunny climate, and said pleasantly, "I suppose you've seen the paintings of Friesz in that charming little gallery in St. Tropez? He's been sadly neglected, partly for political reasons, I think."

Yes, Burton assured her, they had indeed seen Friesz's charming landscapes; in fact, they had seen about everything that there was to look at along the Côte d'Azur. And then he went on to describe their life, not boastfully, or even cutely, not mentioning the sand painters and other international bums, nor even relating their daily existence to the immortal Twenties on the Riviera. What was wrong with the way that he spoke, then? It was, she thought, listening with a sense of growing desolation, that he was already projecting their common existence into the future, to the day when he too would be guest lecturer at the University of Bristol, when he too would run over to Paris with his wife for a week-end's playgoing and shopping, when—worst of all—he would be able to look back with amusement from his comfortable rooms in the George V at the crummy quarters overlooking St. Germain-des-Prés in which they had spent a foolish youthful week, and at the impossibly uncomfortable villa in which they had spent the Fulbright year only because they had been young and silly and Victoria had been "dead game."

Hearing herself described as a brave little soul who was making do without friends, central heating, or decent plumbing, Victoria turned her flushed countenance to the professor and his wife, dreading what must surely be found on their well-bred faces: the horrid recognition that Burton was a stuffed shirt. But no, they were too well-bred for that, if indeed they did recognize the truth; for all that was visible on their smooth pleasant countenances was mild concern for the hardships of these nice young people, and envy for their ability to have so much fun while still so young.

It was only after the eminent couple had bade them farewell and good luck that Burton saw that his wife was biting her lower lip jerkily.

Suddenly frightened, he asked, "Did I hurt your feelings?"

"My feelings! It wasn't me you were insulting. It was yourself."

"But don't you see . . ." he began, and then stopped. "I guess I'm easier to live with when I'm working."

After a while—too long, it seemed to them both—Victoria replied, "I wouldn't say that."

When they got back to their room late that night, Victoria kicked off her shoes and drew the grimy blind. Sitting on the edge of the noisy brass bed and listening to Burton gargling in their semiprivate bathroom, Victoria noticed for the first time the two lemon-shaped stains on the ancient wallpaper and a gnawed corner of the shag rug on which her feet were resting, that had evidently been worried by a dog until it had become unusable elsewhere and so had wound up here; and she knew that she could not stay another day in Paris.

But their encounter in the Orangerie had been working on Burton as well. Long-faced, hairy-legged, serious, vague-eyed without the glasses, he spoke to her around the towel with which he was patting his face.

"Vic, I've begun worrying about what's still undone. *You* know I'm no fun to be with once I get like that." He added frankly, "I suppose we could have squeezed another couple days out of Paris if we hadn't bumped into old Roberts and his wife, but they started the gears grinding, and now I'm itching to get back to work. You wouldn't be too furious, would you, if we—"

"I think we ought to settle up our bill and leave first thing in the morning," Victoria said firmly, and quickly closed the bathroom door on Burton.

They drove south through the dead center of France, down through Lyons on the Route Nationale so as not to have to return again through Grenoble and that difficult road. But the change of scene made no difference. They barely mentioned to each other what they saw from the vibrating windows of the hard-working little car. Burton was already going over his three-by-five cards in his mind; his lips even moved a little as he drove. Victoria sat tensely waiting for the sun and solitude that lay in store for her in her village. The rainy season was over, the best lay ahead, and she ached for the healing hand of the sun as an invalid awaits the arrival of a trusted doctor.

The day after they unpacked, Burton went back to work. He was typing now for the most part, getting up a paper out of some of his researches, and he enjoyed working in the garden; so Victoria took to going out directly after breakfast and staying away, usually at a bench on the dusty Place, until lunch—sometimes, if there was food at home for Burton, for the entire day. Their positions were reversed, and Burton was comfortable in mind with the knowledge that his wife was in the fresh air, marketing, chatting, reading in the shade of the olive tree, perhaps even doing a little sketching.

But Victoria could not sketch with any degree of competence, and as the weeks drew by and the sun grew stronger, she felt her own spirit strengthening as well. Without quite knowing why at first, she began to pay more careful attention to her morning newspaper, and then to the magazines she bought and the books she borrowed from Françoise. These were all in French, because (or so she thought) the English books Burton had brought along bored her; but after a while she had to admit to herself that there must have been a more solid reason for starting in the first place, for taking the trouble to sit with a heavy dictionary in her lap, looking up idioms and marking them down as she read. *I just want to show him,* she thought, *it's childish but there it is. I want to prove that I can learn something too this year.*

There was more to it than that, of course. One sunny spring afternoon she and Burton stopped at the vegetable stand to buy some North African oranges before driving on down to the beach. Burton had his nose in the Word Game of the *Herald,* and Victoria paid for the fruit and accepted it, wrapped in an old sheet of newspaper.

"My God," the vegetable lady smiled, dropping the change into her hand, "but you have well learned the French this year. I think that you have learned better than Monsieur."

Victoria felt her face turning red. She glanced quickly at Burton—but he was gnawing on his pencil, searching for one more five-letter word starting with *e,* and he barely raised his head.

"Yes, yes, yes," the vegetable lady insisted as Victoria shook her head, "it is true. Monsieur speaks as he did when he arrived. But you knew nothing and now you speak with a better accent than he."

Victoria muttered her goodbye and walked swiftly to the car. Could it really be true, or was it just French politeness? But no, what the woman had said was hardly polite to Burton.

She turned to her husband, who was digging in the pocket of his shorts for the ignition key. "You weren't upset by what she said, were you?"

"Upset?"

"Annoyed, I mean. At her saying your French wasn't improving."

He laughed briefly—a little too briefly—before throwing the car into gear and swinging around. *"Je m'en foue.* After all, if I had to depend on the flattery of fishmongers and fruit peddlers, I'd be a pretty sad specimen of a teacher, wouldn't I? I've had a few more important things to do this year than covet their praise, you know."

This extraordinary statement, with all that it implied not only about himself but about how he felt about her, hit Victoria with such force that she almost cried out, as if she had been lashed with a whip. She cranked down the window as they descended the bumpy hill to the plain below and allowed her face to be washed by the cool wind from the sea. When at last she dared to look across at her husband she was astonished to see that he was pouting.

In an instant her furious resentment at his cutting words was dissipated. He was not infuriating, he was simply comical, sitting there hunched over the wheel in his shorts that he insisted on wearing a little too long and waiting to be reassured that he was right and the vegetable lady was wrong. There was no need for her to lose control, no need to answer him in kind; in fact, if she really wanted to hurt him she had only to ignore his implied request for support, or to turn it down. But she had no desire to hurt him, she discovered, nor even the wish to assert herself or explain herself to him. She was simply not interested any longer in Burton, in his work, or in what he thought of her. This in itself was such a shocking realization that it made her feel weak and a little dizzy, and, in the moments that it took for them to reach the wind-scudded seacoast, happier and more lightheaded than she had ever been. So this, she thought, is why I've been working so hard all these long weeks on my French. And it struck her that just as a woman's body will prepare her almost magically to experience the great physical and emotional events of her life, so her mind, deviously, almost furtively, will adjust and retrain itself—if it has any vitality at all and is more than an inert lump of matter—to prepare for new contingencies and unexpected vicissitudes.

"I think," Burton panted, dragging blanket, pillows, oranges and books onto the pebbles, "that it's still a little early for regular bathing. It's so sheltered up at our house that we don't even realize what a strong wind is blowing. It might even be dangerous to plunge in."

"Oh, I don't think so! I don't think so at all!" Victoria pushed her hair into her cap and ran away from him to the green and white sea, blue farther out beyond swimming distance, but within range of the eye and the heart.

Within the week Burton asked his wife to make arrangements for the return voyage. "We'd best take care of it early," he said, fingering his pipe. "When we have a firm date and the petty details are taken care of, we can relax and enjoy the last part of our year. I wouldn't trouble you with all this, but it *does* take some of the household load off me, and you seem to have a talent for detail—for learning irregular verbs and such-like odd things."

It was this last gratuitous remark that hardened Victoria's spirit. He knew, then, what she had been doing while he had been collecting his little data and writing his little articles, and it rankled. Did he suspect the true reason for it? She thought not; and she said nothing to him, partly out of a lack of resolve that was not cowardice but a genuine apprehension that she could be doing wrong and that it was not too late for there to be a change.

But there was no change. She sold their car at a good price; she bought ship accommodations on the date which Burton requested, and at the scale which he had indicated; she went down and got the man to come up and read the gas and electric *compteurs* and paid his bill when it was presented; she assisted the *gérante* with the *inventaire;* she addressed labels until her arm ached and stickered them neatly on luggage and crates; she made a list of all purchases so that Burton would have no trouble clearing customs in New York. And then, the night before the ship was to sail, they sat out on the terrace smoking and saying goodbye to the French fireflies, and Victoria told her husband that she was not going back with him.

He looked at her petulantly, but seemed unable to see her clearly, for he took off his heavy glasses, blew on the lenses, and wiped them with the end of his sports shirt. "That's a hell of a thing to joke about."

"I'm not joking. Look in your passport case—I put the single ticket in there."

Burton reached into his pocket and then stopped. "Say, what is all this? Are you planning on running off to Paris or Majorca with that idiot sand painter?"

"There isn't anybody else."

"No, I guess not. But why, Victoria? What's happened?"

From the reasonable tone of his voice, Victoria could tell that it had not yet sunk in. He heard, but he didn't believe—or if he did, it must have seemed to him like one of those family spats which could be patched up later as the sheets warmed or at worst could be laughed at in the clear morning air after the argument had been reduced to its proper dimensions.

She said coolly, "I've come to the conclusion that we don't have enough in common to stay together. It took me all year to decide, so please don't think you can talk me out of it tonight. You can't."

"But . . ." Suddenly his face crumpled. He said jerkily, "I don't understand. I really honest to God don't understand."

"I'm not sure that I do, either. I think maybe we both expected the wrong things from each other."

Burton jumped up and lunged out with his foot, narrowly missing the cat, which leaped over the garden table to the wall. "If you're serious about this crazy business, have you given any thought to me at all?" His voice rose. "How do you expect me to come home without you, as though you'd died or something, and face my family and your family and—and my colleagues, and our friends. . . ."

Victoria covered her face with her hands. She spoke through her palm. "That's exactly why you're going to have to. For asking a question like that without even thinking to ask what *I'm* going to do, how *I'm* going to get along, what *I'm* going to write to my family. For being concerned not with me, not even with us, but only with your piddling little career."

"But supposing I hadn't gotten the Fulbright. Supposing I hadn't brought you here . . ."

"That's why I'm not angry with you at all, Burton. That's why I'm as grateful to you as I've ever been to anybody, for bringing me here and showing me what another kind of life could be like. You did more than that. You took the greatest gamble in the world—showing yourself to me against an entirely different background from what I am used to, and before I was *so* used to it that I was blind. Well, you lost."

Burton blew his nose heavily, like a middle-aged man. "What are you going to tell your parents?"

"That I like it here, more than I like being with you. That I love it. That I've learned the language, after a fashion, and that I'm going to try to make a living here and a life here."

He turned his back on her. After a moment he said, "I suppose you're going to stay here, in the village. I suppose you've talked about the whole thing already with your gang."

"No, I haven't," Victoria hesitated. "I don't know what I'm going to do, maybe move to Nice and look for a job there working for Americans. Burton . . ."

"Yes?"

"I put the *aspirine*— you know, the ones in the little metal tube—in your trench coat pocket, in case you should need them tomorrow, what with all you'll have to do before you're settled in your cabin. I think you ought to try to get some sleep now—it's going to be a rough day."

"I want to tell you first that you're not the only one who's suffered. I may not have said anything about it all year, but I haven't enjoyed it, your demeaning me and my work. It's not much fun, having your wife look down her nose at you—if I talked in terms of what my work would buy, it was only because that seemed to interest you more than the work itself."

Victoria stared at him.

"I hoped all that would change when we got back home. But I was wrong about that too, wasn't I?" He turned and went inside without another word.

Victoria slept in the garden on a chair. From time to time she heard Burton moving around in the house behind her, and she knew that he was not sleeping either, but she could not bring herself to join him as he stumbled about in the dark. She arose early, her back and legs aching from the unyielding chair in which she had lain as quietly as possible. She found that she was hungry, oddly enough, and almost unbearably tense.

When she entered the house Burton said, without looking at her, "I'd better start now. It wasn't a dream, was it?"

She shook her head wordlessly.

"Well, I'd better start now to hunt up a cab, if I'm ever going to get one to come up here for our—for my stuff."

"I've already taken care of that." She glanced at her watch. "He'll be along any minute—I told him yesterday it was a through ride to Cannes, to the Gare Maritime."

Burton glanced up from the valise he was strapping. "You even arranged for that, didn't you?"

For the first time, Victoria winced. "It was just another one of my chores."

Outside, in the fresh air, there was a clear loud blast. Then it was repeated twice. "Listen," Burton said hurriedly, "I don't want you to go with me. Not to Cannes, not even to the corner—not if you don't want to go all the way. Maybe you thought I'd carry you back bodily. I won't. I'm not like that. But should I write you?"

"If you wish."

"I'll try to write about things besides my career. The kind of letters I might have written if we'd been separated before marriage instead of after."

Victoria began to cry. "Goodbye, Burton."

"Perhaps I'll write and tell you next spring that I'm coming back, not on a Fulbright, but on my own. On my savings, or working my way across if I'm broke."

"Goodbye, Burton."

"Then perhaps you'll write that you've missed me after all, and you'll tell me where I can find you—how I can find you."

"Goodbye, goodbye!"

He bent his long frame almost double to squirm into the taxi with his bags, then quickly straightened up so he could wave to his wife as the cab rattled away. Through the glass he saw her standing in the doorway with her arms at her sides, nodding her head and crying until the cab turned a corner down the hill and they were lost to each other's seeking gaze.

THE PEACOCKS OF AVIGNON

With the wind ripping at her lungs and her eyes streaming tears into the channels of her ears, Terry gunned her Vespa down the highway and onto the main streets of Avignon. It was only when at last she alighted and tried to walk casually away from this one thing in the world that was still hers, this scooter and the little valise carelessly strapped to the rear seat, that she realized how bitterly the wind had bitten at her legs beneath the wool pants and the knee-high socks. Her shins and ankles were nearly numb; she stumbled as she attempted to mount the high old curb and would have fallen to her knees if an elderly gentleman bearing an open umbrella had not been at hand to grasp her elbow.

"*Je vous remercie, Monsieur,*" she said politely.

"*De rien,*" the old man murmured as he disappeared down the drizzly street.

It was not actually drizzling any more, although Terry had been driving through the mushy wetness for hours and hours. It had tapered off to a thick mist, the air was not cold when you stood still, and it was likely that the crest of the flood had passed and that it would be possible to drive northward to Paris without being lost on an endless detour or drowned on the low-lying Route Nationale.

The streets were alive with cyclists, the sidewalks aswarm with pedestrians raising and lowering their black wetly glittering umbrellas as they skittered in and out from under the protection of the shopkeepers' awnings. They were the first crowds Terry had seen since she had run away: the highways had been empty, empty, except for the ominous water gushing along at the side of the road next to her scooter, and the villages had been blank and shuttered. She had felt like an unwanted messenger, herself stricken, bearing news of an approaching plague. But, she thought now, hadn't the plague been inside herself, and not communicable at all?

The bonging of a dozen clocks in the window of an *horlogerie* under whose awning she stood shivering aroused her to an awareness that it was noon, that the hurrying crowds had purpose, and that she too was hungry. She had had a *croissant* and coffee hours before, and it had served to get her started, but it was not fuel enough for a healthy American girl, even one sick at heart and suicidal. Terry had not been living in France long enough to forget the tomato juice, the bacon and eggs, and the toast that used to go with the coffee back home when you were setting out on an expedition.

She stuffed her gloved hands into the pockets of her zipper jacket and walked for some blocks until she came to a workingmen's café. There, ignoring with hauteur (and fright) the stares and the accented wisecracks, she ordered the *plat du jour* and a demi of *vin ordinaire* while she observed her yellowed reflection in the peeling mirror behind the bar, captured for these moments between Byrrh and Pschitt! Perrier. Her face was conventionally pretty, but now particularly long-nosed and grief-stricken, beneath the cap of tight brown curls that had been her late father's too. Her legacy.

After his death eight months before from a brain tumor Terry and her mother had returned, all alone together, to the France they had known and loved when Daddy had been a vice-consul in Nice and Terry herself a hoop-rolling youngster on the Promenade des Anglais, around and around the kiosks. There had been very little money, but since Terry had just graduated from high school and wanted to study art rather than go to college, Florence, her mother, had agreed that they might live together in Paris if they were very frugal. First however there had been the Côte d'Azur for the summer, and since they could not afford Nice, they had settled in a small hillside village rather heavily populated with expatriate friends of her mother's. They were all considerably older than Terry, and much given to alcoholic fretting about the old days, so Terry spent her time either sketching the lower Alps or swimming in the sea and lying on the hot pebbles, thinking how much nicer it would all have been if Daddy had only lived to come back here with them. For some reason Florence was reluctant to leave for Paris, and the summer gave way to autumn.

Florence amused herself amiably enough by studying the application of glaze to ceramics with a young potter named Jean, only son of the widow Marie Bongiovanni who came in to clean and do their laundry once a week. At sixty-three—just thirteen years older than Florence, but looking thirty years older—Marie was really an old lady, sweet-tempered and courteous, but an old lady. She had a whitening beard at the sides of her chin, her face had the color and texture of a rumpled paper bag, and she stank, stank terribly, of dried, never-washed sweat. Even though she was gentle and modest, she reeked of mortality, and Terry could not bear to stand near her for any length of time.

It was not just a cultural void which separated Florence from Marie. Florence was unthickened, still slim-waisted, still fresh and pretty, and sometimes when Terry passed Jean's tiny shop on her way to the beach and saw her mother's blonde head bent attentively over the potter's wheel, next to Jean's long foxlike head with its piercing blue eyes and aggressive hooked nose, she felt as though she, at eighteen, was the worried mother and Florence, at fifty, was the vivacious young art student. Jean was big and swarthy, he had left school early and was shy and ashamed of his ignorance, his hands were always caked and stained with clay and paint, his blue and white striped sailor's jersey and denim trousers were always spotless, and he blushed when he was teased. But Terry had no intimation of what was going to happen before he and Florence went over to the next village and got married.

"I couldn't tell you about it, baby," her mother said when she returned with a scrubby corsage pinned to the left shoulder of her gabardine suit and her young husband waiting discreetly outside on the street; she tried to take her daughter in her arms but Terry squirmed away, hating herself for her inability to accept the caress passively. "You're stronger than I am. You're reasonable and logical, like your father. You would have talked me out of it. And I didn't want to be talked out of it. I wanted some beauty in my life before it's too late."

"Beauty?" Terry cried shrilly, her voice cracking. She blew her nose.

"With that guy? He isn't five years older than I am. You're old enough to be his mother. Have you forgotten, you're fifty years old!"

"I know it every minute of the day. Jean knows it too. You can be reasonable, baby, but don't be cruel. Some day you'll be fifty."

"Maybe, but if I live that long I won't make a fool out of myself with a small-town gigolo who can hardly read and write."

"He is kind and sweet and gifted. Do you know what that means? And he loves me very tenderly."

"He loves your pension and your insurance, you mean."

Florence started to cry, wrackingly. "He knows we're broke. He knows all that's left is yours. He doesn't want our few dollars. We're going to Corsica for our . . . for a few days, and when we get back if you want—"

"If I want I can call him Daddy, is that it? No thanks. I'm going to Paris, and I don't want any money or advice from you or your so-called husband."

Furious, her mother turned on her savagely. "Did you want him for yourself, is that it? Well, he wasn't interested in you, any more than your father was interested in me for the last fifteen years. Your father was a—"

"Don't mention his name to me. Don't you dare to mention his name now. I'm leaving, Florence. I think you'll be more comfortable without me."

In her little cell of a room she had thrown sweaters and underclothes into a zip-up handbag, knocking things off the bed and the walls in her haste to get out, ignoring her mother's terrible cries, "Baby, I'm sorry, baby, I couldn't help myself, baby, baby, I want you to be happy like I wasn't, all I wanted was a little happiness, a little beauty before I get to be an old woman . . ."

Now, less than a day later, her mother's voice still pursued her like the cries of the Furies. It burned, the shame of it burned within her, as she thought of pathetic, foul-smelling old Marie, of her hairy-chested young son, and of the looks on the faces not of the villagers—for they took everything in stride, wars, occupations, adulteries, misalliances, whatnot —but of the foreigners who had been their friends. She shuddered.

Outside the air was a little better. Terry lit a cigarette, retraced her steps to the Square, and realized suddenly that this mighty fortress of Avignon was the old papal palace of the fourteenth century. Or was it the thirteenth? As she stood on the far side of the street and gazed contemplatively across at the towering ancient battlements, lowering before her as though they guarded not heretical remnants but the abodes of the storm gods whose cloudbursts were drowning this whole countryside and her own little family too, she fumbled clumsily in the back of her mind for the jumble of historical misinformation that lay tumbled about, gleaned from school courses, paperbacks, Michelin guides, and artist boy friends. Which popes had lived there? Hadn't they traveled surreptitiously by water across the Mediterranean to and from that little Spanish town that she and Florence had visited a few months ago? Impetuously Terry strode across the Square and up the incline—which had surely been moated once —to the massive doors of the palace. She was not alone, there were many women coming and going with large bundles in their arms, and she was taken aback when a gendarme at the very entrance accosted her and barred the way.

His belted blue uniform was immaculate, but there were smears of dried mud up and down the sides of his leather boots, and his eyes, shadowed under the bill of his cap, were smudged with weariness. For an instant Terry thought that she might have neglected to buy a historic monument ticket, or that the palace was closed during lunch hour.

"I regret, Mademoiselle," the gendarme said, politely but in a voice that was just the least bit clipped, "that this is an area of disaster thanks to the floods. There is a state of emergency and the palace is closed to tourism until further notice."

Beyond his trim shoulder through the gaping doorway, Terry caught sight of two lorries, a row of bunks ranked along the walls of the great inner courtyard, piles of medical supplies marked with crosses, and some old women eating steaming potatoes off tin plates. Then her eyes met the gendarme's, and dropped.

"I—I am desolated," she faltered. "I did not think . . . Excuse me."

She turned and stumbled down the ramp, away from the policeman's eyes. A tourist, she thought, just a bloody tourist. Not a girl running away from home, or a girl awash in a sea of trouble, or a girl who didn't really want to go to Paris. Just a tourist—and a thoughtless stupid one.

She found herself trudging up a winding gravel path alongside one of the immense walls of the palace; it led, she observed, to the park, and although it was quite steep she allowed herself to be carried along with the throng of lunch-hour strollers. She wandered through well-tended gardens, formal to be sure, and made lusher than ever by the endless downpour, but desolate now in the raw damp with the blossoms crumbled and the leaves rotted. Up and up she mounted until she came to a plateau from which suddenly there opened a vast panorama of the Loire valley.

The scene beneath her, as she leaned over the parapet and gazed at the countryside hundreds of meters below, was horrifying—and fascinating. The Avignon bridge seemed to be lying on the swollen waters like a stick floating on a stream. No one crossed it, much less did anyone dance on it. Black and mute on the river that was now a horizon-stretching lake, a shallow ocean of misplaced water, it did not look as though it could ever have served for the stomping fun of the song.

Everything was very still. The water, seen from this distance, did not seem to be moving at all. It was eerie how silently and stealthily it had crept from its placid banks and worked its way across the farmlands, inundating fields, drowning cattle, leaving only gables, house peaks and spires pointing painfully to heaven. Now it lay as peaceful and apparently motionless as a mountain lake. What was missing, Terry realized, was the ominous mood music, replete with growling glissandi, with which the newsreels always embellished their aerial views of similar visitations and devastations. This was the first flood she had ever witnessed with her own eyes, but she had been prepared for something like it by the filmed records of countless similar acts of God and man, and in consequence what was most awesome about the flood was not its unexpectedness or its lack of any parallel in her previous experience, but the stunning absence of portentous musical accompaniment, indeed of any sound at all save for the beating of her own heart.

Leaning on the back of a clammy bench with her cheeks in her hands, Terry felt that a fantastic kind of human courage must surely take life in the very teeth of these catastrophes, that vanity, fear and cowardice flourished only in the *expectation* of disaster and were replaced after it had struck by a stubborn will to go on and render life manageable no matter what stood in the path—flood, fire, pestilence or bombing. Surely the people who lived in those half-submerged houses and farmed the drowned earth were already scheming and striving to retrieve their homes and belongings and to reclaim the land for their plow and their seed, just as these people of Avignon in the very park around her munched and strolled on their lunch hour as though the waters had never risen about their neighbors on the farms around their city.

Then why is it, she wondered, that I still sit here and burn, that the fire of shame still burns in my face whenever I think of my mother? Now that it has happened, now that it is as final and real as the flood, why can't I adjust myself to the idea of my mother and that man and go ahead and make my own life? But the truth was that she could *not* adjust herself, that she felt betrayed and soiled, that her mother and even her dead father were degraded—because she could see no sense, no order, no rationality in the awful thing her mother had done, nothing beyond a momentary upheaval of middle-aged lust like the last ugly tongue of flame in the dying fire of a collapsed house.

And then as she sat there, turning her back to the flood and facing once again the park and the people around her, Terry was startled to see two large peacocks strutting along the graveled walk. For a moment they looked like two dowagers, pursing, preening, chattering to each other as they strolled, surrounded by a retinue of pages, attendants and oglers—schoolboys, linked-armed couples, elderly women with black stockings and little scraps of bread. Suddenly one fluttered, as if aware that the strategic moment had arrived, and opened its tail wide, so wide that in that instant the world seemed blotted out in the sudden blaze of its beauty.

"Oh!" Terry cried involuntarily. "Oh, how beautiful!" Her heart was wrenched within her, and she arose gropingly to follow the birds with the others. The first peacock having displayed itself, the other now pirouetted, almost fretfully, almost as if it wanted willfully to distract all attention from the sullen competition of the flood below, and released its great fan in a burst of radiance surpassing the first. The purple, mauve, magenta and green iridescent circles sworled before her eyes and dizzied her with the wasteful magnificence of their display. There seemed no impulse, for all this dazzle, no motivation, other than a vain and splendid pride.

"*Oh, maman, comme ils sont beaux!*" said a schoolboy in his still-high girlish voice. His matted hair fell across his forehead, his nose ran, a heavy serviceable scarf was wound round his scrawny neck; beneath his bare and bony knees his legs and feet were encased in thick wool socks and ankle-high clodhoppers. Everything about him said farmer's son.

His mother looked old enough, it seemed to Terry, glancing at her, to be his grandmother. Her head was wrapped in a shawl which she held gathered tightly, tensely, beneath her chin; all of her shapeless body was clad in black. She had been crying, or else the raw cold and the air smelling of flood had worked its way into her marrow and loosened her tear ducts; perhaps she had been made homeless by the seeping waters. She replied to her son, almost wonderingly, *"Ah oui, oui, pour un moment de beauté . . . Il faut avoir de la beauté."*

Terry turned away, breathing rapidly, and began to descend by the way she had come. It is necessary to have beauty. Had she ever known that, or, knowing it, had she reserved the hope and expectation of it solely for her selfish self? Still blinking from the wonder of those swaying delicate treasures opened and displayed for her delectation, Terry made her way out of the garden, to the street, and down across the Square to the P.T.T. There she stood patiently in the long queue of those waiting to send telegrams, shuffling like a somnambulist, not consciously aware of exactly what she was doing there until she had reached the wicket and held a form in her hand.

Carefully she wrote, *Forgive me, forgive me, I love you, be happy.* She handed the telegram to the man at the other side of the wicket together with a note which she took from her purse; it was only when he handed her the change and pointed to her printing with a nicotine-stained thumb that she finally raised her eyes and looked into his.

"Votre nom, Mademoiselle."

"Oh, yes." Terry printed her name and rechecked her mother's address. "There."

"Mais . . . vous avez répété deux mots. Cela va vous coûter—"

"Yes, I know." With some surprise Terry listened to her own voice, as gentle as the clerk's. "I repeated it only once, because I have no more money. But to myself I must repeat it over and over, do you see?" she demanded of the puzzled man. "Over and over."

With a lightened step she emerged into the quieter street. There, under the metallic afternoon sky, she mounted the scooter once again and drove off slowly, no longer burning, no longer sobbing, toward her own fate, her own love, her own unknowable destiny.

THE MAN IN THE TOOLHOUSE

Not any more but once upon a time, I used to travel to Buffalo with the kind of exhilaration that children have on the way to a long-awaited circus. It had nothing to do with Buffalo, since the orchestras with which I have been performed in dozens of similar places; but even though I will probably never go there again, the mere mention of Buffalo by a stranger on a street corner can set to rattling in my mind the whole chain of recollections of Rita Conway and Ralph Everett, so that I find myself once again reviewing each link in the chain that will bind me for the rest of my life not only to Rita, but to Ralph and to the Everett home, which exists now only in the imperfect memories of a handful of people like myself.

I think I fell in love with Rita the first time we met, one dark winter afternoon in a rehearsal room of the Eastman School of Music in Rochester. She was seated at a harp, her head bent forward, listening intently to the octaves that she was rapidly plucking as she tuned the instrument, her face so hidden by her long blonde hair that when she looked up at the clicking of the heavy door which I closed behind me, I was stunned by her beauty, and I shifted my violin case from one hand to the other, stammering an apology. She laughed, and I introduced myself.

Rita made it very clear that she respected my musical ability, my metropolitan background, even my poverty. And I adored her hardy delicacy that always reminded me of a wildflower, and her small-town temperament mixing matter of factness with romanticism in a way that charmed me completely.

As I think back now, the years at Eastman seem to me like one of those intense dreams which end so abruptly that you can't remember, try as you may, whether its essential quality was one of frustration or fulfillment. Rita and I played duets together, picknicked together, and worried together about our separate futures. She always knew that I loved her and she was shrewd enough to realize that, since the whole thing was impossible, it was her responsibility to keep everything pitched on a comradely plane so that the inevitable break would not be too painful.

But Rita flattered me by intimating that I was more adventurous than she, as well as more talented (which I knew anyway), and that it was I and not she who faced the exciting prospect of conquering poverty with my music; while she would eventually have to relegate her harp to its proper corner in the parlor, and find a suitable husband.

My impossible dreams ended brutally with an invitation to Rita's wedding, which took place the September after our graduation. Fortunately I was touring that year with a dance band, and I was able to express both congratulations and regrets by mail.

I had met Ralph Everett just once, before I knew that Rita would accept him, and I remembered him only as an engineering student at the University of Rochester, with a shock of black hair. Rita's explanation, made one June evening shortly before Commencement, had hurt me. "You see," she said, "Ralph already has a job lined up in Buffalo, with the Water Department. So that we'll be able to have an apartment, and everything . . . and really, even my parents are quite pleased."

I would have preferred to hear that they were displeased; I suspected that her parents must always have feared that she would run off with someone like me. "And Ralph? Do you love him?"

"I've just never met anyone like him. He's as solid as a rock, and yet he's the most talented person I've ever known."

"In engineering?"

"He writes. I have faith in him, Harry. I'm going to help him become a great writer."

"Is that what he's going to be?"

"Engineering is just a financial crutch for Ralph. He wants to make his father happy, and he knows that it will be years before he makes a living from his writing, anyway."

"When is he going to get all this done?"

"You don't know Ralph. Nothing will stop him."

"Not even a family?"

Rita laughed. "No."

I don't think that Rita really knew what she was saying. I don't think that she knew Ralph at all in those early days, before their marriage; she could hardly have guessed his extraordinary powers of concentration. But his attractiveness, coupled with the security that he could immediately offer, must have impelled her not only to accept him, but to make herself believe in his future greatness.

When I came to Buffalo for the first time after their marriage, I found that they were happy with each other. Rita invited me to dinner; her voice was breathless and warm, and I played through the afternoon rehearsal (I was with the Indianapolis Symphony that year) in a haze of romantic reminiscence.

Rita and Ralph had a flat in a huge old house on Humboldt Parkway. Almost every home along the pleasant street had a large front lawn with an elm tree shading the porch, and a large back yard, with an occasional stable in the rear. The houses looked as though people had been born in them in the days before women went to hospitals to give birth, as though people had grown old in them, died in them, and left the furnishings to their children. It wasn't the kind of street that I would have envisioned for Rita and her golden harp—it struck me that I could have done almost as well for her myself.

"I'm so glad, Harry!" she cried when she answered the doorbell. "I was hoping though that you'd bring your fiddle. Maybe we could have tried one little duet." She led me forward by the hand.

"Rehearsals in the afternoon, a concert in the evening . . ." I almost fell over the harp and the music stand in the living room.

"Care for a drink?" Rita was a little nervous. "Ralph will be home any minute."

"Anything will do."

She smiled shyly. "You can congratulate me—I'm going to have a baby." She turned away and began to make a drink.

"I think that's wonderful."

"I want a houseful. Ralph is agreeable, as long as he can go on with his writing. That way we'll both be able to—well, fulfill ourselves."

I would have said something inappropriate in reply, but Ralph's Ford pulled into the driveway at that moment.

Ralph had grown an aggressive bushy moustache which, together with his straw hat, made him look considerably older than I had remembered him. But as soon as he had removed his hat and accepted my congratulations on his impending fatherhood, he relaxed and grew extremely agreeable. Rita had told me that Ralph didn't have much of an ear for music (about which he apologized deferentially but firmly, like a man asserting that he cannot abide olives, while protesting that he realizes he must be missing something special), but at the dinner table he asked me a number of questions about the relationships between guest artists and orchestra members.

He wanted to know, with a modest air that made me feel as though I were doing him a great favor, all sorts of technical details about the mechanics of touring orchestras.

"You know, Harry," he said, bringing his jaws together on a stalk of celery with a loud snap, "it's my theory that a man can compensate for a lack of imagination in a given field, say in music, by an extra expenditure of effort."

"Do you mean that a fiddler can become a Heifetz simply because he's willing to work harder than the average musician?"

Ralph laughed good-naturedly. "What I mean is that you can learn to do almost anything well if you organize your learning process and utilize every minute of the time you've dedicated to it."

"You may be right."

"Of course he's right!" Rita turned to me vivaciously. "That's how Ralph became a good engineer, even though he didn't care for it."

"Don't mind us, Harry. We don't usually waste time on abstract discussions like this."

Rita and Ralph had tickets for the concert, so we left together in their car, and after the concert they came backstage for me. Rita turned pink when I introduced her to our conductor as a talented classmate; Ralph stood stolidly at her side, his eyes darting in every direction as if to make sure that he would miss nothing.

Later I teased him about it. "You looked like you were soaking up atmosphere."

"The important thing is to observe, isn't it, and to practice at being a writer even when you're not writing? Besides," he added with some hesitation, "I lead a pretty sedentary life. The music business is new to me."

I was impressed and baffled. Rita, wedged between us in the narrow front seat of the car, was tired, but sat contentedly with her head on her husband's shoulder and her hand in mine, unaware of how disturbed I was.

"It's been a wonderful evening," she murmured as we drew up to the house. "Didn't you like it, Ralph?"

"It was a very fruitful experience." In the dark I couldn't tell whether he was being grim or merely funny.

But when we were sipping cold beer on the front porch and watching the Canadian flies slapping restlessly at the yellow lamp, I felt that Ralph was quite humble, and that it was Rita who was sustained by an unquestioning confidence in her husband's secret genius. After a while she arose from the creaking glider and said, "I get worn out early these days." She kissed us both. "Don't talk too late. We all have to get up early."

When she had gone inside Ralph said, "I suppose you envy me."

"Why yes," I replied, a little embarrassed, "I guess I do."

He gestured at the house. "This is the life I've marked out for myself, but only because I can envision something different, something better, for Rita and me."

I suspected that he was thinking primarily of another kind of life for himself, as he teetered back and forth in the rocker and stared moodily at me. And I was startled into a kind of wary wakefulness, because I had been wondering drowsily of the way Rita had cheated herself, or had been cheated by Ralph, somehow, out of the glamorous and exciting life that should have been hers. It appeared obvious to me that it was Ralph who had chosen this quiet humdrum routine, and who was better fitted for it.

I threw my cigarette onto the front lawn, and said rather coldly, "What kind of life do you think you'd like, Ralph?"

He laughed with sudden eagerness. "Oh, I can tell you that. I'd like to travel with Rita, to take her to the places she'd like to see—"

"But how about you?"

"Only because it would give me a chance to meet people, to talk to people. I don't mind living in Buffalo. Any city is interesting, if you take the trouble to learn it. But I do resent having to spend precious time behind a desk checking blueprints that don't mean a damn thing to me."

"You must have known you wouldn't like it, even before you started."

"Of course I knew. I've never had any alternative. Even during high school and college I had to hustle every summer, driving a milk truck or working on a lake boat. And when I graduated—well, there was Rita . . ."

"But if you were writing in a garret you'd probably wish you were leading a normal life."

"Oh, I could never be a starving artist. I think most of those guys are phonies, don't you? Anyway, I have Rita. And it won't be too long before I have my success."

I wasn't sure of what he meant by that, so I said vaguely, "I wish you all the luck in the world."

"Thanks Harry." He grasped my hand. "Too bad we can't get together more often. Sometimes I feel cut off from the people I need—like a spy with nobody to report to."

"Don't you have friends here?"

"One or two. But I don't belong, don't have any connection with other writers—haven't even got time to read their books!" He drained his glass and wiped his mouth with the back of his hand. "Let's turn in, shall we?"

Rita and Ralph had more room than they needed at the time. I had accepted Rita's eager invitation to sleep there rather than at the hotel; but I hadn't foreseen that I would be bedded down in the nursery-to-be, next to their own room. I lay there quietly in the dark, hardly breathing, listening to Ralph removing his shoes (thunk, thunk) and hanging up his trousers (jingle, jingle) and clambering into bed with his wife (a squeak, several murmurs, and a grunt). And after that I wrapped the pillow about my ears. But still I slept very poorly that night.

So it was that, even before the sun came up, I was standing at the window that overlooked the back yard, staring down vacantly at the dewy lawn and at a pair of dungarees flapping mournfully from the clothesline, when I caught sight of Ralph.

He was walking across the damp grass with his trousers rolled up over the ankles, chomping hungrily on the buttered heel of a rye bread and carrying a couple of looseleaf notebooks in the crook of his arm. His shock of black hair stood up angrily, as if someone had used it as a handle to yank him out of bed. He moved purposefully across the yard until he had gained a small frame building adjoining the barn-garage. The rickety door closed behind him with a cool clatter, a light snapped on in the one window beyond the door, and then there was silence.

I shuffled over to the bed and lay down, exhausted. Eventually I fell asleep, thinking of Ralph working alone in the little building and of Rita beyond the wall, a few feet from me, curled into a ball like her unborn baby, her hair unbound on the pillow and her hands clasped warmly between her knees.

It was Rita who woke me. Ralph had already gone to work, but she was waiting to have her coffee with me, her eyes still swollen with sleep.

"I saw Ralph crossing the yard," I said to her, "oh, it must have been hours ago."

"He gets up every morning at four to write. We fixed up the toolhouse so he can work undisturbed."

"I wouldn't have the stamina for that routine."

Rita nodded calmly. "He says sleep is a matter of habit. I only wish he had people to discuss his work with. It's going to be a kind of history of Buffalo, you know, in story form."

"A historical novel?"

"Ralph hates that expression! He's doing a lot of research."

"It's fine that he knows what he wants to make of his life."

"He'll get out of the Water Department some day. We'll both be free. I know we will!"

When I turned at the porch to shake Rita's hand in farewell I felt a sudden ruefulness like a sharp physical pain in the pit of my stomach. Rita was young and fragile in her dressing gown, and it seemed to me that the outline of her pregnancy was just becoming visible. Her hand felt small and warm in mine. "The neighbors must be wondering who the tall dark stranger is."

"I'd better leave now, before you're ruined up and down Humboldt Parkway."

Rita laughed out loud. As I stood on the porch in the pleasant morning sunlight, holding her hand, I realized (more than realized: I had known it all along) that I was not cut out to be a tall dark stranger, in her life or in any other girl's. I had always known it, but nevertheless it was brutal, the way we stood there and joked about it. And then we said goodbye.

Six months later I received an announcement of the birth of a daughter to Ralph and Rita Everett. I must have gone to five or six stores before I found a silver fork and spoon set that seemed suitable. When I dropped the little package down the mail chute, I felt that a chapter of my life had been finished, and that while I was purged now of the anxious desire that had run its course like a long and serious illness, I would never again be really young. A few days later I got one of those little thank-you notes from Rita. It was enclosed with a copy of *Harper's* that contained a poem by Ralph (about the burning of Buffalo in 1812, I think). "Ralph wants you to know," Rita added, "that you're the kind of reader he had in mind. He says it's not so much, just one poem, but I feel as though it's the beginning of a new life for us."

Six or eight months later, Ralph sent me a reprint of a brief article that had been accepted by the *American Historical Review,* entitled (I still have it) "Some Neglected Aspects of the Early Rivalry Between Black Rock and Buffalo." It wasn't the kind of information that you'd go out of your way to learn, but I thought it had more verve than the usual scholarly monograph. And it was proof that Ralph was organizing his time, as he would have said, digging away at the raw material for his book.

By the time I got to Buffalo again, Rita had had another baby, and Ralph's father had come to live with them.

The first thing I noticed when Ralph opened the front door was that the harp was gone.

"You shouldn't have taken a cab," Ralph said. "I would have been only too glad to pick you up."

I put my armful of presents on the couch. At the far end of the room, barricaded behind a baby's play pen, Ralph's father was seated in the easy chair, studying the want ad pages of the *Buffalo Evening News.* The oval peak of his bald head shone under the floor lamp and his high-top black shoes caught the light.

"Father, this is our friend Harry."

The old man arose. "You went to school with Rita."

"That's right." While we were shaking hands I could hear Rita cooing to an infant who suddenly burst into an angry wail. Ralph moved uneasily, but the old man stood still and erect, like a steel engraving out of an old American history book.

He was taller than his son, with a reddish closely shaven face on which time had worn two vertical grooves between his eyes and on either side of his thin mouth. His left arm was missing just above the elbow, and his empty shirt sleeve (he wore only an unbuttoned vest) was pinned neatly back. On his right arm he wore an elastic garter to shorten the sleeve. Despite his complexion and the almost combative cast of his features, there was an aura of death about him that affected me most unpleasantly. He looked as though he were relaxing after having served as a pallbearer at a friend's funeral; and yet he gave the impression that his own end could not be far off. Perhaps the anger in his face, in his whole stringy body, even in his gnarled, veiny, and trembling hand, was that of a man who hated and cursed the idea of death.

Ralph said, "Would you like to see the kids before they go to sleep?"

"By all means. Excuse me, Mr. Everett. I'll let you finish your paper."

He looked at me sourly. "Nothing but bad news anyway."

Rita was diapering the infant, a safety pin between her lips, while the older child stood in her crib, silently watching her mother. "Harry! Give us all a kiss."

I kissed Rita first. Her lips were hot and dry, and the infant squirmed uncomfortably between us as we embraced briefly. I made the appropriate remarks about the children, who were friendly enough; but I cannot remember now what they looked like that evening, except that neither of them seemed to take after their mother. We closed the door quietly behind us and stood in the hall for a moment talking softly.

"You must be working like a dog."

"Ralph gets up with the babies at night. And he *still* manages to write. That's something, isn't it?"

"The harp is gone."

Rita flushed. "Impossible, with the children underfoot. And with Father here . . . it's stored in the attic . . . Come, tell me about yourself while I fix the grapefruit."

Dinner was not a happy meal. Rita had to jump up twice to go in to the babies. She and Ralph wanted to talk about New York, music, books, but the table was dominated by Mr. Everett. The old man hated the world, and he wanted as many people as possible to know before he took reluctant leave of it. He spooned up his grapefruit carefully with his one hand, disposing of as much juice as he possibly could, and wiped his mouth with the back of his hand, using the same gesture as his son. Throughout the meal he stared hard at me, as though waiting for me to make a social error. "I understand you're on the road a lot, with that orchestra." His eyes narrowed calculatingly. "How are conditions?"

I hesitated. He went on quickly. "I'll tell you something. This country is going to hell in a basket."

Rita and Ralph were very absorbed in their food. I said, "I think we're better off than we were a few years ago."

"You wouldn't talk that way if you had to struggle along on a pension. What *are* you anyway," he said with rising aggressiveness, "another Roosevelt New Dealer?"

"Father," Ralph said, "don't you think it would be better if we discussed politics later and let our guest finish his supper now?"

"Later?" He said the word with such anguish that we all looked up, taken aback by his vehemence. "When is that? I might not wake up tomorrow. This is still a free country, isn't it? Well, isn't it?"

"Of course, Father. I just don't want to spoil Harry's dinner."

"I'm only a fiddler," I said. "In politics I vote for the man and not for the party."

The old man's eyes lit up. "That's just the kind of thinking that's softening up the country."

Rita's hand shook as she ladled noodles onto my plate. "Isn't that a little extreme, Father?"

"Extreme? What do you call those professors in Washington? I just hope none of you ever have to exist on a miserable pittance. I went to work when I was eight years old, after my father lost his farm." He glared insanely at me. "Worked hard, saved, all my life, to the day I lost my arm. But they don't encourage thrift and hard work any more. Suckers, that's what we were, suckers."

"More noodles, Father?"

The old man hooked a finger inside his mouth and drew forth a piece of gristle on which he had been chewing as he talked. He put it on the edge of his plate and stared at it somberly. "Now Roosevelt wants a law that a man can't make more than twenty-five thousand dollars a year. What do you say to that?"

"I haven't thought much about it."

"That's how the public gets fooled. They don't think."

"I never expect to earn that kind of money. Or anybody I know."

Ralph raised his eyes and looked at me coolly. "I do, Harry."

"Who cares how much money you're going to make?" Ralph's father chewed savagely on a pickle. "If you had mouths to feed, the incentive would be there, wouldn't it?"

"The opportunities—"

"Don't tell me about opportunities. I've lived longer than you. Rubinoff and *his* violin, on Eddie Cantor's program—I bet *he* makes more than twenty-five thousand a year. There's no reason for the government to confiscate the wealth of those who did make good, just to provide cake and circuses for the ones that didn't. It's high time we quit thinking of ourselves and started thinking about principles."

"I respect your principles, Father," Ralph said, "but Harry hasn't come here to talk politics. Besides he's got a hard evening ahead of him."

"You hear that?" the old man cried out to me. "He respects me—isn't that a hot one? I'll tell you something. To this day he doesn't know what I sacrificed in order to put him through the University of Rochester. He doesn't know the policies I borrowed on, the friends I—"

Ralph's nostrils were dilated. "I must insist—"

"I'm talking."

Ralph subsided, after giving Rita (who was desperately spooning cream into the hollow cavern of her baked apple) and me an odd glance, at once beseeching and encouraging.

His father went on inexorably, "It makes me sick to my stomach to watch a boy with your education wasting his time, getting up at four every morning to write that junk."

"Say it all. You might as well."

"Respect? You don't even respect your wife and children, or you'd try to make that expensive education pay off. You'd try to get someplace in your profession and provide some security for your family."

The old man bent his right hand back against the edge of the table until the knuckles whitened. In the hot silence his swollen finger joints cracked loudly, one after the other. Suddenly he cried out in an agonized voice, like an old minister appealing to his wicked flock, "How do you suppose I feel that the few miserable dollars of my savings has to go to you? You'll piss it away, fooling yourself and Rita into thinking you're a genius. I just wish I could live long enough—"

"You will live long enough." Rita flung her head back challengingly. Her eyes were damp and pained, but I sensed that she had been through crises like this before. "I have faith in Ralph, and I know that you're going to be—"

"I'm going to be dead, that's what. And I wish I could take my money with me." He looked impassively at Rita. "You let him make a fool out of you."

"But I'm happy." Her voice rose dangerously. "I'm happy, won't you believe me?"

At that moment the clear little voice of her older child came floating through the open doorway. "I want a glass of water."

Rita jumped up. The three of us were left at the table in a mist of heavy breathing and tobacco smoke. The old man actually looked pleased with himself, but now it was Ralph who could not let matters dispose themselves so easily; he seemed to have been bitten by a bug of misery which inflamed his entire being with a desire to justify himself to his father. I don't know whether he remembered, or even cared that I was sitting there —or perhaps everything that he said was really directed to me, as the one person who could judge his manner of life against the claims pressed against it by his father. I am not very perceptive about such things—I only know that Ralph spoke to his father like a despairing man.

I heard him say, "I'm trying the best I know to make something worthwhile of my life."

The old man didn't move. His voice was unexpectedly gentle. "I haven't got any future left, Ralph. Maybe that's why I'm so anxious about yours."

Ralph turned pale. "I'm sorry." He made no effort to deny his father's statement; perhaps there was an unspoken agreement between them not to bluff about the older man's life expectations. "I can only ask you to have faith in me."

"You talk like a preacher!" The old man's sudden sneer was shocking. I think now that he was trying to conceal his emotions, but at the time I was angered and embarrassed. "If you had any ability it would have come out by now."

"You're not competent to judge."

"Who is? All I ever saw was one poem in a highbrow magazine that nobody reads anyway."

"So that's it. You'll never be proud of me, because you won't let yourself. If I made a fortune and was praised by all the critics, you'd say it was a fluke."

The old man knocked his pipe into the dessert dish and stared down at the charred fragments of tobacco floating slowly in the remains of his baked apple. "I don't know if they told you. I've got a bad heart condition, I'm apt to go almost any time."

Ralph did not return my glance. He was staring at his father with an expression of concentrated loathing, and in the first stunning instant the thought flashed through my mind that he was disgusted with his father's inability to keep his secret to himself; but then I felt that Ralph hated his father because he was going to die too soon, and so cheat him of his eventual triumph.

"No point in going to my grave," the old man said, "without getting everything off my chest."

"You're not going yet. And you're not going to rush me, you hear? I've got my schedule laid out, I won't let you scare me out of it."

Rita came back into the dining room then. She had put on make-up and tied her hair behind her ears with a ribbon. "I didn't hear any dishes breaking," she said pleasantly.

Ralph said heavily, "We'd better get going. It's not early."

"You won't have to worry about the children, Father, they won't get up."

"Oh, the children. They'll be in good hands—" the old man spoke slowly, so that no one should mistake his meaning . . . "—as long as I'm here."

We went out to the car and then we all turned around, as if by a common impulse. The old man was standing at the parlor window, holding the curtain back with his one arm and staring out blindly at the darkening street.

I was already committed to spending the night at the Everetts'. Now although there was nothing I would have liked more than to have gone off to a hotel, I could not bring myself to decline the invitation which I had already accepted for fear of hurting Ralph and Rita.

After the concert we were joined by two high-school classmates of Ralph's, Jim Bagby, a tall cadaverous fellow, and Ed Herlands, who was fat, well dressed, and had the kind of self-assurance that comes only with inherited money. We spent the evening drinking beer and talking about the cultural sterility of Buffalo. It seemed that it was only this common grievance which still bound Ralph to his old friends, for he held hands with Rita as if to assert his basic separateness from the rest of us.

We were driving home when Rita said, "Harry, I know you're ill at ease about staying with us tonight. But you're one of us . . . maybe you could consider it as a favor to us."

There was an uncomfortable silence—I could think of absolutely no reply—and we finally made our way up the steps to the silent house. The old man was sitting sideways in the easy chair, asleep, his forehead glistening in the lamplight, his stump pressed tight against his chest. His lean mouth had gone slack and his legs were folded sharply at the knees as though they had finally snapped from the long task of holding his body erect. He did not stir when the door closed behind us.

Rita tiptoed across the room, turned off the bridge lamp, and kissed him on the forehead. He stirred and raised his wrinkled lids, and Rita said gently, "I've brought the morning paper."

"That's fine." He cleared his throat. "The children didn't stir. How was the concert?" He looked amiably at me, as though there had been no words between us at all.

"We played pretty well. I hope they enjoyed it."

"All you can do is your best." He arose and clapped his son on the back. "Eh, Ralphie? Then if they don't like what you've done, it's tough, that's all." He chuckled as he waved his good nights and stalked off to the bedroom, the morning paper tucked obliquely under his stump and the white waxy cast of death on his narrow farmer's face.

Ralph stared expressionlessly after him until Rita said gaily, "You see, darling? It's all right."

"You don't understand," he replied slowly. "You don't understand at all."

"Well, I understand that I've got to make up the couch for Harry." She set to work briskly, brushing aside my offer to help, and not quite looking me in the eye as she tucked in the sheets. When it was done I sat down on the temporary bed and looked up at my tired friends. They stood arm in arm, their minds already turned inward to their dark bedroom and their common life. Even the most bitter recriminations bound them closer to each other than I could ever be to anyone.

That night I was untroubled by intimations of my nearness to Rita and Ralph. Before I fell into a heavy sleep, I wondered only whether old man Everett lay in the little bedroom that had once been mine for a night, with the rumpled morning paper lying where his weary hand had dropped it, listening to his son's lively ardent useless movements beyond the thin wall, and cursing his inability either to fall asleep or to die and leave those whom he had given his curse to their damned stupidity.

It seemed to me that I had been sleeping for only a few minutes when I was awakened by a light shining in my eyes. I raised myself on my elbow and peered into the kitchen, where Ralph was outlined before the open refrigerator, whose bare bulb sprayed light rays around his disheveled figure. I called out to him softly.

"Oh, I'm sorry." He turned quickly, digging his fingers through his stiff uncombed hair. "Didn't mean to disturb you."

"How do you do it? An earthquake couldn't get me out of bed after two hours of sleep."

Ralph advanced towards me through the dark dining room, hitching at his half-buttoned trousers, over which his shirttails still hung, and squeezing together a thick sandwich with his other hand. As he reached the couch where I lay with my hands behind my head, I looked up into his red-rimmed unsmiling eyes and realized perhaps for the first time how profound were the differences between us.

"It's just a matter of habit," he said quietly.

"Tell me, Ralph. I don't mean to be rude, but is it really worth it, this kind of life, just to do some writing?"

The circles under his eyes were violet in the pale glow of the street lamp. "Rita would have been willing to make any sacrifice, to go without children, to go out to work to support us, so that I could write. But I couldn't do that to her."

Yes, I thought, that's all very well, but would she? As Ralph talked on about his book, speaking of the sacrifice of sleep, and of the eventual freedom it would bring them, my sleepy mind wandered to Rita, whose smooth cheek even now was buried in her warm soft pillow, and whom some part of me would always love; and I felt that at last I was seeing her through disenchanted eyes. Looking up into Ralph's haggard fanatic's face, I felt that he was crazy, that he was driven by an utterly unrealizable obsession to punish himself day after day, year after year, with this grueling schedule for something which was, after all, just another book.

"My father," he was saying, "hates creative work. He persists in acting the betrayed parent in front of Rita, although he knows that I can't stand to see her upset on my account."

"Maybe Rita's right about him."

"In any case my work will go on, and he knows it." He smiled and extended his hand. "So long, Harry."

I never saw Ralph's father again. He must have been a terrible problem, for not long after my departure he had a stroke which left him bedridden and helpless, a burden to Ralph and Rita and even more so to himself.

In addition to telling me about Ralph's father Rita wrote me that she was pregnant again, and that the doctor had told her to expect twins. She mentioned nothing at all about Ralph, which more than anything else led me to suspect that he had reached the limits of his financial and physical endurance.

I sat in my mother's living room in the Bronx (I never thought of it as my living room), with both my 4-F notice and the letter from Rita in my hand, thinking of old man Everett lying stiff and moribund, cursing the world because he could not be quit of it, and listening to his son tiptoeing off in the middle of the night to his fantastic labors; of Rita, heavy and tired, struggling to keep the two little girls from disturbing the old man; and of Ralph, still adding pages to his endless novel and silently looking through his red-rimmed eyes at his dying father and his taut wife. I was glad that I would not be going to Buffalo that year.

It was Ralph who sent me the next letter from Buffalo, some time later. "My father died peacefully yesterday afternoon," he wrote. "I thought you would want to know although you only met him once. It is just as well that he is gone from this unhappy world . . ." The twins had arrived, and they were both girls: counting Rita, Ralph now had a household of five females.

Old man Everett had left them his pittance, apparently, for they had been able to take over the remainder of the big house in which they lived.

There was plenty of space now, even with the children, and when I arrived in Buffalo the following year, it was taken for granted that I should stay with them.

I was very much taken with the children. The older girls resembled their father in physique, in their stern little faces, and in their slow and thoughtful speech. Penny, the oldest, held out her hand as soon as she saw me and said gravely, "Hello, Uncle Harry. Have you got a nice present for me?"

It was fun, in spite of the war. I even took Rita canoeing in Delaware Park one fine afternoon, with Penny and her younger sister Daisy. Rita stretched out before me, trailing her fingertips in the dusty quiet water as I paddled slowly around the margin of the lake. We reminisced about school, and then I think we chatted about Ralph, but when I asked about his writing, she smiled nervously, reached back to stroke her silent little girls' legs with her wet fingertips, and changed the subject.

But Ralph did not want to change the subject. When he learned at supper where we had been, he said, "Rita and I never have the opportunity to do anything like that. But I'm going to make it possible for Rita to float around in a canoe all day long."

"What do you mean?"

He looked at me in genuine surprise. "There's no contradiction between writing a good book and writing a profitable one. Isn't that one of the reasons why this country is the envy of the world—the fact that excellence is rewarded?"

"Do you believe your book will be a bestseller?"

Ralph didn't even smile. "With all my heart."

How like his father he looked at that moment!

That evening Ed Herlands rolled up to the house in his fine convertible, escorting a frightened showgirl with long legs and a nervous smile. Rita had also invited her brother, who was at the time an Army captain stationed at Fort Niagara for the duration, and his wife. We were a very mixed company.

Rita's brother Fred was a sandy-haired small-town lawyer with a pompous drawl and a way of uttering commonplace statements as though they were new and important. He seemed very pleased with his uniform. His wife was a clubwoman with fluttering fingers and a harassed air who regarded Rita and Ralph as her social equals and me as her superior, apparently simply because I was a New Yorker associated with "the arts." Her deferential manner did not extend to Ed Herlands, despite his obvious wealth, and certainly not to his girl friend, who sat in a corner of the couch with her wonderful legs tightly crossed, chain smoking and trying desperately to look as though she was used to spending her evenings chatting about T. S. Eliot.

Ed was determined to shock the yokels. Obviously Captain Fred Conway and his wife had never mixed with showgirls, and were making an earnest effort to regard Ellie as a girl with a "different" and "interesting" occupation, despite Ed's chuckling assurances that she was just someone whom he was fortunate (or wealthy) enough to be sleeping with. "Ellie and I were having breakfast the other day," he said genially, "and we got involved in a heated discussion—even before we'd brushed our teeth— on the relation of homosexuality to artistic creation." Then he looked around to observe the effect of his statement.

Fred sat with his freckled fingers linked across his officer's jacket, his eyes blinking rapidly and expressionlessly, as if he were listening to a client outlining a legal problem; his wife looked as though she wished with all her heart that she were back home in Fredonia; and Ellie herself, breathing deeply, perhaps from nervousness, perhaps to call attention to her excellent bosom, smiled defiantly, waiting for us to challenge this preposterous account of a conversation that could never have taken place.

But Rita was grinning happily, why I couldn't tell; it might have been that she was not even listening, but was only smiling at the pleasure of relaxing after a long day. Ralph however was nibbling angrily and nervously at his stiff moustache.

"Where's your friend Bagby?" I said to Ed. "I'd half expected to see him tonight."

"He's in New York, studying the dance on a Herlands fellowship."

"Oh?"

"Nothing princely, you understand. But whenever he gets hungry, he manages to let me know, and I send on a check. If you can't accomplish anything yourself, it's nice to know that you can do it vicariously."

Mrs. Conway was delighted that the conversation was being diverted into safer channels. "That's wonderful of you. If only more people of means—"

"It's not wonderful at all. I take it off my taxes. Besides, it gives me a feeling of power." He laughed soundlessly. "I've made the same offer to Ralph, but he's afraid."

"Afraid?" Fred cocked his head with judicial caution, scenting some new buffoonery on Ed's part.

"I told him to go off someplace where he wouldn't be bothered by the kids, where he could write all day and talk all night—for a year, or longer if he needed . . . and I would foot the bills. But as you see he's never taken me up on it."

Out of the corner of my eye I could see Ellie's bust rising and falling, rising and falling. Ralph sat with his lips tightly pressed together.

"But you could hardly expect—" Fred's wife began indignantly.

"That he'd leave his family? Not if he were an ordinary ungifted person like me—or like your husband . . . But don't we always have other expectations of artistic people?"

Rita said sharply, "Ed, I think—" but he cut in swiftly:

"I'll tell you why he turns me down. He's afraid that if I gave him his real chance he'd write a couple tons of junk, or even worse that he wouldn't write at all without the spur of a lousy job and the dream of getting loose from it by making a million bucks.

"But we mustn't forget that Ralph is a very moral man. And if he failed to produce he figured he'd have to come back with his tail between his legs and spend the rest of his life working, like a character out of Balzac or DeMaupassant, to pay me back the money I'd given him, and that I wouldn't particularly want anyway, except for his peculiar standards of rectitude."

Ralph stood up. "Are you all through?"

"Hell, no. Now I've got a good idea for a novel myself, and I suspect that I could really get it done and make a name for myself if I was broke and had your incentive to get at it. By the way, am I monopolizing the conversation?"

Rita said: "Tell us about your novel—I hope it's funny."

"It's deadly serious. My hero is a man who is obsessed by one strange fear, which forces him to change his entire pattern of life."

"Oh, that sounds fascinating." Mrs. Conway looked around hopefully, as if she still expected that somehow the evening could be salvaged.

"My hero has heart trouble. He has to avoid overeating and overexertion. He's grown terrified that one day he'll strain too hard—he also suffers from constipation—and will have a heart attack in the bathroom. This fear of dying at stool is particularly repugnant to him because he is a sensitive man. He has visions, nightmares, of himself dead in an ignominious position, his trousers crumpled around his ankles, his suspenders dangling on the floor, his face pressed against his bare hairy knees, and his thin hair hanging forward so that his bald spot, usually decently concealed, is immediately apparent to the firemen who break open the door and discover his lifeless body. Sometimes he is horrified by the thought that his body will remain undiscovered for many hours, and will stiffen in its ridiculous and ungainly position. He visualizes burly policemen with faces as red as his is purple, trying to straighten out his corpse and draw his trousers up over his flanks. The irony of it is that this fastidious man must go to the most degrading lengths in order to avoid the necessity of evacuating alone. He searches out bathrooms without locks, and uses those primitive arrangements where men relieve themselves publicly in long rows, military style. He—"

"That's enough, Ed."

"More than enough. A compulsive writer could make a powerful thing out of it, couldn't he? Subtly bringing out the symbolism of the man who wants to create alone but can't take a chance." He winked at Ellie, who was nervously rearranging her back hair with arms upraised so that her taut bust, covered with sequins, seemed to blink back at him. "But I enjoy myself so much that I've never gotten past the first chapter."

"Don't play dumb," Ralph snapped. "You're determined to make me look a fool, with this coarse and vulgar—"

"If you're going to be stuffy, old man, I'll withdraw my standing offer of a Herlands fellowship."

"I'd never take a dime from you for a share in my stock. When it comes, my success is going to be my own."

Ralph's brother-in-law nodded approvingly. With his professional smile turned on, he looked like a death's-head. "Your book will be all the better for that attitude."

"I doubt if it will satisfy either you or me," Ed put in blandly. "Ralph operates under the illusion that he can produce a real work of art and make a fortune with it. Mark Twain had reason to believe in himself as a businessman-artist, in his time a Buffalo boy could still make his pile with his pen. But not any more, Ralphie, not any more."

Rita put her hand to her mouth and turned blindly away, fumbling for a candy dish. At that moment I hated Ed with all my heart.

"I think Ralph is entitled to a hobby without being teased about it, don't you?" Fred's wife asked me, as if I could become her ally in averting disaster.

But Ralph turned on her bitterly. "I have no hobbies. I despise people with hobbies. Someday you'll brag that you're my relative."

The three of us were a little constrained at the end of the evening, after Fred and his wife had left, coldly declining Ed's offer of a lift. Ed stayed on long enough to offer to fix me up with Ellie's younger sister (I declined not without regret) and to apologize perfunctorily to Rita.

"He was a monster tonight," she said tiredly, as she stood at the sink in her stocking feet, washing the cake dishes.

"Oh, I don't think so," Ralph replied slowly. "It wasn't an unusual performance. I happened to be handy, so he used me. I don't really care. What the hell, the proof will be in the eating."

Ralph's pudding wasn't ready when I met him next, several years later, but the circumstances of our meeting were so unusual that I didn't think much about his book at first. I was totally unprepared to see him advancing towards me in the bar of the Mark Hopkins in San Francisco, dressed in the uniform of a Naval lieutenant, and without his moustache.

"Great to see you, Harry! Got time for a drink?"

"You seem less surprised to see me than I am to see you."

"I read about the orchestra in the paper." He took off his white officer's hat, and I saw that his stiff shock of black hair had been cropped quite short. He looked ten years younger. "I'd planned to look you up tonight. Didn't you know I was in the Navy? Didn't Rita write you?"

"I've had only one postal from her in the last year."

"I expect she wasn't too anxious to tell you about it. That was the biggest row we've ever had, when she learned that I'd applied for a commission. She'd gotten to like the kind of life we were leading, and she couldn't bear to have anything disrupt it, even though it was inevitable. Probably she'd have been just as upset if I'd allowed myself to be drafted."

"I doubt that."

Ralph turned red. "You're right, of course. What bothered her most was the idea that I was willing, even anxious, to get away. The night I left for indoctrination school—" he hesitated, toying with his glass of beer, "—Rita accused me of deliberately setting out to commit suicide, the way children fantasy themselves dead in their coffins, surrounded by weeping and repentant parents."

"She was overwrought."

"Of course."

"But you look happier now than in years."

"I am. And I think Rita is too. She had visions of me being torpedoed, *spurlos versenkt,* or blown to pieces by a Kamikaze. But here I am safe and sound in San Francisco, presumably doing naval research because I'm a hydraulic engineer, and with leisure to read and meet people for the first time in my life. I suspect Rita's enjoying a vacation from the old routine herself."

"Do you still get up in the middle of the night?"

Ralph smiled shyly. "Only writing I can do is letters to Rita. There'll be time for the book when I get back." He stood up and glanced at his watch. "Rita's expecting a long-distance call from me in a few minutes. Would you like to say hello?"

"I'd love to."

I stood next to the phone booth and watched Ralph drumming his fingers while he waited for the connection. I thought of his father, whom he never mentioned any more, and as I looked at Ralph I observed for the first time that two vertical furrows were grooving into his cheeks, just like the old man's. He looked young in his uniform, but he was not really young.

Suddenly he stuck his head out of the door and said, apropos of nothing at all, "You must know what it means to get some recognition for your work. If only the war was over and I could *finish,* I know in my bones that people like—" he looked into the telephone as though he could not meet my eyes, "—well, like Edmund Wilson, would take me seriously. If they didn't, I don't think I could go on living." His eyes were burning. "But right now I'm concentrating on finding out what the man in the street wants. I want to do a new final draft that will insure me a really big audience. That's why I've been reading a lot of good histories and talking to all kinds of people."

Then he laughed and said, "You must think I'm an egomaniac. What about you? You don't have a wife or anything yet, do you?"

"I was engaged for a while to an OPA economist, but she got sick of waiting for me to make up my mind, so she joined the Waves."

Ralph disconcerted me by laughing out loud. "Tell you what," he said. "Why don't you talk to Rita first? We'll surprise her. Go on, go ahead." He stepped out and extended the earphone to me.

I stood in the little metal chamber, listening to the sharp inhuman voices of switchboard girls all over the country. *Yes Des Moines, The exchange is Linden, L as in Love,* and suddenly I did not want to speak to Rita at all, I wanted to be quit of the Everetts and their crumbling dream world.

But suddenly Rita's voice, clear and yet infinitely small, as though she were speaking from another world, filled me with such anguished nostalgia that I could not bring myself to look through the glass door as I listened. She was frightened and lonely, and she insisted that with Ralph gone, there was no one in Buffalo to talk to. That had been Ralph's old complaint. I clung to the telephone and I wondered. Why must there be someone to talk to? Does it really mean someone to listen, like the audiences I have had all my adult life—so that I have never deeply felt the need of a listener—or does it imply that the listener will answer, that he will say not the things that are better left unsaid, like Ed Herlands, but the things that one needs desperately to hear?

Ralph's smile had faded to a shadow by the time he replaced me in the phone booth, for I had managed to get Rita to say goodbye only by promising to come to Buffalo at the earliest opportunity.

Actually I had no such opportunity until after the Japanese had quit and Ralph had returned from the West Coast. When I did get to Buffalo it seemed to me that Rita must have been overwrought during that feverish telephone conversation, for the Everetts' lives appeared hardly to have been affected by the war. Rita and the older girls had been thrilled by their one visit to the West Coast, and Ralph himself said to me briefly, after he had greeted me at the station and helped me into his car, "Well, I had a very pleasant vacation too—" (This in reply to my remark about a trip to Nova Scotia I had just taken with my brother and his family) "—but it's over now, and I'm satisfied. If the war had lasted much longer, I would have had trouble getting back my work habits."

He had gotten back his moustache too. It was peppered with grey, and I wondered why he felt that he needed it, but that was the kind of question you could never ask of Ralph even if you put it as a joke. Almost as soon as we had reached his home, Ralph excused himself and headed back for the toolhouse, saying over his shoulder, "See you at the supper table."

The girls greeted me with shrieks of delight and led me to the kitchen, where Rita stood with her head bent forward over a mixing bowl, her blonde hair hanging full across her face. When she looked up her eyes were brimming with tears: I was startled and frightened, and for one instant I felt like bolting.

But then she laughed, and as she brushed the back of her hand across her face I saw that the tears had been caused by onions which she was slicing into a bowl of chopped meat. I was overcome with such enormous relief that I stepped forward and kissed her damp cheek.

"Are we going to play some duets while I'm here?" I asked.

"Don't tease me. If it wasn't for our record collection, which is mostly albums you've brought us, there wouldn't be any music in my life at all —except for the girls."

"Are you happy?"

"I'm busy. Ralph has been writing ten hours a day, trying to finish before his terminal leave runs out. I take his lunch out to the toolhouse so he won't break his train of thought."

"And now you're satisfied. I was never really sure."

Rita's hand came down on the kitchen table so sharply that the silverware jumped in the air and fell with a clatter. "Don't you see, Harry? He's almost finished. Suppose it's a failure? What will we do?"

"What you've been doing for ten years. It depends on what you mean by failure, doesn't it?"

"For ten years Ralph has been living for the day when the critics will cheer him. He talks about the money and independence, but it's recognition he's after. Suppose he doesn't get it? Do you think he'll be able to say, Better luck next time? Do you?" Her voice rose dangerously. "Do you?"

"His book might sell moderately well and get some nice reviews, enough to make Ralph feel that he had made a good start."

"A start?" she laughed scornfully. "And then what—back to the Water Department and the toolhouse? We're not kids any more, Harry, neither of us . . . I hate melodrama, don't you? Would you do me a favor—tell

Ralph it's time to knock off? You can go right out the kitchen door."

So I followed the little trampled path that Ralph had made in the grass in his years of crossing back and forth; when I reached the sagging frame toolhouse I hesitated, still uncertain whether I should intrude. Finally I raised my fist and pounded on the iron-barred old door.

But Ralph's voice said "Yup," and I entered his headquarters. The walls of his spotless workroom were whitewashed and covered with old maps of the Niagara Frontier. Ralph was seated at a roll-top desk with his shirt sleeves turned back halfway to his elbows. He got up when he saw me. "You've never been in here before, have you? Let me show you my stuff."

"Rita suggested that it's time to knock off. I didn't want to intrude."

"Let me show you my layout."

His wooden filing cabinets were a marvel of precision. Ralph had cross-filed all of his material the way his engineering reports must have been indexed at his office, so that you could open any drawer and find references to the downtown scene in Buffalo of the 1850s, the clothing of the men, the manners of the women, the shape of the buildings.

The novel itself was in a series of looseleaf notebooks, one chapter to a notebook, and they were stacked head-high on the roll-top desk. "I would have asked you to read it, as a favor to me," Ralph said, "but every time I got a draft out it needed a little more work. After all these years, I'm almost through. I'm sure that if I hadn't had to go downtown to work every day I could have gotten it out in a year or two of concentrated effort."

"Don't you think you're more mature now than when you started?"

"I'm older, that's all I know. Believe me, there's something wrong about grubbing away so slowly in secret, like a hermit crab. I often think how much better it would have been if I had been able to publish regularly years ago, with each book maybe improving a little."

"Haven't you enjoyed it?"

Ralph rubbed his knuckles across his eyelids. "I suppose you're happiest when you don't have time to think about what you're doing. But even if I don't make a dime on my book, even if no one reads it but the critics, they'll recognize that my very best is in it. That's something to be able to say, isn't it, that you've given everything that you have? And that you've done it without stimulation or encouragement, in the lonely hours of the night? . . . You go on, I'll be in shortly."

As I turned on Ralph's lawn to look back at him standing in the toolhouse doorway, caught by the waning rays of the late afternoon sun, I was filled with envy and admiration. Rita was wrong about him—of that I was sure.

Only a few months (perhaps a year) later, I came home to the Bronx one evening from Philadelphia, put down my valise and fiddle in the foyer, and found my mother waiting up for me, lying on the sofa with a newspaper and a bowl of grapes. She had a way of popping the pulp into her mouth so that the skin remained between her fingers—it always made me nervous. She shoved aside the bowl, unable to divide her attention between me and the grapes, and said in a voice at once sad and accusing, "You said you'd be home early."

"I had to catch a later train. What's new?"

She sighed, hauling herself upright with a groan, to register her resentment against being treated as merely a messenger service.

"What should be new? A boy (all of my friends were boys to my mother) called up this afternoon. He *said* his name was Ralph Edwards," she added, as if she was perfectly aware that he had been lying.

"But I don't know any Ralph Edwards."

"From Rochester."

"From—Ralph Everett you mean, from Buffalo!"

"So it was Everett. He said to tell you he was at a cocktail party. He sounded drunk."

"Where? In New York?" Gradually I pieced together from my mother's grudging answers the information that Ralph's book had been accepted by a publisher who had already begun an intensive promotional campaign with a cocktail party. I dialed the Algonquin, but the operator would not put me through to Ralph. Probably passed out cold, I thought, and asked for his wife; but she wasn't registered.

So he had come to New York alone for his first moment of triumph. It was a masculine enough action, and I knew that if the situation had been reversed Rita would surely have taken her husband and children along, like a lady ambassador. But I called the next morning and Ralph insisted that I meet him for lunch. He sounded frightened.

I had to join him in an out-of-the-way spot on Eighth Avenue, and although I was early, Ralph was already waiting when I arrived. "Hell of a thing," he said. "I had to sneak off, or they would have dragged me to lunch too."

"Are you that popular?"

"I need advice," he replied obliquely. "Never realized what I was getting into. Look here." He opened a heavy old-fashioned briefcase and pulled out a bundle of papers. "They've promised me lecture tours— personal appearances in bookstores—radio quiz programs—interviews with columnists I never heard of—"

"That sounds wonderful!"

"There's a catch to it."

"There always is. But it looks like your book is going to be a big thing!"

Ralph looked up, surprised. "Of course. But I didn't figure on a bunch of editors, agents, press agents, book club representatives, and I don't know what the hell the rest of them are, all nagging me to jazz up the manuscript."

"I don't understand, Ralph."

"Probably I'm naïve. I didn't expect to be told I'd written a great book, and then have a bunch of plumbers go to work on it, not paying any more attention to me than if I had been just a yokel, sightseeing in the publisher's office."

"Apparently they want to make sure it will sell."

"But what are they going to make out of me? Yesterday they threw graphs at me to prove they know what makes a book sell. I said, Won't it sell if it's good? And then they gave me reader involvement."

"What's that?"

"They've got figures that show how long people read a book before putting it down. Somebody has even found out what catches people's eyes when they're browsing in bookstores. And my book hasn't got it. My editor says—" Ralph's voice was scornful, and yet uncertain, and he spoke without looking at me, "—I've got to make it longer."

"Longer?"

"I've been thinking about telling them to go to hell. But they're nice people, Harry. They can't understand why I'm not more cooperative, when all that they're interested in is me and my career and seeing that I reach the big public I'm entitled to. All I can say in answer is Yes, but what about the book? It's shaken down now to where they've turned the job over to a girl named Doris. A Wellesley girl, out of Butte, Montana . . . I need your advice."

"If I can only help—"

"They want to send Doris back to Buffalo with me to advise me on a new draft. Doris has the proposed changes lined up in a card index. She's very efficient—used to work for Gallup. Should I go through with it? I've been up all night trying to make up my mind."

"What does Rita say?"

"She thinks it's the chance of a lifetime."

"It *is* your first book," I said. "And it isn't as if you didn't want it to be popular. I remember in San Francisco you were trying to find out what the average man wants to read."

"Sure, but I've already gone as far as I can, maybe even too far, in that direction. Will it still be my book when that Wellesley girl gets through with it?"

"She can't make you do anything you don't want to."

"Somehow I didn't think you'd agree with Rita about this." Ralph began to stuff the papers back into his briefcase. "But I know what you mean. I suppose I have the obligation to listen. I can always say No."

Ralph flew back to Buffalo, and the Wellesley girl went with him. I still have a letter from Rita that describes, with a mixture of fear and mounting excitement, how Doris with her statistics on reader involvement was succeeding in persuading Ralph, despite himself, to broaden his story, work in material that he had previously scrapped, simplify his prose, and inject additional romance. It was on the last point, though, that Ralph balked. Doris explained very carefully, as I gathered, that the firm had had the manuscript mimeographed and pre-tested: there had been strong indications that the reading public would be happier if an aged Iroquois squaw were made out to be eighteen, in order that she might be involved in a romance.

Although he had been going along with Doris's judgment, something about this suggestion made Ralph become really stubborn: he informed his publishers that he was calling the whole thing off. Doris turned to Rita for help, and it was at this point that Rita used a weapon which she had never, in all the years of their marriage, turned on her husband. "It hurt me to do it," she wrote me, "in fact it went against the grain, but I felt that in this instance it was for his own good. I told him that I hadn't skimped and sacrificed all these years just so that he could throw everything away in one quixotic gesture. Of course when I said this I was thinking of Ralph, and of what was best for him, but he took it to mean that I was hurt about the past and frightened about the future—and as a result he has promised at least to think it over."

Ralph's resistance was weakened, but not completely destroyed, by Rita's declaration that if it continued it could only make their years together seem a terrible, useless waste. He wanted, she told me, some assurance from a disinterested person, an artist. "He doesn't *know* anybody. Whom can he turn to, Ed Herlands? It has to be you, Harry. Please call him on the phone and talk to him."

I was very reluctant. I didn't know anything about fiction, or about the merits of the proposal that had so disturbed Ralph. Nevertheless I did feel that I had a responsibility, as a family friend, if nothing more. So I called Ralph. I didn't attempt to pressure him. I simply asked: "What will you gain if you persist? Will you change the manuscript back to what it was?"

"Maybe part-way."

"Supposing you start all over with another publisher, assuming you can get out of your contract. What makes you so sure you wouldn't run into the same thing again? What makes you sure that your way is the right way, or the only way? You've never published a book before, and these people have been doing it all their lives."

"So if you were me, you'd give in."

"I'm not saying that. I'm just asking you what the alternatives are, and whether you've thought them all through."

Ralph didn't say much to that; I think Rita was at his side while he talked. He thanked me most warmly for having phoned, and within a day or two he was back at work on the manuscript. Very shortly thereafter the job was done.

Doris was right, of course. No matter how reasonable Ralph's objections may have seemed to him, the immediate astonishing success of the book was proof that the Wellesley girl (as he persisted in calling her) knew her business.

It seems to me now that before I was actually aware of what was happening, "Queen City" became a national catch phrase. The papers were full of it, I listened to the speculation in Pullman washrooms, backstage at concerts, in restaurants, everywhere, about which Hollywood stars would play the leading roles in the movie version of Ralph's book, and for a while you couldn't turn on the radio without hearing a pun on the book's title or on Ralph's name, to the accompaniment of roars and applause.

In a matter of months Ralph and his book achieved the status of an institution, and I grew used to the feature articles on Ralph's long ordeal and the photographs of Ralph—smiling rather grimly, it seemed to me —seated with Rita and their four famous daughters in the living room, as though he had just been elected Governor. From time to time I thought that I should salute in some practical way my friends' great good fortune, but all I could think of was something ridiculously inappropriate like sending a basket of fruit or a box of flowers. So I did nothing.

The excitement about the book was at its peak when Rita wrote extending me a feverish invitation to spend at least part of my vacation with them at their new summer place in Canada. She made it sound as if I would be doing a great favor by coming up and helping them to enjoy their success. I was flattered and I accepted.

In the club car I picked up a copy of *Life;* it seemed inevitable that there should be a story about Ralph and his novel. The article itself was full of statistics on the number of hours Ralph had spent in the toolhouse, the number of pounds that his manuscript weighed, and the marks that his public school teachers remembered giving him, but there was an omission which struck me with special force: while Ralph's mother, who had died during his teens, was adequately and conventionally described, there was absolutely no mention of his father. And in addition to this there was one sentence that leaped up at me and that I immediately committed to memory, like a musical phrase that would have to recur in my life: "While the final verdict on Ralph Everett's work is not yet in, it must be obvious to the author by now that sophisticates will ignore any work which celebrates the American dream in a manner acceptable to the general public. But their disdain will surely be counterbalanced by the shower of gold now raining down on Ralph Everett as a reward for his long years of solitary labor."

I was intercepted at the station by Penny, who ran into my arms breathless and excited.

"Mom couldn't find a place to park and she's driving back and forth, back and forth!"

We found Rita cruising slowly down the street in a handsome green convertible. I tossed my bag in the back.

"The car goes well with your hair, Rita."

"I hope you won't tease me about all our new belongings. Prosperity has brought more problems than we ever had before."

"What's wrong?"

"I'm terribly worried about Ralph. He's working like a dog fixing the summer place—" she waved up ahead, along the river road on which we were driving, "—and yet he can't sleep nights. He wanders around all night, and the whole routine starts again in the morning."

"Perhaps he can't break his old habits."

"It's more than that. He says the money is a trap for us, and that we'll wind up living like rich people. For a while he talked about our being too provincial, and what Europe could do for us, and how we could sink our roots when we came back, oh I don't know, in South Dakota or some such place. Imagine sinking roots in the Black Hills with four daughters!"

"But now?"

"He's like a man who suspects he has cancer and sits in the doctor's office laughing and joking, and waiting to hear the worst. Ralph has been waiting and waiting for the verdict of the important critics. The more the book sells, the worse their silence is." Rita indicated a pile of magazines that lay between us on the leather seat. "These are mostly quarterlies, college magazines and such. Some of them I never heard of. I'm afraid to look and see if there's anything about the book in them. It sounds crazy but sometimes he acts as though he was ashamed that the book is so successful."

We had turned off the highway and were driving down a narrow sandy road, at the end of which stood a rambling bungalow, half concealed by scrub pines and oaks. As we neared the house I could see Lake Erie glimmering through the trees, perhaps an eighth of a mile away. Daisy, swinging slowly and seriously on an old tire hanging from a tree on the front lawn, raised her arm gravely in a formal greeting. Behind her I could hear Robin and Laura playing jacks on the screened porch.

As we drove to the back of the house I caught sight of Ralph, stripped to the waist and straightening up stiffly from a barbecue pit which he had been plastering. He too waved to us, trowel in hand, and came slowly to the car, sweating heavily and scowling into the sunlight.

I hauled out my bag. "You look twice as tired as when you used to work for an honest living, Ralph."

"I am! But they tell me I'm living the way a successful writer should. Quit my job, you know—I'm an ex-engineer." Suddenly he caught sight of the magazines. His nostrils dilated above the tough moustache and I could see his fine rib cage expand as he wiped his sweaty palms on his dungarees. "Excuse me," he said politely. He reached over and plucked up the magazines from the car seat, then riffled them quickly.

"I've struck gold," he exclaimed. "Not just a review, a whole article. The Problem of the American Writer: Ralph Everett, A Case in Point."

"Couldn't it wait till after supper? I'm sure that Harry—"

"I bet Harry wants to know what this twenty-one-year-old prodigy from Savannah thinks of old Ralph's first book. All Harry's seen is praise from the hacks so far." There was something menacing in his tone. We stood there helplessly in the driveway while Ralph flipped the pages of the journal. "A Case in Point—did you ever think of me in that way, Rita?" Ralph began to walk toward the porch, reading as he moved; Rita and I followed him like two nervous retainers, uncertain whether to follow the master into the bath. But in an instant Ralph turned on us savagely.

"This kid knows more than the old men. 'What can one do but weep,' he says, 'when one examines the career of Ralph Everett? Here is a man, as we are told, who gave his all for his art. He made the accepted sacrifices, cut himself off from fun and frolic, practiced his craft in silence in a drafty toolhouse in the worst hours of the early morning, did not compromise by publishing prematurely, and . . . made a tidy fortune with a book which can only be called a *production*.' "

Ralph looked up from the magazine, his face expressionless. "The boy resents my money. That's the only false note so far. Doesn't he know that it's fashionable for writers to be well off these days?"

"Let's drop it for now, Ralph."

" '*Queen City,*' " he read on, ignoring us, " 'can be viewed in two ways, either as the labored effort of a serious but essentially untalented man, or as a striking example of the effect of the corruption of American culture on its worst victim, the creative man.' "

Rita stared very hard at the keys that she still clasped in her fingers, her brows contracted as though they had suddenly become a mysterious object. Finally she said, "I just don't see why you should be so affected by a youngster, a mere boy, when you've been praised by—"

"Because writing means more to this kid than it does to those old fakers who make a living by patting people like me on the back. I know he gets a childish kick out of sniping at success, but he believes what he's saying. 'The very smell of big money,' he says, 'is on every page of Mr. Everett's novel, and while it would be unfair to conclude from the text that his years of selfless labor were spent with one eye on the eventual reproduction of his story in more popular media, his triumphant reliance on stock situations for characters on whose details of speech and dress he has obviously lavished untiring research would point to the fact that Ralph Everett is a captive, bound not hand and foot, but body and soul, to the culture from which he thought to liberate himself by an intense but hopelessly insecure act of will.' That's what the people I've been waiting for would have said, if they had felt like taking the trouble." Ralph tossed the magazine on a porch chair. "I want a copy of this sent to the Wellesley girl."

"Is that necessary?"

"She deserves a better souvenir than the inscribed book I gave her. If you won't do it, I will. I believe that consciences should be kept functioning. Right now I'm going for a swim."

"Ralph, it's much too chilly—" Rita started to protest, but I put my hand on her arm. Ralph strode swiftly away, down the narrow path to the lake, and Rita and I mounted the porch steps together.

Not long after, he returned to the cottage with a towel draped around his neck and his shock of thick hair standing defiantly on end. "Had a good swim. Did some thinking too—I've made up my mind."

Rita looked at him with fear in her eyes. "What do you mean?"

"I'm driving into town right after supper—going to start work on a new book."

Rita leaped up like a young girl and threw her arms around his neck. "I knew those rotten articles wouldn't get you down!"

At that moment I felt like an intruder. Fortunately I remembered that my mother's only brother, a notions salesman, was in Buffalo on business and that I had half-promised to spend an evening with him, so I said to Ralph, "Would you mind if I drove in with you?"

He and Rita were startled by my request, and I had to explain about Uncle Louis. "But couldn't it keep until later in the week?" Rita asked.

I was on the point of yielding when Daisy came running in to announce that Uncle Ed had arrived.

"Leave it to Herlands," Ralph said. "He always manages to show up at suppertime. But as long as he's staying, I'd like to have you along. I was a little worried about leaving Rita and the kids alone this evening."

Supper was difficult, mostly because of Ralph's abstractedness and Rita's wary desire that the children should not disturb their father; and the dull badinage between Ed and me didn't help much. Ed was just as well pleased to keep Rita company for the evening, since he was obviously anxious to rebuild his frienship with Ralph. "Just make a start, Ralph," Rita pleaded, "and then bring Harry back. After all, you have so much time now."

"I do, don't I?" He kissed Rita fondly, and at such length that even Ed turned away with me in embarrassment; but Penny and Daisy began to laugh, and the spell was broken, and Ralph and I clambered into the convertible. He didn't forget to take the magazine with him.

The evening was cool, but Ralph didn't appear to notice it, and I was hesitant to ask him to put up the top. At old Fort Erie the road swerves sharply and suddenly you come upon the Niagara River and the shallow skyline of Buffalo; seeing it at twilight as we did, it seemed very beautiful. "I see why you've been fascinated by Buffalo," I said.

"We're looking at it now from another country. That makes a difference."

"I think I understand how you can spend your entire life writing about a place."

"Somebody else, not me."

"Then what's your next book going to be about?"

Ralph looked at me dazedly, as if I had been speaking too fast.

"The one you're going to start tonight."

At last he said slowly, "That was just a lie I told Rita."

I hesitated, but finally I asked, "Why are you going into town?"

"I have to get back to the toolhouse. I have to get back there. It's the only place where I've ever had any peace of mind."

"Maybe I shouldn't have come out to visit just at this time."

"I was the one who urged Rita to invite you. I'm glad for Rita's sake, not just for mine, that you're here now."

"When I think of the pleasure you've given so many people, and the pride that your family has—"

"The wrong kind of pleasure, the wrong kind of pride."

"You're very tired, aren't you, Ralph?"

"Why wasn't I tired during all the years I was working on the book? If you can understand that, you'll know how I feel now."

Ralph brought the car to a stop at the American end of the Peace Bridge; the immigration man leaned forward and said to me, "Where were you born?" and then he recognized Ralph. "Hello, Mr. Everett. Back to town, eh?"

Ralph nodded curtly. From the other side of the car the customs inspector said solicitously, "Better put up the top, Mr. Everett. It's turning cold."

"You see," Ralph said, without looking at me as he drove ahead, "I'm even a celebrity for the wrong reasons. They're going to go home and gossip about me."

"That's nothing to be upset about, is it?"

The street lamps winked on as we rolled downtown. "At least there's money," Ralph murmured. "If I never did anything but build barbecue pits for the rest of my life, there'd still be enough for Rita and the girls. Why work? To grind out a shelf full of second-rate books?"

"Just the same," I protested, "your father would have been proud of you."

"Luckiest thing that happened was the old man's dying when he did. He would have laughed his head off at all this publicity. Oh, he would have been pleased for Rita, I suppose. He was very fond of her—just as you are. That makes things easier for me."

He came to a stop in front of my uncle's hotel. "Here you are. You don't mind picking me up when you're through with your uncle, do you?"

"Not at all."

"Just hop in a cab and come over. You'll find me in the toolhouse. Goodbye, Harry." He leaned out of the car and extended his hand. "I've always enjoyed your company. You've been a good friend to us."

I went up to my Uncle Louis's room and we spent a desultory few hours trading jokes and playing cribbage. At last we had bored each other to the point where we were both relieved when I excused myself. I was glad when my cab reached Humboldt Parkway.

But the street was blocked, and when I smelled smoke and saw children running towards Ralph's house, I jumped out of the taxi. The sky suddenly reddened before me, and I felt my heart constrict.

I was much too late, of course. The firemen had kept the blaze confined to the toolhouse, but that was enough. A spaniel-faced old inspector pointed at the flaming shack and said, "We have to figure that he's inside. His car is still out front with the key in the ignition. It's a terrible thing."

It was a terrible thing. They made me identify Ralph when it was all over. I got sick and had to go outside, but the night air revived me—or maybe it was the feeling that Ralph had died in a way that had more dignity than the ugly deathbed scenes with which so many of us reluctantly let go our grip on life. They found him leaning forward over the typewriter as though he were hard at work, and they surmised that when he was sickened by smoke and unable to make his way to the blackened windows or the latched door (which he had locked from the inside apparently to make sure that he would not be disturbed) he returned to his typewriter to await the end with tranquillity and courage. Everyone seemed to agree that while Ralph had been inexcusably careless in dozing off with a lighted cigatette in a wooden shed piled high with papers, what was more important was that he had finished his masterpiece *before* the tragic accident, which could have taken place at any time during the previous decade. As for his files and records, which he had maintained with such scrupulous devotion, they were utterly destroyed. Nothing remained, not his notes, not even the cabinets themselves, nor the framed pictures of Rita and his daughters.

I took Ralph's car and drove back to Canada. The night was cold and I had to concentrate on the unfamiliar road; somehow I found my way to the summer house, where Rita and Ed were sitting on the porch and waiting for Ralph and me. Without any preliminaries I told them what had happened. Rita looked at me uncomprehendingly, then brushed past me and ran down the steps to the empty car, as though I had perpetrated some kind of hideous joke. I stood stupidly staring after her, and it was Ed Herlands who lumbered down and caught her as she fell.

Rita refused ever to return to the house on Humboldt Parkway. The funeral was held from the cottage in Canada—we buried Ralph next to his father—and Rita stayed on there with the children and the nursemaid while her sister-in-law and Ed and I disposed of everything in the house, which we also sold at her request.

I took a room in an ugly boardinghouse in the nearby resort town of

Crystal Beach, and I passed my entire summer vacation with Rita. The girls, as children will, were soon playing happily, unaware of what their gaiety was costing their mother.

"If only they didn't forget so quickly, Harry."

"It would be worse. Life would be unbearable if children lived in the past. And as for us, we have to live in the future, don't we?"

"Ralph did, and for what? I can bear everything else but the thought that he had to die just at the beginning of the kind of life he deserved."

"He fulfilled himself in his children and his book. And he lived long enough to reap the reward for his work. Isn't that more than most artists can say?"

Rita took my hand. "You're very comforting. I know it's hard for you to sit here all summer and listen to me. But who else can I talk to about Ralph? You understand him so well."

At the end of the season I arranged for Rita to take a cruise with her sister-in-law. It seemed only natural for me to meet her at the pier with the children upon her return. By the beginning of the winter I didn't feel too much constraint about asking her to marry me, and I was overjoyed when she accepted.

We have a lovely home in Westchester now, and the children seem very fond of me. When we moved in I surprised Rita by having her harp (which she thought I had sold, along with everything else) placed in the living room. Naturally she approached it with some diffidence, but soon she began to practice regularly, and now our friends enjoy dropping in and listening to our duets.

We often speak of Ralph, and I make a point of impressing upon the girls that their comfortable standard of life is due largely to his unremitting and unselfish labors. The movie made from *Queen City* was released recently, and we all went to see it. Rita cried a little—she says that the stars realized their roles just as Ralph would have wanted—and the girls were thrilled. I like to think that Ralph would have been pleased to see us at the première, which represented in a way the culmination of all his striving. And if he is watching, wouldn't he be happy now to know that not only his great public but his wife and children too revere his memory and respect the fruits of his genius?

THE DANCER

When Peter Chifley left Elyria, Ohio, for New York City, he was twenty-one years old. He took with him all the money he had saved while serving in the occupation forces in Japan, where something had happened which changed the course of his life.

One day Peter had wandered into a movie where one of the early Fred Astaire pictures was being shown. He sat through it three times, and he began to follow the Astaire movies from one section of Tokyo to another: he was no longer the same person. Peter felt that the lightness and grace of Fred Astaire and Ginger Rogers corresponded to something in the daily life of the Japanese of which he had been vaguely aware before; and he recognized that Astaire's trim and airy leaps had released a great creative force within himself.

He decided to become a dancer.

Peter had never learned to suppress his true feelings, and when he stepped into the cool winter twilight after a rapturous afternoon watching *Top Hat,* he was overcome with a breathless buoyancy, and he began to dance at once. The two military policemen who elbowed their way through the crowed of smiling Japanese leaped to the grotesque conclusion that Peter was drunk; and Peter tried to explain without much success that his movements were wobbly simply because he had never danced before.

This incident, and several others, may have influenced the army authorities to return Peter to the United States somewhat early. He hurried home to Elyria, worried about what his parents would think of his new ambition; but they were reasonable people, and when customers gathered in droves at their lunchroom to watch Peter dancing alone in the empty lot next door, they could actually measure their pride and happiness in the ringing of the cash register. However, when they saw that the curious customers never bought anything except coffee, and that Peter was growing restless and unhappy, they reluctantly acceded to his desire to go to New York to study dancing.

It was a cool sunny day, very early in spring, when Peter's bus crossed the bridge into Manhattan, and as he craned his neck to the rear he could see the glowing rays of the declining sun striking sharply against the iron girders of the bridge, like a vision of his bridges burning behind him.

"Look," he cried without thinking, "look, the bridge is burning!"

Everyone turned and gaped. Some of the passengers were disgruntled at seeing only the sunset. A fat man who had been dozing in the seat directly in front of Peter's muttered audibly, "Damned yokel! Man can't even take a nap."

"I'm sorry," Peter said tentatively, "I didn't mean to bother anybody," but no one paid any attention, now that their goal was so near.

Peter alighted from the bus on Eighth Avenue, in the middle of the city, and found himself surrounded by an even greater throng than he had ever seen in Tokyo, which was the only other large city that he knew. These people were carrying briefcases and newspapers, and some even pushed wagons filled with Hershey bars and Chiclets. He decided to approach a shabby smiling man who wore a cardboard hat bearing the words SIGHTSEEING TOURS perched rakishly on his curly grey head.

"Excuse me." Peter spoke, without thinking, in Japanese. "Do you know where I can find a nice clean room?"

"Got much money?" the guide asked coolly.

"No, I don't," Peter admitted, in English. "But how did you understand me?"

"Fortunately you came to the right party, son. I used to coach baseball in Kobe—ran a sex shop on the side." He drew forth a grimy calling card. "Mrs. Blight, who runs this rooming house in Chelsea, went to P.S. 127

with my bookie's sister-in-law. Caters to theatrical people. Tell her Shanker sent you."

"What does P.S. 127 mean?" Peter asked, but the man had already turned away and was calling out softly, as though he hoped no one would hear: "See the secrets of Chinatown, the world-famous Bowery, the tallest building in the world . . ."

Peter picked up his valise and walked slowly downtown in the pale glow of the late afternoon twilight. At Seventeenth Street he took out the card that the guide had given him and surveyed the old red brick houses, some latticed with tough old ivy branches like protruding veins, some with flowerpots on their window ledges. Almost every house bore a small sign: *Furnished Rooms, Rooms for Men,* or *Light Housekeeping Rooms.*

He rang the doorbell of the house that had been recommended to him and was greeted by a small worried-looking woman, who stuck out her tongue at him.

"I'm looking for a room." Peter held out the card. "But if—"

"Oh, Shanker sent you! I thought you were a meter reader. I've been having a feud with the Consolidated Edison Company. Your eyes are going to pop right out of your head when you see the lovely room just waiting for a nice boy like you. At seven dollars a week it's a steal."

Peter followed Mrs. Blight, who was wiping her hands furtively on her meager hips, into a long narrow room that was dark and not lovely at all.

"I'll take it, ma'am. Should I pay you now?"

Mrs. Blight nodded in a motherly way and pocketed the money. "I'll give you a hand-painted receipt tomorrow, Mr.—"

"Chifley. My name is Peter Chifley. I'm going to be a dancer."

"Thrilling! My late husband Benito was an accomplished soap carver—"

She was interrupted by a stout young man who suddenly appeared in the doorway. "An addition to the personnel, Mama?"

"Oh, you startled me! This is Mr. Chickpea. I'll leave you two alone now. Angus, you'll explain about the lavatory and the rules, won't you?" She slipped out beneath his outstretched arm and disappeared down the hall.

"Are you Mrs. Blight's son?" Peter asked.

"Oh no! My name is Angus Mondschein. Like yourself, I am a paying guest. I reside directly across the hall, and I entered to ascertain whether

I might possibly be of assistance while you were getting acclimated."

"That's very kind of you." Peter surveyed Angus more closely. He was perhaps twenty-five, with an extraordinarily large, fleshy, powerful-looking nose, and a pair of thick, well-nourished ears that grew out of either side of his head like cabbages. His eyes were surprisingly large and soft, and his long white teeth were clamped around a fragrant calabash pipe.

"Where do you hie from?"

"I come from Ohio," Peter replied, "if that's what you mean. My father has a lunchroom in Elyria."

"Ah, a native of the Buckeye State. Have your parents too been unable to comprehend your desire for the higher things?"

"I want to go to school. But my parents are being very helpful."

Angus curled his lip. "A false front. You must make a clean break. May I assist your cogitations, as an older student?"

"That's very nice of you, Mr. Mondschein."

"Call me Angus."

"Do you know of a school where I could study dancing?"

"One must avoid a stereotyped curriculum. I myself have explored the offerings of—" he extended his sturdy fingers under Peter's nose and flexed them at the first joint, one by one,"—the New School for Social Research, the Henry George School, the Ethical Culture School, Cooper Union, and at the moment of speaking I am enrolled in several fascinating courses at the Paul Revere School. If you accelerate your unpacking, you'll be enabled to accompany me to said institution. It's within perambulating distance."

"Do they have dancing courses?" Peter asked dubiously.

"They offer a broad schedule of progressive classes. For a dancer it is essential to grasp the Marxist approach to the arts."

So Peter became a student at the Revere School. It struck him at once as odd that the dance class should be known as The People's Dance Group.

"After all," he asked at the first session, "how can you dance without people? I took it for granted that dancing was for people."

This statement created consternation. Almost immediately Peter was characterized as a cynic and a confused aesthete. By the time the class broke up, Peter, who had not even slept one night in New York City, was beginning to think that perhaps he might have done better to stay in the empty lot in Elyria.

"I never would have thought," he said to Angus as they walked home, "that you have to have opinions about the atom bomb. I only want to dance to make myself happy."

"And what about the rest of humanity?" Angus asked severely, escorting him up the steps of Mrs. Blight's house.

"Well, them too," replied Peter, abashed.

The first thing that struck Peter's eye in Angus's room was a charcoal portrait of Joseph Stalin with a pipe parting his moustache in the middle. Below it on the bureau lay an incredible collection of pipes: narghiles, chibouks, meerschaums, skull pipes, South African gourds. On the desk was a jumble of reamers, after-pipe mints, bushy-tail pipe cleaners, moistening pellets, initialed pouches, and back issues of *Pipe Lore.*

Peter looked up at a framed letter that hung above the bed. It was on official United States stationery, and it read: *Dear Mr. Mondschein, While I agree with you on the virtues of pipe-smoking, as one pipe smoker to another I must dissociate myself from your unique interpretation of recent history. I have instructed my secretary to send you under separate cover the Department of Agriculture pamphlet on The Care of Pipes. Very truly yours, I. Angelo Sanes.*

"I received that epistle," Angus stated modestly, "in response to a missive that I dispatched to the Senator containing my views on why we should press for closer relations with our former Russian ally."

"You certainly have a wonderful pipe collection."

"I am in correspondence with myriads of individuals in connection with my collection. And I would not hesitate to asseverate, as I did to Senator Sanes, that Prime Minister Stalin's statesmanship, *and* his military genius, could be attributed to his choice of a curved-shank pipe."

"I promised my father I wouldn't smoke until I was twenty-one," Peter said apologetically, and added, "I certainly appreciate your thoughtfulness, Angus. If you'll excuse me now, I think I'll turn in, because I want to make an early start tomorrow."

At the door, as if it were an afterthought, Angus reached out to his bookcase and pulled out a handful of pamphlets. "You may find it worthwhile to peruse this literature at your leisure, especially if you are addicted to reading nocturnally in the bedchamber."

"Thank you." Peter was about to cross the hall into his own room when a group of young men came bounding along the hallway, giggling and chattering among themselves as they mounted the steps to the floor above.

"They certainly look like they're having fun," Peter said.

"Parties, parties." Angus pursed his lips. "They're very shallow, Piotr, very shallow indeed. If progressives had to rely on people of *their* ilk . . ."

Just then one of the young men looked back from the head of the stairs, raised his fist merrily in a mock salute, turned, and disappeared.

"Well," Peter said, "good night, Angus."

"Good night, Piotr."

When Peter was comfortably settled in bed at last, he picked up one of Angus's pamphlets. *Peace, Plenty, Progress, and Prosperity,* written by somebody named Joe Worker, was a dialogue between a very uneducated man and another man who was completely illiterate. Peter read one paragraph, turned out the light, and fell into a deep dreamless sleep.

The next morning Peter arose early and made his way directly to the Veterans Administration office, where he explained his problem to the Vocational Counselor. The office was enormous. It was a nearly bare loft in which several dozen young men milled about, smoking, swearing, arguing, or merely reading the morning papers listlessly and sleepily, as though they were still resentful at their mothers for having routed them out of bed at such an hour. The floor was littered with hundreds of ground-out cigarette butts, and the walls were placarded every few feet with large red and white NO SMOKING signs.

The Vocational Counselor, who had one piercing eye and one wandering eye, sat with his fists clenched angrily on the glass top of his desk, as though he could barely restrain himself from punching Peter in the nose.

"The tests," he said, in a hard, quiet voice, "will take two or three days. Then we will know definitely whether you have terpsichorean talent."

"What does that mean?"

"Whether you have the ability to become a dancer. If you don't, we'll recommend another line of work."

"But what good will that do?" Peter asked. "I *know* that I'm a dancer."

"You may be wrong." The Counselor smiled bleakly, fixing Peter with his good eye, while his wandering eye gazed wearily about the room.

"Supposing I am wrong? Then you won't even let me dance at all, even though that's what I want to do most. Is that fair?"

"I'm here to help you," the Counselor replied threateningly. "If you persist in being willful, you'll only cut your own throat."

"That's cruel!" Peter burst out, so loudly that one fellow nearby started nervously and broke the point of the pencil with which he was doing a crossword puzzle. "That's like killing a baby before it has a chance to learn to walk!"

"You're being a little harsh, Cheaply. Remember that you're talking to a representative of your Uncle Sammy."

"What's that got to do with my dancing?"

The Counselor unclenched his fist and snapped his fingers smartly as though he were calling for a bouncer. Peter took this for a signal that the interview was over, and left the office hastily.

He returned home, and was about to enter his room when he was once again greeted by the young men whom he had seen the night before. There were actually only two of them this time, but their high-pitched noisy chattering made them sound like a larger company.

"Hul-lo there," said the first, who was exceedingly tall and fair, with two spots of color high on his cheekbones.

His bald-headed companion was plump and moist. He made Peter think of a peeled peach.

"So you're Mama Blight's new boy," said the tall one brightly. "Bert and I thought you were one of the comrades."

"I'm Bert," his moist friend added, "and this is Freddy. We're your upstairs neighbors. If we'd known that you'd moved in, we would have been down for a chat, but we assumed that you were a buddy of Moonshine's."

"Of who?"

Freddy tilted his head at Angus Mondschein's door. "Anxious Moonshine. He tried to convert *us* at first—just imagine!—and he keeps his hand in by propagandizing everyone who moves in."

"He's been very nice to me."

"That's a sure sign he wants to convert you. Has he given you any reading material?"

"Well . . ."

"Oh, let's not stand out here discussing Anxious," Freddy murmured, passing his hand over his pale yellow hair. "We've just come from a fatiguing session at the Unemployment Insurance office. Won't you come up to our digs and have a glass of wine?"

"Thank you, but I've never tasted wine."

"We'll brew some lovely Lapsang tea. *Do* come!"

"All right then."

Peter stepped gingerly forward at Freddy's insistence onto a worn oriental rug, and found himself sitting presently on a studio couch, half-smothered in little pillows and a fur throw of some sort which Freddy tossed across his lap.

"Now Bert," Freddy said, "do hurry and brew the tea, that's a dear. I'm sure that Mr.—"

"Oh, I'm sorry." Peter struggled to sit erect in the midst of the little pillows. "My name is Peter Chifley. It's just an ordinary name, but everybody seems to get it mixed up."

"That's probably because you're an extraordinary person. I'm going to call you Pierre, if I may," said Freddy. "As for us, Bert is a very promising young poet. His grandfather was a merchant prince of San Diego, and *No Quarter* magazine has already printed one of his poems. And I—" he paused to light an Egyptian cigarette, "—I'm trying for a career on the Broadway stage."

"Are you an actor?"

Freddy ran through his yellow hair rhythmically with a small gold comb. "I've done one or two small things at the Cherry Lane Theater in summer stock, but I've been forced to clerk from time to time in one of the Doubleday Book Shops. At present Bert and I have to get along on our unemployment checks, plus what Bert receives from his filthy rich aunt in San Diego."

"Now tell us all about yourself, starting with what brought you to Seventeenth Street," said Bert, who had come in with a flowered tray and was pouring tea into three small Japanese cups.

"I came to New York because I wanted to learn how to dance, but I haven't got very far as yet."

"What kind of a dancer are you?"

"I don't know yet."

"It strikes me," Bert said nasally, "that you're not beautiful enough."

"I didn't know you have to be beautiful."

"It's the soul that I'm thinking of. Your face is too pastoral. I think you lack the *spirituel* quality of our truly great mimes."

Peter did not know what a mime was, but he was too cast down by Bert's words to inquire its meaning. Freddy said, with some asperity, "Sometimes you don't know when to stop talking, Bert. Pierre is just on the threshold of a career. In fact I want him to meet the right people and possibly make a few contacts."

Bert leaped to his feet with a snort and began to prowl agitatedly about the room.

"Oh do sit down, Bert!" cried Freddy. "Someone has to see that Pierre isn't taken in by nuisances like Anxious Moonshine." In the next breath he continued, "While you're at work composing verse I'm going to take Pierre to meet our crowd, and to a few shows, and most important of all he must join a dance group in the Sevenfold School of Theatrical Arts."

Bert remarked coldly, "The only thing you've left out is that we should throw a party for Chipmunk."

"Chifley," Peter said.

"That's a wonderful idea, Bert!" cried Freddy. "Do you have any money, Pierre?"

"A little."

"That's all we need. But we can talk about that later—we'll need to buy wine, pretzels, apples, cigarettes, and soya sticks."

Peter looked up at a painting of a greenish girl seated on a yellow burro. The word Blight was lettered on the girl's buttock, like a tattoo. "Isn't that the landlady's name on that girl?"

"Didn't you know?" muttered Bert. "Mama Blight is a painter. Imagine, she gave it to us for a Christmas present!"

"It's kind of funny looking, isn't it?"

"Ever since she read about Grandma Moses in a picture magazine," said Freddy, "she made up her mind that she's a great primitive. She makes everybody call her Mama Blight, and she paints only naked ladies with burros."

Peter answered suspiciously, "I never heard of a landlady before who was a painter too."

"Well, you have now," remarked Bert.

"You've been very hospitable," Peter said, his hands sinking into several appliquéd pillows as he pushed himself erect, "and I hope you'll come down to visit me in my room soon."

Bert looked at him with renewed belligerence. "Together or separately?"

"Oh gosh," Peter replied, "I don't know. Whichever you want."

Freddy threw back his long fair head and laughed so that Peter could see nearly all his teeth. "Suppose I call for you early in the evening, Pierre, on my way to the Sevenfold School?"

"That'll be all right, I guess. And thanks again."

Peter took the steps two at a time going down to his room. He was restrained from leaping down the entire flight when he caught sight of Angus Mondschein and Mrs. Blight on the landing.

"Hello, Angus," he said. "Hello, Mrs. Blight."

"If it isn't the prodigal!" said Angus, puffing furiously on a short stubby pipe. "Have you been killing a fatted calf with the girls upstairs?"

"Did you happen to notice," asked Mrs. Blight, "the painting that I gave Freddy and Bert?"

"I couldn't help but notice it, it's so big."

Angus yanked his pipe out of his mouth and glared at Peter expectantly. "And what was your reaction?"

"I thought it was kind of crazy."

Mama Blight was not put out at all by Peter's judgment. "You'd better watch out," she chuckled, "or I may not give you a primitive for your room!"

"Fortunately," said Angus acidly, "Mom won't request you to pose, inasmuch as she only portrays naked femmes."

Peter blushed. "I have to go in and clean up now." As he closed the door behind him he heard Angus saying to the landlady, "You fail to recognize that the oppressed multitudes will look to your pictures for a clearer understanding . . ."

Peter felt a thrill of excitement that evening when Freddy led him through the corridors of the Sevenfold School building to a gymnasium where many young men and women were leaning forward at strange angles from bars attached to the wall, and cavorting about like young animals. Peter began to tremble with anticipation; but it seemed to be one of the rules of the school that they register first for a classroom course in the Theater of Tomorrow.

When Freddy and Peter entered the classroom, the students were just settling themselves to listen to a guest lecturer, a huge red-haired man with a voice like a foghorn. An enormous metal ring on his index finger glittered every time his fist flashed through the air. "That's Gripping Rotheart, the big producer," whispered Freddy. "He flirts with the avant-garde."

When the class was over Freddy took Peter by the hand and led him to the front of the room. "Gripping," he said confidently, "I'd like you to meet a new friend of mine, Pierre Chiffon."

Peter was about to correct this when he felt his hand being grasped in a vise of steel. Rotheart squeezed Peter's fingers in his powerful hand as though they were so many grapes. The band of his skull and crossbones ring cut into Peter's flesh so cruelly that he felt the tears start to his eyes.

"Ah, a non-professional," Rotheart boomed, in a kindly tone. "I don't meet many of them."

"We're throwing a little party for Pierre next Friday," smiled Freddy. "Could you drop in for a while—after the show, of course?"

"Love to."

On the way home Freddy spoke excitedly to Peter. "You see? Grip is a force in the theater. Next time he casts a musical, he'll remember you."

"I don't know how to thank you."

Freddy smiled down at him. "Don't worry. I'll show you."

During the next week Peter was truly caught up in the whirlpool of New York theatrical life. It seemed to him at times that he would have drowned if not for the helping arms of Angus Mondschein and Freddy, for he was still not really dancing, and with every passing day he seemed to be further away from his goal. But to tell the truth Angus seemed to be losing interest in him, and indeed to be actually hostile.

This came about as a result of Angus's insistence that Peter invite a homely but progressive Negro girl to go to the Stanley Theater to see a Russian technicolor movie about spores and algae in the Soviet Arctic. "I'd ask her," Peter assured his friend, "except that she doesn't like me, and besides she's so homely. Couldn't I take a nice-looking girl?" "Sometimes," Angus said patiently, "I think that you simply aren't interested in the fight for peace and civil rights." Peter made the mistake of laughing heartily, and replying, "You think I ought to like colored people because they're colored. But I like people because they're people. Isn't that *more* radical? You know, I think you're not radical at all, Angus." To his astonishment Angus was infuriated with this statement, and refused to argue calmly, as he had done on numerous occasions when he had explained that Peter was confused or backward. Peter tried to make amends, but Angus would not yield.

As for Freddy, he took an immense pleasure in escorting Peter to those plays for which Peter could afford to buy them seats, and in introducing him to the members of his set—until the night of the party.

The party was a staggering surprise to Peter, even though he was by now familiar with the habits of Freddy and Bert. When he entered their room, he was stunned by the babbling of voices (some of which were singing a kind of church music) and the thick gray fog of tobacco smoke. He felt quite forlorn, even after Freddy caught sight of him with a gay cry and proceeded to lead him about, introducing him to a collection of strange faces.

In one corner of the room four people were gathered intently about an elderly drunken gentleman wearing suede shoes without stockings, seated in Freddy's sling chair and reciting very rapidly in French with his eyes closed. A few feet away, a young lady with long black hair and a flowing velvet skirt, who looked like a witch, was sitting on the oriental rug, piping sadly on a little wooden recorder. Her knees were drawn up so close to her chin that Peter could see clear up to her crotch before he averted his eyes.

Nearby, under Mama Blight's painting, Bert was declaiming nasally, "*Tex*tual critics, *tex*tual critics," to a knot of intensely angry young men.

None of these people paid the slightest attention to Peter, even when Freddy introduced him as the guest of honor; and Peter was beginning to wonder how he could steal back down to his room unobserved, when Freddy deposited him on the couch in the midst of the little pillows, next to Gripping Rotheart and a beautiful girl.

"Introduce Pierre, won't you, Grip?" Freddy requested.

The producer smiled at Peter in a most friendly way, and for one tense moment Peter feared that Rotheart was going to shake his hand in another crushing grip; but the producer was merely pointing at him with his index finger, on which the skull and crossbones ring glinted grimly. He wore a tuxedo, and a stiff white shirt on which an enormous enameled yellow stone glinted as he swung around.

"Hello again, son," he shouted. "Have you met Imago Parson? Mag, this is Pedro Chieftain. A non-professional."

"How utterly interesting," the girl murmured. She had the roundest face that Peter had ever seen, and the prettiest little nose, and the roundest eyes, which were a wonderful orange-brown shade that made him think of Halloween. They looked at him so intently—in contrast to the supercilious glances everyone else had flung at him—that he felt his face grow hot. Reluctantly he removed his gaze from her smooth face, only to find himself staring at her equally round and luscious bosom, and then at her warm bare little arms.

"Grip," she said, without turning her eyes away from Peter, "be a gem and get me a glass of wine."

"Of course."

"Are you a friend of Freddy's, Miss Parson?" Peter asked.

"You must call me Imago." She smiled, and displayed a number of magnificently even, white teeth. "I went to Bennington College with Bert's sister Electra, a repellent virgin from San Diego. But I'm here tonight because I was eager to meet you."

Imago had leaned forward as she spoke, and now it seemed that she was suspended before him, ready to fall against his chest if she were so much as touched. A springlike fragrance drifted up to his nostrils from the mysterious valley between her bell-like breasts. Peter felt himself growing dizzy, and as he leaned back among the little pillows Imago swung about on the couch so that there should be no room for Gripping Rotheart when he returned.

The rest of the evening was a blur. Thinking back on it later, Peter could remember little except the smoke, Imago whispering flattering words, and the angry frustrated expressions of Freddy and Gripping when he and Imago left together.

Nor could he remember his first view of Imago's little apartment, or even how he managed to remove his clothes in the dark without knocking anything over or otherwise making a fool of himself. But he would always be able to recall his halting reference to his total lack of experience, and Imago's clear-eyed, immediate reply.

"How shockingly refreshing!" she had cried. "I'll be the envy of my colleagues!" and then, "Don't just stand there like Dionysius. Come to bed at once, do you hear? At once!"

In the ensuing hours Peter experienced a portion of that soaring delight that he had first previsioned months before in Japan. Intoxicated by Imago's elastic flesh, he began to appreciate simultaneously the pure pleasure of the selfless spirit, and the benefactions that his dancer's body was able to dispense.

So in the early hours of the morning Imago sat up in bed, the faint rays of dawn glowing on her enchanting breasts, and cradled Peter's weary head in her arms. Pressing his damp tousled hair against her smooth belly, she rocked back and forth, crooning contentedly, "You're a little dear, that's what. A dear, do you hear? A dear, a dear!"

In the following weeks Imago Parson consumed Peter as though she were a flame and he a candle, melting slowly under the fierce heat of her ardor. Her dark warm bed was a temple wherein he performed the mystic rites required of him as dancer and lover. For now he was persuaded that he who danced, loved, and he who loved, danced; and it was the assurance that he was realizing his dream, even if in an unexpected way, that sustained Peter in the more difficult daylight hours with his beloved.

Imago was Lotions Editor of *Chic* magazine. It amused her to demand that Peter call for her, for she liked to have a cab waiting on Madison Avenue, and she enjoyed flaunting Peter at the Hormones Editor, an elderly debutante with whom she was continually feuding. Peter even learned to shop in the drugstores for Imago's personal requisites. He was saddened when he discovered that she took the most elaborate precautions in order to keep from becoming a mother; and it was with the greatest reluctance that he purchased those items which seemed so important to Imago. When he had to wait at the rear of the Boring Pharmacy ("Nothing Ever Happens To Our Customers") until everyone else had left so that he could whisper his order, Peter felt that his love for Imago was stretched to its uttermost point.

Yet he was willing to go on, and indeed he was led to recognize the justness of Imago's criticism of the way he lived. She resented the time that he spent with Mama Blight, Angus Mondschein, and Freddy; and

Peter had to admit that his outside life was irrelevant to the act of creation that he performed repeatedly for her delectation.

Furthermore, Imago was unutterably annoyed, as she put it, when she learned that Peter had answered an advertisement in the *Journal-American* and gotten a job. In fact she became so angry that her Halloween eyes grew bloodshot and inflamed—and Peter could seek refuge from her accusing voice only in his work.

The ad had read: *Wide-awake livewires needed by Market Analysis and Tip Sheet Organization. Big commissions positively guaranteed to young veteran go-getters fast on their feet. L.A.F. earned $185.72* LAST WEEK!!

The President and Managing Director of Matso was a cadaverous, seedy young man named Moe Spleenwell who wore a sweater coat sprinkled with moth holes and who formed bubbles at the corners of his mouth when he spoke. His office was an incredibly small hutch in a rabbit warren on lower Broadway. Peter was astonished to find that the entire building was broken up into hundreds of tiny wallboard cubicles, each fitted with a desk, two chairs, and a telephone. In most of those into which Peter could see, men with dark blue beards were shouting into telephones, scraping the breakfast egg from their flies, or adding up columns of figures in the margins of their morning newspapers. The open glass doors were inscribed with names calculated to bowl over the casual visitor: Global Findings Corp., International Union of Public Opinion Research Interviewers, Hemispheric Federation of Jute, Hemp, and Tweed Importers, and one more modestly lettered, Chaleh Manufacturers' Association of Greater New York.

"You'll do!" shouted Spleenwell, when Peter had done no more than introduce himself. "Pronounce your name clearly—names are basic, Shifty—and extend your hand in a manly grip. I'm going to teach you how to SWING into action." He broke off abruptly and commenced staring out his tiny dusty window at the street scene below.

He stared so long that Peter grew uncomfortable and began to think that perhaps Spleenwell had forgotten all about him, half-hidden as he was behind high stacks of Matso literature. But in a moment Spleenwell leaped to his feet, flinging his lank black hair out of his eyes and crying, "Plans, dreams, plans! Come, Shifty, let's repair to the ready room. There's money to be made!"

He hustled Peter out of the cubicle and down to the street, where he began to march uptown at a great rate of speed.

"Are we going to take a bus, Mr. Spleenwell?"

"No, no, call me a cab!"

Inside the taxi Moe Spleenwell said to the driver, "To the Hotel Splendide, just as fast as you can." When the taxi careened to a stop at their destination, he leaped out and ran indoors with his head lowered, as if it were raining. Peter paid the driver and hurried after his new employer.

The Hotel Splendide was a furtive-looking structure on the ragged fringe of Times Square; the Turquoise Room of the Hotel Splendide was rented by Spleenwell, it appeared, as a classroom for his salesmen.

Matso was a regular bulletin offering inside information on stock market fluctuations, advice on evading federal trade regulations, and suggestions on dumping the surplus war materials of the last three conflicts in which the United States had been involved. It was mimeographed on butcher paper and delivered once a month, wrapped in a plain envelope, by messenger. Peter nudged his right-hand neighbor and whispered, "Why don't they mail it out?"

"Messenger boys are more impressive. Besides," hissed the young man, "don't you know of the penalties for using the mails to defraud? You should—they're listed in Matso."

Peter also learned that Moe Spleenwell put out every issue of Matso singlehanded in his Broadway cubbyhole. This took him about a day and a half each month; the rest of the time he spent at the race tracks, grimly losing the money that his salesmen had earned for him. Peter was somewhat surprised to observe that the Matso Master Salesmen, far from resenting Mr. Spleenwell's deep interest in the horses, admired the skill with which he managed to keep their working hours at a maximum and his own at a minimum.

At the close of the session all of the salesmen arose, linked arms, and chanted the company anthem. Moe Spleenwell blew harshly on a pitch pipe, dropping spittle as he shook his hair out of his eyes, while his agents sang happily, "Matso is tops, it never stops, it never flops! When Moe's got the dope, why should we mope?"

Peter was issued a Matso Minute Man's kit. It included a pearl-gray Homburg two sizes too large (for which he was billed $11.23), a zipper briefcase initialed Z.B.—"for Zipper Briefcase," Moe Spleenwell explained with a chuckle ($6.57), a set of three thousand Matso calling cards ($1.74) on each of which Spleenwell insisted that Peter print his name with a ballpoint pen, and a supply of give-away reminder pads ($9.18) containing useful information for potential subscribers, such as the signs of the Zodiac, the date of Bruno Richard Hauptmann's execution, and the finishing times in the track and field events of the 1912 Olympic Games. If the pages of the reminder pad were riffled rapidly one could catch glimpses on the paper's edge of an unclothed girl engaged in an unmentionable activity.

"Gosh," Peter muttered. "I'll have to sell millions of subscriptions before I break even on what I owe already."

"Good boy!" shouted Spleenwell, who had overheard this remark. "Sour pusses starve, Shifty, but you'll ring the bell."

Peter felt a little ridiculous when he set out, his initialed briefcase sagging with Matso material; and when his oversize Homburg fell over his eyes he was almost run over by a crosstown bus.

For the first few days Peter was unhappy with his work. He would have been extremely lonely, meeting so many people, if it had not been for Imago. And yet something about the city was congruent with his mood: a sense of loss, of something once sought for but long since forgotten, in the faces of all the people, corresponded to his own temper.

One day, while he was hot on the trail of a jobber who was interested in learning how he could legally export to South Africa twenty thousand silk ties hand-painted with obscene pictures, Peter looked down nervously. A little boy of five or six, clutching the remains of an ice-cream sucker, was trying to slip his sticky little fingers into Peter's free hand. He looked straight up at Peter with his grimy earnest face and said, "Cross me, Mister?"

Peter felt his heart turn over. "What's that?"

"Cross me, Mister?" the little boy repeated impatiently.

Peter walked slowly across Seventh Avenue with the child's hand firmly enclosed in his own. At the far side of the street the boy pulled his fingers free as soon as his feet touched the curb. He raised his hand in farewell and ran off without another word, leaving Peter standing on the corner staring after him.

Turning the incident over in his mind, Peter finally decided that he had been so moved because never before had anyone shown such complete faith and trust in him. He could not keep from contrasting the image of the little boy skipping down Seventh Avenue with the memory of himself only the night before, cavorting elatedly before his shadow on Imago's stippled wall. Imago, clapping her hands in delight, had bedecked her glowing nude form with metallic bracelets and, shaking a pair of gaily painted gourds (souvenirs of a Mexican vacation), had rattled out a frenzied accompaniment to his gyrations.

Peter could not wait to speak to Imago about the little boy. At the last minute he decided to visit her that evening instead of going to ballet class.

He inserted the key that Imago had given him in her door and stepped noiselessly into the foyer, intending to surprise her. But there on the love seat only a few feet from him lay a boiled dress shirt, white, rumpled, and shaggy, like a polar bear, with a yellow enameled jewel gleaming dully on its surface, like a polar bear's eye.

Peter recoiled. He bumped into a plaster of Paris forearm splint which Imago had gotten from a lovesick interne so that she could wire it into a lamp, it smashed into smithereens at his feet—and instantly the apartment was ablaze with light.

"How dare you!" growled Gripping Rotheart, sitting erect on the bed, his thick red hair flaming fiercely on his head and chest.

"You've broken my lamp!" wailed Imago, real tears flowing into her fingers as she pressed her hands to her hot cheeks.

Peter picked up the pieces and placed them on the love seat. Then he turned and left Imago's apartment for the last time.

For the first time in his life, Peter was afflicted with insomnia. Night after night he lay in his little room, staring up at the dark ceiling. The disappointments he had suffered were of the kind, he supposed, that people got used to as they grew older—but he didn't *want* to get used to them.

In desperation Peter tried to put himself to sleep by reading the pamphlets that Angus Mondschein had given him; but they only reminded him of Angus (who now avoided him in the hallway), and when they did succeed in putting him to sleep he only had nightmares and awoke sweating and unhappy.

His waking life, selling for Moe Spleenwell, seemed to grow steadily more unpleasant, but for some days Peter could not bring himself to admit that it was anything more than his own depressed state of mind which made so many people appear cruel, acquisitive and cold-hearted.

The crisis came one day while he was wandering through the shiny overheated catacombs beneath Radio City. Turning a bend in the corridor, so that suddenly he could see the rich people, the Europeans, and the tourists lunching under the awnings in Rockefeller Plaza, he came upon a group of sightseers listening to a blue-uniformed girl.

"Three hundred million tons of solid rock," she was saying briskly, "were blasted through, solely that you might stand here and marvel at modern science and American civilization."

"That's ridiculous!" Peter cried. "Even Angus Mondschein—"

Everyone turned to look at him. The guide compressed her lips and folded her arms as though she were waiting for Peter to disappear; but her listeners pounced on him as though he were a sneak thief. One little beady-eyed man pointed his rolled-up umbrella at Peter and said, "Where's your button, Mr. Wise Guy?"

It was true that everyone else wore a large button pinned over the heart. But Peter replied indignantly, "I don't see what that's got to do. I've got a right—"

"Oh no you don't, smarty. You didn't pay, and you've got no right, none at all."

"But I—"

Someone shouted, "Go on back to Fourteenth Street, you troublemaker!"

Disheartened and puzzled, Peter escalated up from the cavern. He mounted a downtown bus that would take him to Fourteenth Street, as they had suggested, and seated himself in the rear.

At Union Square Peter arose and walked to the front, but the entrance was blocked. The driver was engaged in an altercation with a fat Negro woman who had attempted to pay her fare with a five-dollar bill.

"You got a hell of a nerve, lady!" the driver yelled.

"I got nothing smaller."

"I never saw nothing bigger, either. You ought to pay double."

"Don't get smart."

"All right then, here's your change!" He emptied the pennies from his change-maker and hurled them angrily at the woman. Soon the floor was carpeted with coppers which she stooped to pick up, muttering curses while the driver continued to fling pennies at her. At last she could stand it no longer and began to belabor the driver about the head with a heavy handbag.

The passengers sat quietly. Some watched the fight openly, grinning uneasily, but most shoved their faces into their afternoon papers, or simply gazed languidly out the windows at the sweating crowd waiting to board the bus.

"Isn't anybody going to do anything?" Peter asked in a loud trembling voice. He remembered how he had cried out, seeing the fiery sun behind the bus that had brought him to New York so recently. How different his excitement had been then! "People can't live like this. There isn't time!"

"The kid's right." A husky laborer spoke up to the driver. "We haven't got time to horse around. Give her the change and let's get going."

"Come on, lady," another man said to the Negro woman. "My boss is waiting for me. Take the pennies and let's go."

"That's not what I meant!" cried Peter. He stepped between the driver and the Negro woman, holding them apart with his arms. "Why don't you make up? Don't you want to do anything better than this with your lives?"

The bus driver looked up with his arm still extended over his head. "If you don't like it, buster, you can always get off."

"That's right, boy," the woman chimed in, glaring at Peter. "Go on, get lost."

Peter stumbled from the bus. If only he could have explained!

Patches of tar were bubbling in the broiling streets. Women raised their bare arms to push back damp strands of hair, exposing wet bristly armpits. A hot wind blew the sticky wrappers of ice-cream suckers against Peter's legs. He shuddered with a sudden chill and tried to walk faster, but his feet were clinging to the melting tar. On an impulse he turned and passed a Good Humor man who sagged limply at the curb, wailing softly like a muezzin at prayer time, and entered the lobby of an office building at the far end of Union Square.

Listlessly Peter surveyed the glassed-in board which carried the alphabetical listing of the building's tenants. His eye was caught by the firm of Ginsburg and Gainsborough.

"Fifteen, please," Peter said wearily to the elevator operator.

Ginsburg and Gainsborough, Converters, occupied the entire fifteenth floor. The first thing that Peter saw as he stepped from the elevator was a rotogravure blow-up, covering one entire wall, of a modernistic factory. Above its smoking streamlined chimneys was a sign: OUR WOONSOCKET FACTORY. At the far end of the reception room, in front of the long windows, a girl with shoulder-length yellow hair was seated behind a kidney-shaped desk, reading a novel and sucking her thumb.

The book was called *Quean of the Seize,* and its dust jacket displayed a listing frigate and a big sullen girl whose bust was bursting upwards from its sheath like two ripe onions. The receptionist's hand was curled tensely around the corners of the book; her fingernails were tinted an emerald-green.

"Pardon me," Peter said dully, looked down at her model's hostess gown and her gold platform shoes.

"You'll have to wait until I finish this chapter," she replied, without looking up. She had removed her thumb from her mouth: she looked at it carefully, observing how the green nail polish had worn off, shook her head sadly so that her yellow hair swung slowly across her face, put the thumb back in her mouth, and resumed reading.

Peter dropped his zipper briefcase on a chair. What am I doing here? he thought. What shall I ask this girl? Actually he had only desired to escape for a little while from the heat and crush outside.

There was a steady humming coming from some place outside his head. Peter walked cautiously to the far end of the reception room and peered through a small glass peephole set into a leather-padded door. He found himself looking into a large workroom where four rows of elderly women, fagged and worn, were drooping over sewing machines, stitching slowly on large bolts of a glittering fabric similar to the gown that the receptionist was wearing. To the right of the workroom an arched open doorway led into the private office of Ginsburg and Gainsborough, where the two owners sat facing each other across a wide green desk before an open window.

One of them was a tall corpse-like blond, with a monocle screwed tightly into his face and the longest, saddest jaw in the world. The other was a ferocious little bald man whose ears stuck out like handles and whose mashed nose spread out across his face like a pancake. They were both chewing bubble gum energetically—Peter could hear it snap above the whirring of the sewing machines—and they had handkerchiefs tucked around their necks to keep their collars from becoming soiled. They were playing gin rummy with the largest deck of cards that Peter had ever seen. The cards were bigger than seafood menus, so that when they were held up fanwise Mr. Ginsburg and Mr. Gainsborough could not see each other's faces. The blond one peered suspiciously through his monocle around the edge of his cards at his bald little partner, who was keeping score with a piece of red chalk on a tall blackboard that stood against the wall. All around their desk the floor was littered with what looked like little snowballs; but then, as Peter observed them mopping their necks and foreheads, he saw that the little snowballs were wadded-up pieces of Kleenex which the partners flung to the floor each time they wiped the perspiration from their faces.

"My God," sighed the receptionist. Peter started quiltily. "A hundred and two pages and she hasn't even got her feet wet. Although it's true," she added magnanimously, "that four different guys have stripped her clear down to *here.*" And she pointed to her navel, the indentation of which Peter could see quite clearly through the thin sheath of her gown. "It's enough to drive you crazy. What can I do for you?"

"Why . . ." Peter hesitated. "Maybe you can tell me what Mr. Ginsburg and Mr. Gainsborough convert."

"Mostly each other." The girl uttered a short metallic laugh. "Little baldy is Gainsborough, and the tall one with the monocle is Ginsburg. Life is full of surprises . . . What you selling, kiddo?"

"An invaluable periodical for forward-looking businessmen published by Moe Spleenwell of Matso," replied Peter automatically. "Every issue is guaranteed to double the profits of any shrewd operator, including converters."

"There's no profits to double. You're wasting your time here—unless you want to pick me up later and take me to an air-cooled show."

"But what about the Woonsocket factory?"

"That just shows to go you. G and G wouldn't know how to get to Woonsocket if you put them on the train. They borrowed that picture from *Fortune* magazine—it's the newest Finnish suppository factory, in Helsinki."

"But . . ." Peter shuddered as a drop of perspiration freed itself from his collar and crawled slowly down his back. ". . . But what about all those old women working on the sewing machines?"

"They work for a guy named Bulldozer. G and G rent office space from him. They share my services with Bulldozer too, if you know what I mean." The girl yawned, arched her feline back, scratched her shoulder blade with a green fingertip, and crossed her silken legs smoothly, with a soft hissing sound. "What about that movie—didn't you ever play with a girl in the dark, or what?"

"If you'd let me see them for a minute, maybe I—"

"Impossible. They're in conference."

"But I just saw them playing cards."

"They're not seeing anyone for at least two more months. It's too hot right now. As far as that movie is concerned, I'll have to consult my engagement book. Just wait a minute." She uncrossed her legs with the same hissing sound and swung open the door of the typewriter cabinet at the side of the kidney-shaped desk.

A dead baby was lying on its back in the drawer. The little body rested on several sheets of carbon paper; its wrinkled thighs were smudged with ink, its tiny feet tangled in a snarl of paper clips and rubber bands.

A scream rose like a bubble of blood in Peter's throat. He backed away from the desk, unable to look at the receptionist, turned, and ran noiselessly on the broadloom carpet to the door at the far end of the room. He rushed into the workroom where the old women labored at their machines.

"Help!" he croaked. He grasped the nearest woman by the arm. "A baby . . . there's a dead baby in that room!"

The old lady showed him the bloodshot whites of her eyes. She shook off his hand. "I can't quit work. Got to meet my quota." She nodded toward the office. "See them in there."

Peter ran ahead into the office, crushing the little balls of Kleenex under his feet. Before he could say anything, the blond man threw down his giant cards and exclaimed happily, "I knock with five!"

"There's a baby . . ." Peter sobbed.

The bald man cracked his bubble gum and pulled on his jug-handle ear. "Ophelia," he shouted angrily, "who is this interloper?"

"A nut," answered the receptionist, who had followed Peter into the office.

"I'm Peter Chifley," Peter cried. "I'm a man. She has a dead baby in her desk!"

"You're overwrought, old boy," said the bald little man, rubbing his flat nose.

"You got a bad case sunstroke," said the blond man, blowing on his monocle and polishing it with a piece of Kleenex.

"He's hard up," said the receptionist.

"You're both guilty," Peter said imploringly, "if you don't do anything about this."

"I seen once a man at Brighton Beach," the blond man said, "was affected just like this. A vision he said he had, right by where they rent the beach umbrellas. And then he started to jump around like crazy."

"You're the ones that are crazy. All of you."

"You're right, Mr. G.," the receptionist nodded, tugging at her garter. "First thing you know he'll start to dance around the office like Fred Astaire."

"What's wrong with that?" sobbed Peter. "Isn't that better than killing a baby that hasn't even had a chance to walk?"

"You got maybe a point there." Mr. Ginsburg smiled around his monocle. "Let's sit down a minute and talk about it."

Mr. Gainsborough took a small black leather case from the top drawer of his desk, opened it with his thumbs, assembled the three joints of a fine silver flute, and blew one or two experimental notes. "Charms to soothe the savage breast, you know."

Peter stared at the little man in horror. "How can you play at a time like this?"

"The same way you can dance. You *can* dance, can't you, old chap?"

Peter could find no words with which to answer. Ophelia the receptionist stood in the doorway, blocking his path with her aggressive hips; Mr. Ginsburg smoothed down his hair and fanned his long thin face with a Jack of Spades. Mr. Gainsborough dug a piece of wax from the depths of his brawny ear and pointed the embouchure of his flute at Peter.

"Suppose I attempt a few notes of Ravel's Pavane for a Dead Princess?"

"No! No!"

But Gainsborough put the flute to his lips and began to play. While Peter held his breath, he could only hear Gainsborough breathing through his silver flute, and Ophelia breathing through her pores; but as soon as he himself began to breathe once again, the grave melodic line sank slowly, like a baited silver thread dropping down through clear water, into the depths of his soul.

"All right," he whispered, feeling his feet moving slowly along the hot dusty floor, "I'll dance again . . . but not for you!" And with a bound he cleared the distance to the open window and gained the granite ledge that overhung the street, fifteen stories below.

"Holy Jesus," muttered Ophelia, "did you see him go?"

"Come back, sonny!" screamed Mr. Ginsburg, leaning out the window and reaching gingerly for Peter's twinkling foot.

"Should I stop playing?" Gainsborough asked fearfully. "Perhaps I should notify the super, or the cops."

"Call Bellevue," said Ophelia. She moved jerkily toward the telephone.

"Don't stop!" Peter called in. "Keep on playing!"

As Gainsborough blew frantically on his flute, Peter moved easily along the ledge until he was out of anyone's reach. In the clear blaze of the afternoon sun he was sharply outlined against the face of the building, and in a few minutes, while he wheeled, dipped, and spun on the narrow stone, the heads of stenographers and their bosses began to pop out of windows all around him. Peter could even hear their exclamations and their gasps. Far below a crowd began to gather. They collected on the far side of the street, as though they were afraid that Peter might plummet to the ground in their midst.

It was the greatest audience that Peter had ever had, and it increased with every step that he took. He wanted desperately to express the elemental things he had learned in a way that everyone could understand. But it was no use. He could not look at the hundreds of gaping faces, watching him as though he were a chef frying eggs behind a plate-glass window.

And so Peter closed his eyes. As he glided slowly along the protruding lip of the building, the figures of the people he had known rose before him in the darkness like crying statues: Mama Blight and Anxious Moonshine, Freddy and Bert, Imago Parson and Gripping Rotheart, Moe Spleenwell and Ophelia the receptionist.

"Easy now," a startlingly near voice murmured. "Just a few feet more."

Peter opened his eyes. Just a few steps ahead an elderly man in a Palm Beach suit was leaning toward him from a corner window, his bifocal glasses glittering in the sunlight.

"Don't be nervous," the man said, gesturing to Peter with his fingers crooked. "Take it easy."

"But I'm not nervous," Peter replied in some exasperation. "You look a lot more nervous than me. Besides, I have no intention of coming in."

"Wouldn't you like one of these to keep?" The man held out a gaudy pamphlet entitled *Jungle Comics*.

"What for?"

"How about this?" In his other hand the man held an Esquire Girl Calendar which he waved so that it flapped in the wind.

"I'm sorry," Peter said patiently, "I don't know why you think I'd be interested in that. Maybe you ought to see a doctor."

"Now see here—"

Peter turned away and walked back toward the faint sound of Gainsborough's flute; but he had not gone more than a few steps when he saw a blood-red face dangling upside down just above his head. The face belonged to a policeman who seemed to be hanging by his toes from a sixteenth-floor window.

"Look out!" Peter cried.

"It's all right," said a voice from above. A fireman was holding the policeman by the ankles. "We're going to save you."

"That's right," gasped the policeman in a strangled voice. "Just take my hands and hang on. We'll haul you up."

"I don't want to be hauled up."

"Don't you want to be helped?" asked the policeman angrily.

"No!" Peter backed away from his dangling arms. "Help yourself! Save yourself first."

From the other corner of the building the elderly man was making his way slowly toward Peter, a stout rope tied about his waist. He was waving a long railroad ticket in one hand; in the other he brandished a melting ice-cream sucker.

"Look at the nice things I have for you," he said menacingly.

"Go back. Please."

"How would your parents feel if they knew all the trouble you're causing?"

"That's cruel! How could you say anything so cruel?"

The music had stopped. But Peter could not have danced any more even if Gainsborough had continued playing, because the elderly man and the policeman were closing in on him. He took a step forward on the granite ledge and looked up at the heavens, at the sky, last free space in all the world.

Two airplanes were gamboling through the cool blue air, swooping and darting as gaily as two young birds. But then Peter saw that they were not merely frisking; they were engaged in a hawklike duel to the death, streaming trails of white spume as they ferociously intertwined the words PEPSI COLA and I J Fox in a frenzied tangle of melting loops of smoke.

Peter silently asked forgiveness of his parents, of all the people he had met, and of the crowd waiting tensely for his next movement. Then he opened his arms and dove slowly through space, his hair streaming back in the summer sky, his eyes flashing silver tears, as the stone curtain of the sidewalk rose triumphantly on his final dance.

A STORY FOR TEDDY

W hat is it that drives us to consider the girls of our youth, those we enjoyed for a day or a month, those whose scruples we strove and strained to overcome, those who scorned us, those who fled? I am not sure, since even the easy nostalgia arising from the memory of success must give way to other emotions when defeats and not victories come to mind. In the case of Teddy, it was an accident, a typically New York accident, which brought her back to me not long ago, but it is only as a result of my own deliberate life as a writer, and the painful, endless effort to understand, that she has come back with such clarity that I can close my eyes now and see not merely as much but more than I saw twenty years ago.

When I try to recall how I first came to know Teddy, I think back to a double date early in the war, arranged by an acquaintance. Teddy was his date, but my own I cannot visualize in any way—she was surely one of those girls who sit near the telephone, waiting to be fixed up by an attractive cousin. Teddy must have been that cousin. Within an hour of our having met, while the other two danced (we were in some collegiate hangout in Yorkville), I was urging her to go out with me.

Teddy colored. With her fingertips she pushed her ginger ale glass toward my bourbon glass. "You're pretty fast."

"I have to be."

Teddy was not very strong on repartee, and I fancied that I was ruthless.

She was just eighteen, went to college at night, was taking courses in child psychology, and worked by day as a steno for some agency that helped soldiers' families, like Travelers Aid. She lived with her little brother and their widowed mother in an apartment house in a remote fastness of the Bronx. All that mattered to me was that she was lovely.

As for me, I was twenty-three and terribly world-weary. I had worked as a copy boy on the old New York *Sun* the year between college and the Merchant Marine, long enough to learn my way around town. I had only three months before finishing boot camp and shipping out, and I was anxious to waste as little time as possible.

Teddy was not sharp and competitive, like the girls I had known at Ohio State and around Manhattan. She was simple, unambitious, and vulnerable. She made no pretense of being smart or well read, but she was gentle and modest and virginal, and utterly unsophisticated—you might have thought she was the one from Ashtabula instead of me. Her skin was clean and glowing, her blond hair tumbled over her forehead, her lavender eyes were soft and troubled.

I picked up her small, defenseless hand, ostensibly so that I could admire her charm bracelet, from which dangled a little Scottie and a windmill with revolving sails; she had gotten it from her father for her fourteenth birthday. Squeezing her still childish fingers, I said, with a self-pity that was realer than she could imagine, "I've only got my weekends—and not too many of them—before I ship out. Won't you meet me next Saturday? In the afternoon, as soon as I can get in? Say at two-thirty, under the clock at the Biltmore?"

All that week I thought about Teddy. In the clapboard barracks where, like college boys all over America, I was learning with a thrill of despair that my fellow citizens from farm and factory were foul-mouthed, ignorant, and bigoted, it was difficult enough to remember that girls like Teddy still existed. Teddy, snub-nosed and sincere, in awe of me because I came from out of town and had hitchhiked to California and back, and eager to help me forget that hell-hole where I alternately sweated and froze; such a girl took on the proportions of a prize, one I had been awarded without even being fully eligible.

When I pushed my way into the Biltmore lobby through the swirling Saturday crowds, I was struck speechless at the sight of Teddy, already waiting for me. Not only was she unaware that she had breached the code by arriving early, but she did not even seem to notice how she was being sized up by a group of nudging sailors. She was nervous, yes, but only— I could tell—because she was looking for me. The tip of her blunt little nose was pinker than her cheeks, and she dabbed at it with a handkerchief that she took from the pocket of her fur-trimmed plaid coat as she squinted this way and that, searching for me. I realized for the first time that she was nearsighted.

I hung back for just a moment, then stepped forward and called out her name.

With a glad cry she hastened toward me. "I was afraid I might have missed you in all this crowd."

"I was afraid you wouldn't show up at all."

"Silly." This was a word Teddy used often. But she was pleased, and as she pressed my arm I could smell her perfume, light and girlish. "What are we going to do?"

I wanted to show her off. Outside, I led her over to Fifth Avenue, then north, and we paused now and then in the faltering late-October sunlight to look in the shop windows. With Teddy at my side I felt once again a part of the life of the city, secure for the moment at least, as I had not felt wandering forlornly with my false liberty, or hanging, miserable, around the battered ping-pong tables of the USO, waiting for nothing.

At 53rd Street we headed west and stopped at the Museum of Modern Art. The bulletin board announced an old Garbo movie. I turned to Teddy.

"We're just in time for the three-o'clock showing."

"Don't you have to be a member or something?" Teddy looked at me uneasily.

I was still learning how provincial some of these New York girls could be. I led Teddy through the revolving glass doors and took unhesitating advantage of my uniform to get us two tickets; skirting the crowd waiting for the elevator, we skipped down the stairs to the auditorium.

The movie was *The Story of Gösta Berling.* I remember very little about it other than the astonishingly plump whiteness of the youthful Garbo's arms, for I was burningly aware of Teddy's forearm alongside mine. After a while I took her hand and held it through the picture. As our body warmth flowed back and forth, coursing between us like some underground hot spring, I peered covertly at her. She was staring intently—too intently—at the screen; and I knew, as I knew the thud of my own pulse in my ears, that I would never be content with simply sitting at her side. I would have to possess her. Somewhere near the end of the movie, reasonably certain that no one would be observing us, I raised her hand to my mouth, palm up, and pressed it full against my lips. At that she turned her head and gazed at me tremulously.

"You mustn't," she whispered.

She meant the contrary, I was positive. Giddily, I allowed her to retrieve her hand, and when the picture ended I slipped her coat over her shoulders and led her up the stairs to the main gallery.

"I'll show you my favorite picture here," I said. We stood before the big canvas that used to be everybody's favorite in those old days before everybody went totally abstract. It was by Tchelitchew, it was called *Hide and Seek,* and it's too bad it didn't get burned up in the fire they had not long ago. It consisted mostly of an enormous, thickly foliated tree, like an old oak, aswarm with embryolike little figures, some partly hidden, some revealed, some forming part of the tree itself.

Teddy appraised it carefully. Finally she said, "You know what it reminds me of? Those contests I used to enter. Find seven mystery faces hidden in the drawing and win a Pierce bicycle."

I was nettled. "Did you win?"

"Sure. But instead of giving me the girl's twenty-six-inch bike, they'd send me huge boxes of Christmas cards to sell."

By the time Teddy and I were walking south on Lexington, with the wind comfortably at our backs, we had exchanged considerable information about our childhoods, none of hers important enough for me to recall now except that her father had dropped dead in the street during his lunch hour, in the garment center, two years earlier.

"Where are we going?" she asked, clinging to my arm.

"I thought we'd eat in an Armenian restaurant. Unless you don't care for Armenian food."

"I never tasted it. Not that I know of."

No other girl that I knew would have admitted it. Not in that way. We hastened to 28th Street, to a basement restaurant with candlelit tables and a motherly proprietress.

I thought I was doing not badly at all. Over the steaming glasses of tea and the nutty baklava Teddy's eyes glowed, and she held my hand tightly on the crumpled linen cloth. Her face was still unformed, but I observed, for the first time, that her cheekbones slanted, almost sharply, beneath the soft freshness of her delicate skin, and in the shadow cast by the uncertain candle there was a suggestion of a cleft in her chin. I couldn't wait to be alone with her, and I judged that the time had come for me to tell her about my friends in the Village who sometimes loaned me their little apartment for my weekend liberties, as they had this weekend.

"Phil is in four-F with a hernia, but he's nervous about being reclassified, so he's been trying to line up a Navy commission in Washington. Charlene—that's his wife—just found out she can't have children. She's planning to start her own nursery school in Washington if Phil gets into Navy Intelligence."

"If they're your friends," Teddy said gravely, "they must be nice."

I winced for her. Now I know a little better; don't we all flatter ourselves by thinking that way of our friends, when all too often it is simply not true? Phil was not nice; he was a climber. His ambition, combined with his terror of death, drove him to get that commission.

But to Teddy I explained, earnestly and wholeheartedly, "Phil is an anthropologist, and Charlene paints. They've been to Mexico, and their place is full of things like beaten silver masks and temple fragments."

"It sounds lovely."

"Let's go. It's not far—just down on Jane Street."

Teddy was not quick, but she was not stupid either. "Will there be anyone there?"

I knew at once that I had moved too fast. And lying could only make things worse. "They probably won't be back from Washington before tomorrow."

"In that case I think I'd better not." Teddy flushed, and forced herself to look at me. "You're not angry, are you?"

"I wasn't planning on assaulting you," I said, trying hard not to sound sullen. "I mean, the place isn't an opium den."

"I know. It's just that I don't think it would be a good idea."

When we were out on the street once again, walking west into a fall rain as fine as spray from an atomizer, Teddy stopped suddenly before a darkened courtyard and looked up at me anxiously.

"I didn't mean to hurt your feelings. I guess I'm just not very sophisticated about those things."

Pressing her against the wrought-iron picket fence before which she stood, her head tilted, trying to catch some light in my eyes or across my face which would tell her what I was feeling, I folded her in my arms and kissed her for the first time.

I kissed her again, and a third time, and maybe I wouldn't have been able to stop, but Teddy passed her hand across her forehead to brush back her damp hair and said, laughing somewhat shakily, "Don't you know that it's raining?"

So we went on to the Village Vanguard, and then to Romany Marie's, where Teddy assured me, after she had had her fortune told, that this had been the loveliest evening she had ever spent. Like a dream, she said— the whole day had been like a dream.

At about two o'clock in the morning I offered to see her home. She insisted, as we stood arguing by the mountain of Sunday papers at the Sheridan Square newsstand, that she wouldn't think of my riding the subway all the way up to the East Bronx for an hour and then all the way back for another hour. Not when I had to get up almost every morning at five-thirty, do calisthenics, and practice lowering lifeboats into the icy waters of Sheepshead Bay. I yielded, but not before I had gotten her promise that we would meet that afternoon at the Central Park Zoo, where she had to take her younger brother. I stood at the head of the subway stairs and watched, bemused, as she tripped down them, as lightly and swiftly as if she were still a child, hurrying so as not to be late for school.

At the zoo I found Teddy as easily as if we had been alone in that vast rectangle of rock and grass, instead of being surrounded as we were by thousands of Sunday strollers. She was standing in front of the monkey cages with her younger brother, Stevie, a solemn-looking mouth-breather with glasses and the big behind that many boys acquire during the final years of childhood. She whirled about at my touch, her face already alight with pleasure.

"Did you sleep well, Teddy?"

"Like a baby. Such sweet dreams!" And she introduced me to her brother.

What he wanted was to attend a war-bond rally at Columbus Circle, where they were going to display a Jap Zero and a movie star. I think the star was Victor Mature; in any case, on the way to see him and the captured airplane I pulled Teddy aside and asked her if we couldn't cut out for a couple of hours and run down to Phil's apartment.

She stared at me. "Honestly, I think you have a one-track mind."

"Phil and Charlene are in from Washington," I explained hastily. "They'd like to meet you."

"But I'm hardly even dressed to meet *you!*" In dismay she pointed to her loafers, her sweater and skirt, her trench coat, but I succeeded in persuading her.

While we stood in line to see the airplane, Teddy asked Stevie if he'd mind if we left him alone for a while. He barely heard her. He promised to wait for her through the Army Band concert, and we hurried off to the downtown bus. All the way to the Village Teddy kept me busy reassuring her that we wouldn't be barging in where we weren't wanted.

Phil's place was strewn not only with the various sections of the Sunday *Times* but with a crowd of weary weekend loungers who hadn't been there when I left that morning: an unmilitary Army officer and his hung-over girl friend, a dancer in blue jeans from the apartment across the hall who was studying the want ads while she picked at her bare toes, a nursery-school-teacher friend of Charlene's who was arguing heatedly with her in the kitchen about child development. The radio on the bookcase was blasting away with the New York Philharmonic.

Teddy sat primly on a corner of the studio couch with her knees pressed together and a paper napkin spread over them, sipping coffee and nibbling on a Triscuit and speaking only when spoken to. Phil got me off in the john at one point and said, grinning and shaking his head and winking in his nervous way, "You'll never make that girl."

I was annoyed, but I wasn't exactly sure why. "What makes you say that?"

"Aside from the fact that she's a virgin and terrified of you and your highbrow friends, she's too clean. I'll swear she uses those soaps they advertise in *The American Girl.*"

"How would you know about *The American Girl?*"

"I've got a little sister."

I thought of the contests that Teddy used to enter—Find 7 Hidden

Faces—and I found myself hurrying back to her side with her trench coat.

"Yes, let's go," she said. "I'm getting worried about Stevie. If my mother knew, she'd kill me."

"I wouldn't let her do that," I replied manfully.

"I'd like to see you stop her," Teddy said to me over her shoulder on our way out. "You don't know my mother."

I didn't know quite how to answer that, so I busied myself with finding a cab—no mean trick in those days, when they weren't allowed to cruise. I didn't want to know her mother, but on the other hand I wasn't about to come out and say so. When we were settled in the taxi that I had gone several blocks to find, Teddy said mournfully, "Your friends are very talented people."

That made me a little suspicious. "Most of them aren't my friends. And besides, who's talented?"

"Well, take that Army lieutenant. He's an artist. He told me so."

"Rollini? He paints camouflage on the sides of airplane hangars. I don't see that that's such a big deal."

"You know what I mean. I just don't think I fit in with those people. I can't do anything special." She gestured helplessly. "Look at me."

The cab swung sharply onto Sixth Avenue, and Teddy was flung into my arms. I kissed her while her mouth was still open to say something else.

"Wait," she panted, breaking free. "I want to ask you something." She huddled up, very small, out of my reach in a corner of the cab. "Do you really like me?"

"Like you?" I asked. "My God, you're the most beautiful girl I've every known. All week in those cruddy barracks I keep telling myself—"

She interrupted my protestations. "That's not what I mean. I wasn't fishing for compliments. I didn't ask you if you thought I was pretty, I asked you how much you liked me."

Teddy knew as well as I how hard that would be for me to answer. Maybe that was why she didn't stop me when I reached out for her once again, wanting to substitute caresses for words. Only when we were within a few blocks of Columbus Circle did she part from me again, her forehead wrinkled and her lower lip trembling just the slightest bit.

"I just don't understand," she said wonderingly and not very happily. "It's all wrong."

What was I going to tell her—that I wanted to make love to her? She knew that already. Before I could say anything we were caught up and blocked in the traffic of the bond rally that was on the point of breaking up. Teddy darted out of the cab door, calling over her shoulder, "I'll write you!" as she dashed off in search of Stevie. While I stood there in the eddying crowd, paying the driver, the band broke into "Praise the Lord and Pass the Ammunition," and I saw Stevie the mouth-breather, standing with his jaw agape and staring at the trombones through his eyeglasses.

Before the week was over I had my letter from Teddy. I am not going to try to reproduce it her. I will only say that it can best be described as a love letter and that it was so gauche, so overwritten, so excruciatingly true ("I am simply not used to going out with boys like you") and at the same time so transparently false ("my brother Stevie thinks the world of you") that it was immediately, painfully, terribly clear to me that I would never be able to answer in kind, and that there was no sense in my deluding myself into believing that I would. I hope it does not make me sound completely impossible if I add that her words not only released me from thinking seriously about her; they also made it all but impossible for me to think of anything but conquering her.

What inflamed me all the more was that shortly after I found Teddy's provocative letter on my bunk, my entire platoon was restricted to the base for the weekend. Trapped in that raw, artificial place, in its woman-less wooden huts thrown up hastily to house some thousands of frightened boys being converted into sailors of a sort, I spent my mornings bobbing on a whaleboat in the bay, rowing in ragged unison with my freezing mates, and my afternoons ostensibly learning knots and braiding lines but actually lost in an erotic reverie of Teddy—of her slim arms, her tumbling hair, her pulsing lips—gone all wanton and yielding.

By the time we finally met again, I had memorized every line of her, from her slanting cheekbones to her small feet that toed out the least bit —and I could hardly remember what she looked like. We were con-strained then, two weeks after the bond rally, not only by what had passed between us but by the heedless souls shoving us away from each other in the 42nd Street entrance to the Times Square subway station. It was the worst possible place for a boy and a girl to meet on a Saturday afternoon, in that blowing surf of old newspapers and candy wrappers, with the hot, rancid smell of nut stands assailing us. We hardly knew what to say to each other.

She smiled at me nervously, and I was emboldened to take her by the hand. "Let's get out of here." Willingly she mounted the stairs with me to the street, but when we came out onto the sidewalk the raw rain had turned to sleet; it cut at our faces like knives. I cursed the world, the war, the weather.

"But if you were stationed at that Merchant Marine camp in St. Petersburg," Teddy pointed out, "we would never have met."

"Oh great," I said. "Now you're going to do the Pollyanna routine."

"I didn't mean it like that," Teddy replied humbly.

"I want to kiss you, that's all. Are we supposed to stand out here in public and freeze to death while I make love to you? Come on, Teddy, let's go down to my friends' apartment. Like civilized people, like folks. What do you say?"

She could tell I wasn't going to push it too hard, so she laughed and tucked her arm in mine. "Come on, Mr. One-Track Mind, let's get out of the sleet."

It was driving down hard, and we had to run into a doorway, which turned out to be the entrance to a second-floor chess-and-checkers parlor. When Teddy laughed, still gasping a little and shaking off wetness like a puppy, and said, "I wonder what it's like up there," I took her by the arm and led her up the stairs. It never ceased to amaze me how a New York girl could know so little.

Teddy hadn't played much chess, only with her brother (their father had taught them), so I showed her a few openings, but she was frankly more interested in sizing up the habitués.

Later, while we were having a drink at an Eighth Avenue hotel bar (I teased Teddy into having a Pink Lady instead of her usual ginger ale), I asked her if she'd ever eaten a real Chinese dinner. She looked a little disappointed. "We have Chinks in the Bronx almost every Saturday. Sometimes we even take it home with us."

"I'm not talking about chop suey, Teddy. I'm talking about the greatest cooking this side of Paris."

As if I'd ever eaten in Paris, much less in Peking! But that made no difference. I knew a real restaurant down on Doyers Street, and when we got there the headwaiter even remembered me. Or at least he claimed to, which was just as good; and when he followed the bird's-nest soup with platters of crisp glazed duck, Teddy gazed at me in awe.

Afterward we walked off the dinner through the dim, narrow streets of Chinatown, echoing with soft, slurring voices, and then took a subway back up to midtown in order to see Noël Coward's *Blithe Spirit.* We were fortunate to get tickets, and made it just after the curtain had gone up, groping our way to our seats.

Teddy poked frantically in her purse and came up at last with a pair of shell-rimmed eyeglasses. She was seeing bright comedy on the stage for the first time; I was seeing her in glasses for the first time. For both of us it was a revelation. She thought the play was brilliant; I thought she was delicious.

When the play let out, we stopped in at Jimmy Ryan's on 52nd Street, ostensibly for a drink, but actually so that Teddy could see how casually I greeted the boys who were playing there—Pee Wee, and George Brunies, and Zutty Singleton—poker-faced at the drums like Joe Louis—and Art Hodes, whose daily jazz program, I told Teddy, I used to follow on WNYC. But since Teddy's musical background was confined to André Kostelanetz and Lily Pons, she was only impressed, and not overwhelmed, by my acquaintance with the great. I took her across the street to hear Billie Holiday.

We stood at the bar, Teddy's back against my chest, and stared through the throat-tearing smoke at Billie, who sang "My Man" and "Strange Fruit" and "Gloomy Sunday."

Teddy's eyes were wet and shining. She raised her head. "You're opening a whole new world for me."

That was precisely what I was trying to do, but it bothered me to have her put it so patly. It reinforced my conviction that she would always be like that, forever, and that there was no point in my even considering that she might ever be otherwise.

She went on, "And I don't know that it's such a good thing. For either of us. Why should we kid ourselves? It's not going to be my world—it never will."

It was a somewhat melancholy note on which to end the evening, but in a way I preferred that. It struck me that it would be almost diabolically patient to let Teddy stew overnight, torn between guilt and gratitude. The next day was to be the climactic one. I forced myself to kiss her more lightly in parting than I wanted to, and we agreed to meet the next day by the lions in front of the Public Library.

For a change the weather was on my side. The wind was brisk, and Teddy had tied her print scarf around her blond hair babushka-style—it accentuated the slope of her cheekbones when she laughed—but the sun was out. We walked all the way up to the Frick Collection and were lucky enough to get in to the Sunday concert. Teddy had never even heard of the institution and made no attempt to conceal her ignorance.

Although she knew no more of chamber music than she did of jazz, Schubert stirred her, and she held tight to my arm throughout "Death and the Maiden," breathing softly and shallowly while she squinted (no glasses in the daytime) at the musicians. When the recital was over, we walked on up to the Metropolitan Museum, which Teddy hadn't visited since she was ten.

I led her directly to El Greco's *View of Toledo.* "This is worth the trip, this and the Courbets inside. Better to see just these than to get a headache from looking at too many."

How insufferable I must have been, lecturing Teddy first on music, then on painting, about which I knew so little! But she smiled at me gratefully, and let me know by the way in which she clung to me that I was both patient and wise.

As we left the Metropolitan and walked south through Central Park, darkness caught up with us and the wind came up too. Our breaths frosting, we hurried on across Central Park South against the traffic, skipping in and out of the dimmed, blurry headlights until we had gained the rococo refuge of Rumpelmayer's.

Warm, snug, soothed, we spooned up the great blobs of whipped cream floating on our hot chocolates and laughed over inconsequential things, and then suddenly, as if by common accord, we both stopped. I stared into Teddy's lavender eyes, so soft and moist that I wanted to kiss them closed, and she opened her mouth but without speaking, as if she dared not utter whatever it was that she wanted to say.

"I must kiss you," I murmured.

She nodded dumbly.

We went outside. In the dimout across the street the aging men who took you on carriage rides through the park and along Fifth Avenue were adjusting the straps on their horses' feedbags and hoisting blankets over their hides to protect them from the chilly evening. I signaled the leader of the line.

Teddy said apprehensively, "This must be terribly expensive."

Without answering, I raised her up into the carriage and climbed in after her. The driver tucked us in with a warm comforter, swung himself aboard behind us, clucked to his horse, and we were off.

Teddy and I turned to each other so precipitately that we bumped foreheads, searching, in the sudden dark of the covered carriage, for each other's lips. We rode on through the lamplit evening, clinging to each other, kissing, until the current that flowed between us warmed not only our lips but our cheeks and our hands, our fingers and the tips of our fingers.

"You have been so nice to me, so nice to me," Teddy whispered.

I responded by kissing her into silence. It was only after a long time that she could protest, trembling in my arms and frowning, "You shouldn't kiss me like that."

"Like what?"

"You know. It's not right, that's all."

"Nobody can see."

"Silly! I mean, I think it's for married people, or anyway for engaged couples, and like that."

We weren't engaged or like that—the very thought was enough to frighten me out of my ardor—but I had every intention of our becoming lovers, and the sooner the better. "There's only one way," I whispered into her ear, "for you to stop me."

"What's that?"

"Kiss me back the way I kiss you."

Before she could express her shock, I had stopped her mouth again. We must have been near 72nd Street on the west side of the park before we drew apart, panting.

"You know where I'm going to take you to dinner?" I asked.

"Where?"

"Phil and Charlene's. And I'm going to cook it myself. Wait till you taste my soufflé! On the way down we'll pick up some French pastries, and—"

"They're not there, are they?"

"Who?" As if I didn't know.

"Phil and his wife. Because if they're not there, I'm not going. I don't think you ought to take advantage of the fact that you're so attractive and I'm so weak."

I forced myself to be calm and reasonable. "Teddy, darling, what's so terrible about our being alone together for a while?"

"I don't trust myself. Any more than I trust you." She uttered the words with as much heartfelt emotion as though she had invented them —as though no one before her had ever even expressed such thoughts. And she looked more ravishing, more flowerlike than I had ever seen her before, her lips fuller than usual, a little swollen perhaps, her eyes staring piteously at me, her hair escaping from her scarf in little tendrils that clung to her forehead.

"Is it so awful," I demanded, "for two people who care about each other to be alone together?"

"But what you care about isn't me, it's getting me alone." Teddy paused, as if to give me time for a fervent denial.

I could say nothing. I was not the noblest or the most honorable twenty-three-year-old left in the United States, but I was incapable of promising engagement rings to young girls in return for their favors. And this much at least Teddy understood about me. The damnable truth was that I couldn't even imagine myself falling in love with, much less marrying, a girl who would make a big issue out of protecting her virtue. And on top of it all, I had been keyed up for what was going to be a triumph. I still wanted Teddy very badly, but it was obvious that I had failed completely.

After a long while she said, "I think I'd better go home."

She wanted to be contradicted, as with her other assertion that we had left hanging in the air, but I could no more find it in me to protest this time than before. I was too hurt and too shamed.

But so was Teddy, and when we had been brought back in jolting silence to our starting point, she jumped out and began to walk away toward the Sixth Avenue subway so swiftly that after I paid the driver I had to run for the better part of a block before I caught up with her.

"Please, if you insist on going, let me see you home."

"There's no need. Really. And I don't want you to think I'm angry with you, because I'm not. I had a perfectly lovely time. You'll never know how much I loved it—every minute of it. I'm just angry with myself, that's all. You and I are very different, and it's my fault, not yours. I should have faced it right at the beginning."

Still dumb, I shook her extended hand and watched her hurry off toward the subway and the Bronx.

Three days later I stood by my bunk staring at a letter from Teddy, incongruously pink and girlish on the coarse blue of my Navy blanket. For a moment I was afraid to touch it. Finally I tore it open.

It was the letter of a pen pal, jolly and comradely. A friend had given her two tickets to the Columbia-Brown game this coming Saturday. (I was learning that when a girl says a friend she means a boy—otherwise she specifies.) Wouldn't I please be her guest, so she could repay me just a little for all the fun I'd shown her?

If I had been older probably I would have said no. But I was desperately lonely in those barracks, graduation time was nearing for my platoon, and I thought, If I say no, she'll think I'm still pouting. And besides, hope revived: If I turned her down, how would I ever know for sure that she hadn't changed her mind and was using the football game as an excuse, a means of saying I'm sorry, I was wrong, you were right, I'll do whatever you want?

So I awaited the weekend as fervently as I had all the others, and to calm myself on the long, long subway ride up to Baker Field I did a crossword puzzle. Teddy met me by the entrance on the Columbia side, as she had said she would—but so much more real, so much more beautiful than my imaginings of her, that I could almost have believed I not only wildly wanted her but wildly loved her too.

It was apparent immediately, though, that we were to be pals. Teddy was dressed for late November, and for this last game of the season, in plaid flannel skirt and a heavy mackinaw and little fuzzy earmuffs. She looked adorable. When she arranged her small lap robe across our knees I reached around her waist and hugged her tightly to me, but all I could feel were layers of wool and bulky insulation.

"It's my brother's mackinaw. Do you recognize it?"

"It looks better on you than on him."

"This stadium must seem pretty tiny to you after those Big Ten games with seventy and eighty thousand people in the stands."

It did, it did. I could hardly take any of it seriously, the scrimmages, the end runs, the quick collisions, the slow roars, the cheerleading. And especially not the athletes, so puny compared to the hulks on football scholarships with whom I had eaten in my Ohio coop. Not when so many other young men my age were burning and drowning, tapped in torpedoed tankers less than a hundred miles from where we sat cheering. But then it was going to be a long war—everyone promised us that—and these boys on the field would get their chance to die, some of them before the next year was out.

As we shoved our way through the crowds onto the street, weaving in and out of the crawling cars, Teddy turned to me, her face glowing. I had never seen her prettier—or happier.

"That was fun, wasn't it?"

"What's next on the program?"

She laughed. "Know anything about bowling?"

"I know what you're up to," I said. "You're trying to wear me out."

We went to an alley she knew of in Washington Heights where a young crowd hung out—refined, she said, not bums or low-class. To me they looked like high-school graduates waiting to be drafted and their kid sisters. No doubt their younger brothers were working as pin boys. We drank two Cokes and bowled two games. Teddy was a little clumsy, but I loved watching her strain forward eagerly, frowning over the progress of her ball down the alley.

If only, I thought, if only. But I couldn't even plead with her, not when she was content to be surrounded by dozens of shouting kids her own age. Why keep pushing her? I asked myself. Why not leave her to her games and her soft drinks and her soldier pen pals in Greenland, North Africa and Australia?

We had steaks—black market, to judge from the price if not the taste —at a restaurant on upper Broadway, and as I chewed I mumbled, "We've had football and we've had bowling; now all we need is swimming to make our day complete."

"The St. George pool has mixed swimming tonight. Let's go!"

"I see enough water all week. We have to jump into the damned bay with rubber suits on; sometimes they dump out a couple barrels of oil and set them on fire to make it more interesting to swim through."

"I didn't think," she said, crestfallen. "Anyway, it's too cold."

Of course when she spoke like that I had to insist we go. We rode the Seventh Avenue subway all the way down to Brooklyn, got off at Clark Street and went up by elevator straight into the hotel without even setting foot on the street. We parted for the first time all day at the lockers, urging each other to hurry.

I got to the pool first. Teddy came in a moment later, a little shy, tugging at the nether parts of her rented tank suit as she stepped forward on the damp tiles, her pink-tinted toes curling gingerly upward. Her body was slight, paler than mine, and vulnerable. Her embarrassment only increased my own; I turned my eyes away and dived into the water at the deep end. But she slipped in after me and came up alongside me, dripping and cheerful.

"Isn't it great? I'll race you down to the shallow end!"

Actually, although Teddy thrashed bravely, she couldn't swim very well. But she splashed me happily, slipping loose from my grasp when I reached out to paddle her. Laughing and gasping she hauled herself out of the pool and flung herself upon the tiles. She grinned down at me as I hung from the lip of the pool, my legs dangling in the water.

"I'm so glad we came. You were sweet to bring me. Isn't this more fun than all that other stuff? You know what I mean."

"No," I said, "it's not."

Teddy's little bosom was rising and falling regularly; the droplets of water clinging to her bare arms and legs glistened under the lights. I was infinitely touched by the way in which the fine golden down smoothed itself around the soft flesh of her thighs and her forearms. I had never seen her with so little clothing. Her body was not only tender and almost childishly graceful; it was so appealing that it was physically painful for me to survey it without being able to touch it, and I shrank down into the water.

"Why?" she asked. "What's wrong?"

"Everything." I reached up and took hold of her ankle. It was so fine that my thumb and forefinger nearly girdled it, and it seemed to me that I could feel every little interlocking bone as she flexed it in an instinctive frightened withdrawal. "Do you know what I'd be doing now if there was no one in the pool but us?"

Teddy giggled. "There'd still be those people up in the balcony, looking down at us."

"I mean if we had the pool entirely to ourselves . . . I wouldn't even start by kissing you. First I'd peel your suit off."

Her grin faded. She withdrew her foot from my grasp and pulled her knees up tight against her chest, hugging them as if she had taken a sudden chill, or perhaps wanted to hide from me as much of herself as she could.

"I'd pull you down here into the water, both of us naked," I said desperately. "I'd hold you against me so we could feel every inch of each other. I'd run my hands up and down your back, and I'd—"

"Listen," she broke in nervously, "why don't you come up here and sit next to me and we'll talk about something else?"

"Because I'm in such a state I'm ashamed to get out of the water, that's why. Now are you satisfied?"

"I don't know what you're talking about."

"Well, if you don't you're even more childish than I thought."

At that she colored all the way down to the base of her throat. She turned her head swiftly, anxiously, to either side, as if to make sure that the handful of Saturday-night swimmers, mostly older women, could not overhear us.

"Please don't be angry with me," she said. She released her hold on her legs and leaned forward so that she could speak softly, confidentially. The front of her shapeless gray tank suit fell away from her chest, and I found myself gazing raptly into the shadow between her small breasts. She spoke so eagerly that she disregarded my gaze. "If you could get those urges satisfied elsewhere—I mean with some other girls, some other kind of girls —then you and I could just have fun like we did today. Couldn't we?"

"You're joking."

"No, no, I'm not. Not really. I mean, if you wanted it like that—" she sucked in her breath and laughed jaggedly—"maybe I could find a girl who would—you know—do those other things for you. Then you could get off that one track you're always on with me."

I didn't know whether to laugh or to cry. All I could think of to say was, "Here I'm telling you that you're adorable, that it's you I want and not some stranger, but nothing registers. It's obvious that you don't care about me, or you wouldn't say such fantastic things."

"No," Teddy muttered, not looking at me, "it's you who don't care for me. Do you think, if you loved me, that we'd—" She broke off with a quick shudder. The little golden hairs were standing upright on her arms and legs. "See," she said sadly, "I'm all goose pimples. I'm going to take a hot shower. We've done enough for one day, haven't we?"

I remained in the barracks after that, brooding, waiting to ship out into the North Atlantic. I made no effort to get in touch with Teddy. Finally, since I had time on my hands for the first time in months, and access to a typewriter in the Master at Arms' office, where I often stood night watch alone, I wrote a short story.

It was a bitter story, of course, about a young serviceman who, because he is denied physical intimacy by the girl who claims to love him, goes recklessly to his death, a snarl upon his lips.

I made two copies. The first went to *The New Yorker*. After debating with myself for a day or so, I wrote across the face of the carbon copy, *Here is the most I can offer you for Christmas, something I made for you myself, from the bottom of my heart.* I signed my name and mailed it to Teddy.

Within two days the original came back from *The New Yorker*. I stuck it in a fresh envelope and shipped it off to the *Atlantic Monthly*, where I knew from experience that it would rest long enough for me to go off to sea under the happy illusion that it was being seriously considered.

I heard nothing at all from Teddy. After a few days I could stand it no longer, and one night I rang her up from the pay phone in the rec room. She answered, but from her tone, a little frightened when she recognized my voice, I was sure that her mother was there.

"Teddy," I said, "I've been worried by your silence. Are you all right?"

"Yes, I am. Are you?"

"Yes, of course. Is your mother there with you?"

"I don't see what difference that makes." Then she said what her mother must have been coaching her to say, against the moment when I should phone again. "My mother feels I shouldn't see you any more. And I think she's right."

I was so shocked that I forgot to ask about my story. I stammered, "But all I wanted was to see you one last time before I ship out. Does that seem so unfair? For us just to get together this Saturday afternoon?"

"If you had any respect for my wishes," she said stiffly, "you wouldn't press it any further."

I muttered goodbye and slammed down the receiver. But the next day, after a night spent cursing myself for not having let it rest with my sardonically inscribed story, I received a note from Teddy.

She apologized for the way she had spoken (I was right; her mother had been listening) and went on to add that if I still wanted to say goodbye she'd look for me on Saturday at one o'clock in the waiting room of Penn Station. She would tell her mother she was going shopping at Macy's.

It was Teddy's willingness to deceive her mother that encouraged in me the wild hope that maybe my story had accomplished what my physical presence and my pleading had been unable to do. But when I dashed into Penn Station, Teddy came up to me unexpectedly and offered me only her hand and not her lips.

The hand was gloved, but I had the feeling that her fingers would be cold; her lips were pale and bloodless and she smiled at me tremulously.

"You look well," she said. "I'm sorry I can't stay very long."

People were bumping into us in their anxiety to reach the escalator. The vaulted terminal was bleak, drafty and—to me at that moment—terrifying.

"My God, Teddy," I said, "you can't just shake my hand and walk away." I pointed to the bag hanging from her left hand. "You've done your Macy's shopping already. That ought to satisfy your mother. Can't we get out of here? Please?"

"If we could just be happy one last time—like we were for a little while . . ."

"Come with me." I took her by the hand. "I know a good French restaurant near here. While we eat you can talk and I can sit and admire you."

"You'll have to promise that you won't get personal like that."

"Supposing I get personal not like that?"

By the time we reached the restaurant we were laughing together; you might have thought we were just getting to know each other. But in a matter of minutes the laughter had faded away and we were face to face more nakedly than we had ever been before.

We entered the restaurant and passed through the long, narrow bar where three elderly Frenchmen were having their apéritifs. We seated ourselves in the glassed-in garden dining room in the rear courtyard and ordered our hors d'oeuvres. Suddenly Teddy pouted, as one does when one remembers a forgotten obligation. Then she reached into the red-and-green, holiday-decorated shopping bag and handed me back my story.

I stared at her, my spoonful of pickled beets suspended in air.

"Teddy," I said at last, "that was a present. A Christmas present. You don't give back presents."

"I have to. I just can't accept it."

"But why?"

"It, uh . . ." Teddy swallowed. "It was insulting, that's why. Here, take it, please. Then we won't have to talk about it."

"The hell we won't. Do you know how hard I worked on it? Maybe it's not the greatest story in the world, but it's the best I have in me, and you might at least have acknowledged it, even if you didn't like it."

"But I did. I do." Teddy gazed at me in agony. "It's just that you shouldn't have put down all those intimate details."

"I can't believe that you felt like that when you first read it," I began, and then I stopped. A suspicion formed in my mind. "Wait a minute. Did you show that story to anyone else?"

"Well . . . just to my mother."

"I knew it." I was too sickened to be triumphant. "You might as well give me her literary verdict. I'm sure she had some memorable comment."

"She said it was dirty."

I jumped to my feet and flung down my napkin, knocking a knife and a fork to the floor. My legs seemed to be entangled with my half-tipped-over chair. A French family at the next table looked up in surprise from its *pot au feu.* So did three ladies on the other side of us.

With her knuckles at her lips, Teddy asked, "Where are you going?"

"I'm leaving. What did you expect?"

She began to cry. Ignoring the tears that were welling from her eyes and dropping onto her artichoke hearts, she whispered, "Please, please, please, don't go. Don't leave me like this."

Frightened by her tears and by the enormity of what I was about to do—walk out on a sobbing girl under the disapproving gaze of a roomful of people—I hesitated.

Teddy went on. "I promise not to say anything more to upset you. All I ever wanted was for us to have fun together, without hurting anybody, before you shipped out."

I sat down. Weeping softly, Teddy told me that I had expected too much of her from the start, that she wasn't like all the other, older girls with whom I had been intimate (there had been only two, but Teddy imagined scores).

"I suppose the trouble was," she mused sadly, somewhat more under control, "that it was all just a little too cold-blooded. If I had felt that you cared for me . . . I couldn't lie to my mother about that. Don't you see, maybe she's not so smart, but she's all I've got, she and Stevie, and I have to live the way she expects me to. The way she wants me to."

If before Teddy had made me enraged, now she was making me squirm. Seeing this, she reached across the table to touch me lightly on the arm and added, "Don't ever think I'm not grateful. You can't imagine how much you've done for me."

Mollified, I disclaimed any special virtue, and we left the restaurant almost as calmly as we had entered it. We strolled up to 42nd Street and then east through Times Square to Bryant Park, stopping under the movie marquees to study the stills of the Ritz Brothers and the Three Stooges, of Lynn Bari and Jean Parker.

We sat on a stone bench under a leafless tree in Bryant Park, discussing books and observing the types on their way into the library. We were careful not to talk about ourselves, or about Christmas, or about what the new year would bring; when we bumped knees, we excused ourselves. But then it began to rain again, the fine but mean rain of a Manhattan December, and as we looked hopelessly at each other and then at the forbidding bulk of the library, I remembered the movie houses on 42nd Street.

"Come on," I said. "I'll take you to see *Intermezzo.*"

"I really must go home. I'm expected."

"Not yet." I tugged her off the bench. "You yourself told me Ingrid Bergman is the most beautiful girl in the world. You bragged about seeing her in front of Bloomingdale's."

Laughing and protesting, Teddy allowed me to hurry her to the theater. But *Intermezzo* was a mistake. We had to sit through the last hour of an anti-Nazi epic, plus a newsreel of Mrs. Thomas E. Dewey launching a Liberty ship, before we were rewarded with Leslie Howard making love to Ingrid Bergman. They went off together to celebrate their illicit passion in a sun-kissed Mediterranean villa, knowing—or at least Ingrid knowing —that it could come to no good end and that she would have to tiptoe out of Leslie's life in order to spare him for his art.

I sat with my arm around Teddy's shoulders, but I might as well have clasped a statue. She held herself absolutely rigid and stared fixedly at the screen through the little shell-rimmed glasses she was no longer self-conscious about wearing, her elbows tight against her sides, her fingers locked together in her lap. By the end of the film I was intoxicated all over again with the odor of Teddy's damp blond hair and lightly fragrant perfume, and she was biting her lips, fighting back the tears as Ingrid took leave of her unsuspecting lover. The theme music swelled to a crescendo, and we groped our way out to the street.

It was almost pitch-dark, the dimout was on, and the rain was driving directly into our faces. Luckily I captured a cab and we tumbled gratefully into it, slammed the door behind us and waved the driver on. Then, to my astonishment, Teddy flung her arms around my neck, held me so tightly I could hardly breathe, and proceeded to kiss me as I had taught her to kiss.

My God, I thought, have I won at the last possible moment? And when the driver called back, "Which way, folks?" I whispered to her, "Let's go down to the apartment. Now!"

I have thought since then that if I had been a bit more mature, more masterful, if I had simply directed the driver down to Jane Street, I might have won out. But I doubt it. For Teddy shook her head fiercely, even while she continued to caress me, and muttered, "No, no, no, I'm going home, I'm saying goodbye to you here."

We remained clasped in each other's arms all the way up to the Bronx. In front of her apartment house, while I stood, distraught, counting bills into the cab driver's hand, Teddy ran a comb unsteadily through her hair and apologized for the expense of the long ride.

"I'm the one who should apologize for never taking you home before," I said. "Let's go on up."

In the back of my mind, I suppose, was the final hope that Teddy's mother and brother would be out. The old red brick building was shabby, with peeling hallways; but what was worse, it was a walkup, and Teddy lived on the top floor.

We climbed slowly and awkwardly with our arms around each other's waists and on the fourth floor Teddy told me, blushing, that we still had two more flights to go. "The higher you go, see, the cheaper the rent is."

As we moved dreamlike up the last flights, I thought how often she must have flitted up and down all these steps—no wonder she was so slim!

When we reached the top floor she indicated silently the door which was hers: 6B. But before she could say anything I unbuttoned her coat —my pea jacket was already open—and pulled her close to me. As I began to kiss her she went limp. I was kissing her hair, her ears, her eyelids, her cheeks, but when I pressed her lips to mine she did not respond with the ardor which had so surprised me in the taxi; and even though she opened her mouth under the pressure of my lips, she remained absolutely passive, drooping like a flower deprived of sun, her eyes closed, as I raised her unresisting arms and slipped them around my neck.

For some reason this passivity drove me wild, and I tore at her woolen dress, searching for the zipper and the buttons, until I had worked my hands through. Her underthings slithered to my touch, and in a frenzy I pulled up handfuls of her slip until my fingers reached the smooth flesh of her back and her belly. She remained motionless, neither assisting nor opposing me, as I worked open her brassiere and freed her breasts.

My hands roved frantically, attempting with desperate speed to discover what had been denied them for so long. Her body was more delicately wrought than her wistful, pretty face, and I was stunned to feel the sharp, childish wings of her shoulder blades, the fragile bones of her rib cage behind which her heart was throbbing, the pathetic soft buds of her breasts.

Suddenly I was crying. "Teddy, Teddy, Teddy," I whispered, and I felt her give way in my arms. In another moment we would both have sunk to the cold stone floor; but at that instant the steel door of 6B swung open and Teddy's mother flew into the hall like some great bird of prey.

She could have been no older than I am now, but she seemed a dreadful old bag, a harpy, her hair half crammed into a net, her eyes darting venomously out of a craggy face slimed with cold cream. As I released Teddy, she pulled her coat together to cover her gaping dress, and then, yanked forward in her mother's iron grip, stumbled blindly into the sanctuary of their apartment. Her mother flashed me one scornful glance —part rage and part pure triumph—before she slammed the door.

I stood there dripping rain and sweat, too shocked even to be conscious of frustration. My eye was caught by the Macy's shopping bag, stuffed with gaily wrapped Christmas presents, that had fallen from Teddy's hand to the floor. I bent to pick it up when the door opened again. Teddy's mother snatched the bag from me without a word, and before I could open my mouth she had slammed the door.

No doubt it was the shopping bag, decorated with holly and mistletoe, that reminded me of my story, my gift to Teddy. As I made my way slowly down the long flights of steps, pulling myself together to face what had to be faced in the world beyond Teddy, I discovered that I did not have the manuscript she had returned to me. It must have been kicked under the table at the restaurant, and as I swayed out into the dreary street I thought, Well, I'll never see the restaurant, I'll never see the story, I'll never see her. Never again.

I was right, of course; at least in that limited realization I was right, if in nothing else. But a few weeks ago I had to see an editor about a manuscript, and I drove into New York and pulled into a West Side lot. It was a raw wintry day, with the soundless wind rushing papers about the streets to remind one that beyond the solid brick and stone, nature still strove to do you down. I gave myself one more moment of my car heater's warmth before braving the cold, and while I was checking the contents of my briefcase and putting on my hat to protect my bald skull, I was overcome by the eerie sensation of having been here once before, in some different incarnation, younger, hatless, without a briefcase. But in an empty lot?

The attendant rapped on the car window with his knuckles. "What do you say, Mac? I haven't got all day. Leave the key in the car."

"Wait a minute," I said. "Do you live around here?"

"I was born exactly two blocks down the street." He was an underslung, argumentative Italian, remarkable only for his long nose and for his pride in the place of his birth. "Anything you want to know about the neighborhood, ask."

"What used to be here, before the parking lot?"

"Rooming house, like everyplace else on the block. Restaurant on the first floor."

My eyes began to smart. I closed them for a moment. "A French restaurant?"

"French, Italian, what's the difference? A restaurant."

I got out of the car and shuddered in the chill wind as loose sheets of paper plastered themselves against my shins. They were not likely to be pages of the story I had left behind, a story which had surely turned to ashes with the restaurant, and probably long before. The story was gone; so was the little blonde who had sat just here, weeping as she handed it back to me—and so was I, the would-be writer, pompous but still unsure of his craft and his magic charm.

We have all three died, as surely as if the war had done us in; but did we really die forever? Teddy still lives in my mind as she was then, whether she has gained the chairmanship of her P.T.A. or not. And I, too, live again in my mind as I was then, whether or not I have won my way to what I dearly desired to be. Only that well-meant and ill-written manuscript, that rejected gift, deserved to die forever. It is *this* story—called up by the sudden stinging recollection of two young strangers, the boy and girl at the last table of the garden restaurant, yearning for everything but understanding nothing—that is the real story for Teddy.

SOMETHING A LITTLE SPECIAL

Sitting at the Genoese sidewalk café with his bearded chin cupped in one hand and a glass of cool white wine in the other, Sam Keller glanced at the bowed blond head of his pretty wife, bent industriously over the *conto* for the luncheon of *frittura* and rolls, which she had ordered in a brave and hardly faltering Italian. If it were not for the camera dangling in its tan leather case over the wire back of his chair, and the new open-top Fiat glittering in the spring sunlight at the opposite curb, with their luggage strapped to its rear, they might have been old-time residents or expatriates, he thought happily, instead of mere tourists with just two weeks of vacation travel ahead of them before they turned around and headed back for San Francisco. For the first time since their honeymoon four years earlier, abbreviated to accommodate his budding career, they were utterly free—with the exception of one little obligation. At the thought of it, Sam frowned, and as Ellen looked up, satisfied with her calculations, her sharply observant eye caught his uneasiness.

"What's the matter, Sam?"

He concentrated on paying the black-coated waiter, counting out the tip carefully to familiarize himself with the money. Then he said, "Not a thing." Knowing what her response would be, he persisted nevertheless. "I just wish that we hadn't promised Nick to look over his property. Couldn't we just go on to Como and Milano? And maybe afterwards—"

"Afterwards! And you're the big planner! The farm is practically on the way to Torino—you know that. Unless we go there now, we might as well forget it. Besides, it'll be fun. An adventure. Sometimes," she added, a bit coldly, "I think that you chose your profession to give you an excuse for regulating everything. Why not take things as they come, and get some pleasure out of doing a little favor?" Then, as if to take the sting out of her words, she squeezed his arm as they approached their auto. "You only child, you."

But it wasn't his being an only child, he knew, that worked on her nerves. It was his insistence on keeping remote from family and family responsibilities; it was his refusal to make up with his father ever since their last shouting match, which Ellen had witnessed as a shaken bystander. Why did his throat get dry every time that scene arose in his mind? He swallowed.

"It's not that I'm being stuffy," he said, knowing that he was being just that. "It's simply that I wanted the two of us to be all on our own. A kind of honeymoon."

"We will be. From tonight on we'll be able to do whatever we feel like."

"You know what I want to do tonight? To celebrate our arrival in Italy? I want to make love to you on foreign soil for the first time."

"You'd better," Ellen threatened. But he was pleased to see that beneath her mock toughness she was actually blushing a little.

Then why, he thought, driving as casually as if he were at home through Genoa's northern industrial suburbs and its beach towns, and then onward to Savona, why did the idea of this little favor fill him not with expectation but with dread? Was it Nick? Or Nick's need for family souvenirs?

Nick's property was above a hill town, high on a mountainside not too far from Cuneo, on the southern slope of the Italian Alps. To get there they would have to drive from Savona up the autostrada—here Ellen consulted the map while he wound the wheel through green, lovely hills not unlike their own in northern California—then, after the end of the autostrada, up successively narrower roads until they came to a monastery not marked on the map because it was abandoned, but known to the nearby villagers. It was ten minutes' walk, Nick had said, from the monastery, where they'd have to leave their car, to his ancestral acres.

Nick diGrasso was somebody the Kellers had met by chance one Sunday afternoon while they were driving around back of Sonoma, looking for a family-owned winery where they might picnic and take home some good table wine. They had stopped in at a small restaurant to inquire on the off chance that the proprietor would know of such a vineyard nearby. The proprietor was Nick.

He had taken them into his hearth, bade them taste the wine that he bought for his own table, given them a note to his vintner, and introduced his wife, Betty, and their four small children, each born within a year or so of its predecessor. Nick was just Sam's age, although he looked younger, clean-shaven and with a mop of curly black hair. Betty and Ellen were of an age also and spoke the same language, even if Ellen's Italian had come from her junior year abroad, while Betty's had come from the family kitchen on Grant Street.

Although Sam and Ellen drove out quite often after that, sometimes with friends, they didn't really have much in common with the diGrassos. Sam had gone to Stanford and done his graduate work at MIT, thanks to his father (who never tired of reminding him of it), while Nick's education had stopped short of the *liceo*, after his widowed father had been ambushed by the Social Republicans, the last-ditch Fascists in northern Italy. Sam had a strong sense of profession; Nick, who had beaten his way to the USA with the aid of a GI after the war, would try almost anything for a buck. He'd apprenticed himself to a pastry cook, taken business management at night at San Francisco State, worked weekends at a crab stand down on Fisherman's Wharf, and saved. When the chance came his way to buy up a small restaurant, he was ready.

But if Sam had done none of those things, not even saved (they'd sold some of Ellen's bonds for this European vacation), he'd read a lot of books and listened to a lot of music which Nick had never heard of. This was perhaps why Nick admired Sam inordinately. He made you feel, Sam often thought, as though he had been waiting impatiently all week for you and your wife to pay him the honor of eating his cooking and passing a few cheerful Sunday-afternoon moments with his lively family.

"I'll tell you something else," Ellen had said when Sam had mentioned this talent of Nick's on their way home from his restaurant one Sunday evening. "He makes me feel as though I'm beautiful."

Unwilling to admit that he was shaken, Sam had replied promptly, "But you are," and peered hopefully at her, curled up in the dark beside him.

"You would say so," she had murmured almost scornfully, and then added, "Besides, I don't mean exactly that. I mean, he makes me feel I'm voluptuous. And don't tell me you think I'm that."

Well, pleasing women was supposed to be an Italian gift. And Nick, who played up to Ellen's love of Italy (as well as to her vanity), was overjoyed when he learned of their vacation plans.

"You're just the ones," he had said excitedly, "to find out for me. Wait till you get up in those mountains above Savona. Man! It won't take you too long, and you're gonna see something different, I promise you, something a little special."

The farm where Nick had lived until he had run off to America had been his since the death of an uncle some years ago. It was tenanted now by a fellow named Ugo Fannini, with whom Nick had played as a boy and who had never left home; Ugo lived there in the diGrasso house with his wife and small boy, his father and mother, and worked somewhere nearby as a mason or roadmender. The question was, Had Ugo kept it up? What was the place worth now? There had been a fine stand of horse-chestnut trees; and no matter what might have happened to the property, the view was really sensational. Sam was a big expert: when he looked it over, he'd be able to say whether the property ought to be sold or converted into something more modern.

"No point in tying up money in the old country, right? It brings me in next to nothing. I could use the cash here in my business."

It was the sort of responsibility Sam hated to take on, the sort that relatives continually asked of you—if things turned out badly, they always blamed you—and if this had been Nick's sole request, he would have sought a way to get out of it, even though Ellen had practically consented as soon as the words were out of Nick's mouth. But Nick had been shrewd enough to realize that he could really commit them by making a more sentimental demand.

"What I'd like is a souvenir of the tribe—you know what I mean?" He had leaned forward confidentially. "Ugo wrote me he's been keeping everything. If you could bring back some pictures of my family—you know, the old folks—especially of my father, *mio caro padre . . .*" And he had lapsed into Italian with Ellen.

Sam was more annoyed than he dared let on at Nick's using Ellen in order to get at him, and at the use of family piety to milk him for a professional opinion on that land. He and Ellen had not had as easy a time of it as people thought who only saw them clam-digging or holding hands at concerts: She had been stunned by the discovery that he and his father could say the things to each other that they had. What was more, she could not understand why he should shrink from her father's generosity ("What do you mean, he's trying to buy you? That's paranoid!"), as if it were simply the converse of his father's meanness. Despite the messed-up lives of her sisters and brothers, she insisted that it had been fun growing up in a large family, and she resented friends' assumptions—assumptions she dared not deny as yet—that she was still childless because she and Sam were not ready to "settle down."

So now, having duly turned off at Savigliano, in quest of a place he was not eager to find, Sam said hesitantly, "Maybe Nick thought he was doing *us* a kindness."

Ellen glanced up from the map, puzzled. Then her brow cleared. "Maybe it'll be a kindness all around. I bet the Fannini family will be glad to have news of Nick."

"If we get there."

For a while it looked as though they wouldn't. Finding Santa Maria dei Fiori was easy enough, yes. At the public washbasin in its unpaved square, women in black balanced baskets atop their heads, old men in berets and felt slippers gazed at them incuriously, a mangy dog yelped as they slowed down, a spavined goat tied with a rope to a rickety cart raised its tail to drop its beanlike black excrement onto the dust. Three small boys came running out of a churchyard with books under their arms and heavy wool socks dropping down their calves, chasing one another and crying shrilly until they caught sight of the new Fiat.

"I'll ask them the way to the monastery," Ellen said.

Laughing, the boys nodded as Ellen spoke (even to Sam her Italian sounded harshly Nordic), and they vied with one another to give directions. *A sinistra, a sinistra,* that much he got, but just where to turn left he could not make out. After saying *grazie* three times and punctuating her thanks with candy bars, Ellen turned to Sam happily.

"At the end of the village, a real steep road, not paved, goes straight up to the sky."

"They said all that?"

But at the end of the village the road petered out into a mountainside meadow, with no ascending road in sight. They turned about and still did not find it; they asked an old man, but he had no teeth in his head and seemed to be mumbling, according to Ellen, the opposite of the children's instructions. They tried it his way and found nothing, and by the time they reached the town square yet again, Sam was ready to go on to Torino.

"Once more around," he said glumly, "and the old ladies at the wash-tubs will think we're out of our minds."

"I'll get out and ask them. They must know."

Ellen came back confidently. "The kids were right. We must have missed it. We have to cross the river."

They had been bemused by the glorious stream, carrying melted snow from the Italian peaks all the thousands of meters down to the Mediterranean, from which they had mounted an hour or two earlier. It leaped like something alive, from boulder to boulder, singing dangerously to distract you from the insignificant road which snaked over it on a trembling wooden bridge and promptly bent out of sight around the mountainside.

So they crawled over the bridge in low gear, and then around and up a stony track so eroded that it should have been strewn with the cracked axles of wrecked carts, abandoned after they had bent and slipped to death part way up the mountainside.

"We're ruining a brand-new car," Sam grumbled, but actually he was happy, with Ellen crying out in delight and clutching his arm as they swung out over seeming emptiness, with the leaping stream now fifty, now a hundred feet below.

"If we keep on going, Ellen, we may wind up in Switzerland."

"Or in heaven."

"Well, where's the monastery?"

"You need faith, Sam, if you want to encounter the house of God."

"Faith in God, or in the car?"

"In yourself. That's all I've ever wanted of you," she said cryptically. "Look, there it is."

The brick-and-plaster monastery stood squarely on a grassy knoll, the one level spot on the mountainside. The only unusual thing about it was that it should be there at all, hulking and bulbous as a Victorian exposition hall, utterly unlikely in this remote corner. It seemed to be quite deserted.

But as Sam swung the car about on the hard-packed dirt in the shade beneath a jutting bay, a strolling couple came into view. A farm woman in a shapeless and all but colorless dress, her arm hooked through a heavy woven market basket, walked beside her husband, a sunburned, knotty-looking man whose collar lay open and whose shirt sleeves were rolled up to expose his white neck and arms and who looked younger than his wife, perhaps because of the proudly careless way in which he bore their little boy high on his shoulders, like a prize he had won at a village fair. They strolled on, too shy to stop and stare frankly at the strangers, alone in the empty square.

Sam pulled up the handbrake. "Let's find out if they know where the Fanninis live."

Ellen had already snapped open the car door and scrambled out to confront the couple, who awaited her in silence. Addressing them eagerly in the dusty piazza, the wind whipping her pink skirt about her thighs and the sun glinting on her lacquered toenails in her Sausalito sandals, she might have been a child of this workworn couple, come back from California with news of a new world. It was startling to think that his wife, talking bravely in her high, clear, unyielding American voice, was probably as old as this couple, who looked as though they might have been cast, centuries before, out of some hard and ruthless material.

Ellen turned to Sam while he was striving to disentangle his long legs from the babylike shell of the little car. "Sammy," she cried, "these are the ones!"

They confronted him now, not cold or inhospitable in the least, but wary, like forewarned children, waiting for proof that he had not come from the bank or the government.

"*Buon giorno,*" he said uneasily. The little boy sat still on the man's shoulders, gazing down from that height as unsmiling as his parents and with the same smoldering black eyes. Sam stuck out his hand, although it felt as awkward and artificial at the end of his arm as a divining rod. "*Sono un amico di* Nick. Nick diGrasso." Desperately he turned to Ellen. "Was that right? I wasn't ready to start talking."

But the man was pressing his hand with his own, which felt as though it had been carved from oak. His brown face was wrinkling like a bent leather glove. "*Benvenuto,*" he said, "*benvenuto a* Santa Maria dei Fiori."

I'll be damned, Sam said to himself. It works! "What do you know," he said to his wife. "I can understand. He says 'Welcome.'"

Ellen was already exchanging greetings with the little boy, who dimpled at her as his father swung him down to the ground, and his mother, suddenly worried about appearances, bent to wipe the child's nose. Ellen had learned the boy's name at once and was rummaging in her handbag for more of those candy bars, cooing at the child, "Eh, Gian Paolo, *cioccolata!*" and demanding belatedly if his mother objected to his being stuffed with Hershey bars.

Sam reached quickly into the car for the camera which Ellen's father had given them for a going-away present. At once the family began to primp, as though they had gotten dressed up for a ceremonial family photograph. Sam did not wait, but while Ugo Fannini dug his thick calloused fingers into his tough wiry hair in an effort to pull it into place, and his wife tucked her child's blouse into his shorts and pulled up the dangling folds of his heavy woolen stockings from his clodhoppers, he clicked, wound, clicked. Ellen said angrily, "Has it occurred to you that you're invading their privacy?"

"They don't seem to mind," Sam replied, and then said to the Fanninis, pointing to the camera, *"Per* Nicolò. O.K.?"

Ugo Fannini nodded animatedly and said something Sam could not catch.

Ellen explained, a little tight-lipped, "They'd like us to come up to their house."

Sam extended his hand to the little boy, who was already leading the way, waving them on with his Hershey bars.

They had to climb up one more hillside which a jeep could hardly have mounted. The path proceeded jaggedly through the woods at sharp herringbone angles, unsupported by wall or balustrade. Its flagstones, embedded in dirt and enlaced with wandering roots, were worn hollow, like the pavings of an old church, by generations of plodding feet.

"We're in a different country, at last," he said to his wife. "I can feel it under my feet."

But Ellen was conversing earnestly with Ugo's wife, leaving Sam to tramp along stolidly with Ugo and the skittering little boy. He wanted to ask, but did not know how, if these trees through which they were making their arduous way were the chestnut grove that Nick had asked him to examine. He had looked up the word "chestnut" earlier, in their cabin, when Ellen hadn't been watching, but now it escaped him completely. Still, these must be the trees. They were old, potent, sturdy as the people who chose to remain among them. Greening once again and twinkling in the clear spring light, they rose splendidly through the thin mountainous air toward the blue bowl of the sky.

Then the stone-and-plaster cottage came into view just below the crest of the hillside. At the final few steps Ugo Fannini reached down, as though it were something that was always done, like crossing yourself, and clasped his boy's hand to swing him up these last couple of feet. For a moment Sam was stabbed with a queer pang of irrational envy.

The sound of their coming had roused a silky-haired hunting dog and the older Fanninis too, who came out together from a barn which faced the farmhouse and was tied to it by a rotting, unpainted grape arbor under which stood an uneven work table, a wooden bench and several copper kettles. The old lady (no more than sixty, maybe, but she could have passed for eighty) began to shell peas nervously, more to keep her hands occupied than to finish the task, revealing as she smiled—the wrinkles around her eyes deepening into channels—that it was she and not her husband whom Ugo resembled.

The old man did not smile. He seemed to have grown up out of the ground like the grapevine before which he stood, gnarling, twisting and darkening over the years, his skin seaming with the seasons like the tough bark of a deeply rooted vine. Even his clothing—the shapeless beret wedged between his ears, the blue work shirt bleached almost white, the flannel trousers flapping over the frayed carpet slippers—seemed always to have been a part of him, and added to the sense he gave off, almost like an odor, of stolid permanence. His gaze, fixed and impersonal as he attended, with no sign of interest or comprehension, to his son's rapid introductions, came from but one eye, for the other had been enucleated. In its place he had plugged a colorless twist of cotton wadding, the end protruding villainously from the socket into which it had been stuffed.

The forbidding gaze from his one blue eye was more than patriarchal; it was ferociously piratical. Or maybe, Sam thought, I am romanticizing. But the next instant, as Ugo was saying something about Nicolò, the old man leaped upon Sam.

The dark wrinkles of his face splitting into a smile, old Fannini began to pummel, pinch and shake him, all the while emitting a startling high-pitched wheeze. It was an ardent greeting—it could be nothing else—for the old man slapped Sam's cheek affectionately and even tugged at the point of his short beard, cackling, "Hey, *barba, barba!* Hey, *barbato!*"

Sam wanted desperately to thrust aside the old man, who was no longer just a carving of someone's idea of a father but a live peasant, smelling powerfully of dried sweat, garlic fumes and stale pipe tobacco. But he dared not move. As he submitted passively to the embrace, little Gian Paolo jumped up and down, like his barking dog, which was careering wildly, leaping into the air as if possessed. His grandmother stood expressionlessly by his mother, her wrinkled hands folded before the waistband of her apron. His father, Ugo, was conversing rapidly and jerkily with Ellen.

Sam muttered to her, "Would you please get this old man off my back?"

But Ugo was taking hold, talking loudly to his father and, over his shoulder, more slowly to Ellen.

"Sam," she said. "Grandpa is deaf. He thought his son said you were Nick, when he was only saying that you were from Nick."

The old man released him, his eye gone suddenly blank and guarded again.

Sam put his hand to his face. "What was that business of grabbing my beard?"

"Just teasing. He hadn't seen you since you were eleven—I mean Nick, of course."

Sam could not exactly brush off the old man's lingering imprint, not with everyone looking at him as though in truth he had suddenly been changed into someone else. The grandfather had resumed his original stance, exactly as though he had never done that wild capering, and so completely unembarrassed by it that now, only moments later, Sam could hardly bring himself to believe that he hadn't imagined the entire episode.

"Now that you've had your fun," he said to Ellen, a little more stiffly than he had intended, "would you ask Ugo if he'd mind showing me around?"

Motioning to him to follow, Ugo trudged off, the tawny dog trotting along at the rundown heels of his fiber sandals.

Ugo led him up behind the house on a sloping path through the vegetable garden until they had attained the highest point of the diGrasso land. From this small clearing they had a spectacular view. Had they been giants they could have leaped, it seemed, over the beets, cabbages and beans and landed directly on the roof of the Fannini cottage; and from there one more great bound would have taken them yet farther down, to the dome of the monastery beside which stood, alone on the dusty piazza, his little toy of a car, glittering in the spring sun, and far below that, sharply separated from them by the jagged white lightning of the mountain stream whose torrent they had crossed on the way up, the rooftop tiles of the little village of Santa Maria. What was more, it was easy to discern, with the aid of the defining sweeps of Ugo's arm, the limits of the diGrasso property, the grove of chestnut trees which Nick had spoken of with such deserved enthusiasm. It was a fine few acres, but it was hardly likely that the property could be put to much better use than that which the Fannini family was making of it now.

With the aid of gestures and a few English words, Ugo explained, stumbling and reddening, that he was frightened by the implications of the Kellers' visit. Was Nick unhappy with the terms under which the Fanninis were living on his property? Did he have something new in mind?

Sam tried to protest that he was not in on Nick's big decisions, that he was simply looking the place over for Nick.

"What you do?" Ugo asked, pointing to Sam's hands. He wanted to know, it appeared, what Sam did for a living. Sam did his best to explain what a city planner was, but he might as well have tried to explain bird watching or polo playing to Ugo, who, Sam feared, understood only that his visitor was some kind of landlord's agent.

Nevertheless Ugo was polite. Sam was truly pleased to be able to explain, even haltingly, how he would tell Nick that his property was in good hands.

Sam was pleased, too, with the knowledge that he was not kidding himself. There was really no more practical use for this mountainside than the maintenance of the Fannini family. The chestnut trees looked healthy, but there weren't enough of them to log, and in any event the hauling would be too hard; it was a glorious site for skiers, but again it was much too far from any place remotely fashionable; and the land itself, although you could keep a kitchen garden or even a subsistence farm of sorts, was too steeply pitched for anything more ambitious than what the Fanninis were doing. Nick's best bet would be to leave things as they were, even if the Fanninis paid him no more than a couple of dollars a month.

Scrambling down the garden path with Ugo, Sam found himself disposed to admire the simple improvements the Fanninis had made in the years since Nick's departure—the freshly plastered walls, the new timber supports for the trellis, the drainage ditches dug behind the old folks' living quarters to protect them from flash floods.

Ellen, on her knees in the dust, had been playing with Gian Paolo, the boy laughing shrilly as he sought insincerely to flee, his mother red with pleasure, the grandparents watching remotely in the shade.

"He's a love! A perfect love!" Ellen cried as the shadows of the two men fell athwart her and the child. "These are nice people, aren't they, Sam? I'm so glad we came. Did you have any trouble making yourself understood?"

Sam shook his head.

"Signora Fannini wants to show us through the house—she's been waiting. Come, let's go." And she nodded to Ugo's wife, who led the way into her cramped parlor.

The ceiling was so low that Sam had to duck. Indeed, there was hardly room for the six of them and the little boy, but as they moved on to the kitchen, with its massive wood-burning stove, and to the one bedroom, dominated by a high narrow bed and a loud chromo of the weeping Christ above Gian Paolo's ancient blackened crib, he could not resist the fore-taste of his description of this tour when he returned to his colleagues on Post Street.

Their hosts seemed more dutiful than proud. It was only when Ugo took them across to the other building, which sheltered both his old parents and his cow, that he lost his taciturnity.

Flinging open the split door to display the somnolent beast, which was indoors because it had only recently calved, Ugo said, proudly, *"Nostro migliore possessione."*

Sam would have liked to see how the old people lived, in the dirt-floored one room separated from the cow by a partition and warmed by the heat of the beast, but Ugo's mother unexpectedly barred the way. Wrenching her veined hands, she shook her head violently and muttered something that Sam could not catch.

"It's not fit, she says," Ellen said.

"What's not fit?"

"Their home. For visitors."

"Then let's say our goodbyes and shove off."

But Ugo was bringing out wine and setting a tray on the table under the arbor. This was the real proof, Sam felt, that they were being regarded not as accomplices of a far-off landlord, but almost as friends. Ugo wiped the dark bottle carefully before drawing the cork, his wife pressed water tumblers on them, and little Gian Paolo helped his grandmother pass a dish of hard speckled cookies. Only the grandfather stood aloof, wineglass in hand, his blue eye shaded by his beret and by the trellis under which he remained.

"*Salute!*" Sam said boldly, raising his glass. Then he turned to his wife. "How am I doing?"

"This is our chance to ask for that souvenir—the pictures, remember?"

Sam was suddenly touched by a vague sense of alarm. "I wouldn't do that. Nick can get along—"

"Nonsense. Didn't you see all those old pictures by Gian Paolo's crib? They're of the diGrasso family, not of these people."

Before he could ask how she was so sure, Ellen had proceeded with an explanation of Nick's request. Ugo and his wife listened intently. Then Ugo said something to his wife, who hastened back into the house, wiping her hands on her skirt.

"You see? They're probably glad to get rid of the pictures and to send Nick something a little special at the same time."

It was too late to argue. Sam gave Ugo an American cigarette (the old man declined with the merest horizontal gesture), and they were lighting up when Ugo's wife returned, bearing a green embossed box the size of a Whitman's Sampler.

"*Ecco!*" said Ugo Fannini. He opened it for Ellen, saying something about how glad they were to return these pictures Nick had left behind. "With our compliments." At these words, Gian Paolo burst into tears and, as Ugo cried out in mortification, pounded his fists against his father's leg.

Astonished, Ellen released her hold on the box, photographs fluttered through the air like dying moths, and the little boy scrambled about swiftly, trying to catch the photographs as they fell, tripping over his dangling laces and bumping into Ellen as she stumbled back in an effort to stand clear.

"I didn't mean . . ." she said helplessly, but stopped, for everyone was talking at once, the Fanninis apologizing, the old lady saying something incomprehensible as she grabbed at the lopsided table against whose legs Gian Paolo was colliding. A tumbler half full of wine tipped over; the dripping red pool fell into a sticky puddle at the child's feet.

It was the old man who swooped down, grabbed his grandson by the arm, yanked him half erect and cracked him viciously across the behind.

"Hey!" Sam started in anger as the little boy uttered a scream. He took a step forward to protest. It brought him face to face with the glaring old man, separated from him only by the body of the squirming, squalling Gian Paolo, held by the middle under his grandfather's arm like a slippery little pig. Ugo was attempting to explain, but his wife seized her child and carried him away into the cottage.

The old man now retreated once again, just as he had when Sam's identity had been made clear to him. Sam turned from him to expostulate with Ellen, who was helping Ugo to retrieve the photographs.

"I told you we shouldn't have done this." Sam knew that the reminder would annoy her—she could never stand being told that she had been forewarned—but he couldn't help himself, not with the old man's eye still fixed on him.

From her squatting position Ellen said shortly, "It was just that the child was used to playing with these."

"Then why do we have to take them away?"

"They're not his."

"For God's sake, did we come here to teach the kid property rights?"

"His parents want us to have the pictures. And his grandparents. I don't think we can refuse them now. I offered to take something else of Nick's —they wouldn't hear of it."

"You're ruthless, you know that?"

Ellen rose. She smoothed out her skirt and, accepting the green box from Ugo, said quietly, "Better that than weak."

Sam was infuriated. But then Ugo's wife was back with the child, amazingly fast, with the boy's face washed and wiped, quite composed, and with every trace of jealous hatred gone from those great black eyes. It was fantastic. Why, Sam thought, in wonder at how the memory came unbidden, when my father slapped me for stealing pennies I bit his hand; but here was Gian Paolo, peaceably accepting Ellen's placatory presents. Rummaging through her purse, she brought out ticket stubs, packets of

Kleenex and photographs of Sam himself, younger, *sans* beard or wife. Gian Paolo, neither snuffling nor snubbing her, accepted Ellen's random and hurried offerings with a pleased grin.

Everyone was mollified; there were smiles, smiles wherever you looked —except for the old one, who remained grim and motionless, almost as though he were standing in judgment, even when Sam hoisted Gian Paolo up onto his father's shoulders as he had been when they had first met down behind the monastery. Ugo offered to walk down the path with them to the piazza, but Sam demurred. "He climbs the hill often enough," he said to Ellen. "Tell him it'll be more pleasant to remember them all this way."

After she had explained, Ellen said, "Now you can take that family portrait."

The old man, however, either did not understand or refused to budge; in any case, the others had to cluster around him. His wife stood on one side, still somewhat tense, his daughter-in-law on the other; before the three Ugo knelt, with little Gian Paolo still grinning atop his shoulders. Sam shrugged and focused swiftly, and was startled to see, when he peered through the view finder, that the cow in the barn behind the family had stuck her ruminating head out the upper half of the stable door.

"I have it," he said and snapped the picture. It was only after he put down the camera that Sam became aware of how the old man had stubbornly hung back, hands behind him, chin against his chest, blue eye in shadow, the string sticking out of his empty eye socket like a wick ready to be lit and so to set him afire.

Sam made no effort to shake hands with the old man after he and Ugo had said their farewells. Ellen kissed Gian Paolo, embraced his mother and then took Sam's arm for the precipitous walk down through the chestnut grove, with the family slowly waving farewell.

At the car door she released her hold on his arm and turned to look up, although the trees separated them from the Fanninis. Her face was flushed—whether from the walk or the excitement, he could not be sure —and it struck him, even in his annoyance with her, that she had never looked prettier. He was going to say it, but Ellen jumped into the car without even giving him the chance to hold the door for her, and he saw that she was clutching the little green box very tightly.

"Listen, Ellen," he said as he clambered into the driver's seat and started up the motor, "I'd appreciate it if you'd leave that box behind."

"That'll be the day."

"There's nobody else around. They'll find it here in the piazza."

"I don't doubt that."

"If you won't put the box down here, we'll have to leave it for them in the village. Or mail it back."

"I have no intention of sending it back. It's Nick's."

He released the clutch so swiftly that the car almost stalled as he swung it about. "What's the matter with you?" he demanded hotly. "You saw how much those pictures mean to the kid."

Ellen held herself rigid in the lurching car. "Look who's talking—shooting off that damn camera in their faces as if they were monkeys in a zoo. Everything is a project for you. You had to take pictures to prove to the idiots in your office that you were here."

"And what do you have to prove with that box you're hanging onto so tight? You don't care about those people up there—it's Nick you care about."

"I knew you'd throw him at me sooner or later."

"Why not? It's the truth." Even in second they were descending too fast, and he had to hit the brake while he wrenched at the wheel. "All you want those pictures for is to ingratiate yourself with him. And if Nick doubles the rent on those people, or evicts them, you couldn't care less, could you? What matters is having Nick slobber all over you for bringing those silly pictures of his dead old man in a soldier suit."

Ellen's face was contorted. She shouted at him over the wind and the rising babble of the mountain stream below them. "You're not jealous just of me. You're envious of Nick, because he loves his father, because he's happy with his family. Because he makes babies."

Sam shot out his right hand and twisted Ellen's bare arm so brutally that she dropped the box. "How do you know I can't make babies? How do you know?"

"I've been waiting four years. Betty DiGrasso didn't have to wait four years."

"And you're not Betty. How do I know it's not you? You wouldn't go to a doctor, would you?"

"I've got news for you. I don't have to. What do you think of that? Watch the road!" she cried as he bent down to retrieve the box. "Give me back those pictures. You and your noise about the kid's playthings. He doesn't even miss them. I saw how you envied his father. And hated his grandfather. Yes, hated that poor old man! That's when you give yourself away. Just because he made a simple human mistake and tried to put his arms around you!"

"I didn't hate him. He smelled bad, that's all."

"Like your father, I suppose. Is that why you haven't talked to *him* in all these years? The whole human race smells bad to you, and all you can do is lie to yourself."

"You're the honest one, you and your Conversational Italian, swiping a kid's toy just to be able to suck around Nick."

"You lie to yourself. Not just to me. To yourself. You hate happy people like Nick because you're not happy, you hate men like Nick because you're not a man. Beard or no beard, you're a spoiled baby. Talk about little Gian Paolo. Look at you—jealous of your own wife because she speaks Italian!"

"You're not even honest enough to say why. You have the soul of a cheat."

Ellen began to laugh. It was that laugh, defiant, bitter, unyielding, that enraged him past the point of any restraint; it goaded him on to destroy her mocking superiority.

He lifted the green box high to pitch it into the swirling stream swinging into sight below as the car careened on down the swerving road. With a cry Ellen was at him. She managed to deflect the sweep of his arm so that instead of soaring through the air and disappearing into the river, the box sprang open as it flew upward, showering them with pictures.

Half blinded by the fluttering photographs that glinted as they tumbled topsy-turvy about him, and thrown off balance by the sudden weight of his wife's straining body, Sam lost control of the wheel. The car bounded from left to right, once, twice, thrown from rock to rock as though flung by the same hand that sprinkled the glossy, sparkling prints through the air; and as he heard his wife's high wailing scream rising and then declining with their violent thrust through space, he was hurled forward, his head smashing against the glass of the windshield at the impact of the car against the great gray boulder which impaled it so that it hung helpless, its wheels spinning uselessly, above the wild blue-white torrent fifty feet below.

Then, as the blood began to trickle down his forehead, oozing hot and sticky like spilled wine in the afternoon sun, his wife flung herself into his arms, sobbing wildly. Clinging to each other fiercely in the sudden still-ness, they sat listening to the pumping of their hearts and to the waters rushing away beneath them.

BOBBY SHAFTER'S GONE TO SEA

I t was on a T-2 tanker, some years ago, that I became a particular friend of the steward. He was a stocky, smooth-spoken young man of about thirty, of mixed Negro and Indian and Irish ancestry. His name was Bobby Shafter, and what happened to the two of us, one steamy night in Panama, I am only now beginning to understand.

We had been knocking around the Caribbean for some months—Aruba, Curaçao, Galveston, La Guaira, Mobile, Paramaribo—but with very little port time in any single place. So we were delighted with the news that we'd be laying up at Balboa to wait for engine-room parts.

Nevertheless, Panama City—and the Zone—soon wore itself out for me. There was an air of malign vacancy about the broad, empty tropical streets that was oppressive and even sinister. There, in all their nakedness, gaped the tourist traps, bulging with Dutch gin, Swiss watches and English woolens that the inhabitants could not afford and had no use for anyway, and the grog shops sprinkled with drunken sailors and pregnant prostitutes. Even sex turned sour after I was accosted at four o'clock in the morning by an adolescent girl at least six months gone.

If there is no revolution afoot, life in these latitudes must imperceptibly degenerate for the visitor into the kind of lethargic vegetating that the existence of the inhabitants seems to him to be. So it was with me.

I did join nighttime crowds, squatting in their white ducks and huaraches and laughing without comprehension at old Marx Brothers movies thrown onto improvised bed sheets in village plazas; I did follow, from a hunger for both music and love, youths strumming guitars and singing romantic Latin ballads through half-deserted back streets—until they saw me and closed their mouths; I did buy a pretty parakeet from a sandaled Indian who knew how to squeeze for an extra balboa; I even tried to enter the lives of some of the whores at the Villa Amor, my closest connection with the republic. But you cannot buy conversation any more than you can buy intimacy or love, and finally, appalled by the utter absence of any strenuous ambition, by the seemingly absolute unawareness of even the possibility of any largeness of social prospect, I found myself lapsing into the torpid colonial mindlessness of those around me—sailors and savages, Yankees and Indians—my days punctuated only by the rains that from one afternoon to the next came pounding at us all with the relentless insistence of death itself.

I was more than ready for anything Bobby had to propose. One afternoon I ran into him in a cantina, impeccable in his gold-braided dress blues and white hat. He shook his head sadly at my loud sport shirt and stained khaki trousers and drew me aside. "I've got a date for Friday with one of the sharpest babes on the Isthmus." He winked. "We're in love."

I congratulated him.

"Nita's a Nicaraguan, and very proper."

"You like them that way."

"True, but it raises problems, pal, problems. For this ball she insists on bringing along her two sisters."

"You'll be a busy man."

"So will you. One of them has a husband; the other'll be your date."

Bobby was already married, to a square chick from a shanty town outside Nashville; I had seen pictures of her, and I knew that when they had been married, in a formal Catholic ceremony, she had cried for two hours from shame at her own ignorance and fear.

Bobby could joke about his Catholicism to me as he couldn't to anyone else aboard ship: "Man, there was a time when you scored zero on the turf if you didn't belong to the Church. And if you did, you made the society column, dig?" Yet the ceremonial of the Mass touched him deeply. He enjoyed the white man's religion and the white man's church; still, he retained a lively contempt for his fellow Negroes who wore out their mouths trying to suck their way into the white man's world.

Bobby had been born and raised in Florida. His grandfather, a Seminole, had bequeathed to him his copper coloring and his name. His father had worked for the express agency, his mother had taken in washing, his sisters had studied bookkeeping and stenography and had nevertheless wound up as maids. Infuriated, he himself had gotten out while the getting was good, expelled after one year from a Negro agricultural and mechanical college. He was more specific about his early sexual adventures: pleased by my incredulity, he insisted that Southern white girls were allured by Negro men.

"During the ten months I worked as an orderly in the state hospital, there wasn't a week passed that I didn't make out with one of the nurses."

"White nurses?"

Bobby laughed at me. "You think there was any other kind? The first few times I couldn't believe it, but later I got to taking such crazy chances, it makes my hair stand on end now to think back."

"How old were you?"

"I turned seventeen that year. A wild kid. Once we were parked out in some stump-jumper's field, and when he snuck up pointing his flash I had to take off with my pants around my ankles, shaking like a treed raccoon. I left for Harlem the next week."

When he hit 125th Street, he had already been tempered by his audacious nights with the aggressive nurses, by the money he had earned as a kid selling bootleg corn to and for white men beneath the grandstand of the local ball park, and by the bitter knowledge that his parents and his sisters were grinding their lives away because they were both frightened and resigned.

Because Bobby was neither frightened nor resigned, he threw himself into the labor movement, picketing the cafeterias whose tables he bussed and the docks where later he longshored. The Communists took him up, and for a while he took them up. The idea of a career as a leader of the oppressed—planning, telephoning, haranguing—had its appeal for someone who hated being shoved around as much as he hated work, but Bobby was too shrewd to let himself he exploited as a kept boy. He broke with them, but delicately, without destroying those connections that might later prove useful, and moved on to new fields.

He ran numbers, and then jobbed hot cargoes from his longshore friends; afterward there were stimulants, from pep pills to goofballs, and then party pictures. At one time he was living with twin sisters, and three really frantic show girls were working for him part-time. All these activities brought him more and more into the odd zones of the white world, from Cancer to Capricorn, so perhaps it was understandable that it was precisely during these years that he joined the Catholic Church—just as it was at the height of his involvement with the party crowd that he bumped into poor little Ceelie Mae, cutting through the Greyhound Bus Terminal on 34th Street. Bumped into her as she was waiting tensely to roll back to Tennessee, conned her into staying, and married her.

"It was a revelation," he murmured, fondling their wedding photograph, "that a girl could be so pure. I mean, she didn't even know what she had it for. And for once I managed to restrain my appetites. In fact I couldn't imagine touching her until we were married."

He and Ceelie Mae lived happily on Sugar Hill. She knew nothing of his activities, whether for human rights or for his bank balances, and had never gotten over her original Cinderella bewilderment at their fine apartment, or the splendid clothing that he chose for her.

Then suddenly he shipped out to sea. It had nothing to do with Ceelie Mac, who was no doubt as bewildered by it as she was by Bobby's other activities and who accepted it (he assured me) as she did everything that he decided to do. I suspect that it was some nastiness connected with either the party pictures or the profits from girls, or both. Within a few years he had worked himself up (probably with the help of well-placed friends) to chief steward on this tanker.

The one great thing that had happened since then was that at last, only some six months before, during Bobby's most recent shore leave, Ceelie Mae had succeeded in becoming pregnant. It was the one fruition that Bobby had always wanted of his marriage but had never been able to admit that he yearned for; and now he was happy.

So we sat in his cabin, more often than we did in mine, because he had a record player, and we talked about all this while we listened to his record collection. Bobby had no use for jazz and didn't care for classical music. He did love operettas, and he adored the little encore pieces of Fritz Kreisler. There was one record called "Kreisleriana." How can I ever forget those evenings with the sentimental Viennese waltzes sobbing away, the moonlight floating through the porthole as our ship knifed through the warm black waters of the Caribbean, and Bobby confiding in me about daisy chains in Central Park West duplexes at dawn, and the lovely twins who spoiled him, bought him delicately engraved gold slave bracelets and white leather driving coats, besides turning over to him half of their earnings. He made it all sound not vile or even sordid, but like something out of André Gide.

Bobby's expenses were heavy, and he turned to unorthodox ways of augmenting his income. He and the Old Man had agreed to split the kickback on the ship's stores which Bobby was responsible for purchasing. It was not a particularly unusual arrangement; what made it so in this instance was that the captain was from Georgia. But as Bobby said, "If you can show a cracker how to make a buck, he can be mighty big about prejudice. The long green is the one color line he won't draw."

Bobby had other ways of making money. He bought cut marijuana in bulk from *campesinos* who grew the weed undisturbed in the fields of their tiny farms on the fringe of Panama City. Occasionally he took it aboard on his person; sometimes he had it carted aboard with the ship's stores. Brisbane (which was where we were headed, sooner or later) jumped with cats who had developed a taste for tea during the Yank invasion of World War II and who would pay a dollar for a box of twenty cigarettes. So every evening after dinner he spent a quiet hour locked in his cabin, whistling between his teeth while he stuffed cigarette tubes with marijuana, clipped the ends and packed them neatly in the more elegant boxes—Benson & Hedges, Sheffield, Melachrino.

After we became friends I kept him company while he rolled his cigarettes, although some obscure, indefinable compunction held me back from helping out. As he worked he chatted about some of the strange things he had done in his time and about his hopes for his unborn son, who was going to be called Bobby Shafter, Jr. His manicured fingers worked nimbly, his soft, deceptively innocent countenance glowed with pleasure as he regarded the ornately framed wedding photograph. And behind us, the *zigeuner* music filling the night air, causing Bobby's liquid eyes to fill with tears for very pleasure at all the beauty that the world contained. What a sentimental man!

On Friday evening he shamed me into wearing my only suit for our date. He found me swiping halfheartedly at my brown-and-white shoes. In mock anger, he reached out and plucked the cloth from my hand.

"For God's sake, man," he drawled, "you so cheap you gotta stoop to shining your own shoes? The liberty boat's alongside. Come on, I'll treat you to a first-class shine."

He did, and after that we clambered into an enormous old Cadillac cab that he had commandeered, slanging a little with the adolescent Negro driver in broken Spanish and island-accented English as we chattered through streets still soaked from the afternoon rains.

Bobby dug me in the ribs with his well-ironed elbow. "Better than riding like a smelly sardine in a chiva, eh?"

He never rode the chivas, those nickel-a-ride buses converted from superannuated Chevy panel trucks into crumbling rust-eaten jalops with two facing benches, each side holding, squeezed tightly, four Indians, Negroes, goats, chickens and their assorted smells; he knew that I did, and he couldn't resist teasing me about my stinginess.

We cut across a part of the city that I had never bothered to explore and rolled to a stop before a modest white stucco cottage set in a row of similar houses, each with a tiny lawn, a cactus and a flowering geranium or two.

I took Bobby by his uniformed arm as he was telling the driver to wait for us. "Did you let these people know that I'm white?"

He flashed me a confident but wary smile. "They'll accept you, just the way your friends would me."

That was equivocal enough—maybe not for the captain, but for me. I followed Bobby up the steps and on inside.

Bobby's almost-fiancée Juanita, a terribly young girl with huge, dark, frightened eyes, was seated on the very edge of a sagging couch with a young woman a few years older, whom I took to be her sister, and a very handsome if severe-looking young man who was surely the brother-in-law. They were an attractive trio, gotten up for an evening out in semiformal dress, a little nervous, their complexions—more Latin than Negro—a trifle strained. Across from them, stiffly upright in a worn barrel chair, sat a mountainous Negro lady. It was hard to guess her age from her impassive black face, but she was at least ten or twelve years older than the others and seemed to have nothing in common with them; even her shapeless dark dress bore no relation to the frocks of the young ladies. A neighbor woman, perhaps? Or an aunt?

Bobby rubbed his hands together. "Hi, everybody, *buenas tardes,* here's my buddy, Nita, her sister Maria, Maria's husband, Evan Jones, and sister Concepcion."

I gaped. Was *this* my date? I turned to Bobby, appalled. The only thing that got me over the next few terrible minutes was the realization that Juanita and her sister and brother-in-law were almost as ill at ease as I. One or two desperate attempts to communicate with Concepcion exposed the final horror: she knew almost no English. It was no go, despite the fact that Mr. Jones, an extremely well-mannered Jamaican whose Spanish was excellent, did his best to help.

"Have you been living here long?" I asked her. I waited, miserable, while the brother-in-law made this important question clear to the lady.

Old Stone-face nodded once. "*Si.*" That was that.

I tried again: "I suppose all three of you work?"

"Yes." Nothing more.

I gave up. When we got out on the walk and helped the three sisters into the back of the cab (Bobby and I were to sit on the jump seats and Evan Jones up front, next to the grinning driver), I grabbed Bobby and whispered, "Why the hell didn't you tell me?"

He smiled blandly. "I didn't think you'd be color-conscious."

"It isn't that. She's old enough to be my aunt. And I can't talk Span—"

He waved me into the car with a flourish and said to the driver, "To the Jockey Club, man, and steer like a deer."

The Jockey Club was maybe not the most exclusive supper club in the area, but it wasn't the cheapest either. I had certainly never been there for dinner and dancing under the stars, which was obviously what Bobby had in mind; I was more easily satisfied. What was more, it was certainly Gold and not Silver. The social life of the Canal Zone was built around these two fantastically artificial designations. Gold for the whites and the wishful-whites; Silver for the hopelessly dark Negroes from the islands and the Indians from the backwoods and the jungles. There were Gold rest rooms and Silver rest rooms, Gold commissaries and Silver commissaries, Gold swimming pools and Silver swimming pools. I was no agitator. I used the Gold facilities, but it always left a sour taste in my mouth. And the Jockey Club was about as Gold as you could get.

This was not lost on the women or on Evan Jones, all of whom looked at Bobby with such trepidation that he started to laugh. "What's the matter? This is a big night. Relax."

The unworthy thought had already crossed my mind that Bobby had invited me to join his family as his front man to gain them angry admittance to forbidden ground. But I didn't dare tax him with this, certainly not in front of his guests.

It was only when the big cab pulled up in front of the Jockey Club and a uniformed Negro doorman handed us out that I began to get the picture. For not only was the doorman deferential; so was the scuttling Negro headwaiter; and we were shown to a table that was quite near the Latin American band and well in the clear of the palm trees that fringed the unroofed dance floor. Only then did I really try to see the six of us through the eyes not of one who passed through the Gold doors perhaps wryly yet really unfeelingly, but of one whose every waking moment was colored by the unending dreary decisions to be made every time his hand reached for the Silver door and his eyes lingered on the Gold door.

We could all, save for big, black, stolid Concepcion, have passed for light enough to be acceptable in a world where the line had to be drawn not between white and nonwhite but between approximately light enough and impossibly dark—and by someone not too exigent, someone who would do almost anything to avoid trouble. And that someone would have deftly arranged—as in truth our black waiter did—for Concepcion to be seated at the darkest and most inconspicuous corner of the table, from which she might appear to inquisitive eyes as perhaps a hired chaperone or superior kind of mammy, with our party but not really of it.

The Jockey Club was favored by American naval officers. I counted four junior-officer submariners with their dates, young civil-service stenos or the adolescent daughters of Zone employees (in any case, looking as emptily fresh and untroubled as their cousins in the country clubs back home). There were also a number of tourist couples and businessmen of the type who could afford this kind of evening out. They all took their turn in whispering about our party, in gesturing surreptitiously—and sometimes not so surreptitiously—at the six of us.

But I detected no obvious animosity, nothing more than curiosity or bewilderment, and after a while I began to enjoy the new situation. The puzzlement on these well-bred faces, so used to the easy pegging of their fellow creatures, gave me a kind of secure pleasure. Who were we? Was Bobby an Indian? A South American naval attaché out with his wife? The Joneses, he with his acquiline nose and neat mustache, she with her large-eyed loveliness and good grooming—maybe consular visitors from one of the islands? And I, with my precious skin so patently and painfully fair that I could not expose it to this tropical sun for so much as half an hour without its shriveling and dying? As for Concepcion, it would be no more than a poor pun to say that she was beyond the pale. She was quite simply unthinkable, and all around us our fellow revelers were peeking in uneasy bafflement.

This was fun. I felt a bit of a celebrity and I enjoyed watching Bobby, his arm casually draped across the back of Nita's chair, his face wreathed in a genial smile of self-satisfaction.

Evan Jones, I learned, was a bacteriologist from Barbados, now working at the Gorgas Hospital in Ancon, from which he and his quiet but very sweet wife had come up for this night on the town. As yet they had no children, and they shared one great dream: to get away from the artificially imposed restrictions of this colonial outpost, steaming with prejudice and tropical lassitude, and to make a new start either in New York City or in Rio de Janeiro.

Their chances were very slight indeed. Evan and Maria were painfully realistic about this—yet still they dreamed. They had no notion at all of the rank slums and isolated provinciality of Rio, about which I tried to tell them a little; but maybe they were right in not taking me seriously, for they had both already forgotten more than I could ever learn about such matters, and they were concerned not with those familiar miseries but with escaping the abomination of the color label.

I got through a little better about New York; but even here they opposed me with a stubborn disbelief that I just couldn't understand, until they pointed to the reason for their willful infatuation.

"Harlem, like the upper East Side, is exciting only for the rich," I remarked sententiously. For the first time Concepcion was following me, at least when Maria bent over and whispered rapidly into her ear. "The limitations the whites impose on you are still there, for the few rich Negroes too."

"I can't believe this," Evan replied. "I see the evidence against it."

"Evidence?" I stared at him, uncomprehending. "Where?"

He nodded toward the dance floor, where Bobby and Juanita, the most attractive couple on the floor, were executing a nifty tango.

"*There* is a different kind of Negro." Evan's hands were clasped tautly, dark against the expanse of white tablecloth. "You can't know what that means to us."

Unexpectedly, Maria leaned forward, her face alive with excitement, and placed her delicate fingers on my arm. "You see, none of us is like Bobby. He has self-assurance. He walks in with us where we would never go. He looks not to one side or the other. He has no fear, he does not lower himself. You see?"

To my amazement Concepcion, after listening to a machine-gun burst of translation, slowly turned to me and nodded. Her black face glistened in the dim glow of the torches around us; she was perspiring heavily. Had I been wrong about her also?

"Yes," I said at length, "I think I do."

There was no point in my adding that now I understood too their real hopes, which were not for themselves but for their little sister, who was still young enough and for whom now a golden door had been opened by the bold young American. Even if they did not admire him so, they would have been duty bound to flatter him and to encourage her.

"Well," Evan said, "if you'll excuse us. I want to give Maria a whirl."

We arose and he took her in his arms and twirled her off in the direction of Bobby and Nita. I said to Concepcion, "Would you like to dance? To dance?" and pointed toward the floor, now quite crowded with gliding couples. To my relief, she shook her head slowly and gravely.

So I sat down. With my planter's punch in one hand and my good cigar in the other, I leaned back grandly and surveyed the scene before me. Those who had been staring at our table, at me and Concepcion, lowered their eyes or glanced too quickly in another direction, but I felt no triumph. I felt instead rather sick for Nita.

If I didn't share the Joneses' admiration for Bobby, it wasn't because I was censorious of his past. I could even understand why he enjoyed romancing gullible girls with vague hints of a life together under the shelter of the American flag. But now, having met one of these girls and her family . . . How crushed these gentle people would be!

I determined to take Bobby aside to tell him that I wouldn't be a party to this game any more, even though I knew he'd persuade me not to spoil the fun for the others. But I had no opportunity for even this much conscience-salving; instead I was thrust almost immediately into a posture

of solidarity not just with Evan Jones and the three sisters but with Bobby
too.

What happened was that after the dance set Bobby and Nita returned
to our table, hand in hand and glowing. As Evan and his wife came up
too, Bobby, driven either by pity for Concepcion or by a belated readiness
to relieve me of my burden, bent gallantly over Concepcion's chair and
demanded of her the privilege of the next dance. I was astonished to see
Concepcion smile slowly at him, then hoist herself out of her chair by
pressing down hard on the arms with her palms, as heavy people will. I
stood there for a moment, transfixed.

Partly to cover my confusion, I asked Juanita to dance with me. We
all moved off—Nita and I, Evan with Maria, and Concepcion solemn as
ever, but flexing her great haunches with surprising grace as she followed
the tricky steps executed by Bobby, who grinned shamelessly.

I didn't have a tenth of his deftness, even though I was a little drunk,
which is ordinarily helpful. So, although I was anxious to talk with Nita
about her sister and Bobby, I didn't open my mouth once during the three
numbers we danced together for fear (or so I told myself) of losing count
before all the watching eyes.

One thing I was bent on, however, was testing Concepcion. As soon
as the dancers had drifted off the floor, I accosted her and Bobby.

"My turn," I said. "How about us switching partners?"

"Como?"

Bobby laughed. "The mate wants to navigate with you, baby."

Nita whispered rapidly to her sister, who shook her head and finally
smiled broadly, showing me two gold incisors, then, murmuring something, placed the palm of her hand approximately over her heart, on her
massive black-draped bosom. Juanita turned back to me. "She says she's
tired, she's out of breath."

Bobby took Nita by the hand. "Tell her she'll sleep better. Greatest
thing in the world for her." And he clapped me fraternally on the back
and sailed off with Nita as the music started once again. Perhaps Concepcion's spirit had toughened. She presented herself to me, and as the
tourists and naval officers gaped—she dark, looming and indomitable as
an aircraft carrier, I skinny, lost and tense as a sailor on his first encounter
with a woman of the streets—we worked our way somehow around the

floor, not bumping into the other couples only because they carefully cleared a path for us.

After the first number Concepcion detached herself from me with absolute firmness. Once more her hand went to her bosom; this time, having gained my little victory, I was willing to concede. At our table we were shortly joined by Evan and Maria, too considerate to leave us trapped with each other, and later, when the music had stopped, by Nita and Bobby, who summoned our waiter with an upraised forefinger.

"Repeat for everybody, man."

When the waiter had returned with the drinks, Evan raised his glass. "Ladies and gentlemen," he said, then paused while his wife translated for her older sister, "I should like to propose a toast. To Bobby and to—"

He stopped abruptly. The waiter had been leaning over Bobby's shoulder, whispering urgently. Suddenly Bobby straightened in his chair, took the startled waiter by the lapel of his mess jacket and spoke out in a perfectly audible voice.

"Put that in writing."

The waiter stared at him in dismay. "I can't hardly write."

"Go tell the captain what I said. And if *he* can't write, let him deliver the message in person instead of sending you to do his dirty work."

Evan jerked about to stare at the retreating waiter, then returned his gaze to Bobby. "What is this?"

"Never mind. Drink up."

"Please tell us what it's all about."

Bobby ground out his cigarette in the conch shell ashtray and looked us over almost disdainfully. "They want to put conditions on our staying here."

"Conditions?" Evan placed his hand to his mouth as if to hide his lips, thumb to one corner, index finger to the other. "Of what sort?"

"Let the captain tell you when he comes."

We all drank then, without a toast, in a newly oppressive silence. Evan gave his wife a light; she had to steady his hand with her fingers in order to draw flame to the tip of her cigarette.

After a long moment the headwaiter hove into view, with our waiter tagging wretchedly behind. The headwaiter, who minced as he moved, was a Negro too, but many shades lighter and many years older than our original waiter.

He worked his way around the table, skillfully, so that he could stand between Bobby and me. "If I could see you two gentlemen alone . . ."

"Knock it off, Jack," Bobby replied coldly. "Spit it out loud and clear."

"I only wished to explain the management's wishes in regard to your pleasure. If you gentlemen—" he indicated Bobby and Evan—"wish to dance with the ladies you are escorting, or with this lady, that is fine. And if this gentleman—" he inclined his head in my direction—"wishes to dance with either of your young ladies, there is no objection."

Bobby jabbed his thumb at Concepcion and me. "But you don't want her to dance with him. Right?"

"We would prefer not."

"Why not?"

The headwaiter stared at us miserably. He did not answer.

Bobby repeated the question. "Why not?"

The waiter extended his pink palms pleadingly. It was as if he were demonstrating the evidence of his color. "Maybe if we step into the lobby . . . There is no need to disturb the other patrons."

Evan picked up his wife's wrap. "Bobby, I do not enjoy being where my family is not welcome. Nothing will be gained by making a scene."

"That's what you think." Bobby showed his teeth.

"Wait," I said. "I'm the one whose behavior is questioned."

"I assure the gentleman . . ." the headwaiter muttered.

I stood up. "I'll sit with whom I please and dance with whom I please." At last. I felt virtuous.

"Don't waste your breath on this joker," Bobby said. "We'll talk to the manager. Period."

The headwaiter was trembling. "He will speak to you by the door."

"Never mind that jive. If he can't come here there's only one place I'll meet him, and that's the kitchen." Bobby put both hands on the table and stood erect. "Clear? Now shove off."

Evan Jones shepherded the sisters, stunned by the abruptness of it all, away from our table and toward the kitchen, which opened off the lobby. He touched Bobby's elbow. "None of us will enjoy prolonging this. Can't we leave quietly? Why the kitchen?"

"Just let me do the talking."

Head up, Bobby marched into the kitchen leading all of us, and the two waiters, as smartly as though he had earned his uniform at Annapolis. He paused at the great chopping block and allowed the headwaiter to scuttle before him with his funny crablike gait. There we found the manager, a fat Panamanian with an octagonal diamond that glittered on his little finger, and an eye both sad and greedy.

The manager extended his hand to Bobby and nodded gravely. "I'm afraid we have inconvenienced you."

Bobby ignored the hand. "I bet this is the first time you ever had Gold and Silver dancing together on your floor."

"You understand, to me it makes not a particle of difference."

"Oh sure."

"But we simply cannot afford to disrupt our guests."

"Maybe we educated them a little tonight. But I'm not concerned about them." Bobby raised his voice. "I'm concerned about my own people."

He aimed his finger at Evan, at Maria, at Concepcion, at Juanita—and then at the kitchen help, the cooks, the pearl divers, the busboys, the waiters, the musicians, all dark-faced, all beginning to grin and whisper. Suddenly we had an audience of over a dozen; and it grew every second, as more waiters came through the swinging door and pressed against each other in order to see and hear. Then I knew what Bobby was up to.

"We proved tonight," he said, "that if you are determined, you can do things that were never done before. We proved that you can be a man, if you really want to." He snapped his fingers at our waiter, who stared at him openmouthed. "What do you think about it, man?"

"I guess that's right."

"You *guess?* Don't you want to be a man before it's too late, before you're nothing but bones in a box? Black man can be just as much man as white man."

"That's right!" a voice called out.

"You tell them, Yankee man!" cried a squat black dishwasher in an ankle-length rubber apron, in accents as British as those of Evan Jones.

"All right, I'll tell you," Bobby shouted above every kitchen noise, above splattering faucets, clattering dishes, rattling silverware. He waved aside the enraged manager.

"I'll tell you that I wouldn't work in a place where my black brothers were insulted. I wouldn't work where my black brothers weren't served. I wouldn't work—" he dropped his voice to a virtual whisper, now that he had us— "where I had to be the one to tell a black man or a black woman to sit in a corner.

"I know you've all got mouths to feed. But you can refuse to degrade yourself or your people. Right?"

"Right! Right, man, right!" They pronounced it *mahn, mahn,* but I knew what it meant.

They pressed on him from all sides to shake his hand, to clap him on the back, to touch his gold-ribboned arm, laughing and shouting with pride and delight. I found myself jammed against the great wooden door of the meat locker, with Evan and Maria squashed breathless against me, gasping and shining-eyed.

"You see?" Evan demanded. "You see? He's champion, simply champion!"

I looked down into his little wife's glowing eyes. Yes, I had to see. I looked across, beyond Bobby and his cheering admirers, to Juanita, who stared with silent adoration at her laughing, perspiring hero, and to Concepcion, who, despite the monumental impassivity with which she stood, arms folded across her vast bosom, now exuded an air, almost an aroma, of justification, like a mother who has lived to see her maligned boy vindicated at last. If I had known a little less, I too would have been wholehearted in my admiration for the way in which Bobby—a live symbol of the intoxicating possibilities of freedom—had so swiftly engendered this renewal of faith and self-confidence.

Then the manager, after a tense and voluble consultation with his headwaiter, came up, his fury reined, and asked us please to consider that we had all been his personal guests. Cheap at that if it would get Bobby out of the kitchen and his help back on the job. But Bobby capped the evening.

"We don't want any free rides. You know what we want? To be treated exactly the same as anyone else. That shouldn't be too hard to understand, should it?" And he draped his arm almost paternally around the manager's pudgy shoulders. "Now if you'll just let us square our bill, we'll be on our way."

Out in the street five minutes later, Evan and the three sisters were still hardly able to believe that they had been a part of Bobby's feat. I whistled up a cab; this time Concepcion insisted on hoisting herself into the front seat, obviously to let Bobby ride in state between Maria and Nita, who held his hand in quiet rapture while Evan and I perched on the jump seats.

Evan could not contain himself. "This has been one of the greatest evenings of my life. How rare to find a man who is personable, charming and brave. One of our own! With fifty, a hundred, a thousand men like that, what couldn't we accomplish?"

At the sidewalk in front of the girls' home, we chatted for a few moments more, in order that Bobby and Nita might have their parting embrace alone in the shadows. It was just getting to be uncomfortable when Bobby came bounding out, dancing a little soft-shoe routine and patting his lips with his handkerchief.

"Let's go man, go," he called to our cab driver; and we took off with a jolt.

Bobby dragged deeply, with a contented exhilaration, on his cigarette as he drummed his fingers rapidly against the window. He turned to me, bright-eyed. "Maybe we ought to dig up a couple chicks to finish off the evening."

"Not tonight. Let's sack in. I stand watch in the morning. Tell me something, Bobby: You set up the whole show tonight, didn't you?"

He looked at me blandly. "Son, I wouldn't know what you're talking about. How could I know they'd kick up such a breeze?"

"You knew damn well Negroes don't go dancing at the Jockey Club."

"Maybe they will now. And maybe the help will be a little more aggressive." He looked me over challengingly. "Is that bad?"

"Not for Evan. But is it good for the sisters?"

"Are you going to turn preacher on me now?"

"I suppose you're going to marry her."

"I could do worse. She's neat and clean, and she loves me. I wouldn't be the first cat to keep two households going. I'm really a family man at heart." He winked at me. "I can't bat around night in and night out like you single guys."

"You know something, Bobby? You stink."

He laughed out loud. "If I thought you meant that, I'd poison your cornflakes. I do want to thank you for coming along tonight. You helped me out of a spot with Concepcion."

"I was the fall guy."

"It didn't hurt, did it?"

"Come on, here's the pier."

As we strolled toward the liberty boat bobbing on its line, Bobby clapped me on the back. "Buck up. Maybe one of these days you'll be my best man!"

But when we got out to our anchorage and climbed aboard, a telegram from Ceelie Mae was waiting for Bobby. He was the father of a baby boy, named Arvel Shafter, born prematurely, weight nine pounds two ounces. Tears of joy sprang to Bobby's dark eyes as he stood in the companionway clutching the telegram.

"I'm a father," he whispered. "I'm a father."

I murmured congratulations, trying to make up for our words of a few moments earlier.

"Come into my suite, man, and let me break out the VSOP. You wouldn't refuse a nightcap with a new papa at a time like this."

So we started to drink all over again. It must have been something like four o'clock in the morning.

"The situation calls for my Fritz Kreisler favorites."

"It's your party, Dad."

Bobby laughed. "I like that: Dad! You know I was just kidding about that little Juanita, don't you?"

"Sure."

"I mean to say, at bottom I'm the kind of square john that needs romancing even more than he does a roll in the hay." He raised his glass. "Mud in your eye, baby."

As I listened to the tremolo of the sentimental violin for the hundredth time, quite drunk and very sleepy now, something made me say, "That's a mighty big baby, Dad."

He smiled proudly. Then his face clouded. "Say, how would you know?"

"I'm an uncle twice over. Average babies run six, seven pounds."

"Maybe, but I've been building up that little chick with buttermilk and chocolate shakes."

I looked at him. "Two months premature, wasn't it?"

"So she says." Suddenly his hand shot out blindly, like a snake's tongue, and fastened itself in a painful clamp on my wrist. "Do *you* think it's possible? Do you?"

"Let go."

He stood over me, glaring down at me. "Do you?"

"I don't know. I guess not."

"The stupid little chippy. Not even enough sense to lie about the weight."

"Wait. Don't jump too fast."

"What kind of a sucker do you take me for? She named him after her old man, not me. You know why? Because nine months ago I wasn't home. I was five thousand miles away on a goddamned tanker. So she moves up the date to when I *was* home—for three weeks—seven months ago."

"Bobby, it doesn't sound like the girl you described to me."

"Weren't you giving me the same bit about Nita? Do you think she'd be any different? They all smell the same between the legs. If anybody ought to know, I should."

"The least you can do is give her a chance to explain."

"Explain!" Bobby hurled his glass to the deck in a rage. As it broke, a thin pool of Scotch trickled along the fiber rug between us. "Listen, baby-face: When I paid off after the last voyage, I found her in the apartment with a sailor, a homely little jerk. Cousin Willie from Nashville, she said. Five foot four, black as the ace of spades, never finished grade school, eighteen years old. Would you think that a girl I picked up in a bus station, and put a silver-blue mink in one closet and seventeen pair of shoes in another, would shack up with an ugly, undersized, seasick teen-ager? Why, the poor shnook threw up every time his DE passed Ambrose Light. He asked me for a recipe for seasickness."

"Maybe Ceelie Mae wasn't used to being alone. You told me how dependent she was on you."

"I had to ship out. That's one thing I don't discuss."

The record had finished. The needle was swinging wildly across its smooth core—*ticketa, tocketa, ticketa, tocketa.* I caged the arm.

"You were very happy about this baby," I said, "until it got born. You told me you'd been trying for years."

Bobby glared at me wildly.

"Maybe Ceelie Mae wanted a baby even worse than you did. And maybe she knew how much it would please you to have a son, even if it had to be from a kid—"

Bobby was already shoving me to the door. "Go on, get out of here. Take off, get lost." He gave me a push that sent me stumbling over the coaming. "You're just as superior as all the rest." He slammed his door.

The next day we sailed for Australia. Bobby's supplies were swung aboard early, so there was no need for him to go ashore again, or even to turn up on deck.

In any case he did not, not for three days thereafter. We were worried about him in the saloon, but the purser assured us that he had spoken to him through the door. The captain would have been just as pleased if Bobby had died in his cabin, so nothing was done.

One day at sunset I stood at the fantail, idly watching our wake and thinking about Evan Jones and the sisters, when I felt Bobby at my side. I turned to find him rather drawn and bloodless, but composed.

"Can I apologize?" he asked.

"Forget it."

"It's that last crack I made. I was upset. I really don't feel that way."

I shrugged in some embarrassment. "What are you going to do, Bobby?"

"I could kill her—that's one possibility. Or I could pretend to believe the whole silly story and play Daddy. Or I could go back to Panama and marry Nita, at least long enough for her to do the same thing to me."

"Oh, come on."

"You know something? No matter what I come up with, I can't win."

The one thing he did not say was that I had pushed our friendship too far, that I had presumed on an acquaintance that was, in the nature of the situation, unbalanced. It was just too easy for me to be superior; in fact, he understood it all better and more bitterly than I ever could.

We passed some quiet hours after that, he and I, on the long voyage to Australia and then on through Suez; but there were no more long sessions in his cabin, with the record player spinning sentimental music and Bobby snowing me about his conquests, and I asked him no more about his wife than I did about how he disposed of his cigarette boxes. When at last we tied up at the slummy nethermost reaches of Staten Island, supposedly home but in reality as far from our dreams of home as Tierra del Fuego, we paid off in the saloon and parted with a handshake, leaving unspoken the common realization that it was only now, in our own city and on our own soil, that we had to part.

"So long, kid," he said, reaching out to straighten my carelessly knotted tie. "Don't rush into agitating—or marrying."

In fact I did marry two months later and gave up the sea. And with it gave up the possibility—or so I begin to feel now, after all that has been happening in a world beyond my reach and my personal involvement—of ever again being as close to another troubled wanderer as I once was to Bobby Shafter.

WHERE DOES YOUR MUSIC COME FROM?

When I was sixteen and a junior in high school, my whole life changed. Until then I had led a very ordinary existence, growing up in the postwar years with my younger sister on an elm-lined street in the house in which my mother had been born. I had a Rudge bicycle, a chemistry set and a crewcut, and the only thing that marked me out from the rest of the kids on the block, apart from my height, was that I really liked my piano lessons and shone at the annual recitals of Miss Wakefield's students. Indeed, I used to daydream of going to New York City and playing the Grieg Piano Concerto under the stars at Lewisohn Stadium, with thousands cheering me as they did Artur Rubinstein.

My father, an uneasy real-estate broker, regretted an enthusiasm fostered mainly by my mother, and tried to steer me from music toward medicine, starting with the chemistry set and later taking me on long Sunday-morning walks in the course of which he tried to convince me, man to man, that there was nothing like being your own boss. He ran his business from a wooden cottage attached to the back of our house, so he was home a lot, between phone calls, and he probably exercised more of an influence on me than most of the fathers on the block did on their kids.

It was only after I finished junior high and began to flounder around with swarms of strangers in Franklin Pierce High that I discovered how many different worlds lay beyond the placid, comfortable one of Buchanan Street. There were boys who smoked marijuana and girls who got pregnant; longhairs who did math problems in the caf while the others fiddled with their jalopies and hot rods; Negroes who disappeared after school as though they had been swallowed up; jocks who stayed until it got dark, playing soccer or jogging around the track as if they had no homes to go to and no pianos to practice. I didn't settle into any of the cliques, because I wasn't ready to limit myself. Belonging to almost any of them would only have confirmed me as being what I already was on Buchanan Street, and I was getting a little tired of that.

So, with the seamless illogic of the sixteen-year-old, I limited myself almost exclusively to one boy's company for so long that people used to kid us about going steady, as if we had been of different sexes, or about being twins, as if we had been brothers.

In fact Yuri was a twin himself, and he walked to school every day with his sister Yeti (born Yetta), the ballet dancer. Yeti's beauty was so immediate that it was frightening. She had long, straight, shimmering blond hair that hung uninterruptedly down her back to her waist, eyes the color of delphiniums in July, set shallow and slantwise above her Slavic cheekbones, and skin smooth as eggshell. She walked with the characteristic half mince, half prance of her craft, toeing out as she advanced, she was as slim and flat-chested as a boy, and because of her self-absorption she was—besides being my best friend's sister and therefore inviolable—as close to being absolutely uninteresting as any girl I had ever known.

Yuri was something else. He was bowlegged, his tough and kinky brown hair barely grew above my shoulder (after a while they called us Mutt and Jeff), and his thick, passionate lips were usually twisted in a cynical grin. He played the fiddle—which he carried with him nonchalantly in its weathered case wherever he went, even into the john—with dazzling fervor and dexterity. He had been the concertmaster of our school orchestra since his freshman year, but I hesitated to approach him not only because he was so good but because of that grin. The other members of the string section said he was decent enough, if somewhat condescending, like a big kid playing for an afternoon with little ones. They said too that his mother awoke him at dawn so he could practice for two hours every morning before school—later I found that this was true.

One day after ninth period I was in the music room practicing on the Mozart A-Major Concerto, the K. 414, the first movement of which the conductor, Mr. Fiorino, had promised me I could play with the orchestra for the spring festival, when Yuri Cvetic sauntered in and leaned his elbows on the tail of the piano.

He listened for a while, his fiddle case wedged between his torn sneakers, that grin showing the spaces between his front teeth. Finally he said, "Ever do any accompanying? I got a Brahms thing here we could try."

Within days we had exchanged confidences never before revealed to anyone else. Everyone took it for granted that we two would eat together in the cafeteria; and when, because of homework or music lessons, we couldn't see each other after school, we would talk on the phone, more quietly than our sisters but just as lengthily.

Yuri never came to my house more than once or twice. My father complained that he couldn't bear the squeal of Yuri's fiddle being tuned up to the piano. It was no more legitimate than his shouting, after we were in tune, "I can't hear myself talk on the telephone when you guys are playing." I knew I was losing respect for my father when he came out and said that he mistrusted Yuri not only because he encouraged me to have musical ambitions but because he came from the other side of Pierce High, from Cotter Street, a noisy neighborhood of teenagers tuning up go-karts, women arguing loudly in foreign tongues and drunks too shameless to go on indoors.

Yuri shrugged it off with the grin that I suspect bothered my father more than anything else, for it bespoke that wise invulnerability that can unsettle an adult more than any adolescent surliness. After that we hung out together at the park in fair weather, at his house in foul. His family never objected; they were always delighted to see me whenever I turned up at their second-floor flat.

In addition to his twin sister, who, when she was around, was usually polite enough, in her self-centered way, there was a younger sister, Helen, a freshman when I first met her. Not only had her parents used up their inventiveness on the twins' names, but they also seemed to have taken one look at their last-born and decided that a ballerina and a violinist would be enough and that this time they would settle simply for a daughter. Helen was a nice enough girl, with a sweet, even smile and dark, gentle eyes unlike Yuri's and Yeti's in that they were always shadowed, as if she didn't get enough sleep, but she had no interest in music or dance and she never opened a book. She appeared content just to get by in school and to keep the household going while her parents were off working and the twins were off practicing. And besides, she was buxom; she gave you the feeling that if she didn't watch herself, she'd wind up looking like her mother.

I think that was what put Mrs. Cvetic off her youngest and convinced her that it would be profitless to push Helen into the arts as she had done with the twins. Mrs. Cvetic, a practical nurse, was a heavy-breasted, shapeless woman who breathed through her open mouth and waddled so alarmingly that you could practically feel the friction of her thighs. She always wore a wrinkled and stained uniform, not quite white, its pockets bulging with Pall Malls, wooden kitchen matches and professional samples of Anacin and Bufferin, which she chewed as other people do gum or candy.

"Hiya, boy," she would greet me on those occasions when she happened to be home of an afternoon. "You gonna play some music with Yuri today? Okay, stay for supper."

If I declined, she would wave aside my hesitations, the long cigarette bobbing from her lips, ashes sprinkling the bosom of her uniform, while she growled at Helen, "Move away the goddam ironing board so the boys can practice. And let's see how much goulash we got for supper."

The ironing board had no legs. Sometimes Helen would balance one end of it on a kitchen step stool, the other on the edge of the upright piano, and press away at her mother's uniforms (I never could understand why, since Helen was always ironing them, the uniforms were never clean). When I wanted to lift the keyboard lid, she would take the ironing board and lay it on the round oak dining-room table. When she had to set the table for dinner for the six of us, she'd set the plank against the wall. But Mr. Cvetic had bolted a full-length mirror and a long section of three-inch galvanized pipe to the wall for Yeti, and when Yeti hung onto the pipe with one hand, doing her ballet exercises, Helen had to drag the plank, heavy as a painter's scaffold, out to the front hall, where it teetered at the head of the stairs, announcing to you as you mounted the worn rubber runners to the Cvetic flat that Helen must be busy doing something else.

Often it was the meals which, while her mother tended the afflicted and her sister flexed her back, Helen prepared by herself and served as well, eating off in a corner like a European mama, only after she had made certain that the rest of us were taken care of. More than once Mr. Cvetic, having worked overtime, came in when we were already on our dessert and had to be served separately. But Helen never lost her composure, even if her father complained that the meat balls were no longer piping hot. It confused me that a girl so downtrodden should look so contented.

In our house the dinner-table conversation was predictable. If mother had the floor, it would be cultural, with quotations from the day's speaker at her club, John Mason Brown perhaps, or Gilbert Highet. If father was in a talkative mood, and nothing of note had happened in his business during the day, he would inform my sister and me of George Sokolsky's opinion in the afternoon paper, or of what Galen Drake had philosophized about on the auto radio.

At the Cvetics, you never knew. They ate noisily and greedily, as though each meal was to be their last, and they talked fast and loud—all except Helen, who rarely spoke—about whatever popped into their heads. Slender Yeti put away enormous quantities of everything—three slabs of seven-layer cake were nothing for that girl, whose bare arms, when she reached for more, were like match sticks—and she rattled on, in a voice as thin as her arms, about Madame Tatiana's yelling fight with the accompanist at ballet school. Yuri, chewing fiercely, mocked Mr. Fiorino's efforts to conduct Von Suppe ("You'd never catch me doing that, teaching fifth-raters to play fourth-rate music"), and simultaneously, in counterpoint, his mother gave us free professional samples of the folk wisdom she had picked up from her years of nursing chores.

"Gertie blew up like a balloon, poor thing," she would say, spooning up her soup with a loud trill, "and when the doctor stuck the drain in her belly the smell was like the stockyards. But sometimes you got to do that, you got to let out the poison. Helen, bring in the rest of the cauliflower."

Her husband was small, wiry, wizened, and good-humored. I never saw him (but once) in anything other than working clothes—a brown leather jacket over khaki shirt and trousers—just as I never saw Mrs. Cvetic (but once) in anything but that wrinkled white uniform, size forty-six. Mr. Cvetic worked as a journeyman plumber—actually as a plumber's helper, I think—on the new housing projects that were going up; he drove a clanking old Ford with a busted muffler, and you wouldn't have thought that he would be mad for theosophy.

I hadn't been in his company more than ten minutes when he asked me what I knew about Rudolf Steiner, and when I said, Wasn't he the man who wrote the operettas? I was in for it. Yuri groaned rudely and Yeti wandered off to do her bar exercises before the mirror, but Mr. Cvetic ignored the twins and plunged ahead into a basic description of the anthroposophical life view. It was all very confusing—it seemed to take in everything from organic farming to better kindergartens—but after a while I took some comfort in observing that it was confusing to the rest of the family too and that even Mr. Cvetic himself grew hazy when it came to details.

"But I learn," he would say to me, snapping the calloused fingers of one hand while he picked his teeth with the other. "That's the big thing, to learn from the great minds of the ages. You'll see some day how beauty comes from unity."

"From unity?"

"And unity comes from variety. The flower comes from the seed, the seed comes from the flower. Where does your music come from?"

"I don't know. From the composer?"

"The mind comes from the body, the body comes from the mind. You get me?"

Mr. Cvetic took magazines I had never heard of. In our house we got *Reader's Digest* (my father would still be reading the February issue when the March one arrived) and *Harper's* and *Book of the Month Club News.* But Mr. Cvetic read *Tomorrow* and *Manas* and a magazine the name of which escapes me, published in some town in Pennsylvania and dealing with compost gardening, even though he didn't have so much as a potted plant. He liked to read, moving his lips as he did, about subjects that he didn't agree with or even understand, which startled me, and what was more he was always grinning with happiness over the wonderful variety of material for argument. He stayed up late making notes (for what purpose I never found out), while his wife shuffled about in house slippers the heels of which had long since been crushed to death under her bulk, dropping ashes on the bare floors and opening windows so the kids wouldn't have tired blood and sluggish bowels.

Yuri was fed up with all this, just as I was growing tired of the atmosphere in my house, but at least his folks didn't quarrel with what he was doing; they were proud of it and encouraged him in fulfilling their jumbled-up expectations. Besides, they accepted me practically as a member of the family and were frankly proud that Yuri's best friend was from Buchanan Street and a musician to boot.

"Man, when the day comes," Yuri said to me one afternoon in his quick slurred way, running the words together between tongue and full lips much as his father did, "I'm going to have an apartment with Oriental rugs so thick you can drop a golf ball on them and never find it again. I'm *sick* of bare floors just because they're supposed to be closer to nature or better for Yeti's posture."

I tried to sympathize, when actually I envied him. But what did he mean about when the day came? We both had our dreams of glory and were bound together by the discovery that our separate daydreams could interlock so beautifully, but I didn't really see how our exchange of confidences and intimacies had anything to do with money or Oriental rugs.

In Yuri's eyes I was, I began to realize, like a boy who fantasies great success with girls—rescuing them from drowning or halting their runaway horses, causing them to fall madly and pliantly in love with him—but dares not visualize a consequence consisting of marriage, children and passionless slippered evenings yawning at TV over a can of beer. If for me our music was going to make us famous, that fame would serve only to make us more desired and more famous—and so on, into Carnegie Hall and Lewisohn Stadium, in tails and smiles. But for Yuri the fame was going to bring him Oriental rugs.

It was disconcerting to learn that he was so practical, but I started with the recognition that he was the better musician and that he was the soloist too. What was more, he took the initiative with my mother, who was a little awed by him, in getting us invitations to perform Schubert, Brahms and Bartok for her clubs and her friends' clubs, for the Soroptimists, the AAUW and the Matinee Musicale Society, some of which got us excused from school, others of which actually paid us. We were big shots in a small way, and I wasn't the only one to realize that I owed it to Yuri. Even my father had to admit that Yuri wasn't doing me any harm, if I didn't get a swelled head from the recitals, which wasn't likely to happen as long as I was merely the accompanist.

One unusually hot June afternoon we were ambling along Cotter Street after a final exam in Spanish, licking at Dairy Queens and sizing up the strolling girls in their thin summer dresses. We came into Yuri's front hallway and looked up to see Helen's broad, soft behind undulating gently at the head of the stairs; she was on her hands and knees, scrubbing the steps. At the sound of our entrance she turned, raising her dripping hand to brush away the dark hair from her forehead, and regarded us with a still childish gravity.

"Hi, Helen," I said.

Then she smiled down at us. "I was trying to do the steps before anybody got home. Where's Yeti?"

Yuri shrugged. "Probably downtown, seeing *Red Shoes* for the fourth time." He stepped over her pail and waved me onward, calling back over his shoulder, "Make us something cold to drink, will you, Helen?"

The rooms were half bare, as usual, the floors strewn with a knocked-over heap of Mr. Cvetic's magazines. Usually I loved entering that apartment, but now it struck me for the first time as somewhat bleak and airless, smelling still of Mrs. Cvetic's cigarette butts. We went on out to the front porch and flopped onto the glider.

I said, "Why do you give Helen such a hard time?"

"You don't mean me, you mean all of us."

I was embarrassed. "I mean, we could have gotten our own drinks from the icebox."

Yuri shrugged again, drawing back his full lips over his teeth. "Division of labor. My old man works for the rent and the groceries. My mother works for the music and the ballet lessons. Yeti dances and can't spoil her feet, I fiddle and can't spoil my hands, and Helen takes care of the house. What's wrong with that?"

I wasn't quite sure. Maybe, I thought, everything was taken for granted just a little too readily. But Yuri waved away my discomfort.

"Never mind that stuff. You know something? There's room in this town for another kind of music besides rock-and-roll and Schubert. What future is there in Schubert? Fifty bucks a night, two nights a month? All we need is four, five more fiddles, bass, percussion, couple horns, and we're in business. Then, with a booking agent and some stylish arrangements—"

"What kind of music are you talking about?"

Yuri blinked rapidly, as though he were signaling me. "Strauss waltzes, gypsy fiddle music, things people can dance to without being acrobats and hum without being self-conscious. I could be like a strolling violinist, and you could conduct from the piano."

Helen was standing in the doorway with a pitcher of lemonade. She spoke before I did, in a tone that I had never heard her use. "Is that what everybody's been knocking themselves out for?"

Yuri turned on her swiftly. "Who asked you to listen? What do you know? You're fifteen years old, you still think I can go off to Europe and win one of those international prizes and live happily ever after. I'm trying to be practical."

He was, too. At seventeen we weren't ready to organize the kind of society orchestra he had in mind—but in a few years we would be. And in the meantime he knew, better than I, that we simply weren't up to the cut-throat concert world. Given his teaching, his instrument and his practicing, Yuri would at best qualify one day for a first-desk job with the city symphony. In order to supplement his income he would either have to teach ("What a drag! Look at Fiorino!") or play hotel music, which at least had some of the glamour that he thought we had been talking about all these months.

Unlike me, Yuri was daydreaming, I began to see, not about impossibilities but about reality. It troubled me as much as it did Helen, maybe because Yuri was beating me to the cold compromises involved in growing up. And I could not put out of my mind the way the lemonade pitcher trembled in Helen's hands before she set it down by the glider and hurried away.

Yuri spoke no more of the dance orchestra that day or for a long time thereafter. I got a summer job as a camp counselor, and Yuri, who had wanted to go to Tanglewood or Marlboro, had to take a paying job with the Civic Pops Orchestra, which did a summer season in the municipal park.

When we came together again as seniors in the autumn, we were both anxious to make up for lost time. We resumed our duets at once. I had almost forgotten the intensity of the pleasure you could derive from making such music with a friend.

But then, starting as an undiscussed eventuality and looming larger as the year rushed by, there was the prospect of my going away to college. My father, who had managed only a year of college before the depression caught up with him, worked at convincing me that in a Big Ten school "You'll make contacts that will be invaluable to you in later life."

When I made the mistake of repeating that to Yuri, it broke him up.

But his mocking laughter jarred me, and I began to think not about how square my father was but about what it might be like, really getting away from Buchanan Street once and for all.

Yuri was bright, school was easy for him, but he couldn't have cared less about going to college. And it wasn't simply sour grapes. I knew his parents would do without necessities to send him to a conservatory, but they hadn't brought him up to face the prospect of being one more poor fish in a great big pond.

"I'm not kidding myself," he said when I raised the subject. "The best I could do after Juilliard, or one of those trade schools, would be an audition for a job with a big orchestra. What's so big about that? I can do better right here with help from people like your mother and without getting gray waiting for a break."

I stared at him. I said, "Are you satisfied to stay here forever? Don't you even want to try to make it in the big time?" I was on the point of adding, What else have we been dreaming about all these months? but something in his face stopped me.

He extended his hands. "Why throw away a sure thing for a mirage?"

He was pleading for more than understanding; he wanted me to tie my future to his. As my best friend, he was hoping against hope that I would turn my back on my father's ambitions for me. It wasn't just that Yuri wanted my moral support and my physical presence. What he wanted even more, it struck me with ferocious suddenness, was the kind of real help from my mother and her friends that would depend on my sticking with him.

I was hurt at Yuri's readiness to use me in this way; I would rather he had come out and said what he wanted from my mother. But that would have involved different admissions on his part, so I held my tongue, and we went on more or less as we had.

More or less, except that even while we were reading duets and rehearsing for recitals, I was studying for my finals and trying to decide among various Big Ten schools. When I finally made up my mind, and then was accepted by several, I didn't run to tell Yuri or his family, as I might have a year earlier. Nor did he bring up the matter with me again.

Yeti too was itching to be out of school. She had been running with a show-business crowd, or the nearest approximation that our town could boast (little-theater actors, modern dancers, and a part-time beatnik group just coming into its own), and after a number of auditions, including one breathless trip to New York, she caught on with the road company of a Broadway musical. She was to join it directly after graduation, and she was trembling with the first real excitement I had ever seen her display.

If Yuri was not particularly impressed, and Helen, smiling very enigmatically for a sixteen-year-old, said nothing, at least their parents seemed pleased. The twins, they decided, were entitled to a big graduation party.

"Listen, boy," Mrs. Cvetic said to me, "you come next Friday night for sure. We're gonna have one hell of a big blowout."

"You couldn't keep me away," I said. "You know that."

"Okay, but this time bring a girl."

I was a little disconcerted. The few girls I could take to movies or concerts wouldn't have known what to make of the Cvetics. So I mumbled something about seeing whether I could dig up a date.

I didn't even try, but on the evening of the party I took the steps up to the Cvetic flat two at a time. In the hallway the noises of many voices talking at once sounded reassuringly familiar; the odors of Mrs. Cvetic's and Helen's cooking smelled familiar too—stuffed cabbage, eggplant salad, savory pudding.

But when I walked in I felt that I had entered a strange house. The noise wasn't coming just from the family but from a throng clustered here and there all through the apartment, which had been decorated like a dance hall with twisted streamers of crepe paper, Chinese lanterns, and life-size pencil drawings of Yeti in her tutu and Yuri with his fiddle.

I recognized some kids from the school orchestra and the glee club. In addition there were a number of middle-aged strangers, friends of Mr. and Mrs. Cvetic, I guessed, and a gaggle of bony girls and slim-hipped boys from Yeti's ballet school.

It was fairly early, but the air was already exhausted, fogged with smoke, and as I blinked my way through the mob, peering around for Yuri, somebody cracked open a can of beer under my nose and swung it about, lashing a circle of suds onto the bare floor. Girls shrieked, but Mr. Cvetic, ignoring everything, had a classmate of mine pinned to the wall and was exhorting him, as near as I could make out, to eat eggshells for their mineral value. When he caught sight of me he waved, his hand clutching a stuffed cabbage transfixed with a skewer to a slab of rye bread.

"Hey, go by the dining-room table," he called out amiably. "Helen and the missus have got food there for an army."

He wasn't kidding, but I wasn't hungry. I took a beer and went on to the piano, where I found Yuri, with a new haircut and a new sport shirt, surrounded by a crowd of kids from school. They were egging him on to do–an imitation of me accompanying the glee club.

Yuri mussed his hair to approximate mine, and, flinging his hands over the keyboard to make them appear long and scrawny like mine, pounded out the Rudolf Friml medley from *The Vagabond King.* Everybody was laughing. I had to myself, in order not to look like a stuffed shirt, although I didn't think it was all that funny. When Yuri caught sight of me he stopped and held up his hand.

"Here, you do it," he said, making room on the bench. "This is your instrument, not mine."

I was stuck for quite a while after that. The gang pressed more beer on me so that I would give them the cocktail-hour classics that they wanted, but finally it palled and I begged off. I shoved through the knots of dancers and talkers and found myself pushed smack up against Mrs. Cvetic, who was fishing stuffed cabbage out of a Pyrex bowl. She thrust a steaming plate at me.

"Whatsamatta, boy," she asked, squinting to fend off the smoke from her dangling cigarette, "you on a hunger strike or something?"

I made a pass at eating and congratulated her on the party.

"The kids deserve it, they didn't let me down, they worked hard all this time. Besides, you only graduate once, right?" She dug me in the ribs. "So have a good time, the party is for you too."

I wandered on through the apartment, very confused. Mrs. Cvetic was more unselfishly hospitable than my own parents. But was she really doing the twins a favor, making such a big deal about high-school graduation?

At the end of the long hallway I entered the kitchen, intending to leave my plate on the counter and maybe leave the party, since I felt out of place. But as I put down the plate I heard a step behind me, and I turned to face Yuri, who was standing in the doorway, grinning his grin.

"Looking for something?"

"Helen is the only one I haven't said hello to. This is where she punches the clock, isn't it?"

"Stick around, she'll turn up. Can I get you anything in the meantime?"

"Not a thing. Great party." I could see that he expected more, so I added, "I was accepted by two colleges this week."

Instead of asking why I hadn't told him before, he said negligently, "Make up your mind yet?"

"I'm waiting to hear from one more before I decide for sure."

"In any case you're going away. That's it."

"That's it."

I hadn't meant to be flip about what was terribly important for both of us, but Yuri seemed to want it that way. Scratching at the fiddler's rash on the underside of his left jawbone, he said, almost as if it were an afterthought, "I didn't hurt your feelings before, did I? I mean, imitating you at the piano."

"Don't be silly."

"Okay then. Let's split a beer."

I was going to protest that I was full, but something in his face stopped me. I held out a glass, and Yuri poured half a can into it. We drank in silence, not looking at each other.

"Well, I've got to circulate. Anything you don't see, just ask for it." And he swiveled about and walked out of the kitchen.

I should have left then. But it was true, I told myself, that I still hadn't seen Helen, and she was one person whose feelings I didn't want to hurt. So I wandered through that crowded apartment one last time.

By now the guests had progressed from talking to shouting—about the Korean fighting, which had just broken out, about homosexuals in the ballet and the State Department, about compost heaps and wheat germ —and from dancing to banging beer cans together in rhythmic accompaniment of a monotonous folk singer. Helen was not in sight.

I made my way on through the dining room and the living room to the front porch. The awning was rolled down and the living-room blinds were drawn, and it took my eyes a moment to grow accustomed to the darkness. Then I saw that several couples were embracing against the railing at either end of the porch. I was about to retreat and leave them to their business when I realized that a girl was sitting motionless on the glider, hands folded in her lap. It was Helen.

When she heard me she looked up and smiled and motioned to me to sit beside her. I was a bit uneasy, but she insisted, mouthing the words, "It's all right. They won't care."

I glanced to my right. I was a little shaken to see that the blonde digging her fingers into the hair of the boy pressing her against the railing as though he was trying to shove her over the falls, his leg between hers, was Yeti.

"She won't care either?" I whispered, gesturing at Yeti.

Helen shook her head mildly. "It's just her boy friend."

"But what are you doing here? Don't tell me you're the chaperone."

"It's the only quiet place. I worked pretty hard getting the food ready."

"I bet you did." I had to bring my head closer to hers in order to keep my voice low. "I've been looking for you all evening."

That wasn't strictly true, but it was becoming true as I looked at her. Perhaps because of the heat or the long hours in the kitchen, she had put up her thick dark hair; her face was more mature now, calm, self-assured. She smiled at me again, her cheeks rounding, and she was no longer just Helen; she was someone strange and beautiful.

"I don't think you'll be seeing much more of us," she said, "after this summer."

"What do you mean?" I asked stupidly.

"You'll be going off to college. And then . . . people grow away from each other."

"Not good friends. Good friends stick together." Something made me add, "Besides, I'm not a hundred per cent sure I'll go away. Why can't I go to college here? Right now I'd rather be here with you than any place else in the whole world."

"You mustn't talk like that," she said agitatedly. "Not when you've got the chance to go. Anyway, you'll see. You'll see, when you make new friends you won't need the old ones so much."

Her insistence, stubborn as a child's, was charming; and yet I was touched by a sudden premonition that Helen, unlike Yuri, knew more than I—and always would.

Suddenly her dark eyes filled, and I was in terror lest she begin to weep. "Yuri loves you," she said, "you know that? I hoped you would influence him to be idealistic like you, to use his talent for the best. If it turned out the opposite, and he was the one to influence you . . . it would be better for you if you never saw us again."

"I promise you one thing," I said. "No matter what, I'll never forget the Cvetics. You've been nicer to me than my own family."

"We just like you, that's all."

Encouraged, I added what would never have entered my mind five minutes earlier but now seemed profoundly true and important. "You know something? You're not only the nicest one in the family—" I pressed forward, whispering so that Yeti should not be able to hear— "you're the best-looking."

Helen shivered, as if taken with a sudden chill, and grasped her bare upper arms defensively.

"What's wrong?" I asked. "Are you cold? Here, let me rub you."

I touched her smooth flesh with my fingertips and discovered that it was not cold but blood-warm, not goose-pimpled but satiny. Helen released her grip on herself and raised her eyes to mine.

As we sat there staring at each other, with my palms on her soft arms, we could hear the shuddering sighs of the embracing couples on either side of us, and the rich wet sound of lips and tongues meeting, sticking, parting. Helen drooped toward me, I slid my hands around her back, she raised her hands from her lap and began to caress my temples. When her fingers reached the back of my neck I pulled her to me, overcome as much by the unexpectedness of what was happening as by the beauty of the moment.

Just as our lips swelled and touched, each to the other's, in that instant of exquisite revelation, the porch door swung outward. I opened my eyes to the startling beam of light and raised them to meet those of Yuri, who was standing in silence, his fists clenched, staring at us.

How can I ever forget the look on his face? His glare was compounded of rage, disgust, contempt—and a strange, frightening kind of envy. And in the next instant there glinted in his eyes, I could have sworn, a scheming flicker, a swift calculation of the possible advantage to him of what he saw before him.

Helen sat motionless, not from fear or shock but as if time had come to a stop for her and she did not wish it to start again. Her arms hung free, no longer clasping me; her face was pale but quite composed. It was impossible for me, though, to remain impaled under Yuri's stare. I arose awkwardly, mumbled something, and shouldered past Yuri and on out of the apartment.

≡

Helen had been right, of course, about me and her family. After I was settled in college I sent her a picture postcard of the bell tower, saying that she would like the quiet, regular, pealing music that it made; but even though I printed my return address, she did not reply. The only acknowledgment I got was a postscript at the bottom of one of Yuri's letters: "Helen asks to be remembered to you."

I wrote Yuri in some detail, but without undue enthusiasm, about my new life. Yuri's occasional letters, on the other hand, struck me as not only provincial (anecdotes about classmates I had hardly known) but increasingly desperate, as if now that I was gone he was discovering, in the blind, lonely thrashing that he preferred to conceal behind a mask of amused contemptuousness, that the times were wrong for what he wanted out of life. I began to think that maybe I had never really understood Yuri.

Then came a last letter in which he told me cryptically that he had joined the Marines. All I could think of at first was that he was trying to beat the draft and in a typically sardonic fashion, fiddling his way through the Halls of Montezuma. But he put it to me in a lower key, in terms of his maybe taking advantage of a new GI Bill for Korean veterans to study conducting "when I come marching home." Maybe he was just saying what he thought might please me or renew my confidence in him. I have no way of really knowing, because after that we lost touch with each other.

It was my father who sent me, many months later, the clipping from the afternoon paper which announced, not without pride, that the gifted young violinist, Yuri Cvetic, who had gone straight from Parris Island to Pusan, had been captured by the Chinese Reds. The best I could do, when I came home in June, was to talk to Yeti and her mother on the phone, for my father's business had turned sour and I had to leave town almost at once for a resort job as pianist with a dance band.

More than once, at the silly hotel by the lake, I reflected on the irony of the fate that found me making a necessary buck out of my music while Yuri was involved in the miserable consequences of a larger decision. I wrote him about this—why not?—through the International Red Cross, because I thought that it just might bring back to his face—even at my expense—that mocking grin.

But he did not reply, and in truth he may never have gotten my letter, for not long after, word came of his death in a prisoner-of-war camp; and

I found myself crying, alone in my room, at the idea of his permanent silence. Where had our music gone to?

The papers of that time were full of angry words about the betrayal of the heroic Marines, and in our town the tragic fate of Yuri was coupled with the implication that he must have died a hero's death. I don't know that this was ever substantiated, any more than was the stronger rumor to the contrary when his body was finally shipped home for burial: that Yuri had simply turned his face to the wall and died, as if his capture itself had been a symbolic yielding up of life, which he would not want to have undone any more than he would have wanted to go on living if the joints of his fingering hand had been frostbitten and amputated.

His interment took place on a rare and lovely April afternoon. Yuri was entitled to burial in a military cemetery, but his parents preferred to have him in their own family plot, painfully bought (like his musical education) with their own sacrificial payments. I had just arrived home for Easter vacation, and in fact was not in time for the services; but I borrowed my father's car and hurried on out to the suburbs.

It took me a while to find the cemetery. I got to the graveside just as an honor guard was lowering the flag-draped coffin into the ground. All I could think, as I stood off to one side, away from the family and the faithful friends, inhaling the ineffable fragrance of fresh-turned earth, was that if through some miracle of this heavenly day the dead could draw just one breath, they would burst open their coffins and climb, happily reborn, from their tombs.

I turned to walk away, convincing myself in the usual cowardly fashion that it would be better if I called on the Cvetics later, when they had had the chance to compose themselves. But Helen, walking with a strange doughy-faced young man, caught sight of me, and I could only wait for her to approach. She smiled at me sadly, very white-faced in her mourning costume, and extended her hand with no word of greeting. Her sadness seemed to encompass not just the wasteful death of a young man but, I thought, the tragic quality of life itself for those compelled to go on.

"I'd like you to meet my fiancé," she said to me.

I shook the hand of the young man, who was not only embarrassed but restlessly anxious to get back to his salesman's route before he lost any more commissions.

There was nothing for it then but to await the others, who had not as yet seen me. Mrs. Cvetic, quite bowed over by grief, was being half led, half dragged away from the graveside by her husband and Yeti, whose veiled hat had been knocked somewhat askew by the exertion. As they neared me on the flagstone walk, their figures dappled with the spring sunlight filtering through the river willows, I could hear Mr. Cvetic panting shallowly under his burden and his wife sobbing jaggedly, like a wounded animal, with each step. They stopped to take breath, and suddenly Mrs. Cvetic, in black instead of white, for the first time, raised her head and caught sight of me.

She broke free from the restraining arms and lurched toward me. Before I could move or even think of what to do or say, she had hurled her heavy, sagging body at me, gasping and sobbing.

"My God, my God, my God!" she cried.

I tried to put my arms around her, but she was shaking and crying and pounding at me with her fists. It struck me with a thrill of horror that she was greeting me not with affection but with hatred.

"His best friend!" she screamed. "You were his best friend!"

Clumsily, I strained to pat her heaving back, but she cried loudly, "Best friend, why didn't you stop him? You didn't even try, you didn't go yourself, why didn't you try to stop him? Who's going to play duets with you now?"

Even if I had been able to think of something to say to her, I would not have had the time. Yeti, her head averted, and Mr. Cvetic, shrunken into an unaccustomed Sunday suit and mumbling something either incoherent or in a foreign tongue, took up their burden again, pulling and dragging her by the elbows. Her wails floated back over her shoulder in the spring sunshine of the silent cemetery, and Helen, nodding an apologetic farewell, hastened after her family, her ankles flashing in their black nylons, her escort hurrying along at her side until they had all disappeared from my view.

From my view, but not from my mind. For years I wondered, Was Mrs. Cvetic right? Should I have tried to stop Yuri from going to his death? Yet I must admit that when I think now of the family that changed my life, my feeling for Helen and her fate affect me just as strongly as my feeling for Yuri and his fate. As for the music, it is enough that I hear it in my mind. Where it has gone, along with my youth, I think I know; but where it came from, during those passionate months of performance with Yuri, I doubt that I shall ever know.

A HOT DAY IN NUEVO LAREDO

L ouise Ridley's main reason for driving rather than flying to Mexico— or at least the reason she had given to those who asked—was that she wanted to be able to show Dickie more of Mexico than just Monterey. So, two days after he had finished fourth grade at the day school, she had packed her only child and their valises into the aging station wagon and they had set off for their first trip abroad and—thanks to his father's cooperation—a Mexican divorce.

Actually she had wanted to be alone with her son on this leisurely trip so that he might gradually accustom himself to something even she could hardly comprehend—that from now on they would be alone together. Alone, with no Roger to call out, "I knocked off work. Who's for caulking the boat?" or "It was too hot in the office. Who's for a swim?"

But it had been too hot in the car, after the initial exhilaration of getting away. It had been too hot in Carolina and too hot in Georgia, and long before they had gotten to the Alamo, deep in the heart of downtown San Antonio, Louise and Dickie had lapsed into the sullen rather than companionable silence that tends to surround immobilized travelers squeezed together too long. They were bored with the South and with the somnolent heat, and so they grew bored with each other. Since Dickie was not romantically patriotic, the Alamo—except for the old firearms in its little museum—had proved a disappointment to him, and as they strolled along the banks of the river that meandered sweetly through the heart of the city he had solaced himself with greedy descriptions of what he would be able to buy once they were in Mexico.

A fielder's mitt was what he wanted, specifically a second-baseman's glove, because that was what his father recommended. Roger, who in his time had been a great fan of Charley Gehringer, had adjured him in parting—as if he couldn't think of anything more important to say to his son—that leather and silver were the things to buy in Texas and Mexico. "Ask your mother to pick out a second-baseman's mitt, Dickie, and I'll get you a real major-league baseball to go with it."

The idea of the mitt had kept him busy, or at least animated, most of the dull way down from San Antonio to Laredo. Staring out the windshield at the dusty sun-baked countryside, with no cowboys in sight, no cattle, no nothing, not even oil wells, Dickie would mumble ruminatively, in the nasal, rich-boy's drawl that was all too reminiscent of his father, "It's not the padding in a fielder's mitt, it's the flex-i-bil-i-ty. You've got to have soft leather for that."

And if, gazing fixedly at the flat strip of highway enclosed by her gloved hands and the white arc of steering wheel between them, she neglected to express agreement or even interest, she succeeded only in calling down on herself a nagging reminder: "Mommy, you promised. Don't forget, you promised me the mitt. Are you listening?"

At last Louise decided that it was her job to make a more sustained effort than she had felt up to so far to tell Dickie what lay in store for him. For them, in fact.

"Dickie," she said patiently, "I'll get you that glove. A promise is a promise. But you're big enough now to realize that once we're living together, just the two of us, things will be different than they used to. I'm not going to be able to buy you anything that comes into your head."

Dickie twisted about to face her, shocked. "I know that. Don't you think I know that? But the glove—"

"We'll look for one in Mexico. I just want to make sure that you understand. Nagging for things won't do you any good—it'll only make us angry with each other. There's no point in running after a glove the minute we cross the border, because you wouldn't be able to use it there anyway. We'll probably pick it up on our way back, so we won't have to carry it around with us."

The boy's face had closed.

"Dickie," she said sharply, "are you listening?"

"Yes," he said in a tone that disclosed nothing. "I'm listening."

"You know, when we cross the border, you're going to see things you never saw before."

"I know."

"I wish you wouldn't be quite so sure of yourself. It's one thing to look at film strips, or even to listen to Mrs. Weinberg in social studies, but it's quite another to see things with your own eyes. I could tell you from now to doomsday about the less developed countries. Like the reasons why they're poor and we're rich. But it wouldn't mean anything compared to what you're going to see for yourself. That's one reason," she concluded, sick of her own sensible voice, "that I decided it would be better for us to go to Mexico than to Nevada. For the divorce, I mean."

"Whatever the reason was, I'm glad."

That was somewhat reassuring. They cruised into Laredo at dinnertime and pulled up in the main square before the biggest hotel in town. At that it was nothing fancy, but it promised a better night's sleep than anything they could get on the other side. Or so she explained to Dickie, when he asked why they couldn't keep right on going and spend the night in a foreign country.

"I'm tired from the driving, honey," she said as they ascended in the elevator to the top floor. "Right after breakfast we'll cross over the bridge into Nuevo Laredo. And we can walk around there before we drive on towards Monterey. Look out the window," she said as they entered the room. "That's Mexico, Dickie."

Ignoring the bellhop, Dickie ran to the window. "Man! You mean that little thing is the Rio Grande? It doesn't look so grandy to me."

She tweaked his ear. "Let's get washed up for dinner."

Seated across from her innocently amiable son in the hotel dining room and picking at a plate of cold chicken salad, Louise found herself wondering once again why she hadn't just flown off with him and gotten the divorce over with, instead of wandering through strange towns that she had no desire to visit and that seemed to bring Dickie no visible benefits. Obviously she was putting the thing off; even now she was delaying their entrance into his foreign land on the excuse that she wanted a night's sleep—when sleep never came any more without aspirins and tranquilizers.

It wasn't that she didn't want the divorce. If anything, she should have broken the marriage off years ago, when she had first had to make excuses to Dickie for Daddy's repeated absences. Clinging to that feckless man had done her boy no good that she could see; it had gotten to the point that now, nearing thirty-two and with a long-legged boy who all too soon would be taller than she, she could not even remember why she had married his father or what there had been about Roger that had ever made her think she loved him.

To conceal the trembling of her hands, Louise fussed with her bag, digging about in her change purse for the tip. "You want to pay the check?" she asked. "Then finish your milk."

As soon as they were out on the sidewalk he said, "Can we go to a movie?" but with no real hope in his voice, and when she replied, "No, but you can stay up in the room until eight-thirty," he did not protest, but fell into step with her as she strolled, without aim, from one lighted shop window to the next. The Fanny Farmer candy boxes in the drugstore windows and the Early American driveway signs (The Smiths Live Here) in the hardware-shop windows were no different from those in Montclair, and if that was all there was to see they might just as well have never left home—except that at home you couldn't buy divorces.

The men's furnishings stores, though, of which there were an unusual number, were flamboyantly Texan and aggressively masculine. Hats and boots, hats and boots—who would have thought that the putty-colored men in this scrubby border town could drift into such stores and slap down seventy-five dollars for a pair of hand-tooled boots, or one hundred and twenty-five dollars for a Stetson? Suddenly she caught sight of her reflection and her son's in a mirror behind these overpriced peacock displays.

She looked tall and pale, pale and sexless, sexless and unloved—a lanky and uninteresting woman in a wrinkled linen dress and soiled cotton driving gloves. Beside her stood the boy who resembled her so strongly that she felt sorry for him. Long-armed, long-legged, short-waisted and broad-shouldered as she was, he stood staring at the cowboy boots as she did, with his hand pressing down hair as straight and mouse-brown as her own. Even his expression in repose, now that he was not pleading for something or frowning over a book, bore that deprived look which she hated in herself. At least I earned it, she thought angrily, my father didn't leave my mother and me to chase blondes, he died on us and left us broke;

what has happened to Dickie, except maybe me, to make him look so hangdog, as though something vital had been withheld from him?

In truth, however, his face reminded her as much of Roger as it did of herself: those large jug-handle ears, that classically carved but bridgeless nose that grew straight from his short forehead. And those nervous athlete's hands . . .

Louise sighed. "Enough, Dickie," she said. "Let's head back." And she was dismayed to see how amiably he obeyed her, how eager he was to please in the small things—just like his father.

Back in their room he propped up the pillows behind him and disappeared into one of his endless collection of Hardy Boys books while Louise washed her hair and rinsed out their underthings in the bathroom. At least, she thought, he did not seem lonesome or shaken up—not yet. But that would come later, no doubt, when the vacation and the sightseeing were over and he had to face up to a fatherless routine.

"Time's up," she called out. "Turn off your light."

"I'm writing a letter. As soon as I finish."

When she had draped shorts, panties and nylons over the shower curtain rod, she stepped back into the bedroom, prepared to bawl Dickie out for not listening to her. As she opened her mouth, however, she saw that he had fallen asleep over his letter, with the light on. His book, the sheet of hotel stationery and his ballpoint lay on the quilt by his outstretched hand.

She switched off his bedlamp, smoothed out the covers and took the letter over to the bathroom doorway to see what he had written.

Dear Daddy, she read, *We got to the border. We can see Mexico from our room. Tommorow we will ride over the Bridge and we will be in Mexico. Mommy says they are poor there. Everything is cheap. So I will get my mitt there instead of in Texas the lether is just as good, mommy says. It is stiffling here just like in Georgea. It is going to be a hot day in Nuevo Laredo. love Dickie*

Louise placed the letter on the bureau and scrounged through her purse for her pills. If only, she thought, someone or something could reassure her that all this would come to an end; if only she would not have to be reminded so brutally of Roger every time her son struck a pose, caught a ball, wrote a letter. Even his poor spelling came from his father. When there was no longer any necessity for the letters, there would be phone calls, visits, weekends together. Then why the divorce? Only because it would free Rog from the obligation to make those eternal excuses and apologies, and it would free her from having to ask herself why she remained tied to someone who was not merely unfaithful but shallow and foolish to boot.

It was not that she hated Rog or even disliked him any more. It was rather that he made her dislike herself, made her wonder if she really loved her only child. Was she deluding herself now about Dickie as she must have been about Rog, when he had conned her into giving up her hard-won Cornell scholarship for marriage, with only one year left for her degree? What could have possessed her? She had not been impressed with his looks—on their first date she had thought him funny-looking—or with his money—she had known boys with more. He had been persistent, that was all, and so blandly convinced, that young man who had always gotten everything he wanted, from catboats to tennis cups, that he had wound up by convincing her too.

Was that all? Was there nothing about him that had charmed her, seduced her, bowled her over? If so, the very memory of it was gone now. Instead she recalled with shame those evidences of his true nature that had been manifest even in the earliest days of their courtship—his turning to appraise other girls' legs when they were out walking together, his grinning mockery of her attachment to those large ideals from which he had gradually won her away. But then she couldn't even say that she had loved him for his weaknesses, as other women had so obviously married because their men were drunkards or mother's boys begging for redemption. Roger hadn't dissimulated—he was what he was—while she . . . Louise touched her fingertips to her eyelids and lay quietly, awaiting the sleep that would carry her away from all the questions.

Finally it came, but it was soon over. Dickie was up at dawn, eager for his new country. Once she was fully awake, in fresh clothing, and with the sun not yet too high, Louise too began to share his anticipation. They packed swiftly, checked out, ate a more rapid breakfast than she would ordinarily have countenanced, and drove onto the international bridge with Dickie clutching their birth certificates bravely.

"Well, we made it," she said after their car had been stickered and they were saluted ahead. "Does it feel different?"

"It sure does. Doesn't it to you?"

Louise laughed. "I'll let you know in Monterey. I'm going to run into the tourist office to ask a few questions and get a map. Will you come in with me, or would you rather wait in the car?"

"I don't want to go in any old office. It's more fun out here. You won't take long, will you?"

"I'm sure I won't."

But when she emerged onto that dusty street, that poor, cheap flyblown imitation of the American streets across the river, the sun was already blindingly high overhead and Dickie was no longer in the station wagon. Taken aback, Louise slipped on her sunglasses and peered anxiously up and down the block.

She was relieved to see Dickie's unmistakable figure framed in the blank daylight at the end of the street, and she hastened toward the shop before which he stood, his nose virtually pressed to its dirty window. The sidewalk was crowded with tobacco-colored women carrying bundles and babies, bony dogs already listless in the baking sun, and barefoot, mud-stained children, none as pale or long-legged as her boy, who turned at the sharp clear sound of her heels and gestured eagerly.

"Hey, Mommy, look here!"

As she approached him, slowing her pace, so did the street urchins, beggars and vendors bearing boxes of junk jewelry and chewing gum. If she did not remonstrate, they would continue to cluster around her and Dickie as thickly as the insects that buzzed about them all.

"*Vayase!*" she said sharply, waving them away, and then, to Dickie: "You mustn't give them anything, or they won't leave us alone."

"Mommy," he demanded, pointing, "look at the leather stuff here. Look at those neat holsters! And that saddle! That's all they've got here is leather, nothing but leather. I bet we can find a mitt inside."

"Well, we're not going to look."

"Just for a minute? It'll only take a minute."

"I told you yesterday, there's no sense in carting a baseball glove all over Mexico."

"But, Mommy, we've got a great big station wagon. I can tuck a mitt away so you won't even notice it. Please, Mommy, can't we just look?"

Louise did not honestly know whether it was his logic or his whining that annoyed her more. "I said I'd get you one on the way home. Not now. It's a matter of principle."

"Please?"

"And I told you not to nag." She was beginning to perspire. "When you're ready to behave like a ten-year-old instead of a five-year-old, you can come along with me for a walk. Until then, wait in the car. Here are the keys."

And she strode off without looking back, determined not to yield, but sweating with the guilt that breaks out when the inflicting of punishment affords unforeseen satisfaction. Never mind, she thought, I'd rather accuse myself of harshness and unfairness than of overindulgence; one Roger is enough.

It was hellishly hot. She had to force herself to go on past the seedy arcades, dabbing at her face and neck and glancing into the gloomy grogshops, the side-alley groceries and one-man barbershops without customers, the nameless stores with no signs saying what they sold. And the last-chance bargains stacked up as they were all over the world in every last-hope town at the end of the line—watch charms and wineglasses, bracelets and bookends, ashtrays and earrings, scarves and serapes, baskets and belts, monkeys woven from wicker, pillows embroidered "Souvenir of Mexico."

Her head ached, flies rose droning from the horseballs in the gutter, importuning voices whistled Señora, Señora in her ear, a Spanish lover sang tinnily in the cavernous cantina, clouds of dust blew like powder, carrying the wail of a baby, the hoarse quarreling of two men, the last-ditch pleas of the sidewalk merchants. The medley of noises that filled the ramshackle streets, not just unfamiliar but frankly foreign in its steady persistence, deafened her for a moment to the wail she should otherwise have recognized at once.

She whirled about. Dickie stood where she had left him, but his hands were gripping his gut, and he swayed as though he had been shot on this preposterous Southwest movie set. His face was contorted; his usually pale features flamed hotly.

"Dickie!" she cried, her voice quavering. "Dickie, what's wrong?"

As she ran unsteadily toward her son, cursing herself, the half-circle of Mexican children that had formed around him wavered and broke.

"Dickie, are you all right?"

Before he could answer, a bold little boy with flat Indian features thrust a box at her and cried in English, "Chiclets, lady? Jus' one peso?"

She turned from him to her son, but a girl who came only to Dickie's shoulder loosened the greasy black rebozo which she wore like a parcel, pulled back its edges, and revealed a baby whose face was covered with sores. Louise recoiled and drew Dickie to her.

"Have you got cramps?" she demanded.

Dickie shook his head wordlessly. Tears were coursing down his cheeks. The Mexican children looked on interestedly, offering suggestions, making comments she could not catch. The boy with the box of chewing gum wore sandals made from truck tires; the others stood barefoot in the dust.

Louise cradled Dickie's head in her arm and pressed his abdomen with her fingertips. "Let's make sure it's not appendicitis," she said, the words sounding ridiculous even as she uttered them. "You might have a touch of food poisoning."

"I'm not sick," he muttered, shuddering. "I'm not sick."

"Then what is it?"

"I can't stand it," Dickie buried his boiling face in her blouse. "They're so poor."

Louise felt her legs give way. As she slipped to the curb, pulling him down with her, she heard him say, "I gave them twenty-seven cents. It was all I had. I divided it up. What else could I do?"

"Of course," she murmured. She could not remember when she had last cried like this, helpless and broken by the loss of innocence. But no, that was not true; the twanging spasms of her boy's sobs were her own. They revived in her now the stifled memory of the undead past. Her father, fallen out of life without warning, like a precious coin flung carelessly into a fountain, and she weeping in Roger's arms. That fraternity boy, who laughed uncomprehendingly at her infatuation with the distant poor, proved to her how instinctively, without guidance or instruction, he understood the terror of deprivation when it shook and retched within the circle of his arms. And because he proved it, she believed gratefully that he had proven himself, and she fell in love with him.

"It's hard to explain, Dickie," she said to her son. "I tried to, but it was a bum try. Particularly since I didn't realize whom I was talking to. You'll have to forgive me. Here, blow your nose and we'll go look for a mitt."

"I don't want it! I don't want it any more! Don't you understand?"

Louise gazed at him pensively. If she did now, she had not before—that was sure. And it struck her that it was not Roger's early compassion but its perpetuation in his son that was his best gift to her. Now that she was grateful again, maybe it would serve her better.

"I'll try to," she said to Dickie, "if you'll give me another chance. And it looks as though you'll have to, because you're stuck with me." As she arose, drawing her son up with her, she added, "For the time being, anyway. Come on, Dickie, let's head for Monterey."

CLAUDINE'S BOOK

Not so long ago, in the town of Phoenix, a shopping center for upstate New York and western Vermont farmers since the days of the American Revolution, there lived a very bright young girl named Claudine.

Claudine's father, Fred Crouse, was a widower. He had brought his unmarried sister Lily over from Loudonville to cook and keep house for them, which she did very well, except that she was high-strung and got to feeling that she was wasting her life away in an old eleven-room house with no closets but a cupola big enough for a fancy-dress party. As soon as Claudine was old enough for school Lily got a part-time job, working at the local library four afternoons a week. It kept Lily in touch with the higher things and made her feel more worthwhile, but it meant that Claudine was left alone a lot.

Claudine didn't mind. She liked best hanging around her father's Mobilgas station on the state highway, but he didn't want her making all those crossings between school and the station; besides, the language of the truckers was apt to be kind of vulgar for a little girl's ears. Claudine didn't bother to tell her father, who worked thirteen hours a day and was harried with many worries, that she knew all those expressions already. Nothing ever happened in Phoenix was the main trouble. In fact, nothing ever had, not since Joseph Walker, whose widowed mother drank and took in sewing, got drafted and was captured in Korea and then wouldn't come back when the war was over. A turncoat, Aunt Lily called him, and said that when it was in *Life* Magazine about his refusing to come home from China, two New York reporters had interviewed his mother, his school friends and the librarian. But all that was before Claudine was born. Nothing else had happened since Joseph Walker had come back, which he finally did one day, to dig footings for contractors when he felt like working, and looking like the most ordinary man in the world.

But then Claudine looked like the most ordinary girl in the world. At least, you wouldn't have guessed from her appearance that extraordinary things were going to happen to her. Lily always said that Claudine's eyes were her best feature, which is what you always say about a girl who isn't pretty. She was long-legged and short-waisted, so that she seemed always to be groping up through the tops of her jumpers, like a giraffe reaching out over the fence; her nose was long, with widespread nostrils, like her father's, and had a tendency to run with the first frost. What was more, her short upper lip (Aunt Lily said that she had been a thumb-sucker) made her teeth seem unusually long, like Bugs Bunny's. Over all, she looked woebegone—although she rarely felt that way.

Claudine had only one friend. The other children at the consolidated school thought she was stuck-up, or funny-looking, or even dumb. When they caught her making faces at herself in the mirror of the girls' room —even though they did it sometimes themselves—they decided that Claudine was queer and left her to herself.

There was Robin Wales, though. He found none of these aspects of Claudine annoying, maybe because he had his own problems. First of all there was his name: it did him no good to bring up Robin Hood or even the great pitcher, Robin Roberts, because he didn't even try to hide from his tormentors the fact that he despised baseball. "It's boring and stupid," he said, and that finished him off in Phoenix, which prided itself on fielding a good Little League team.

Besides, Robin had no use for people who tried to push him around or play rough. "I'm not afraid of those guys, Eddie and Walter and the others," he told Claudine, and she knew that this was true, that he simply preferred going his own way, doing what she liked to do too.

In addition to his being more intelligent than any other sixth-grader, Claudine thought that Robin was quite handsome, despite his ears, which looked like the handles of a cream pitcher, and his mouth, in which there glittered a fat silver brace. The only thing about Robin that really bothered her—aside from his constantly trying to boss her, simply because he was a boy—was his transistor radio, which he wore suspended from his braided Indian belt that had his name spelled out defiantly and which he never turned off. All his allowance went for batteries, because he loved to surround himself with sound (just as Claudine, when she was not playing with him, loved to surround herself with silence).

"Weather in a word," he would shout when they met after school, "sultry!" But at least he knew what the word meant, and what the pollen count was, and underground testing, and Cambodia, as well as every rock-and-roll hit on the Top Ten from week to week and the Bargain of the Day at Giveaway Gordie's Used Carnival.

Much more important than his ordering her around when no one else even tried to, or constantly banging things in time to the noise that came from his beltline, was his ingenuity in figuring out new places to build huts. Neither could remember when they had started, for it seemed to them that they had been building huts forever. It was Robin's scheme to make a treehouse in the fork of the old hickory above the roof of the Crouses' barn and to make a lookout lodge out of Claudine's cupola where nobody ever went, not even Aunt Lily to store winter stuff. And to build a hut in the back of the abandoned diner off Main Street, using some of the things that Robin's Uncle Burgie, who sold secondhand stoves, sinks, iceboxes, sump pumps and hockey skates, couldn't get rid of, after they'd been standing outdoors for a season or two.

Like many married couples, Claudine and Robin derived separate benefits from their joint household arrangements. What was unusual was that Robin's pleasures were those you would commonly associate with a wife (although there was nothing sissyish about him), while Claudine's were of the kind ordinarily thought of as a husband's (although again she was no tomboy but an almost fragile girl, with those large, wondering, rather bulbous blue eyes). That is, what Robin enjoyed was the planning involved in making each place livable: finding scraps of carpeting, making pictures to hang on the walls, gluing up chairs out of abandoned camp stools, even rigging up hammocks for their sleeping bags, and then decorating with the boat paints and lacquers he grubbed from his father's garage.

But Claudine, although she cooperated willingly enough, was at bottom attached to the huts as sanctuaries. Just as a man will come home from a hard day in the world of affairs in search not of distractions but of a quiet zone for reflection and refreshment, so Claudine looked forward to her hours alone, when she had no obligations at home and Robin was busy feeding his hamsters or taking his accordion lessons.

It was from Robin's Uncle Burgie that Claudine got the big stack of old business diaries. They had some whitish mold on the binding part, and they dated back to 1926, but as Claudine pointed out to Robin, the inside pages were absolutely clean even if the days of the week didn't correspond, and lots of them were personalized with initials and enhanced with fascinating facts, like: Bleriot Crossed the Channel This Day, or Hebrew Feast of Pentecost Begins This Day. Robin wasn't interested in these facts, however, or even in doing much with the diaries.

"Don't you want to find out who Bleriot was? Or what the Hebrew Pentecost is? If you came to Feb twenty-two and it said G. Washington Born This Day and you were a foreigner, wouldn't it arouse your curiosity?"

"Everybody knows Washington. Even foreigners. Besides, I'm not a foreigner. The reason I got the diaries, they'll look good on the shelf."

"What shelf?"

"I know where to get the shelving. If you help me cover it, I'll put it up for you."

In return for her cooperating, Robin turned the diaries over to her. Standing there in rows, they posed a challenge beyond looking up Charles G. Dawes and Gertrude Ederle: all those blank pages cried out to be filled, while she was alone, quiet and sheltered, in one of the huts through which they had scattered the shelving and the diaries like so many branch libraries.

At first Claudine simply copied into them things that she liked. Sometimes it would be a special story out of the newspaper, like the one about the eleven-year-old girl who got up every morning at five o'clock to practice figure skating for two and a half hours before school so she could try out for the Olympics. Then, increasingly, it would be a poem or a stanza from a poem in one of the books that Aunt Lily was always bringing back from the library: live ones like Richard Eberhart and Horace Gregory, dead ones like Mallarmé (because his name sounded like marmalade) and Keats (because his mask was cool and his poems were not). She liked to copy down parts she didn't understand, because often they sounded the best. Sometimes she would look up the words in the dictionary; so she got to know not only Bleriot and Dawes but "sacrosanct" and "hyperbolic."

It took a good three or four months, and a couple of diaries all filled, before Claudine got up the nerve to put her own stuff in them. She started with what she called Wondering. "I wonder," she wrote, "why that girl Nanette got up every morning at five o'clock to go ice skating. Did she set the alarm herself? Did she make her own breakfast? Did she want to show her father she could be the greatest skater in the world? Why didn't the newspaper article tell all the things you would want to know?" Or: "I wonder what made Horace Gregory write that poem about the girl sitting at the piano. Was it just because he saw her once, in his own house? Maybe he made it all up. If I knew where to write to him, would he tell me, or would he think I was crazy?"

When she saw that Robin was really not interested in using the diaries, or even in looking at them, Claudine began to make up things out of her head for them.

"Sayings All My Own" was what she called them at first, and they fitted nicely into the one-day space of one diary, if she didn't write too small. If she was feeling businesslike, she would note that "The weather this day continues brillig and fine for Father's business. It makes people restless, so they get out on the road." Or, if she was moody and somewhat ingrown from having been left alone by her father, Aunt Lily and Robin Wales, she would allow herself to become abstract and general: "Grownups believe that grownup is a babyish word. They prefer to call themselves adults. They don't think of children at all. They worry about them and they yell at them, but they don't think of them. It's more like putting them out of their minds. PS: Where does the expression come from, putting somebody out of his misery? Ask Robin."

But then when Robin asked her one day, "Say, Claudie, are you using those diaries?" she was almost ashamed to reply, "Yes, I put sayings into them."

Robin didn't seem to think there was anything odd about that, though. Claudine became all the more eager to fill the diaries, for now that they had become hers alone, she felt a funny responsibility to fill those hundreds of empty pages with her own words. Copying or pasting would be cheating.

She decided to make up a story with all kinds of things in it, descriptions of herself and her daily life, Robin and his radio, their mutual enemies, so that when she got to the end the diaries would have everything in them, like a good long novel.

"Today begins my life story," she wrote on New Year's Day. "My father was a very brave soldier, wounded during the Battle of the Bulge. Now he is the prop. of a very big service station, the biggest Mobilgas station within a radius of 30 mi. He is 53, the oldest father I know of. My mother was a beautiful French girl named Adrienne who came to live in Phoenix with my father but could not have any children until I was born after 9 yrs of married life. She named me Claudine after her dead sister and then died herself before leaving the hospital. It was a tragedy of life for my father. I never knew her but Aunt Lily has lived with us ever since and is like a mother to me. Everyone says so. She is 48. Cont. tomorrow."

Next day, alone up in the cupola, Claudine curled her feet beneath her and began to write. "What do I look like? I am four foot nine inches tall and weigh 87 lbs. Aunt Lily says that if I hold up my chin and straighten my shoulders some day I will be a distinguished looking woman. But right now I am homely, and I bet anything I am always going to be homely."

She paused to reach for a hand mirror that Robin had gotten from his Uncle Burgie. It had a fancy curved plastic handle, but the back had fallen off and a piece of the silver foil had peeled loose, so that when you looked at yourself in it there was a little hole smack in the middle of your forehead. You could squint through the hole clear to the tree outside the window, so that instead of seeing the skin on your forehead there would be a chickadee sitting freezing on the bare branch. "It goes to show," she wrote, "that once you can see not only the outside but the inside of your head, what you will find is a bird sitting on a branch where your brains are supposed to be." And while she was at it, she made up a poem about the mirror with the hole in it that showed you the world as well as your face.

Not long after this, Claudine brought a newspaper clipping up to the cupola and stuck it in the diary with LePage's paste. It read: MODERN KIDS KNOW TOO MUCH, STATE PROF CLAIMS. Underneath the headline she wrote, "Why is he so sure. If he went to my school he'd claim just the opposite. Those kids don't know anything except the Top Ten." She hesitated, and then crossed out the last four words out of loyalty to Robin.

"The real trouble is, they see more and more on TV, but they know less and less. They act wise but they think stupid."

When there was nothing special in the newspapers, Claudine wrote about her teachers ("Miss Bidwell wears stretch support stockings but she makes fun of other people"), her father ("I wish he didn't have to work such long hours, but what would he do at home? He never knows what to talk about to me or Aunt Lily"), and how she was changing so much every day it made her dizzy, even though when she looked in the mirror there she was, with the same popeyes and the same hole in the middle of her forehead. The only person she didn't describe, for reasons that weren't quite clear to her, was her Aunt Lily, who had to be in there when she wanted to write about food or clothes or books.

In about six months the diaries in the cupola were all written in. Claudine had to bring in the ones from the hut behind the diner and those Robin had wrapped in a poncho for her in the treehouse hut, and before she knew it they were filled up. Spring had come, and Claudine had been keenly aware of it, deserting the diaries for days on end to go fence walking and bike riding with Robin; but always she returned, when she was alone, to the diaries. It was almost as if without them she would have no excuse for being alone—or even for being.

And indeed it was strange that, once she had finished writing in the last of the diaries and brought her story up to date, putting on paper practically everything she had ever wanted to say, Claudine fell ill.

It was a tremendous worry to Mr. Crouse, who couldn't cope with sickness, especially when the doctor wouldn't put an exact name to it. Despite everything his sister did, from making broths and compresses to reading to Claudine by the hour, her fever did not abate and at last she had to be taken to the hospital. There her weakened condition and lassitude were labeled as probable infectious mononucleosis, a very popular disease with children, but nobody would commit himself for sure. All they knew was that it seemed likely to be a long, slow business.

For Lily Crouse the house was now unbearably quiet, even though Claudine usually kept to herself when she was home. Just the idea that Claudine was up there in the cupola, doing Lord knew what with the Wales boy or even all by herself, had been comforting; but to come home from the library to that huge, ugly house and find it absolutely empty was almost more than Lily could stand. She would even have welcomed

Robin's noisy presence, his piercing whistle and jangling transistor, but he never came by now—she was more likely to bump into him in the corridors of the hospital, where he came regularly to bring Claudine the gossip about Eddie, Walter, Miss Bidwell and others.

One day, driven by uneasiness and loneliness, although she tried to tell herself that it was simply a desire to track down a lost library book (Gavin Maxwell's book on otters, actually, which Claudine had loved), Lily climbed the steep steps to the cupola. She had never once gone there during all the time that Claudine and Robin had been using it as a hideaway. Maybe Claudine had actually asked her not to, and she had promised—she couldn't quite remember. In any case the funny room looked absolutely unfamiliar; the kids had festooned the place with political posters and crepe paper left over from old birthday parties. A tatty, grease-stained straw mat lay on the floor and, against the wall, a lopsided bookcase was propped at one corner with broken ends of brick. In the bookcase were three rows of old diary volumes. Lily pulled one out and began to riffle its pages idly.

Several hours later, Lily crept down the stairs, her legs aching from having squatted for so long in one position. She went directly to her room and sat down at the desk where she kept the household accounts and mailed out statements to Fred's customers. Now she addressed an envelope to Josephine Schaefer, a classmate who had been working in New York for some years as a secretary in a large and aggressively successful publishing house.

Dear Jo, she wrote, *Under separate cover I am mailing you a carton of diaries which I have just found. As you will see, they are numbered in consecutive order with little pieces of adhesive tape. They are the work of Claudie, who has apparently been doing this writing on the sly for quite some time. I don't exactly know what to make of them—which is why I am taking the liberty of imposing on you. Is there someone in your office whom you could show them to?*

Lily gnawed at the corner of her mouth, and then added: *The thing is, Claudie has been in the hospital for some time (that's why I haven't been able to get down to the city) with an undiagnosed illness from which she is recuperating very slowly. I have a feeling now that it is all mixed up with what she's been writing, but anyway I don't want her to know I've been reading her private diaries—much less that I shipped them out of the house for anyone else's eyes. I'm sure you understand. Forgive me for not writing sooner, but as you can imagine things have been difficult here, what with Fred having to have a quick dinner and then scoot off to the hospital. Say hello to Janie—yours ever—Lily*

It seemed to her only days later that the phone was ringing, wildly and demandingly, as Lily entered the empty echoing house. She hastened anxiously to the telephone, reaching out for it as she ran.

"Lily, it's me—Jo. Mr. Knowles says he sat up half the night with Claudine's diaries, and he wants to talk to you about them. All right?"

"Why, yes," she said uncertainly, "I suppose so."

In a moment a man's voice was saying, "Miss Crouse, I am grateful to you for sending us your niece's diaries. I would like very much to publish them, exactly as they are, and I think the firm will agree with me. They're a find. They're brilliant, they're unspoiled, there isn't a false note. Still, I have to ask you something."

Lily wanted very much to speak, but no words would come out. She moistened her lips, but it was no good.

Fortunately Mr. Knowles did not seem to expect a formal reply. "Miss Schaefer tells me that you're a librarian, Miss Crouse, and that Claudine is a small-town child, never been to New York more than once or twice, to Radio City Music Hall and the Metropolitan Museum. Can you assure me that you haven't had anything to do with her manuscript—I mean in the way of suggesting things to her to include or to leave out, or to change in any way?"

"Mr. Knowles," Lily said heatedly, "I never even knew those diaries existed until a few days ago. I never changed one word before I mailed them in to Jo. And if you don't believe me—"

"Your word is more than enough. I would like to take a run up to visit you, though, if I may. And Claudine, of course. When would it be most convenient, Miss Crouse?"

All she could think of to say was "Claudie is a very sick girl."

"Then we'll be in touch. Perhaps when she's well enough to travel, you can both come down here, as guests of the firm?"

That was the way it stood when Lily made her next visit to the hospital —she tried to space her visits between those of Fred and of Robin Wales. Claudine was propped up on two of those long, flat, slablike institutional pillows, her head so small and unsubstantial that it looked like some doll's carelessly placed in the middle of the bed. The pallor of her lengthy confinement accentuated the glitter of those pale prominent eyes, grown even more bulbous during the illness. Her forehead, too, jutted more sharply than ever (I'll have to make her bangs, Lily thought; surely that will help), while her body seemed scarcely to exist beneath the hospital blanket. She had been reading *A Tale of Two Cities,* which lay beside her on the coverlet.

"I like this," she said, pointing to it but scarcely opening her eyes. "Can you bring me some more Dickens books?"

"Listen, Claudie," Lily said determinedly, "I found your diaries."

Claudine gazed at her blankly. "They weren't lost."

"I mean, I read them." More unnerved by Claudine's silence than she had been by Mr. Knowles's talk, Lily added lamely, "It wasn't that I meant to pry. I was looking for a library book, and I just wondered what was in those old diaries, and then when I did open them . . ."

Claudine stared at her, expressionless. She did not protest, or indicate that she had any intention of interrupting. Finally Lily added, "Well, I thought they were just fascinating. Claudie, I do hope you're not angry."

"Why should I care?" Claudine gazed at her in puzzlement. "Listen, no fooling, can you bring me some more Dickens books? Like *Nicholas Nickleby?* I hear that's real good."

Lily stood helplessly at the bedside. It would be better to have Fred there, she guessed, before trying to explain about the publisher; and the doctor too—maybe she oughtn't to reveal anything more without consulting him. "Of course," she said. "I would have brought them with me now, except that I was a little, well, flustered."

Claudine could not have said why, but this announcement of Lily's, which only a month or two ago would have made her so angry that she would have been tempted to throw a babyish tantrum, now gave her a comfortable and comforting sense of relief. Is it like a secret that you don't want to tell but are sick of keeping and are glad when someone else finds it out and relieves you of the responsibility? It was almost better, she thought sleepily, snuggling down into the blankets, than the pills that the nurse gave her to swallow every evening and that made her drift off to sleep as though someone were paddling her off into the darkness on a Venetian gondola. As she heard Aunt Lily's footsteps fading away down the corridor, Claudine found herself thinking dreamily, It's over, it's over, and I'll get well now.

As soon as she awoke, refreshed and clear-headed, Claudine remembered those drowsy speculations. She had been right—it was all over—and she was restlessly eager to get out of the hospital. But the funny thing was, she observed in the next few days as she became more aware of others around her, that now Aunt Lily seemed to be suffering from the same symptoms that had afflicted her.

"I hope Aunt Lily didn't catch that bug from me," she said to her father when they were alone at home together, with Lily off to the library once again.

"Tootsie, what are you talking about?" Mr. Crouse demanded. "She's not sick or feverish. In fact she's back at work."

"Yes, but she's acting far away, like I was when it was first coming on. In fact . . . so are you."

And her father refused to look her in the eye. What was it, then? He was stubborn, like all adults, and there was no point in pressing him any further.

But Claudine knew she was right, and her suspicions were confirmed that Friday when she found her aunt furiously cleaning the house, as it had never been cleaned for as long as she could remember. What was more, Aunt Lily had made her a new corduroy jumper and bought her a blouse to go with it. Both had to be worn on Saturday morning, when Aunt Lily herself came out of her room with a brand-new outfit and two bright red spots on her cheekbones that might have been rouge but more likely were just plain excitement.

"What is this, the Fourth of July?" Claudine asked and was immediately sorry, for her aunt looked stricken.

"You know my friend Jo," Aunt Lily said, all in a rush. "Well, she is going to stop by for a bite of lunch with her boss, Mr. Knowles. He looks forward to meeting you."

"Me?" The whole thing sounded fishy. But it wasn't; it was all just as Aunt Lily had said. When it was over with, when Jo and Mr. Knowles had driven off in his little white sports car, Claudine couldn't even wait to wave goodbye to them before she was off to explain everything to Robin, who had been forbidden access to the house, much less to the cupola, for the entire day.

"He's a great big stoop-shouldered man with the most beautiful shoes you ever saw," she explained to Robin when she found him at last, up in the treehouse. "They look like they're hand-made out of that cloth they use to put over loud-speakers—you know, with the little nubs in it."

"What's so great about that?"

"He wants to publish my book."

"What book?"

Claudine had to tell him the whole business of the diaries, which in fact she had almost forgotten about until Mr. Knowles brought up the subject.

"Wait a minute," Robin said wisely. "Wait a minute. You mean that guy came all the way up here from New York City just to see those old books I gave you? Just because you wrote some stuff in them?"

"He read it already. He wants to call it *Claudine's Book.* He says it's one of the best books he's read in a long time, and anyway I'm the youngest person he ever heard of to write a whole book."

"Are you going to get money for it?"

"I don't know. We didn't talk about that. Anyway my father would keep it for me, like he does my birthday money. Mr. Knowles was more interested in how I wrote the book, and where I wrote it, and all that. He made me take him up to the cupola and show him just how it was."

Robin was eying her somewhat suspiciously. "Did you tell him all about our huts?"

"Only what I had to. I mean, about your giving me the diaries and things like that. He didn't care about the huts, he just wanted to make sure I wrote it all myself."

"Who did he think wrote it? Me?"

Claudine shrugged. "What's the difference? I told him you were my very best friend, and that was why you gave me the diaries, and he said if I wanted to I could dedicate the book to you, instead of to Daddy or Aunt Lily."

But Robin had already lost interest, which was all right as far as Claudine was concerned, because in her heart she was even more surprised than he that anyone else, particularly a grownup, should be all that interested in what they had been doing. Robin had a pretty grandiose plan for a dam that would convert the little creek behind the Wales house into a fish hatchery.

They put a good part of the summer into the dam, with very few arguments except when Robin insisted on being insufferably bossy, and Claudine felt no great need to be off by herself, clipping newspapers and writing thoughts down—the way it was last winter, she reflected, when I was younger. They never did exactly finish the hatchery, because school started before they had collected all the stuff for the dam. And then, a couple of months after school had begun, Claudine's book arrived.

On the front of it was a great big picture of her with a dopey expression and her hair pulled back with a ribbon, and underneath in big letters, *Today begins my life story . . .*

"Gee, I look awful," she said to her aunt.

Lily stared at her, astonished. "Aren't you excited? Aren't you proud?"

"I guess."

"Wait till the other children see the book. And your teachers! Then you won't be such a cool one."

It was true: the fuss was really something when the books turned up all over Phoenix. Kids that had ignored her for years wanted her to sit with them in the cafeteria. She was elected vice-president of her home room and made playground monitor. And Miss Bidwell—the old faker!—acted like she and Claudine had always been dear friends, and even asked her to sign her autograph on the title page of the book.

"But you know something?" she said to Robin as they pushed through the piles of heaped-up leaves on Genesee Street on their way home. "I think the whole thing is a pain in the neck."

"This is only the beginning, folks!" Robin shouted at her. "You ain't seen nothin' yet!"

"I'd rather be left alone."

"Then you shouldn't have written all that. Who forced you to do it? Nobody twisted your arm. When you make your bed you have to lie in it."

"That's a cliché. You don't even know what a cliché *is.*"

But it did make her uneasy in the days that followed, being stopped at her father's service station or in front of Dohrmeyer's Meat Market by total strangers who wanted her to pose with them for pictures, or sign things, or tell them what she would be when she grew up: was it really all her fault for writing in Robin's diaries? Claudine became more irritable as the demands on her got worse, and finally she took it out on Robin, mainly because instead of sympathizing he kept giving her more clichés.

"If it hadn't been for you and your Uncle Burgie and all those old diaries, I never would have gotten into all this trouble."

Robin was very hurt. He said she was ungrateful and bratty, and he wasn't going to play with her any more. In fact he wasn't even going to talk to her. She could hang out with her new fair-weather friends instead.

In the middle of all this a group of strangers checked in the Al-Rae Motel up the street from Mr. Crouse's Mobil station and fanned out from there like a bunch of G-Men after a kidnaper—as if everyone in Phoenix didn't know what they were up to even before they had unpacked their bags. There were four of them, three men and a young woman researcher. They were all employed by a big picture magazine—the bearded Hungarian, weighted down with leather tote bags, was a photographer, the cynical young man with pockmarks was a writer, and the man who spoke in a whisper (as though, Claudine thought, he was ashamed of his own voice) was a consulting child psychologist.

The girl researcher, who was pretty, with a big wide mouth and an Irish grin, turned up everyplace you could think of, the photographer trotting along after, muttering in Hungarian and measuring the air with his light meter. They walked right into the school as if they owned it—you could see them through the seventh-grade window—and took millions of pictures. Then they went off in their rented Ford to the F. Crouse Mobil station, and the next day, which was Saturday, they were prowling around Robin's huts, even trying to climb into his treehouse. Claudine was afraid that Robin would think she had tipped them off (actually, they must have studied up on the huts in her book) and would get twice as sore. But he was keeping to his promise not to talk to her.

The other two, the pock-marked writer always grinning skeptically, as though he didn't even believe that the world was round, and the whispering psychologist, were much less in evidence. For a while Claudine didn't even know where they were, and it wasn't until they came to her house and sat down in the parlor with Aunt Lily that she got wind of what they were up to.

Aunt Lily thought Claudine had gone to the movies with Robin to see a Charlton Heston movie about God, so it was easy to sneak in through the kitchen pantry and listen. The child psychologist was doing most of the talking, in his tiny baby voice, and Aunt Lily, all dolled up with coral earrings and toilet water and her silk scarf, was sitting on the edge of her chair ready to fall off, listening so hard her earrings were practically standing on end.

"Surely it is obvious to a woman of your intelligence, Miss Crouse," the child psychologist was whispering, "that you have been responsible for the upbringing of one of the most remarkable children of modern times. That is, assuming that Claudine did all of the writing of the book herself."

"Why did you add that?"

From her vantage post Claudine could not see the psychologist, but she was in line with Aunt Lily's bust, rising and falling very fast, and with the pock-marked writer, grinning like an absolute fiend.

"Because in all of my years of experience, both in the clinic and in the field, I have never encountered such a combination of insight and steadfastness in one so young."

"You have to remember, Dr. Fibbage (that was what the name sounded like to Claudine), she has been very ingrown. She's had only one real friend, and no one but me to turn to for books and ideas."

The writer broke in, "Miss Crouse, I must say that it is your ideas and your sensitivity that I find in *Claudine's Book.*"

Claudine was fascinated by the expression that stole over her aunt's face. It was exactly like that of Aunt Lily's fat friend Marie Klemfuss when someone tried to tempt her off her crash diet with a slice of angel-food cake—a mixture of fear, greed and calculation.

"Well," her aunt said slowly, "if Mr. Knowles believed me when he first decided to publish it, I don't see why I should have to explain any further."

"Mr. Knowles couldn't have known you as we do."

Aunt Lily turned red, and the writer, Mr. Craft, added hastily, "I'm not suggesting that you would ever deceive anyone. But in addition to being an intellectual, you are a very modest person. Obviously you would be reluctant to confirm the extent of your influence on little Claudine."

Little Claudine! All of a sudden she felt like throwing up. She tiptoed backward, pulled open the screen door soundlessly, and bolted off down the street. When she got to the Waleses she went right on into the kitchen without knocking and almost bumped into Robin, who was running his thumb around the inside edge of a jar of Skippy peanut butter.

"Don't tell me you're not going to speak to me," Claudine said breathlessly, taking advantage of the fact that Robin's mouth was stuck with peanut butter. "If you heard what I just did, you'd want advice too."

He listened quite impassively to her description of Aunt Lily and the two visitors, and even turned down the volume of his transistor. But when she reached the part where Aunt Lily got the hungry look in her eye, Robin held up his hand.

"Just a sec." He twisted the dial to a roar. "And now the one you've asked for, the Madmen singing the number-one hit of the week, 'Weeping and Wailing.' "

Robin turned off the radio and said, very practically, "It's all clear to me. Those people are out to make trouble for you. They'll hound you worse than the Beatles."

"Don't you think I know that?"

"They're just zeroing in on you now—I heard all about the technique on Long John's program. First they interview your friends, then your enemies, and then your family. By the time they get to you, they know all about you and you feel like they've been reading your mail or listening to you talk in your sleep. Well, that's the way the ball bounces, Claudie."

"You and your expressions. They'll be after you too, watch and see."

"They were already. Where do you think they came before they got to your house?"

Claudine stared. "What did you tell them?"

"Nothing special." Robin was very casual. "I told them I got the diaries from Uncle Burgie for decoration for the huts. I told them I never knew what you did with them. I told them you had a good imagination, almost as good as mine."

"Thanks."

"They asked me about your aunt. I said she was the smartest lady in Phoenix, smarter than all our teachers put together, starting with Miss Bidwell."

"That wouldn't take much." Claudine thought for a moment. "Got any crackers?"

"Just Ritz."

"I like them." She dug deep into the box he offered her. "I can tell you've got an idea."

Robin nodded. "As long as everybody thinks you did the book all by yourself, they'll be after you. People like that Mr. Fibbage—"

"Dr. Fibbage."

"What's the diff? He'll hang around studying you like you were in a bottle. And they'll keep on pointing at you wherever you go. When you get to high school all the teachers will say, Well, Miss Crouse, I should think anyone who could write a whole book could do better than eighty-two on a simple test. And if you want to go to college—"

Claudine shuddered. "I could change my name, though."

"They're on to you. You think Jackie Kennedy could change her name?"

Claudine listened intently. Robin had a crazy imagination, but he was very smart when it came to practical matters. Smarter, in fact, than her own father, the only other person in the world with whom she might have consulted about this thing. Her father would be of no help at all. He meant well, when he was around, but he had never been able to bring himself to say anything to her about the book (as if it was dirty), so this was a decision she would have to make by herself. Ever since the business about the book had come out, Mr. Crouse had taken to looking at his daughter peculiarly; and now that it had gotten out of hand, he seemed positively frightened of her, as though he had fathered a witch.

Claudine walked home slowly. By the time she got there, the pock-marked writer and Dr. Fibbage were standing on the porch saying good-bye to Aunt Lily, who was clenching her hands tightly together, as if she held something between them, like a little bird, that she was afraid would fly away.

"Well, well, well," whispered Dr. Fibbage, "and here is Claudine. Just the very person I'd like to see."

"Would you like to see us, Claudine?" asked Mr. Craft, grinning at her as if he were about to eat her. The way he put it, she would be chicken if she said no. "I'll buy you a soda downtown if it's all right with your aunt."

"If Claudine would like to go . . ." Aunt Lily said faintly.

"Sure I would." Before anyone could say another word, she was leading the way to their shiny rented car. "I'll be back soon, Aunt Lily."

"We won't keep her long."

"A very unusual woman, your aunt," the psychologist whispered to her from the back seat, and peered at her intently.

"That's for sure," Claudine said.

"You're not so very usual yourself," Mr. Craft remarked as he headed the car down to Main Street. "Muscling in on my racket like that. I got enough trouble with the competition without having to fend off eleven-year-old kids."

"I'm almost twelve."

"Big deal."

"Say, Mr. Craft," she asked, "do you like writing?"

"It beats working, I'll tell you that. But then I'm not famous. Just well known. How about you?"

"Oh, I got bored with it by the time I finished up the diaries. I don't think I'll do any more."

"What makes you say that?" the doctor demanded eagerly.

"I just told you. It's boring. Besides, I got sick of my aunt nagging at me to fill up all those diaries."

"You what?" All of a sudden Dr. Fibbage was panting like a dog in the summer sun. "You mean your aunt knew about the book while you were writing it?"

"Hey," Claudine said to Mr. Craft, "stop here, at O'Molony's Pharmacy. They've got the best ice cream, with the little chunks in it, not the Softi-Freeze stuff."

"Wait a minute," Dr. Fibbage whispered at the top of his lungs as they stood in front of the drugstore. "You haven't answered my question yet."

"Can I have my sundae? Then we can talk some more."

In the booth, after she had ordered a Phoenix Monster Sundae, Claudine said to Dr. Fibbage, "Why did you get so shook up when I told you my aunt knew about the book?"

"Because it was supposed to have been as much of a surprise to her as it was to the rest of us, later on."

"Oh, she's just modest. You said yourself she's very unusual. The fact is, she thought up the whole thing, practically. Mr. Craft, be careful, you're spilling coffee on your tie."

"My hands are shaky. That's what too much writing does," the writer said to her. "I thought I heard you say the book was your aunt's and not yours. Isn't that silly of me?"

"Well, if you'll promise not to tell anybody . . . I mean, I promised my aunt I wouldn't tell anybody. But I don't think it's fair for me to keep getting all the credit and have people buying me sundaes and taking my picture and everything, when actually most of the good stuff in the book is Aunt Lily's. She loves to make believe. It was her idea right from the start, except she was afraid people would make fun of her, so she decided to put everything in my name."

She looked across the table at the child psychologist. "Dr. Fibbage," she said, "you look like you just saw a ghost. Did I say something wrong?"

He reached out uneasily to pat her hand. "I'm unused to such honesty from someone so young."

"Claudine is a red-blooded American girl, that's why," Mr. Craft said heartily. "Here you thought you could watch Emily Dickinson grow up under your microscope, Fibbage, and instead you found yourself buying Monster Sundaes for a healthy, normal seventh-grader. Am I right or wrong, Claudine?"

"You couldn't be more right, Mr. Craft," Claudine replied after she had licked off her spoon. "You know something? You talk very sensibly, for a writer. I told my friend Robin Wales that writers could be as sensible as architects—that's what he's going to be. I'm beginning to think maybe some day I'll be a writer after all—I mean a real one, not an imitation. Well," she said, rising, "goodbye now, and thanks a lot for the sundae. I promised Robin I'd play with him if all the reporters and photographers would leave us alone. And I guess now they will, won't they?"

At the front of the drugstore, Claudine turned to look back at the two men who stood at the cashier's counter, their feet nailed to the floor, staring after her. She waved farewell to them and, whistling the "Marseillaise," ran off down the street in search of Robin.

TEASE

For many years I have told a story on myself, the point of which was, I supposed, that as a young man I was a good-natured fool. Now, however, if I regard what happened not as a joke on me but as a revelation of what we are all capable of, I remember something very different. It is as though my young protagonist were no longer the self I cherish with such wry and amused fondness, but had become instead a stranger—a wild and predatory stranger. But here is the story as I used to tell it:

When I was twenty-one a college classmate and I got temporary jobs in the Panama Canal Zone, jobs that seemed glamorous beforehand but turned out to be drab and routine. Only the after-hours night life was fun, and even that palled after a few weeks.

One night we decided to change our luck by crossing the Isthmus and spending the night, and our money, in Colón instead of in Panama City. Not that the program there would be any different. Rum-and-Cokes while we watched the jugglers, the tango teams and the imported strippers, and tried without real hope to make the B-girls, hired to separate tourists, sailors and other fools from their wallets without yielding up anything more than a smile or a dance. It made no more sense than going, say, from Brooklyn to Newark in search of novelty. But at least the décor, the faces and the bodies would be different.

So we went off on the Toonerville railroad that joggled us across the thin strip of jungle separating one ocean from another. We bought round-trip tickets, to make sure that we'd get back, but for the rest of it we decided to leave things to chance.

"Let's make a pact," I proposed to Tommy. He was the kind who could appear calmly sober all evening, and then amaze people who didn't know him by passing out with his face on the table top, or slipping slowly to the floor. "We'll take along twenty bucks apiece and go as far as we can on it. Agreed?"

He understood me. We were already weary of those cold-blooded whorehouses—the Villa Amor, Las Tres Palmas and the rest—where, although you could drink at your leisure and dance with the girls before-hand, you were rousted unceremoniously from their cubicles in order that they might hurry down and hustle up the next customer. We were tired too of the streetwalkers. It was true that they were not supervised and hence were more human: They led you languidly, even at dawn, into the rabbit warrens where they lived and fornicated, down endless ramshackle open corridors teetering above the littered courtyards alive with scrawny squawking chickens, past room after doorless room, one with an Indian mother vacantly suckling an infant, another with a pipe-smoking toothless grandfather opening a mango with fingers gnarled like roots, a third and fourth with a nude couple snoring as they slept or scratching themselves as they quarreled above a wailing phonograph, until finally you reached the girl's own room, her very own because she earned it by flinging herself down on her back on the pallet, yanking her print dress up over her naked belly and giggling as she beckoned to you with her brown hand. Yes, they were all too human, but if they complimented you on your manliness, they could give you no faith in your personal charm.

For that we had turned to the B-girls. The Americans resident in the Zone had promptly discovered, as such people always know such things, that Tommy and I were not even candidate members of the colony but were only transients, and therefore they protected their daughters from us, with perfect justification, as if they knew that our motives were the worst. Those waxen-looking girls living lonesomely in the tropics—of whom we were told by a bartender (citing no authority) that they were pale because they menstruated twice a month—were as unappealing to us adventurers as, say, pygmy women to explorers on safari. They were safer than they knew.

And so we had taken up the game of trying to conquer Latin night-club hostesses who, although they were hired to please, had no slightest intention of allowing themselves to be conquered, no matter how much money, energy and charm you invested in them. Practiced in capturing your interest on the dance floor or at the little tables across which they leaned to display their shadowed charms, they sensed precisely how many drinks of colored water they could con you into buying them, at a dollar a shot, before your patience or your funds ran out, or before the last floor show faded away late in the night. These professional persuaders were more firmly determined to avoid genuine intimacy, we had learned at some cost, than the most carefully nurtured Yankee maidens. But the more we—unlike the tourist suckers—knew of their determination, the more we were tempted to overcome it, not by buying them but by winning them. That was why Tommy understood at once what rules I was proposing for the old game we had tacitly agreed to play in new surroundings.

When the train pulled in, we strolled about and had a leisurely dinner. Before it was fairly dark we were pub-crawling.

I cannot recall anything about the first places we went to. One drink at each sufficed to convince us that they were no different from those of Panama City. The one we finally settled at, though, remains fixed in my mind, because it was there that I encountered Isabel.

When we drifted in the band was just finishing "Begin the Beguine," behind a horribly grinning, lacquered male singer. As we pushed through to a ringside table they went into a fanfare, not for us but for an American stripper introduced by the singer as Pepper Mint, or something of the sort. The lights went down and the girl came out bathed in a green spot, and began to glide sinuously before us, the horizontal bands of cigarette smoke shifting in the poor light as she disturbed them with her weaving arms, hips, and legs.

She was extraordinarily good, gifted at what she was being paid to convey. In a few moments she had wriggled down to nakedness, or to very little more than high-heeled pumps. Her body was magnificent, and it was most disturbing to have that greenish torso twisting and flexing before us within arm's reach. Tommy was breathing so hard as she skidded offstage, her dimpled buttocks winking farewell, that he could not find his voice to dismiss the two B-girls who sidled up and slid and into the empty chairs at our table.

"You like to buy us a drink, yes?"

I shrugged. "One round. We're not rich tourists."

The blond one, who had seated herself at my side, laughed unaffectedly. "Was too much for you, the dancer?"

"Not for me," I protested, and sat up to examine her. She was a grinning, self-confident woman in her late twenties. Her dyed hair went well with a creamy skin the color of light coffee. She had slim, quick fingers that flicked and snapped like her eyes when she spoke, and teeth that showed irregular but very white when she smiled her oddly reckless smile.

"Isabel. I call you Toby, you look like a cat with those fat cheeks, okay?"

She had me. She was an impudent one, and maybe it was because of that that I was challenged into making her see me, and admire me, not just as a source of revenue but as a man.

Once the floor show was over we started to talk. My Spanish was impossible; her English was like a movie Mexican's, good for a million laughs. Between laughs, and drinks, I learned that she was in fact a Mexican, or so she said, from some hopeless village near Veracruz, where she had waited on tables and earned just enough, entertaining sailors in waterfront bars, to keep from prostitution. She had beaten her way down to Panama for reasons as vaguely stated as mine, but her safari must have involved a nerve that I wasn't even sure I possessed. Now she was selling not exactly her body but her sensuality and her whimsical appeal.

In fact, in precise proportion to the degree that she charmed me, I wanted to charm her, to impress her, to make her like me. Tommy, stimulated no doubt by the luscious memory of the stripper, was more concerned simply with making out with Luisa, a chunky and matter-of-fact woman who could be gay, as she was paid to be, only by some effort of will.

The catch, though, was that in order for Tommy to make out, he had to be charming; and in order for me to be sure that I was really a charmer, I had to make out.

So Tommy allowed Luisa to make admiring sounds as she felt his biceps, and bought her more drinks. And I, good old Toby, bought Isabel more drinks too. The more we drank, the later it got, the more Tommy and I had invested in our endeavor. Isabel and I did not dance even once, although we had the opportunity all evening long on that crowded dance floor to press the lengths of our bodies against each other.

Why didn't we? I didn't want anything so easy, I didn't want to be paid in installments, and as I looked over Isabel's shoulder, sliding so warm and brown within her semitransparent white blouse in time to the band's rhythm, and watched Tommy grappling doggedly with hefty Luisa, dragging her like a sack of maize across the floor already cluttered with sailors and their B-girls, I knew, as though it were written out for me like the printed prophecy that pops out at you from a penny scale, that Tommy would get nowhere, while I—well, I had a chance.

"It's getting late," I said to Isabel. Then, smiling with all my heart: "Let's be serious. You know what I want. I want to go home with you tonight."

"Toby, you sweet, you can't do that." She shook her head solemnly, but softened the refusal by showing me her white, white teeth.

"Don't read me the rules." I reached out for her forearm and took it tightly in my hand. It was almost the first time I'd touched her; I felt a shock of pleasure and was warmed to see her face turn grave. She knew that she could not just put me off. Gripping her arm until I could feel her pulse, I said, "I'm not buying any more fake drinks unless you tell me yes. I don't want to buy you, I like you too much, you savvy? I want you to like me that way."

"I do." Her tone was absolutely unfeigned. Even the fact that she didn't look at me, but sat with lowered lids, gazing thoughtfully at my fingers on her arm, convinced me. Then, as if coming to a decision, she glanced around, checking on the waiter, who was busy at another table, checking on the *patron,* who was bawling out a bartender at the register, and finally fixed her brilliant liquid eyes on me. "You can't go with me —but maybe I can go with you."

"Don't say maybe. Say for sure."

"All right, I say sure, if you buy us a room. But don't tell your friend."

I was happy to promise. I even bought the next round, although it was Tommy's turn. We were both close to being drunk, and closer to being broke, and we arose with exaggerated politeness as the girls went off together to the john. It was late, the crowd had thinned out, and the drummer saluted our gallantry with a ruffle and a spinning of one of his sticks high in the air, grinning and showing us his gold teeth as he caught it.

"*Salud!*" Tommy called out, raising his drink. But to me he said, "The women are fixing to dump us."

"How do you know?"

"Luisa's got a bicycle parked out back. She and Isabel come to work on it, with Isabel sitting on the back fender."

"So?"

"They got to go home the same way."

I had to laugh. "Listen, pal," I said, "if I get Isabel out the front door, you think you can cope with Luisa and her two-wheeler? You think you can cope?"

"I'll tell you one thing," Tommy replied with dignity. "I'm going to give it the old college try."

The girls were already on their way back to the table. I said hastily, "Here's luck. And check your wallet for the train ticket—it's a long walk back."

We made it very clear to the waiter that our spending was over. The *patron* had no cause for complaint; he looked up from counting dollars and balboas and even mustered a greasy good-night smile as his girls checked out. A couple of cabs were drowsing at the curb, and I hustled Isabel into the nearest one before she could change her mind. Laughing and squirming, she twisted about so that she could blow a farewell kiss to Luisa through the back window.

I had my hand on the bony shoulder of the sleepy Negro hackie, but I hesitated before pressing him on, in order that I might get one last glimpse of Tommy and Luisa. I was rewarded. While we craned our necks, Luisa emerged from the shadows of the alleyway next to the night club, whose neon sign had just been cut off. As she pushed her bike to the sidewalk, she was evidently arguing with Tommy, whose head was shrinking down like a bull's to protect him from the rain, which was starting to patter, then to bounce off the ground. She thrust her chunky body forward, climbed aboard and began to pedal off, with Tommy trotting along beside her.

Isabel was laughing, softly at first, and then wildly, her head back against the upholstery, her breasts shaking as she clapped her hands. "*La lluvia,*" she gasped, "the rain!"

"What about it?"

"The more it rain, the faster she go. The faster she go, the harder he run. You know something, Toby? He never gonna catch her."

"I never thought he would." I was torn between guilt and gloating. "Never mind them. Where should we—"

Isabel gazed at me sweetly. "I know nice hotel. Brand-new."

"I can hardly wait."

"But we got to stop first. Not too far. I got a girl friend—"

"Another one?"

"You silly! I meet her sometime after work. Poor. No money. In the rain . . ." She looked at me pleadingly.

"You're breaking my heart." There was nothing I could do. Besides, I was curious. "What are we going to do with her?"

"Maybe we get a sanvich."

"It can't be anything more than that. I blew all my dough on your phony drinks."

"No-no, you'll see." She leaned forward and shot a stream of Spanish at the driver, who nodded drowsily, threw the car into gear, and released the clutch with a jerk.

We were pitched against each other. At last. Breathing in her fragrance, a mixture of some cheap lilac perfume and the friendly odor of her warm body, I pressed her to me. She smiled luxuriously and murmured something I did not catch.

"You do like me?" I asked. "Really like me?"

For answer she raised her hand and ran her fingers through my hair. She was a little weary, not so eager as I, and five or six years older, maybe more; but her answer was yes, of that I was convinced. Reassured, I bent to kiss her lips.

But the taxi stopped joltingly. I looked up, annoyed. From the shadows of a darkened store front there stepped forward a big sullen-faced girl with wet hair half plastered to her skull, a terrible complexion and a man's zipper jacket flung carelessly over her shoulders. She opened the door of the cab without being invited, as though she had been expecting us.

Isabel introduced her to me as Gertrudis or something equally ugly—any name would have seemed ugly—but it made no difference, since her lack of interest in me bordered on the absolute. Wedging her wet bulk firmly into the back seat, she launched at once into a lengthy speech none of which I could understand, partly because of that Central American way of speaking as though Spanish consisted of nothing but a run-together series of liquid vowels. Although she salivated as she spoke, and gesticulated broadly with her mannish, reddened hands, she did not betray any genuine animation in speech or gesture. All that mattered anyway was that Isabel was far more excited by her than by me.

We had gone no more than a dozen blocks when the driver brought us to a halt before an all-night milk bar. The girls scrambled out and hurried on inside, their heads bent against the raindrops, leaving me to deal with the cab driver, who had already slumped over into a foetal position, chin against his chest and hands pressed between his upraised thighs.

"*Cuánto cobra usted—*" I began, but the driver interrupted without even troubling to open his eyes.

"I wait."

I glanced through the dripping window at the milk bar. Isabel, laughing and chattering, was urging her friend to eat. It was becoming painfully clear that the whole scene had taken place before. Well, I was damned if I was going to give up now. I clenched my teeth and went on in.

Isabel patted the leatherette stool at her left. "Toby, you better eat too. Is late."

"You're telling me?"

I had a soft drink while I waited and watched. Isabel was sipping at a milkshake in this oasis of light in a darkened city and hanging on her friend's words—uttered between huge gulps of bread and cheese—as though each one was precious. Gertrudis was a big eater—a second sandwich soon went the way of the first—but she seemed to derive no more satisfaction from this than from her talking, which made Isabel's eyes sparkle and from time to time doubled her up with laughter. I might just as well not have been there. At least, not until it was time to pay the *cuenta*.

Isabel looked away with a new-found delicacy as I fumbled through my pockets. The bill was less than I had expected, though, and I managed a smile as she thanked me. Her friend, the boillike blemishes standing out garishly on her sullen countenance in the lavender light of the fluorescent tubes, did not bother to acknowledge me, but simply shrugged the zipper jacket over her meaty shoulders. Before she slouched on out to the taxi, she threw a farewell remark at the counterman, who mumbled something casual around his dry, dangling cigarette butt as he cleared away our little debris. Apparently they were all buddies.

When I re-entered the cab, though, grimly ready to outlast my new antagonist, Isabel snuggled into the crook of my arm and pressed tightly against me as we drove off.

"Now we go to hotel."

"I don't want to rush you," I said. "It's only four A.M."

"You funny." She murmured to Gertrudis, *"Está burlesco."*

Her friend didn't crack a smile. It had been clear enough since she had come into my cab from out of the rain that she didn't like men. I released myself from Isabel.

"The rain has stopped," I said. "Isn't it about time that we dropped off your friend?"

"We get out first," she replied equably. "Then her."

While I was thinking this over, I had a chance to survey the slick, silent streets, which seemed to be getting a little familiar.

"How does this guy know where to go," I asked Isabel after a while, "if nobody tells him?"

"He knows," she said simply. "I already tol' him."

"Well," I said, "you better tell him to go the old-fashioned way. We've already passed this plaza twice. Once more and I'll own the cab."

She leaned forward and spoke sharply to the hackie, who gave no indication of discomfiture, but continued to drive us sedately through the night while the blotchy-faced girl droned on in her unpleasant way. Even though Isabel was leaning against me as she listened, I was growing sleepy.

At last we pulled up before a squat, freshly stuccoed building which, save for its vertical neon HOTEL SUPERBA, might have been a veterinary clinic. Blithe as if we were off to a Sunday picnic, Isabel hopped out, leaving me for the moment with Gertrudis, who was smoking a little brown cigarette and spitting tobacco shreds onto the floor mat.

"I go in first," Isabel called to me. "You pay him, yes?"

I paid him, all right, after a miserable effort to argue. When I put back my wallet it was practically empty, but it was worth all of it, I thought, to see the last of that rude and sulky young woman, who said nothing as I hastened eagerly after Isabel.

I found her in the lobby, shaking the night clerk, who was trying obstinately to stay asleep in his tilted chair, with the immutable stubbornness of the stoically enduring. He had no protection, and no equipment beyond a freshly sawed table desk sitting on opaque glass blocks. Behind his nodding head hung a raw, unfinished rack for depositing mail and room keys. The dark cubbyholes gaped emptily. It was like staring into the vacant sockets of a jaw from which every tooth has been extracted. Isabel and I, it was plain, were alone with the desperately sleeping Indian in a building that might have been put up just for this one night.

I yanked his chair upright by its left leg.

"Numero once," he groaned, scratching his bare brown belly with one hand—his embroidered white shirt hung unbuttoned to the navel—and with the other extending a key hooked to a hard rubber ball so huge that you couldn't stuff it into a pocket even if you wanted to. Someone had painted the number 11 on it in white.

"Hold on." I was very conscious of exactly how much I had left in my wallet. *"Cuánto?"*

He spread the fat fingers of one hand and displayed them. *"Cinco."*

I looked at Isabel. She had helped a lot of people to my money: not only her boss but also the cabbie, her peculiar girl friend, the counterman at the milk bar, and now the hotel clerk. From each, from all, no doubt, she took her cut.

But then, she had earned it. And I had stuck it out. What mattered, after all, was that she really and truly liked me. At least that was what she seemed to be saying to me as she stood blinking a little in the bare light, her fine legs apart and her bare arms akimbo, daring me not to like her, not to admire her for her dash and her nerve, not to pay. I drew a deep breath and, turning back to the clerk, exchanged money for key.

"Por dónde?" I demanded, my voice echoing through the empty hall.

He pointed his dirt-caked thumb dead ahead and then let the arm fall back against his belly, the fingers working their way into the folds of his flesh, like piglets searching for the teats of their recumbent mother.

"Come, Isabel," I said, leading her down the bleak uncarpeted corridor which, relieved only by grilled doors at regular intervals, had the clanking monotony of a cell block. Six, eight, seven, nine—we had the last room on the floor. I unlocked it and let her in.

With incomparable grace, Isabel held out her arms to me in the quiet of our ultimate sanctuary. A familiar gesture, but she endowed it with a rich and wonderful mystery. Our bodies close, we whispered, not because we had to but because it did not seem right to rupture the before-dawn silence. At last, I thought, at last, I've won! And I kissed her slowly, savoringly, deeply.

Isabel pushed at my arms, and as I lowered them my jacket fell to the chair at the side of the bed. She tugged gently at my loosened tie until she had it in her hand, then unbuttoned my wrinkled shirt and slipped it off too. I stood naked to the waist. As I stepped out of my loafers to more nearly equalize our heights, I began to fumble with the buttons of Isabel's white blouse.

She laughed a little, helping me. "You got big fingers. *Sin arte.*"

"That's because I'm nervous," I muttered. By the subdued light of the bed lamp I stared at her newly exposed throat and soft upper bosom, bronze-gold above the lace of her slip. "I'm dazzled. Isabel, Isabel, Isabel."

"Toby, you nice boy," she chuckled. "You do me one more favor."

I drew back in order to look at her, but did not answer.

"We get a room for my friend. She have no place to stay."

"Now you ask me? Why now?"

"I promise to. Gertrudis can't ask you herself. *Tímida.*"

"She looks it."

"What you say?" Isabel demanded, with just a touch of impatience. "I got to tell her, she's waiting with the taxi driver."

"She'd better stick with him—he's got the last of my dough."

Isabel was gazing at me sorrowfully. I unbuttoned my hip pocket, pulled out my wallet and spread it apart with my fingers. "You're looking at my train ticket and my last dollar bill. If you sandbagged me you wouldn't find anything more."

Even as I spoke, Isabel was buttoning her blouse. She tied the little bow at her throat and picked up her purse. "I go tell her," she said.

"You do that."

"You lie down, you look tired. Okay, Toby?"

"Okay."

After she had slipped out I lay down dizzily and waited, staring up at the frieze of cobwebbed cracks running along the upper wall of the plastered cell, hardly finished but already falling into disrepair. I might have been lying in the bare bedroom of a bleak new garden apartment in Bayside, Long Island. But not alone. Not all alone.

The time passed very slowly. I said to myself, She knew I didn't like that girl. Who would? The fact that I had no money left, for her or for anyone else, was more than just fate. It was her responsibility as much as mine.

But I could not go on talking to myself. I got up in my stockinged feet and padded out into the hallway. It was empty. I could see clear down to the sleeping clerk with no obstruction, human or otherwise. I started to run.

Without pausing at the clerk's desk I went right on to the door, which I struck with my shoulder, skidding to a halt on the slippery sidewalk beyond it. I peered first this way, then that. For as far as I could see, the length of the street in both directions was absolutely bare, and drying out here and there where it was touched by the first flush of dawn.

I walked back slowly into the Hotel Superba, my socks soaked through and plastered to the soles of my feet. I took hold of the snoring clerk and shook him awake ruthlessly.

"Did my girl friend go out?" I demanded. "Did she go away in the taxi?"

"No home," he mumbled. "No home."

I released my hold on his shirt. He fell back to sleep at once and I proceeded on down the blank corridor to its end, my wet socks leaving footprints on the unwashed plaster dust of the still unfinished tile flooring. Inside my room I stripped off the socks and, drawing the blind against the early dawn that was already seeping through the window, I threw myself down on the bed once more. Unslaked, my lust turned—like a glass of milk left undrunk—to a sour, hateful curd. I lay for a long while, burning and seething, frustrated, shamed, humiliated. It was only after seemingly endless hours that exhaustion overcame me, and I fell asleep.

But when I awoke, bewildered for an instant, alone in the strange room, I was finally able to laugh at myself.

That, in essence, is the story I have told others not once but many times in the years that have passed since it—or something like it—first happened to me. Presumably I tell it on myself when I want to show what a sucker, what a fool, a young man can be.

And when people press me—as some do—about what happened afterward, I tell them truthfully that I ate a cheap and greasy breakfast, caught the lurching train back to Panama City, and confessed laughingly to Tommy, once he had admitted that Luisa had outraced him on her bicycle, that I had wound up not with Isabel but with the morning paper.

But observe, as I do now, what a charming self-portrait I have succeeded in painting, what a wholesome person emerges from this "true"
recital: good-natured, sporting, able to laugh at himself, and above all
charitable. The only thing I have suppressed is the brief epilogue which
I must now relate.

Some days after that fruitless evening, Tommy was ordered to the other
end of the Isthmus, to Cristobal, for several days' work. The minute that
I heard this, I began to think of Isabel, whose very name I had put out
of my mind. All of my shame and resentment at being victimized came
rushing back, and I was taken by a rage for revenge.

With great casualness I said to Tommy, "I want you to look up Isabel
in Colón. You remember, the tease."

"If I get the chance," he said. "But you know, I can't afford that stuff."

"Who can? That's why I want to scare her out of pulling the same trick
on anyone else. Tell her I'm good and angry. *Furioso. Frenético.* Wait!"
I swiveled about in my chair and jammed a letterhead sheet into my
typewriter. Rapidly I typed out, in Spanish: "Señorita: I have not forgotten. You shall pay for your treason." Then I yanked it out and scrawled
an indecipherable signature beneath.

"There, that looks official. Tell her I'm negotiating with the proper
parties to have her taken care of. Physically."

"My Spanish isn't that good."

"Hers is. You won't have to draw a picture."

Tommy was a good fellow, if a little dull, but I couldn't predict whether
he would go through with it. So it wasn't until his return the following
week that I learned what had happened. Part of it I could see on his face
as he pushed through the swinging doors of the Pacifico, where I was
having the usual, Myers rum and Coke, before dinner. He wore a dubious
expression, as if he weren't quite sure what to say to me (as if, I thought
before casting the notion aside, he were reluctant even to greet me); and
the freckles on his forehead had darkened and grown blotchy.

"How did it go?" I asked him.

"Same as here." He waited until the bartender had brought him his
drink before adding, "I saw your friend."

"You gave her the message."

"Oh yes. She smiled at first. Either she didn't understand or she figured I was joking. So I took out your note. She stared at it and stared at it. First I thought maybe she was illiterate, but no, she began to jabber a mile a minute. In order to stop her I told her what you said, about hiring the Mafia to knock her around. Well, she started to tremble, you know, and her eyes filled with tears. She was pale, and biting on the letter as though—"

"Biting on what letter?"

"On your letter. The note you typed. Then she turned around and ran out of the bar like a deer, by the side exit, at the corner of the bandstand. I thought I'd better go after her—I didn't want to carry it too far—but when I asked the bartenders where she lived, they made out like they didn't know what I was talking about. I said to them, When she comes back tell her I was only kidding. But I don't know that she ever came back. If you ask me, by now she's on her way to Tampico, or wherever it was she came from."

I couldn't think of anything much to say. Tommy gulped down his drink a little more swiftly than usual and wound up, looking at his glass instead of at me, "I can't stick around tonight. Fact is, I've got a dinner date. I'll see you."

Why did I do it? None of the excuses that I can muster up even approaches adequacy. Just because she had humiliated me, did that give me warrant to terrorize her? I had accepted the rules of the game. I knew when I started that her livelihood, her very life, depended on her countering aggressive men with all the cunning she could conjure up.

No doubt it was to Gertrudis that she had turned, in miserable panic, for help in fleeing from those bandy-legged little Indian soldiers, strapped into their Sam Browne belts and serving both their provincial masters and whatever rich gringo could afford their services for a job of pistol-whipping. Isabel and Gertrudis knew in their bones what I understood without ever being honest enough to make explicit to myself: that the cards were stacked in favor of the Tommys and the Tobys, the rich, careless Yankees who, if they were outwitted in the skirmishes, could always win the wars simply by whistling up the apparatus of terror and repression that had been invented precisely to crush the victimized and the rebellious.

Well, if Isabel could only know it, this is one time she won. For, despite all my efforts to bring back just that one night when she charmed me and I tried so hard to charm her, to win her not by her rules but by mine, not with money or force but with the assertion of my simple manhood, I cannot really call her up in her mature and weary beauty. All I have, instead, is what I have earned for myself: the woman whom I never saw, but who remains nevertheless indelibly imprinted in my mind's eye, pale, trembling, fearing me, hating me and cursing me, now and forevermore.

THE HACK

Sooner or later everyone who writes, and publishes, is bound to be approached by a supplicant who writes but does not publish. "Would you read this? And be honest with me: Have I really got it?"

Such a plea for reassurance goes straight to the heart, for it is one that every writer has uttered, once upon a time, if only to himself. What could be more natural, in a trade without diplomas, licenses, or name plates? Sometimes there comes a more extreme demand, the most painful of all, and the most painful to answer: "Should I go on?"

A negative answer is implicit in the very uttering of the question. If you do not believe in yourself, even beyond the boundaries of sanity, no one else will. But the cruelty of replying with absolute frankness is easy only when you are young, desperate to assert yourself, and so prove your own gifts, if necessary at the expense of others.

Just before I came of age, I met a man in Ann Arbor named Harold Bangs who threw these questions into relief and so, I gradually came to see, altered my conception of myself. The funny thing is that, far from being unsure of himself, he was fanatically certain—like many eccentrics —that he held an exclusive option on a certain corner of the truth.

After my sophomore year at college I had gotten a summer job as lifeguard at a Michigan beach resort; but instead of spending my evenings making out with the girls at the casino, I had sat up late, night after night, in a kind of fever, writing stories about the people around me, the busboys, the waiters, the lonely wives, the weary worried husbands. By the time fall came around I knew that this was what I wanted to do, more than anything in the world, and I was convinced, in the way that you can be only when you are very young, that I was greatly gifted. Anyway, I had to find a single room, off in some quiet place, so I could write all night, if I wanted to, without disturbing anyone. That was how I met Harold Bangs.

Mrs. Bangs was the one who answered the doorbell of the unprepossessing, run-down house in a courtyard only a few blocks from the Michigan Union, and led me on up to the attic room. Thin, shy and puckered at the lips as if she had just bitten into something bitter, she stood in the doorway of the narrow room and rubbed her hands up and down her flanks.

"I know it's not very big," she said, blinking rapidly in what I later realized was a tic, "but you did say you wanted a real quiet place."

Mrs. Bangs must have had a first name, but I never learned it, nor could I ever have thought of her as anything but Mrs. Bangs, not young, not old, not interesting, just an overworked rooming-house keeper whom I never saw in anything but a J. C. Penney house dress, ankle socks and white open-toed buckle-strap Enna Jetticks, and who always smelled of ammonia and Bab-O while she scrubbed the endless steps to my room and the toilet next to it.

Even the mail, which for her consisted principally of utility bills, catalogues and a weekly letter from a Mrs. J. C. Hurd of Ishpeming, Michigan, was invariably addressed to Mrs. Harold Bangs, that drooping-breasted, down-dropping woman who never relaxed, seldom smiled, and ran the house alone, as if she were a widow woman.

In fact it was the mail that first brought Harold and me together. There were eleven of us roomers in that dark, cool and faintly moldy old house, not counting Mr. and Mrs. Bangs, and it was customary for the one who first spotted the postman stuffing the box to bring in the mail and lay it out in piles on the oak hall table, under a hand-lettered poem, a souvenir of the Chicago Fair, entitled "That's Where the West Begins." That was how I knew about Mrs. Bangs's mail; and that was how Harold came to know about me.

The building, so I was told by two forestry students who'd roomed there the year before as well, had been willed to Harold Bangs by his mother. What was more, he got a monthly pension (I saw that, too, in the front hall) for almost total disability—he had been gassed in the war. Apparently Harold figured that the house and the check for his lungs were sufficient contribution on his part, and that if his wife wanted to eat regularly it was up to her to put in a fifteen-hour day in the rooming house. But I hardly set eyes on the man, who was as indifferent to my existence as he was to the ten other roomers barracked over his head—until the day early in October that two of my literary efforts came back from *Story* Magazine in the very same mail.

All the winey fragrance of the autumn afternoon leaked away as I dropped my load of library books to the oak table and stared miserably at the creased manila envelopes that bore my name and address in my own handwriting. There was no need to open them. I knew their message by heart: *Dear Contributor, This alas is a rejection slip. And heaven knows the editors have had their share . . .* You're no good, you're no good, the two envelopes shouted at me. Yes, you are, yes, you are, screamed the defiant starlings, black, bold and unrepentant in the courtyard elm that grew all the way up past my attic window.

I closed the front door behind me and picked up my books and rejected stories, clenching for the long climb up the dark rubber-treaded stairs to my solitary room. Suddenly a voice called out to me from Mrs. Bangs's quarters.

"Hey, Tommy."

Mrs. Bangs never addressed me by anything other than my last name —after all, it was I who paid her once a week, and I whose room she dusted and swept. But this was a man's voice, thin and twangy, coming from beyond the end of the hallway, where I had never ventured, from the dining room, whose sliding doors stood somewhat ajar.

"Come on in."

Harold Bangs was sitting in a pool of light at the far end of the round mahogany dining-room table, before an old L. C. Smith office typewriter with a metal circle of keys, the kind of machine that you used to see in pawnshop windows wedged between banjos and golf clubs. He was a long-limbed, lank-jawed man in his middle years, with protruding shoulder blades that pushed out the back of his shirt like hidden wings, and swollen knuckles that he must have cracked a million times, sitting humped over the typewriter. He wore black garters above the elbows to hike up his shirt sleeves past wrists that looked as though they connected his hands to his arms not with bones but with twisted cotter pins. The shirt itself had no collar—I thought they'd stopped making them years before. His skinny shanks were crossed, exposing bare skin, hairless and white as bird droppings. He wore no socks under his plaid carpet slippers.

Although it was bright daylight, the bile-green shades on the dining-room windows were drawn down so far that their wooden spring rollers were revealed. As I approached, he squinted at me across the goose-neck lamp with shrewd frankness. Or at least frankness was the impression he seemed to want to convey; actually, I thought, he looked fanatically self-assured, like an evangelist, although of course I had no way of knowing why or to what end.

"So you scribble too," he said, sizing me up with his ice-blue myopic eyes.

My temper shifted at once from depression to fury. I detested that word; besides, who did he think he was to couple us like that? But, since I could not think how to express any of this without sounding impossibly snobbish, I said nothing, but tried unsuccessfully to glare as I advanced into the circle of light cast by the student lamp, exactly like those with which all the other rooms in the house were furnished. It was now that I observed that his face and neck were covered with a week's growth of graying stubble which further hollowed his already cadaverous cheeks and made him look toothless, when in fact he was equipped with a garish set of store teeth that intensified the fixed insincerity of his welcoming smile. It was only later that I learned that the teeth were a gift from the Veterans Administration, just as I was to learn, from continuous observation, that Harold was one of those rare birds, like Gabby Hayes, the old cowpoke in the Hopalong Cassidy movies, who was never clean-shaven and never bearded but somehow managed to maintain a continuous seedy stubble.

"This is where I work," he said. "Right now I'm knocking out an adventure yarn about two prospectors in the Andes. Going to try it on the *Post* and then on the men's mags."

Still I could find nothing to say. Around the typewriter the dining-room table was piled high with copy paper, manuscripts, carbons, envelopes, and back numbers of the *Writer's Guide* and the *Information Please Almanac*. Over everything hung the foul odor of dead cigarette butts, thousands of them, heaped in dime-store glass ashtrays which had surely not been emptied since his last shave; obviously Mrs. Bangs, always moving through the upper floors with dust mop and toilet brush, was not allowed in this sanctum.

"Tell me straight," Harold demanded. "How does *Story* treat you?"

"I don't know what you mean."

"Do they give you a prompt reading? I haven't tried to crack that market yet." He laughed hollowly, coughed, and spat out a crumb of tobacco. "Not that I've got anything against them. It's just that, according to the *Yearbook* payment scale, they're pretty far down on the old totem pole."

"I wouldn't know. I haven't had anything from them but rejections. Form rejections. They return my stories pretty fast, but that's no help."

"Sure it is." Harold cracked open a carton of Wings, pulled out a fresh pack, and offered me a cigarette. "You should keep a tally of your submissions, like I do." Between us lay an open notebook whose pages were ruled off in columns headed TITLE, DATE SENT, POSTAGE SPENT.

My head was spinning. "I haven't thought much about anything that systematic."

"But you should! Aren't you a serious writer?"

"I think I am," I said. I thought I was the most serious writer in Ann Arbor. "That is, I'm trying to write about serious things."

"Who isn't? I had a feeling, even before I saw your manuscripts in today's mail. When I heard you pounding your machine up in the attic night after night, I knew you weren't just doing term papers. It's too early in the semester," he added, shifting the wet cigarette with his tongue, "for that much schoolwork. I been running a rooming house long enough to know that."

I could feel my face reddening. "I hope the noise hasn't bothered you or Mrs. Bangs."

"The missus turns in early, right after Lowell Thomas and 'The Shadow.' Me, I put in a long day. Fourteen, fifteen hours at the machine is nothing for me. Nobody knows what's involved except another writer, right? Working out plots and outlines, making copies, studying your markets—there's no easy road to riches for us guys. It's a very time-consuming business."

By now I had edged back to the sliding doors. "If you'll excuse me,"

I said, "I'd better get back up there and start scratching away again, Mr.—"

"Call me Harold, Tommy. That's the spirit. Don't let those rejections get you down—I've got drawers full. And, say," he called after me, "any time you want me to read over some of your stuff, don't hesitate."

I fled.

But that was to be only the first of many such encounters, although I never took him up on his offer. Harold got to know my class schedule, and approximately when I would be returning to the house to drop off books, or change clothes, or do some writing; and all too often at those times he would leave the dining-room doors ajar in order to entrap me.

Just as Mrs. Bangs seemed always to want to wish herself out of my way, blushing when she collided with me as I shuffled out of the toilet in the morning and shrinking against the wall when I clattered down the stairs in the evening, Harold, seemingly nailed to his squealing swivel chair before the L. C. Smith, sought out excuses to lure me into his den. I never saw the two of them together—it was like those mystery movies where you discover that the real reason is because they are both one and the same person, a master at disguise and a master at crime. Except that Harold and Mrs. Bangs loomed larger in my life than did Lon Chaney or Boris Karloff.

Harold, I found out, wasn't all that eager to read my stuff. What he did want was for me to read his, and more than that to reassure him by my camaraderie that we were both members of a very special fraternity.

"I invested a lot of time on fillers," he informed me one day. "Fillers, jokes and funny coincidences. Matter of fact, I even hit 'Keeping Posted' one time. Not bad, hey? That's the top of the market, you got millions of readers going for you there. But you're dead unless you can concentrate on that exclusively. It doesn't pay, Tommy, take my word for it."

He lit one cigarette from the end of another, and dropped the short one in the butt cemetery without bothering to stub it out. No wonder the room stank.

"Besides, I think my forte is in yarns. I've got a tale of the sea here, about two brothers, Alaska salmon fishermen, with a powerful story line and strong romantic interest. So far I've had fourteen turn-downs, all printed, not one personal note. It beats me. Want to take a look at it and tell me your honest opinion?"

I put it off as long as possible, and finally came back with some miserable half-assed corrections of his typing and spelling (even when I am an old man I will remember with sour satisfaction that Harold Bangs wrote "wearwithal" and "medeival" and "irregardless"), but I could not bring myself to discuss his plot, which was incredible even if you accepted its premise—that a New York society girl would go to Ketchikan in search of adventure. Or its characters, high-flown on one page and mealy-mouthed on the next.

All I did say was "Harold, when were you in Alaska?"

"Never. But I got it down pretty good, didn't I?"

"Why don't you write about something you know, like the world war?"

Harold cracked his knuckles. "Tommy, I knocked out fifteen Flying Aces yarns—they're all in that corner." He gestured with a blackened fingernail. "Dogfights between Spads and Fokkers, Jennys and Messer-schmidts, I wrote them all and never hit once."

"I didn't know you were in the Air Corps."

"I wasn't. I was a plain old doughboy—that's how I got gassed. But nobody wants to read about the Argonne woods any more. You got to know your readers and your markets."

Harold shifted his bony frame in the swivel chair and drew back his lips, showing me not only those store teeth white as his shanks, but his pale-pink gums as well. "You like to think you're sitting up there and writing for posterity. But first you got to get published, right? You know what James Joyce went through with his stories? Here, take this copy of *Writer's Digest* and see what the editors of *Blue Book* have to say."

The worst of it was that when he gave me something to read I was under obligation to return it and so start a whole new round of conversations. Once I tried to outsmart him by leaving the magazine on the mail table in the hall with a note of thanks. All that happened was that next time I passed, Harold called out, "Hey, Tommy, you don't have to stand on ceremony, I'm always here. And you don't have to worry about inter-rupting me. I can always pick up where I left off."

All through that autumn I lived half in anticipation, half in dread of those sessions in Harold's den. Businesslike and implacable, he went on writing his unpublishable yarns about lean, silent adventurers and red-lipped maidens on the Amazon or the Yangtze, and I struggled on too with my unpublishable college romances that make me cringe when I recall their ineptitude. Night after night I heard his typewriter, and he reassured me that the sound of mine was music to his ears.

Finally it got to be too much for me. Not the writing, but Harold's belief that he and I were engaged in the same kind of enterprise. The more I heard his machine, knowing that when it stopped he would seek me out for what he called "shop talk," the more it graveled me. And so, because I was constrained to leave the rooming house and find another place to write, I regard it as Harold's doing that I went out and fell in love.

The closest campus building to my rooming house was the old music school, which I had had no reason to visit before. Now as I wandered through its seedy corridors in search of a quiet corner where I could write undisturbed, I was charmed by the mishmash of sounds that filtered out to the hallway—fiddles tuning up like cats in pain, cellos clearing their throats, clarinets showing off, sopranos trilling loudly as if terrorized— sounds that happily bore no relation to my work.

I chose an empty practice room, slipped into a chair with a writing arm in front of the piano, and was deep in my work when a girl walked in and said, "I'm sorry, but I signed up for this room for this period." She didn't sound at all sorry.

"You want to practice?" I asked. I was a little stupid not just from surprise, but because she was an excitingly attractive girl, downy, dark and snapping-eyed.

"It's not just that I want to," she explained, zipping open her briefcase and placing a Czerny volume on the piano rack. "I have to."

I persuaded as hard as I could, and finally succeeded in getting her to let me stay on and work while she did her exercises. Elaine was intrigued with my having selected such an unlikely place in which to write. At four-thirty, when she had finished her stint, I walked her to her dorm; then we had dinner together and walked the streets, telling each other about ourselves, until eleven o'clock. The next morning we met for break-fast, and in two days we were in love.

Now we did together what before we had done alone. We embraced on a bench late at night at the edge of town, and I read Yeats aloud to her by the light of the street lamp. Because I had given her *The Tower*, Elaine attuned me to the passions of the Schubert Trios in the record room of the Women's League. We arose early, anxious to come together, and met at dawn where we could hitch a ride from the milk wagon, breakfasting as we clattered along on a sackful of jelly doughnuts and a container of milk sold us by the driver. We walked, walked, walked, alongside the Huron River, through the Arboretum, past the stadium and on out into the country, on the railroad tracks, under viaducts, across golf courses and meadows, stealing pumpkins and, back in town, scuffling through heaps of leaves piled up for burning.

The happy surprise was not only that I was loved (although I could not stop wondering that I, I of all unlikely people, should cause such a girl's face to come alive when she caught sight of me) but that I could still do all I had before, and more. My schoolwork flourished, and I found that, sitting alongside Elaine while she frowned over her scores, I was writing more fluently than ever before.

As winter came on, though, Elaine and I were driven from our meadows, lakeside paths and park benches, and we grew to detest the icy ivy wall of her dormitory, where we ended our days at one o'clock on a Sunday morning clinging not alone but in concert with rows of other gasping, groping, miserable couples. It was then that I began to realize how much more bold and resourceful than I this seemingly fragile girl was; and it was disconcerting to have to admit to myself that worship and awe were not enough, that I simply did not understand women in general and Elaine in particular. I could not reconcile her delicate frame, her narrow bones, and the way she fitted into the circle of my arms, with her cool determination that we find a way to be alone together. She was only nineteen and had been too busy with her music to run around much with boys, but her eagerness for absolute intimacy gave me the uneasy feeling that she must already have had a string of lovers as long as my arm.

A premonitory shudder went through me, and not just because of the danger involved. But the inflaming vision of the two of us alone together in the darkness, warm, safe, locked in a fast embrace, overwhelmed the compunctions of inexperience. I had already told Elaine all about my rooming house, about the fellows on the second floor who knew that I was trying to write undisturbed and never came up to the attic without knocking, about Mrs. Bangs, who always turned in early. And about Harold, always tapping out his yarns at the dining-room table and leaving the sliding doors ajar so that he could collar me for shop talk.

"It's perfectly obvious," Elaine said coolly, "that if you don't want me to slip in behind you and go on up while you engage him in conversation, you'll have to put it to him man to man and see if he'll help us."

Man to man! Even the wicked glance with which she accompanied that cliché could not quite remove the curse from it. Still, it was worth trying to win Harold's support, considering that his wife was a devout Methodist Episcopalian, much involved with the Epworth League when she was not mopping or scrubbing. So, after all those weeks of avoiding him, one day I brought Harold his mail.

He had been wondering, he said, why he hadn't seen me lately and hadn't even heard my portable clacking away. Was I in a dry spell? He had never had that trouble himself, but he did have a book about writers' block, put aside for such an eventuality.

No, I assured him, it was just that I had taught myself to write longhand. "The reason is," I wound up, with none of the dash of Robert Montgomery or Melvyn Douglas, "I've got a girl."

Harold cracked his knuckles and scratched speculatively at his stubble, then flicked a kitchen match across his gritty blackened thumbnail to touch flame to the damp butt that hung from the corner of his mouth. He was not the sort to get his kicks from prying into others' sex lives. "Well," he opined, releasing smoke through his nostrils, "as long as it doesn't interfere with your work."

I hastened to reassure him. And I went on, with a glibness that surprised me, to tell Harold how Elaine had inspired me, and how well we worked together, and what a shame it was that she couldn't keep me company in my room while I typed just as I did her while she practiced her scales and sonatas.

Without changing expression, as though he hadn't been listening, or simply wanted to change the subject, Harold mumbled, "The missus has got an Epworth League meeting this Saturday night, right after supper. Myself, I'll take advantage of the peace and quiet to lock myself in here and get some typing done."

My temples started to pound when I realized what Harold was telling me. The next few days passed in such fevered anticipation that I scarcely noticed how matter-of-factly my sweet Elaine took Harold's clearing the coast. When I think of it, she was not unlike those coeds I hear about nowadays, who move in and out of their boy friends' rooms as casually as if the boys were their brothers. People weren't all that different when I was in school; it was just that love was a little more difficult, and you had to be more circumspect—unless, like Elaine, you were born self-assured and knowing what you wanted.

After the first rapturous nights we grew almost careless, up in our hideaway. Once I concealed Elaine in the shower when Mrs. Bangs suddenly shuffled up the steps bearing soap and a light bulb that she had forgotten to bring up earlier; another time I had to throw on a bathrobe and run my fingers through my hair at eight-thirty in the evening to answer Mrs. Bangs's buzz—two short, three long—summoning me to the telephone.

But we managed to keep our rendezvous all through the winter without being discovered, thanks not only to the tact of my housemates (some of whom were envious, others amused) but even more to my accomplice and accessory in fornication, Harold Bangs. Never once did he become sly or leering when he made his offhand remarks about his wife's comings and goings. All he asked in return was that I continue to acknowledge our literary fellowship, which I could do only in the most begrudgingly reluctant manner.

Neither of us had been having what you might call a smashing success with our respective efforts, unless you were to count the handwritten note of encouragement I'd gotten on a story rejected by *Esquire*. But Harold was unquenchable, and unchangeable in his absolute self-assurance that one day the gates would be opened for him by the elect, while I, if somewhat more prey to self-doubt and occasional despair, was buoyed up by Elaine's avowals of faith in me.

Elaine liked the idea of my being a writer. "I want success for you even more than I do for myself!" she cried one night, and I was transported. When the Michigan *Daily* announced a spring writing contest, Elaine went after me to enter it. I had never gotten mixed up with the campus literary crowd, even to the extent of submitting my stuff to their magazine. To Elaine I explained that they were a bunch of poseurs, big-city intellectuals trying to impose their tastes on us provincials; but in my heart I dreaded the possibility of rebuff. It was one thing to be honorably rejected, no matter how often, by unseen editors in high places, but it would be quite another to be brushed aside as unworthy of publication even in a campus magazine by people of my own age.

I don't know whether Elaine understood the real reason for my hesitancy. In any case, she swept away the ostensible ones, and by repeated assurances of faith convinced me that I should enter the competition, which called not for a short story or a piece of journalism but for a character study, a portrait of someone unusually odd or interesting. The winner was to be awarded a hundred dollars plus publication of his sketch.

If I say that it was Elaine's idea for me to write about Harold Bangs, I hasten to add that I accepted it enthusiastically and gave it all I had. To be sure, I changed his name, calling it "Howard: Portrait of an Unsuccessful Hack"; I changed his habitat from a rooming house to a trailer, in which he wrote science fiction while his wife was out demonstrating kitchen ware at neighborhood parties; and I doctored him up in other small ways that would, I felt sure, prevent his being recognized by anyone but the other fellows in the house, such as giving him a wooden leg instead of bad lungs. But I retained the essentials, the stacks of incoming and outgoing manuscripts, the clattering old typewriter, the glass ashtrays choked with butts, the smell of dead cigarettes and the feel of falling hair, and above all the look of Harold the happy fanatic, with his sleeve garters, dead-white skin, and cadaver's growth of whiskers, tapping out his malformed fantasies at the mahogany table from which he never rose, embedded forever in that gloomy room like a dead dictator in a wax museum.

Well, I won. It was a sweet day, with a girl to embrace me on the street when I told her the news, with teachers and other skeptics to call out congratulations, with the spring air invading even my stuffy attic room while I composed my letter home of pardonable triumph and vindication. Then came word that the *Daily* had sold my sketch to an intercollegiate press association for syndication across the country.

For a day my article was everywhere, and for a little while I was a hero, at least to Elaine and to myself. But then my stories began coming back, seemingly faster than ever, with the same printed rejection slips. And one night as I was sorting through the dismal mail on the hall table, a voice called out to me from beyond the dining room's sliding doors.

"Mr. Harlow, would you come in here?"

It was Mrs. Bangs. But what would she be doing asking me into Harold's sanctum? With the bad news tucked under my arm, I moved uneasily down the hallway to see what was up. To my astonishment Mrs.

Bangs was standing beside Harold, her red and roughened hand resting on his rounded shoulder. Before she could say anything, however, he spoke.

"Congrats, Tommy, on the prize and the sale. I knew you'd hit if you stuck at it." For once he was not smoking, and his hand seemed to tremble as he passed it along his bristles. His shoulder blades jutted like a twin hump.

I peered at him across the student lamp, but before I could thank him Mrs. Bangs said, her voice shaking. "You have chosen a poor way to repay confidence and friendship. Harold is too polite to say it, but you have disappointed us both."

I was sick with embarrassment. I stammered, "I'm afraid I don't know what you mean."

"Don't say that," she said, blinking rapidly. "You knew who you were writing about. It would have been different if we had been mean to you, or intolerant. But you never had a better friend here than Harold. Isn't that true?"

What did she know? I stared at Harold. Had he told her? Nothing like that showed in his face. He looked wretched, but not as though he had given me away. On the other hand, how did I look? Fortunately his den had no mirror.

"Yes," I said to Mrs. Bangs, "it's true. Harold has been very loyal."

"And you made a joke out of him for your own gain." Mrs. Bangs had tears in her eyes, but she wouldn't stop.

Oh God, I said to myself. Aloud I said, "Honestly, I didn't think of it that way."

"Well, you should have, because I do. I work hard to keep this house nice, and quiet for my husband so he can concentrate on his writing. And you come along and treat it all like some kind of dirty joke. My husband is nobody to laugh at, Mr. Harlow." Now she was weeping openly.

"Harold," I said miserably, "I didn't mean—"

"It's all right, kid." Harold cracked his knuckles. "The missus just got upset, what with me not having any luck lately with my own stuff. But I'll hit one of these days, just like you did."

"I know you will," I said. "I'm sure of it."

"It's just a question of time. Maybe I won't make it like you did, but I'll make it. You and I work in different ways, is all. I have to make things up. I couldn't write about what happened to me, or about my family or friends. I couldn't do that."

Even as I backed out of that artificially lit, artificially lived-in room, mumbling apologies to the couple whom I was seeing together for the first —and last—time, my heart was hammering triumphantly in my chest. Harold had put his nicotine-stained finger directly on the difference between us, a difference on which I was ready to stake my life.

For when the chips were down, Harold would never dare; and I always would. Even on his own limited terms, his caution condemned him to failure, since, immured in his dark study and his immature fantasies, he shrank not just from human beings but from the materials of his own life; while my ruthlessness, of which I had not known myself capable, assured me that, with all the failures in store for me on all the hall tables of my future, I was bound for certain ironic petty successes (even though they were to be most gallingly belated), bought at a price Harold would never be prepared to pay.

And so, victory strangely mingled in my heart with self-disgust at seeing that it was Harold and not I who had defined the boundaries separating us, I slunk from his room and from his wife's contempt and despair. I could be bold on paper, I would be bold on paper again, I was certain of it now. But I would always be a coward in other ways.

A few weeks later the semester was over and I tiptoed out of the Bangs house with my two valises and my laundry bag, leaving the final week's rent in an envelope on the accursed table so as not to have to face Harold or Mrs. Bangs again. And that summer, my love affair with Elaine already dying, I returned to the lifeguard's job and to my typewriter.

THE BALCONY

Their room had seemed ideal at first sight. High-ceilinged and airy, it had a cool, shabby, clean appearance that was most inviting. Madeline stepped to the jalousies and tugged at them gently, and as the sun came streaming through, outlining her slight figure, she turned to smile at her husband.

"It *is* nice," she said. "It looks out on the street. Very lively."

Brian nodded to the hotel owner's wife, who stood at his side, the huge door key in one hand, a scrubbrush in the other. *"Muy bueno, Señora. We'll take it."*

But they should have known better, for it was hardly their first day in the country. No sooner had Brian lugged their bags up from the lobby, and Madeline shaken the wrinkles out of their folded clothes, than they were stunned by a roar that started at the corner two stories below and seemed to increase in volume and intensity as it blasted through the open window, driving directly at them. They stared at each other, almost frightened. Then Madeline walked to the window and looked down.

"It's one of those trailer trucks—what did you used to call them in Kansas?"

"Semis. But for God's sake, it sounds like he's driving it right into the bedroom."

"It must be because the street is rather narrow and the walls are so high. They almost seem to slant inward, toward the street, as they go up, so maybe it's—" Madeline seated herself in the wicker rocker and rubbed at her ankle—"something like an optical illusion, only for the ears."

"Always the invocation of science. Has it struck you that the Avenida Juarez happens to be the main drag for all the bus and truck traffic out of town?"

"Did it strike you? It was you who marched us up here from the bus station because you didn't want to be right in the town square."

"I wanted to save money. And it just occurred to me about the highway." He was about to say more when the air was filled with a shrieking whine, punctuated with a series of rhythmic rattles. Brian winced. "They're zeroing in on us." He raised his voice. "Madeline! Pack up that stuff and let's blow. I never heard anything this bad in Florence, not even in Rome."

"It never did us any good to move in Italy, either. We could never afford the kind of place that was quiet, could we? Come, let's go for a walk and look over the market. Maybe it'll be quiet tonight, after supper."

But the city, for all its pleasures, was no more quiet than any other Latin town. Children played tag, women bickered in the market, an old Indian hawked noisemakers, a young blind beggar girl moaned from her shawled huddle on the spittle-stained sidewalk.

They bought a pair of unyielding huaraches made from old truck tires for Brian, an impractical comb carved by hand from one piece of wood for Madeline, and a kilo of red bananas that they could peel and munch on as they strolled the musical streets. They tried to figure out the tub of humming insects casually guarded by a yellow-toothed old lady, and what the dignified and distant Indian squatting on his shredded serape could earn even if he were to sell every one of his little pyramid of speckled apples. Then the seasonal afternoon rains came, and they paused, taking shelter under the hospitable awning of a sidewalk café for a leisurely coffee. But there, across the road, under the overhang of a building that hardly protected her from the straight down-driving rain, knelt the blind girl in her black tatters, her rebozo stretched tautly across the narrow curve of her shoulders. At her side a naked baby a year old, perhaps two, a stick of bamboo clutched in his small fingers, dabbled his other hand in the water that gushed furiously from the drainpipe next to him, while his mother continued to move her lips in the singsong whining chant that was now inaudible above the drumming of the summer rain: *"Por amor de Dios, por amor de Dios."*

In sudden fury, Brian grasped Madeline by the forearm. "Do you see that? She doesn't even stop her pitch in a thunderstorm. Nobody to listen, nobody could hear her anyway, but she keeps right on wailing."

"I'm sure the poor thing was trained to beggary from childhood. It's particularly horrible when you think that there's no need for it any longer."

"I suppose you mean atomic energy and all that crap. Well, in the meantime I take it as a personal affront. If I emptied my pockets into that baby's dirty little paw, what good would it do?" He held up his hand to forestall her reply. "I know, I know, charity isn't the answer. But I don't want to write to my congressman, I just want to paint."

"You might have thought of that before you suggested that we come to an underdeveloped country."

"Logic again. Why is it that your logic is always based on sentimentality? You know, I read someplace that they rent those babies by the day, the beggar women. Very effective with the tourists."

"Brian, you go to the most disgusting extremes to protect yourself from pain. Even if that was true, would it make the baby's plight any the less terrible? Or her mother's? Or this girl's?"

"How would you know? You're worse than your mother, always exhibiting her self-satisfaction by making like a mother. You haven't even got the excuse that she does."

Madeline said, almost inaudibly, "And whose fault would that be?"

"All right, I shouldn't have said that. But you know, I think if you lived in a world without misery, you'd have to invent some in order to be happy."

"I'm getting out of here. The rain's stopped."

Brian folded some bills under his saucer and hastened after Madeline, who was already striding up the street. He took her arm and slowed her pace as they crossed the Zocalo. There was noise there too, but it was more what they had hoped for, the rattling soulfulness of a strolling mariachi band, and with the help of the players the time passed more pleasantly until the late dinner hour.

After they had eaten, however, they were both very tired and ready for bed, and there was no excuse for them to stay away from their room. The hotelkeeper barely inclined his bald dome away from his vacant contemplation of the evening paper as they passed before the desk and mounted to the second floor. At the head of the broad stairway they came abruptly upon the hollow open square off which opened the dozen rooms of the second story. The emerging stars and the wedge of moon, riding slowly through a soft bank of clouds, illuminated the begonias and cactuses in their terra-cotta pots on the margin of the open square.

"Be careful, Brian," Madeline murmured. "The tiles are still slippery from the rain. A cactus spike can really hurt if you fall on it."

"It isn't the rain that worries me, it's the noise." Brian closed their door behind them. "I know you've heard this routine before, but if they're going to be pounding at us all the time, what kind of work can I get done in the next couple of weeks?"

"Sometimes I wish that we could trade places. I wish that you had to listen to those seventh-graders snickering while you were trying to show them color values, and trying to think what to make for supper, and where to go that would be cheap on our vacation. If you had to, you'd do it, that's all." Madeline turned back the bedcovers and began to step out of her skirt.

"That's what you said in Mexico City, and I still couldn't draw a line, with all that racket. The difference between you and me is that you love what you do, *especially* when it's unpleasant. But I hate to paint, I admit it, it hurts. I welcome any little distraction."

"Haven't I always done my best to protect you from distractions?"

"Yes, you have, baby, and I love you for it. Now do you mind if I read for a while?"

"The light won't bother me. But I do need my sleep."

"Of course you do. How else could you have the strength to take care of me?"

Somewhere below, the doors of a cantina swung open, and a roar of laughter, followed by a tenor raised in romantic song and a bellowing protest, floated up to their window. Madeline raised her head from the pillow to stare anxiously at her husband. His lips were set in a thin line; his large pale eyes stared unseeingly at the book before him.

"It'll surely stop soon," Madeline whispered. "After all, they need their relaxation too."

"From what? You don't have to whisper—*they* can't hear *you.*"

"Do you really believe that rotten propaganda about them sleeping in their sombreros all day? Because if you do I—" She could not finish; at that instant a semi came blasting up the highway and shifted gears at the corner beneath them with a grinding clatter and a rising howl that seemed aimed deliberately and directly at their hearts.

They stared at each other, united in despair.

"Maybe if we closed the windows part way . . ."

"Part way won't do."

"Then let's—" Madeline raised her voice as a motor scooter howled and howled higher and higher, straining as it swung around the heavy truck.

Brian hauled himself out of bed and clopped to the window. "If I close these jalousies we'll stifle."

"We can open the door."

It was a bad night. They tried everything, but in the end it was useless. If they barricaded themselves they could not breathe; if they allowed air in, they were engulfed by the shock waves of the street noises. Only toward dawn did the sounds subside at last, so that they could drop off finally with nothing but the calls of the awakening songbirds to punctuate their fitful slumber.

Early in the morning two small girls began to play with an inflated rubber ball in the open patio beyond their door. The ball smacked sharply each time it struck the terrazzo, with a loud report like gunfire, and the voices of the little girls were shrill.

"Those damn brats. Let's get up and have breakfast."

"Brian, I'd try to find us a place in the country, but where? What will you do? You claim you can't work without stimulation."

"*I* claim. How about you? Don't you like to see different faces sometimes too?" Tugging at his trousers, Brian stared red-eyed at his wife. "Are you going to start in on me before breakfast? Are you going to tell me what I know better than you, that I ought to be painting all year instead of just trying to sketch in the summer? Are you going to put in for a medal because you haven't saddled me with kids and a mortgage?"

Madeline replied in a very steady voice, "I am going downstairs to see if they can't give us a quieter room."

"The idea being that we could fight better on a good night's sleep, is that it?"

"If you like. I'll see you at breakfast."

Somewhat abashed, Brian temporized. "I'll order breakfast while you negotiate. Would you like *huevos rancheros?* Papaya?"

"Lime with the papaya, please."

There was a vacant room on the far side of the court, the quieter side; its small balcony overlooked only the local street. After breakfast they packed up and hauled their stuff across the sunny patio to the new room.

The morning sun, streaming in through the open windows and throwing the intricate shadows of the wrought-iron balcony across the woven-fiber rug, made everything seem at least bearable, and hopefully even pleasant.

"I guess this might do, don't you think?" Brian asked his wife.

Madeline replied, a bit doubtfully, "The movie house is just across the way."

"At least it doesn't open until four o'clock. Then I think you get a triple feature for your four pesos and you go home."

What they did not know was that the blind beggar woman was in the habit of stationing herself with her baby on the sidewalk in front of the movie theater every afternoon.

It was several days before Brian himself had this brought to his attention. He and Madeline did in fact sleep better in the new room and in consequence were in a good humor to explore the city at leisure, to sketch and read in the parks and plazas, and occasionally to swim.

One afternoon, when they had returned for a siesta in the shade of their high, dark, airy room, Madeline stepped onto the balcony to hang their bathing suits out to dry. As she glanced across the street, she uttered an involuntary cry.

"What's the matter, Madeline?"

"Oh, nothing. There's a blind woman in front of the Teatro Alhambra. She looks just like the one that's always at the entrance to the public market."

Brian jumped to his feet. "Let's see." Wrapped in a towel, his bare feet slapping on the tiles, he joined his wife and peered down, following the direction of her finger. "That's my girl friend. And there's the baby. He sits there sucking at that damned sugar cane as though he'll never have a care in the world. Dopey little bastard."

He took his sketch pad and pen from the round wicker table and dragged the armchair forward so that its front legs hung out onto the little balcony. Then he sat down and began at once to draw.

Madeline watched over his shoulder for a moment as the figures began quickly to emerge from the blank pebbled paper. She touched her fingers tentatively to her husband's sparse, wind-ruffled hair, smoothing it into place, and said almost shyly, "You'll get arrested if you don't put something on."

"Later, later," Brian muttered impatiently, and continued to sketch swiftly, whistling almost soundlessly through his teeth as he worked.

Pleased, Madeline tiptoed back inside, picked up an orange-backed Penguin novel, and stretched herself quietly across the bed.

Every day thereafter Brian took up his post on the balcony, sometimes sitting, sometimes leaning against the wobbly wrought iron, staring down at the lively panorama below him and occasionally, but less and less frequently as the days slipped by, trying to draw: brown women with pale-green woven baskets on their heads, barefoot children slapping at flies and at one another as they ran laughing around carts and burros, sunglassed and sombreroed tourists staring impatiently, pink-faced, at the unconstrained life around them—and always, shortly before the movie opened its doors to the townsfolk and peasants, the blind woman squatting in her tatters with the nude infant at her side and her terrible empty eyes upraised, keening softly her dreadful demand.

"My window on the world." Brian extended his arm in a grandiose gesture. "I envision myself as an old man here, complete with pipe and slippers and sketch pad, jotting down my observations on those still climbing the hill."

"How about the meantime?"

"You couldn't resist that crack, could you? It's easy to be demanding when you're safe yourself—there's never been a lady painter who wasn't a second-rater. Yet I don't see you even trying to sketch, and you went to art school just like I did. What's the matter, are you so worn out from baby-sitting those seventh-graders that you can't even pick up a Conté crayon?"

"I wouldn't want you to feel I was competing." Madeline spoke between pinched lips. "All the best handbooks say it unmans an American husband."

"You want to know what unmans me?" Brian tore the topmost sheet from his sketch pad, crumpled it and threw it over the balcony railing. "It's that goddam blind female, scrunched up there, mumbling about love and God. She won't let me work, she sits there daring me to ignore her or to love her and help her—and I can't do either."

"I suppose that's as good an excuse as any. It's better than the ones you had in Perugia and Cagnes and Torremolinos. Poverty should be as challenging to an artist as to a social scientist."

Brian swore. "It must be wonderful to be so liberal-minded that you can wipe out the smell of misery with one of those little cliché catchalls that you carry around with you like a spray deodorant. I wish I had your faith in progress. I could explain to that flea-ridden, half-starved bag of bones over there that her underdeveloped nation must make the leap into the industrial age. That she should petition for increased participation in UNESCO and bigger grants-in-aid from Uncle Sam. It's so much more reassuring to pin a label on her wretchedness than to give her the price of a handful of *garbanzos,* isn't it?"

Madeline replied in a trembling voice, "I never stopped you from giving her charity. If it would make you feel better than painting her—which is what you've been trained to do—you could wrap up your dinner in a napkin and give it to her every day."

"You know what I'd like to give her? A swift kick. I'd love to give her a boot and say, That's for tormenting me. That's for rolling those blind venereal eyes and blaming me that nobody put drops in them when you were born. That's for picking the busiest corners in town to do business, but not having the guts or the strength to raise your voice to the customers above a whining whisper. Then I'd give her one last shove, for borrowing a lousy little brat that hasn't even got sense enough to cry, but just sits there in the dirt all day like a corny prop for a proletarian movie." Brian sighed, shudderingly, and fell back in the heavy chair. "Now you know what I say to myself every day when I come out here and look."

"I'm sorry. Maybe we ought to go home, Brian. It was a good idea up to a point, but—"

"But we've passed the point? Or missed it? Well, even if we have, the apartment is rented till Labor Day, remember?"

"All right, then. We'll continue to sun ourselves and stare at the beggar girl—is that the program? If only I could convince you that I've never lost faith in you! Wouldn't that mean anything? Wouldn't that help?"

"Not as much as a little honest skepticism. Have you ever thought of trying that?"

They might have continued as Madeline had indicated, save for a rather ridiculous accident. The next afternoon, after Madeline had gone shopping, Brian padded over to the balcony to bring in his plaid bathing trunks from the railing. He felt a drop on his bare shoulder (he was wearing only dungarees and huaraches) and glanced up; yes, the rain was beginning a little early. He was about to turn away to push the armchair back into the room where it would be safe from the rain when it seemed to him that from the corner of his eye he could espy the blind woman feeling her way along the rough stucco wall of the movie palace, inching forward to her post with the infant wrapped tightly in the shawled crook of her arm.

Brian leaned forward to make sure and accidentally brushed his trunks from their resting place, straight down to the sidewalk two stories below. He peered down through the bars at the little particolored bundle lying like a discarded rag on the sidewalk, then shoved the armchair back into the room, slammed the long windows closed, and hastened across to the open patio, which was already slick with rain and darkened with the reflection of the metallic sky above.

Rather than cling to the shelter of the wall and its little overhang, he decided to cut across the patio to the main stairway. Halfway there, he felt the drizzle quicken to a downpour; Brian spurred his gait to reach the sanctuary of the covered staircase, but instead his foot suddenly went flying out from under him. He landed in a wet heap on the slimy smooth stone, his right leg bent grotesquely beneath him.

He twisted himself into a sitting position, but when he attempted to rise, his leg flamed with pain. Huddled weakly under the pounding of the tropical rain, he began to sob aloud.

As he sat, soaked and trembling, his head against his knees and his arms wrapped tight about his calves, the two little girls who had disturbed his sleep on the first day of his arrival stuck their heads out of their room and regarded him curiously. He raised his head and glanced at them, only half recognizing them and so only half acknowledging their existence, but they came all the way out onto the patio, wrapped from braided hair to ankles in plastic ponchos.

They approached him warily, one on either side of him, as if his injury might have made him dangerous. Chattering with soft rapidity in Spanish, they knelt and took him firmly by the arms. He could not say to two small children, Leave me, I want to be left alone, so he allowed them to help him to his feet. His right leg buckled under him, but by bending the knee deeply in a kind of swoop and at the same time stepping delicately on the ball of the foot, he found that he could make his way with their assistance through the blinding rain to his bedroom door. With mature dexterity they maneuvered him over the ledge and through the door, which they worked open, to his bed, where they held him gently while he lowered himself to a prone position. Then, before he could protest, the older one had knelt at his side and removed his soaked huaraches, while the younger sister, whose front teeth were still missing, brought him a towel from the washstand to mop the rain and perspiration from his bare skin.

"Gracias, gracias," he mumbled as they stared down at him unsmilingly from either side of the bed, their dripping ponchos falling away from the braids that hung to their shoulders, the delicate gold hoops glinting below their pierced earlobes.

He leaned over to the bedside table and took from it the paper sack of huge, sugar-sprinkled cookies that Madeline had bought to indulge a bedtime sweet tooth. But when the girls reached, tentatively, each for a single cookie, he tossed the entire bag to them. *"Tómate esa!"* They accepted it gravely, without protest, executed a funny little bow, as though they were retreating from royalty, and backed out of the room almost at a run.

After that Brian lay there, without moving, listening to the sounds of the moviegoers filtering up faintly through the closed windows, for what must have been several hours. When Madeline returned at last, the rain had stopped; the sun had returned too, and it sparkled through the windows onto the chair where his sketch pad lay abandoned.

"Hello," Madeline said. "I almost got caught in the shower. But there was this crazy parrot—" She stopped abruptly. "Why are you so wet?"

"I fell, with my leg under me. Now I don't seem to be able to move."

"Oh my God, I'll get a doctor. Are you in pain?"

"Not as long as I lie still. Those two little girls next door practically carried me back in. I was going down to get my swimsuit—it fell off the railing. Did you happen to see it on your way in?"

Madeline laughed a trifle hysterically. "You're the one who's always calling me naïve. If you dropped a washrag, it would be gone in two seconds."

"Take a look out the balcony," Brian insisted. "Humor me."

Madeline peered through the window. "No," she said after a moment, "there's nothing down on the sidewalk. Nothing."

"Now see if you can spot the blind one and the baby over by the box office."

"Why?" But, not waiting for an answer, Madeline craned her neck. "No, no sign of her. Does that make you feel better?"

"Worse. Don't be malicious."

"I'm sorry. I didn't mean it that way. I'm going down now to see about a doctor."

"Which we can't afford."

"Don't be ridiculous. Can I get you anything while I'm downstairs?"

Brian shook his head. "Unless you want more cookies. I gave the bag to the kids for helping me in."

Madeline stammered something incoherent and hurried out. It seemed hardly a moment before she was back, breathing hard and looking a little peculiar.

"The Señora says the girls told her about you, and she took the liberty of calling a masseur. He is supposed to be here any minute."

Brian started to laugh. "If he can't help, maybe they'll send a voodoo doctor."

"Do you suppose," Madeline asked nervously, "we could explain to him that it was a mistake, when he arrives? Otherwise we'd just have to pay him and start all over again. You ought to have an X ray—we don't know if you sustained a fracture."

"Sustained?" Brian laughed again. "I sustained worse than that. But I didn't break any bones. Sometimes I think I don't have any to break. I could use a good rubdown, though. As a matter of face, so could you. When he gets here, let's ask him if he has a special rate for aching couples."

"Please don't make any more jokes. It's no better than seeing a chiropractor, or a naturopath. What'll we tell him when he gets here?"

"I don't know about you, Madeline, but I've had a bellyful of science. I'd like the touch of a healing hand for a change, instead of just a diagnosis and a prescription."

"Oh, Brian . . ."

There was a knock at the door. Brian said politely, "Please let him in, dear."

Madeline opened the door to a big-bellied, jovial man of fifty, with a wrestler's neck, a gold tooth, and a large black bag, which he gripped in his muscular brown fist. In the other hand he held a panama hat, as immaculate as his white blouse, which was delicately embroidered at the cuffs, the throat, and along the front and back panels.

"Good afternoon, I am sorry I am so late." He spoke a heavily accented but very rapid English. "I am mostly retired. My wife takes the messages when I go out. You have trouble with the leg?"

"The right one. Madeline, would you get a chair for Señor—?"

"Call me Tony, I am known widely as Tony." He flashed a smile. "No chair is necessary, Madam."

"Can you tell," Madeline demanded tensely, "if the leg is broken?"

The masseur bowed. "I am thirty years in the business, eighteen years at the Chicago Athletic Club." He manipulated Brian's leg tentatively but tenderly. "If there is a break, we have to have splints, no? But I believe not here. How you fell?"

"In the rain. I was starting to run." Brian went through the ludicrous episode again, keeping his gaze on the masseur, away from Madeline.

"And it hurts here."

"Yes!"

"And here."

"Yes. Not as much."

"But not here?"

"No. You see, I can walk on it, if I keep my leg bent." He glanced at Madeline. "I can limp around quite rapidly, and without any pain at all, except that I must look like some god-awful freak, a Quasimodo or a boogeyman from a nightmare."

Madeline closed her eyes. Her fists were clenched.

"I know what you mean." The masseur nodded sympathetically. "Lady, will you leave us alone, please."

"Alone?"

"I must remove his garments so to examine and to give him the treatment."

"Oh. Yes, of course." She picked up her purse. "I'll go down to the corner and have a coffee."

"Make it a tequila," Brian advised her. "You could use it."

The door closed behind her and the masseur set to work. Removing his embroidered shirt, he proceeded to don a short-sleeved white blouse which buttoned up the side of the throat and gave him the look of a dentist, a Latin tooth-yanker with big biceps. Then he took a bolt of unbleached muslin from his bag and unrolled it alongside Brian half the length of the bed.

"Now we take off the trousers." He gentled Brian out of the dungarees and out of his shorts as well, and then rolled him onto the muslin and covered his loins with it, exposing the length of his leg. Brian lay back with his arms tucked behind his head.

He asked lazily, "Can you tell what it is?"

"You know the anatomy?"

"I used to know the name of every goddam bone and muscle."

"How come?" The masseur regarded him solemnly, almost with suspicion. "You studied?"

"That's right. I'm an artist—of sorts."

The masseur's broad face cleared. "You paint the nudes."

"Once upon a time. Then I did their insides, but I wasn't very good at the essence either. Then . . . Never mind. What does it look like to you?"

"I think is a ligament, a muscle sprain. Bad, hurts like awful. You know what they call? A Charley horse. Hurts, but is going to be better. Now we use the pressure."

He opened a bottle of liniment and poured some into his clean cupped palms, then proceeded to work the fluid slowly into the soft parts of Brian's leg. The insistent pressure was almost voluptuous. Brian closed his eyes and responded willingly to the masseur's directions to turn, flex, lie still.

Slowly, painstakingly, methodically, he worked over and over the area, stroking, rubbing, pressing with his large, bent thumbs, coaxing away the pain. As he worked he chatted, softly, smoothly, in a liquid, slurred English as soothing as his moistened hands.

"You know Chicago? Art Institute, lots of paintings? Eighteen years I work there. Brr, I freeze in winter. Terrible town to be broke in winter-time, no friends. But then I meet rich men at the Athletic Club. Soon I got money in the bank."

"Are you married?"

"Sure. Not to American girl. Too flashy. How I know they want me, not the bankbook? So I come home for vacation, I marry a girl from here, I take her back to Chicago. Seven years we live there. You know what? Little by little she gets like a flower when you take it out of the ground. Finally she says, Tony, I can't stand the snow in the face on Michigan Boulevard, is not for me. So I take her home. Now I'm retired, but they come down from Chicago, they pass the word. Still I'm in demand, still the services are requested. You got responsibility, people ask for you, you got to go."

"I suppose so. I wouldn't know." Brian raised his head from his arms. "Tony, do you think it's a bad thing, having a wife make sacrifices for you —so that even when she doesn't remind you of them because she knows you can't stand it, you can still see them in her eyes?"

The masseur's vigorous brown hands paused above Brian's leg for an instant, then resumed their hypnotic rhythm. "I can do good for the leg. Maybe when you move around better, you can do good for your wife."

"It's a little late for that."

The masseur showed his gold tooth. "Never too late."

"Didn't your wife look at you cross-eyed, those winter nights in Chicago?"

"*Look* at me? She cried!"

"So you gave in. You took her home."

"Only after I saved up enough money, so we wouldn't live poor in my own city."

"But doesn't it bug you to have the poor all around you, pleading for help—" Brian gestured toward the balcony—"when you know that even if you gave away all your loot, it wouldn't do a damned bit of good?"

The masseur continued to work, and to talk, in the same high good humor with which he had begun. "Nobody can do everything, not even Jesus. Everybody can do a little. I make you feel better, maybe you paint better, you make your wife feel better. Then she make babies."

Brian sat up abruptly. "Are you almost through?"

"Couple minutes more. You like it here, before you hurt the leg?"

"It's more beautiful than Chicago. Nicer people, too."

"But poorer too, huh?"

"You ought to know."

"That's right. You and me both. It's good for us to know."

"Why?" Brian stared at him curiously.

"The better men think about the poor ones. Okay, we're all finish for now." The masseur reached into his hip pocket for his heavy tooled wallet and drew from it a small engraved card. "You want me tomorrow, next day, I come again or you come to me. Maybe we have to strap, but I think no."

Brian accepted the card and struggled into his trousers. "I'm very grateful. How much do I owe you?"

"We make it forty pesos, all right? And don't put weight on the leg yet. Stay still, make the wife work." He smiled, almost secretively, as he rolled up the muslin and the blouse and tucked them away in the bag with the liniment. "When she gets mad, you jump up and run after her. You feel better then."

"I seem to have only a few pesos," Brian said in embarrassment. "Would you mind stopping at the café opposite the movie house and asking my wife to pay you? And would you tell her that I need her?"

"Sure. Let's open the window, give you lots of fresh air."

When the masseur had closed the door behind him, Brian turned his head to observe the setting sun throwing its last beams against the blank plaster wall of the cinema across the street. Already the neon sign had winked on; and although from his prone position he could see nothing of the life on the street below, he could hear quite distinctly the sounds of the motors, the sidewalk vendors, the excited children, and a supplicating mendicant woman. Closing his eyes, he lay back against the pillow and waited for his wife to return.

MY CONEY ISLAND UNCLE

nevitably our parents are the bearers of our disillusion. After they have ushered us into the world, they must bring word that Santa does not exist, that camp is out of the question, that Grandma is dying, and that they themselves are flawed by spite and unreason. Sometimes it falls to another grownup to renew in us for a time, through disinterested kindliness, that original seamless innocence, the very notion of which can otherwise become a sour mockery. The lucky ones among us can be grateful for a childhood graced by an unencumbered relative—a bachelor uncle, perhaps—who enjoys us not for what we may become, or may one day owe to him, but simply because we exist. I had such an uncle.

We lived, my parents and I, in a small frame house not far off Main Street in Dunkirk, New York, which is on Lake Erie about halfway between Buffalo and Erie, Pennsylvania. My father had inherited a hardware and agricultural-implements store to and from which he walked every day, and where my mother joined him to keep the books and wait on customers during the hours when I was in school.

My mother was a good sport, I think now, about a life that she could not have foreseen when she fell in love with my father on a summer vacation at Lake Chautauqua. She had been a New York girl with musical ambitions; she often exercised her light and agreeable soprano voice of an evening during my boyhood, accompanying herself at the Aeolian Duo-

Art piano father had given her on the occasion of the arrival of her firstborn—me, Charley Morrison, who also turned out to be her lastborn. Mother solaced herself with introducing me to "the better things" (Friday-night poetry readings at her Sorosis Club, piano lessons with Miss Letts, and reproductions of the Great Masters), traveling to an occasional concert in Buffalo, and taking me to New York every year to visit her three brothers, my uncles Al, Eddie, and Dan.

Uncle Dan was the one who mattered. I can't remember why he happened to be visiting us when I entered kindergarten on the very morning of my fifth birthday. What I do remember, so vividly that the sunlit-noonday thrill of it is still almost painful, is the sight of Uncle Dan coming toward my mother and me on the cracked sidewalk before our little house, which sagged, a bit askew, like my father, as we returned from that terrifying first day of school. He was leading an Irish-setter puppy by a braided leather leash.

Aside from our family doctor, who had bad breath and wore high-top shoes, Uncle Dan was the only real doctor I knew. He might not have been an outstanding physician, but he did know, even though he never married or fathered a son, what could turn the trick with a small boy. As I ran up to him, still trembling from the strange lonely newness of the classroom, he unwound the leash from his fingers and flipped it at me.

"Here you go, Charley boy," he said. "Here's a puppy dog for a good student."

And he stood there, stocky and self-possessed, smiling around his cigar, ignoring my mother's shocked surprise and nudging amusedly at my bottom with his toes as I dropped to my knees to caress my new dog. "Just treat him right, Charley boy," he said, "and you'll have a real friend."

I didn't know how to tell Uncle Dan that he was my favorite. The other New York uncles were all right, but they had wives and children of their own; he was the one who I felt belonged to me. People said that I looked like him, which was beyond my understanding—he was a burly man with an impudent mop of reddish-brown hair (my father had almost none that I can recall even from my earliest childhood, and I couldn't even tell you the color of the fringe around his ears), and an even more unlikely mustache, full, square, and bristling. How could I resemble a middle-aged man—he must have been in his thirties at that time—with a big thick mustache? It was enough that he would give me a dog, and an occasional boot in the behind, to show me that he appreciated what I didn't dare to tell him.

As the years passed, I came to believe that he would have understood, had he been around, far more than my parents. Not that they didn't try, in that dull and drowsy community. But in the cruel way of children, I often felt, particularly as the depression invaded our lives like a prolonged state of mourning, that they—immured in their dark semibankrupt store that smelled of iron filings and bird seed—had no notion of how they ought to treat me. Else why would they have lied to me after they had my dog put away when he went into distemper convulsions? And why did they take it for a kindness to let me oversleep the grand opening night of the circus, the only halfway exciting event of the year in Dunkirk, after I had worked to the point of exhaustion for a pass, a ticket which they could never have afforded, in those lean days, to buy me?

I was going on thirteen that summer, sullen and rebellious after the circus fiasco, when my father informed me with clumsily evasive tact that, as a reward for having done well in school and helped out at the store, I was to be sent to New York. Alone.

I was old enough to know that my parents could not have come to this decision by themselves. Mother's family had to be consulted, if only because they would have to put me up. My mother had already forgone her annual visit home, but this, as well as the matter of who was paying for my ticket, was something that simply went unmentioned in our household; to bring it up would have been like asking if you were going to get a Christmas present, and how much would be spent on it.

Besides, I had a strong hunch that it was my Uncle Dan who was footing the bill. He was the one with the fewest responsibilities, and it was he who scrawled me the postcard (he never could manage a whole letter) asking if I'd like to batch it with him for a while.

If they had fixed it up not with my Coney Island uncle but with the Manhattan uncles, Al or Eddie, I probably wouldn't even have wanted to go at all. Not that I was spoiled or blasé about New York. But mother and I had always stayed with Uncle Al and Aunt Clara, mother sleeping on the studio couch, me bunking with their boys.

They were all right, but as far as I was concerned there was nothing glamorous or big-city about them. Uncle Al was seldom home except Sunday evenings, when he'd slump down morosely before the radio to listen to Ed Wynn, and Aunt Clara was in the kitchen baking all day, gabbing with mother. She wouldn't let my cousins own bicycles, they didn't even know how to ride, and they never ceased needling me monotonously as a hick. We'd stand around in the concrete courtyard of the apartment house, not a blade of grass in sight, bouncing a sponge-rubber ball back and forth in the little clear space to one side of the corroded green fountain of a nymph with jug that never worked anyway, and taunting each other out of boredom and aimlessness.

"Is this all you guys ever do?" I'd ask. "Isn't there anything else to do in New York, except follow the horseballs in the bridle path in Central Park?"

"Horseballs yourself. Is it true you still got Indians running around loose in Dunkirk? Aren't you afraid of getting scalped? Why do you always say faw-rest and George War-shington?"

And then my mother, with her relentless passion for intellectual improvement, would haul us off on the bus to the Museum of the City of New York to look at dolls costumed as dead mayors' wives, or to the Museum of Natural History to study the pasted-together bones of brontosauruses and tyrannosauruses. After five or six days I was more than ready to go home.

I just knew that it would be different now, staying with my Coney Island uncle. From the moment that father bade me goodbye in the unwashed bus depot that smelled of depression and defeat, stowing his rusty Gladstone in the rack over my head, shaking hands with me shyly, and smiling a reassurance that did not conceal his perpetual somberness, I settled into the new mood of freedom and adventure. All through the long ride down across Pennsylvania, Erie to Warren to Coudersport to Towanda to Scranton to New York, I pitched and rolled on the torn leather seat with the stuffing oozing out, exalted as though I strode the deck of a Yankee clipper. Even the discovery that my uncle was not at the Manhattan Greyhound Terminal to meet me, as he had promised, was exhilarating. I kept a good grip on the valise, as father had advocated, and while I was looking about for Uncle Dan, a lady from Travelers Aid came up and asked if I was Charley Morrison.

"Your uncle is tied up in an emergency. He says to come right out to his place. Now you can take any line of the BMT, can you remember that? Don't take the IRT, you'll get all mixed up."

It was like Uncle Dan, I thought, not to send some stooge relative after me, but to trust me, even though it was already well into the night, to find my way out to Coney Island. I got there without trouble, hauled the valise down the steps of the elevated into the street at Surf Avenue, and walked straight up the block, milling and restless as Times Square, even at midnight, to the corner where Uncle Dan's signs hung in all his second-floor windows. Just as I was reaching out to punch his night bell I heard my uncle's familiar voice behind me, deep and drawling.

"Charley boy! Have a nice ride?"

I swung around. Uncle Dan was standing there smiling, medical bag in his left hand, cigar and door key in his right. His hat was shoved back on his head, and his Palm Beach suit was wrinkled at the crotch; he had put on some weight and seemed tired, but otherwise he looked the same.

"Let's just throw our bags in the hall, so we can go out and grab a bite."

He led me around the corner and up the ramp, gritty with sand, to the boardwalk. Above us the looped wires of bulbs drooped like heavy necklaces, the neon lights of stores and stands slashed on and off, some hurling their arrows hopelessly after each other, others stabbing into the sky like red-hot sparks, and the night was so illumined by them all that you could follow the smoke from the skillets of the hamburger joints high into the air before it disappeared into the darkness, along with the hot steam of the coffee urns. Amidst the acrid smell of burning molasses, before salt-water-taffy machines swaying rhythmically as they pulled the fat, creamy ribbons to and fro, girls opened cupid's-bow mouths to receive huge wobbling cones of cotton candy extended eagerly by their sailor boy friends. The ground shook beneath me with the thudding of thousands of feet on the wooden boardwalk, stained in spots from the wet footprints of late bathers and the spilled soda pop of boys my age who shook up the open bottles and released their thumbs to aim the spray at the unsuspecting before they fled. And over it all the intermittent roar of the plunging roller coaster across the way at Steeplechase Park, its electric controls rattling as it raced down below the horizon like an express train to hell.

Uncle Dan led the way to Nathan's hot-dog stand and said to a Greek counterman, "Two franks well done, Chris, for me and my nephew." He turned to me. "You take yours with sauerkraut? I forget."

I said boldly, "I like mine with everything." Mother would never have let me eat a spicy hot dog in the middle of the night, much less with all that junk smeared, rubbed, and squeezed on it.

"That's your nephew, hey, Doc?"

"Come in from the West to keep me company for a while. We're going to have some fun, us two bachelors." My uncle took a huge bite; I had never before seen anyone handle a hot dog, a cigar, and a toothpick all at once. "And listen, Chris, if this boy comes by with a hungry look during the day, his credit is good."

"I got you." The counterman extended his bare arm, hairy as a gorilla's. "Have a knish, kid."

We washed down the hot dogs and knishes with big shupers of root beer. The glass mugs were heavy as sin, frosty, with foam running down the sides; Uncle Dan blew off some of the suds at me as if we were drinking beer, which was just what I had been secretly pretending. As we strolled on he asked, "What time do they make you go to bed back home?"

I hesitated. I wanted to add thirty minutes to my weekend late limit, but then something made me answer honestly.

Uncle Dan screwed up his face. "That sounds awful damn early to me. At least, it is for Coney Island. Tell you what, if you promise not to snitch to your mother, we'll just forget that curfew stuff while you're staying with me."

I could hardly trust myself to reply.

"Your mother's a good woman," Uncle Dan remarked, in a thoughtful tone that I had never heard him use before. He took me by the elbow and led me to his apartment through the midnight crowds, thicker than we had even for circuses back home. "She's got her troubles, you know, like all of us. But she's my favorite. I mean, your uncles are all right, they're not bad fellows, but they've made a couple mistakes. Number one was when they got married."

As he threw away his cigar, he added, "Number two was when Al and Eddie left Brooklyn. In Manhattan, you don't even realize that you're living on the shore, on the edge of the ocean, the way you do here."

He fell silent, and I, matching my step to his, could not remember when Uncle Dan had ever talked to me so much all at once. After a while he went on, "This is a good place to live. You'll see."

In the two minutes that it took me to fall asleep, I observed that Uncle

Dan came to bed beside me in his drawers. It was a practice that my mother condemned as disgusting, but I resolved to put my pajamas back into father's Gladstone next morning. Mother thought too that you couldn't get really clean in a shower, and at home we had a monstrous old claw-legged tub that we filled part way with kettles of boiling water from the kitchen stove, in a bathroom so drafty that we stuffed the casement with rags and plugged in two electric heaters from the store ten minutes before bathtime. But Uncle Dan's shower stall, into which I leaped when I awoke, with Uncle Dan already halfway through his office hours down the corridor, had a ripply-glass door with a chrome handle, the first I'd ever seen outside of the movies, and water that kept coming out hot, forever.

I did get a rather haphazard tourist's view of New York in the days that followed—waiting in line with the other out-of-towners on Sixth Avenue to see a Marlene Dietrich movie about the Russian Revolution at Radio City Music Hall, riding the elevator to the top of the Empire State Building to peer down at the tiny pedestrians who might be Uncle Al or Uncle Eddie ("from up here your uncles look like ants")—but what entered deep into my being was a sense of the variety and richness of possibility in the city, a sense of how one could, if one only wished, enter any of a number of communities, each as unique as the single one in the small town I had left behind.

Uncle Dan did this for me, and without even realizing it. All he knew was that it might be fun for me to tag along with him for a while. It never occurred to him that just by exposing me to his daily round, which to him was not particularly exciting but pleasant enough so that he had no deep incentive to change it, he was presenting me with motives for persisting in this confounding, fascinating world.

If my father knew everyone who came into his store, everyone knew Uncle Dan when he stepped out onto the street. But there was a difference. On our way to his Buick, which he kept garaged a few blocks away, on Neptune Avenue—I cannot remember whether it was the first or the second day of my visit, for by now everything has blended into a generalized memory of that liberating week, as if the revolution I was experiencing was far more than the sum of its insurrectionary incidents—we were suddenly stopped by a pleading woman.

"Doctor, doctor!" she cried, gasping for breath, holding out her empty reddened hands as though she were extending something precious and hot, like a freshly baked cake. It occurred to me that if she had been carrying something, anything, even a little purse, in those swollen hands, she wouldn't have looked so wild.

"Let's take it easy," my uncle said. He addressed her by some Polish or Slavic name. "Is it your husband? Casper?"

She nodded, trotting alongside us as we approached the car. "He beat up on Mrs. Polanyi. He knock her down, he try to kill her."

"I warned you it was going to happen, didn't I?"

"What I can do? I can send him away? How we going to eat?"

"Well, now you'll have to do it. No two ways." He held open the front door of the car. "Hop in."

She shook her head vigorously. What was this? Why wouldn't she get in? My heart thumping, I stared at the frightened woman, who stood there with her chest heaving, refusing to sit in the front seat.

But Uncle Dan understood. With a sigh he yanked open the rear door. "OK, let's not waste time."

She crawled into the back, and as I settled myself beside my uncle, he muttered, "She thinks it's not polite to sit up front next to the doctor. It's a wonder she'll ride with us at all."

In a few minutes we had pulled up in front of her house, a red-brick tenement indistinguishable from all the others on the block except for the crowd gathered before it. Uncle Dan leaned on the horn with one hand to clear the way as he reached back with the other for his satchel. "Come on, Clara," he said to the woman, who had been crouched on the edge of the seat as if afraid that she might soil it, "we'll go take care of Mrs. Polanyi. Charley boy, you keep an eye on the car."

I couldn't just sit there on that baking Brooklyn street, not with the neighborhood kids staring at me. So I got out and thrust myself into the crowd.

In its midst a girl of about my age, one of her twin braids half unwound, was crying against the bosom of a gray-haired woman.

"What happened?" I asked boldly.

A boy answered wisely, "It was her mother." "Huh muddah" was the way he pronounced it, and it took me a second or two to understand. "The nut stomped on huh. He's a real nut. You the doctor's son?"

Before I could answer, a thin-faced sallow man came out the front door and sauntered down the stoop, pausing only to light a cigarette with a wooden kitchen match. Although he was tieless, he wore a sharp striped suit with a grease stain big as a campaign button on his left lapel; his fly was open. The crowd moved off even while the flame of the match still flickered, before he blew it out. He came directly to me, placing his face so close to mine that I could see the pores on his fleshy nose, and fixed me with his very pale, almost colorless blue eyes. I had the feeling that he was looking through me, at something just behind my head, rather than at me.

"You the doctor's boy?"

"I'm his nephew." I heard mutters from the crowd, which had drifted back to either side of us.

"He's a great man. Man of science. You know science?"

"Not much."

"It powers the world. You know science, you got hidden power. Mrs. Polanyi, she was tuned in. She was wired for sound. They send her messages against me. Man, she could have destroyed everybody. You know Mrs. Polanyi?"

I shook my head wordlessly. I knew, suddenly, who he was, and what was wrong, but I was not frightened. I was simply curious and fascinated. After a few moments of odd disjointed talk my uncle tramped out in his heavy, solid way, lugging his satchel and blowing on a prescription blank. He beckoned to the crying girl.

"Hey, Jeanette! Take this to Rudnicki's drugstore and get it filled. Your mother'll be all right—I'll stop by tomorrow." He winked at me as he shoved a fresh cigar into his mouth, then turned to the man who had been talking with me. "Casper, you got to go for a ride. You met my nephew already?"

"Sure. He's a smart one. Science, like you. It powers the world." His pupils were the merest pinpoints; his jaws were clamped as if with a wrench; when he smiled it was like a dog baring his fangs.

"Amen. Come on, Casper, let's go. Here comes your wife."

Her handkerchief to her face, she stumbled down the steps and through the ranks of the curious.

"I'm going to need you to sign the commitment papers, Clara. . . . Close that door, will you, Charley boy?"

And we were off to the hospital, my uncle making easy talk with the wife, and me sitting beside the demented husband who had almost murdered a defenseless woman. It did not take long for him to be removed to the barred retreat where for all I know he still paces, hunting for the secret wires of science.

After we had finally left his wife, in the charge of a sister, weeping in terror at the prospect of feeding her family without her husband's wages, Uncle Dan took me into the precinct house, where he had to make out a report. Then we drove across the length of Coney Island, from the hump of Sea Gate, sticking out into Gravesend Bay, over to Brighton Beach, to that corner of it which encloses Sheepshead Bay, and there, on a street of bay-front cottages smelling not of traffic exhaust, dumbwaiters, and dark metallic elevators, but of clams, salt marshes, oakum, and rotting bait, I met a sword swallower.

Mr. and Mrs. Alvarez might have been, superficially, customers of my father's. She was a childless but motherly woman with the bosom of a pigeon, but her flashing eyes were those of an opera singer. When we arrived she was just removing a sheet of cookies from the oven. While her husband, who greeted us in his bathrobe with the *Daily News* dangling from his left fist, was squeezing my hand so hard that it brought tears to my eyes, Mrs. Alvarez was already pouring me a glass of milk and setting the cookies before me.

She stood over me and stroked my hair while I ate and drank, saying, "You come from a nice part of the country, kiddo. Many's the time Alfredo and I played the fairground circuit all in through there."

"What did you do?"

She laughed, her bosom shaking. "You wouldn't think it to look at me, but I used to be a bareback rider. Since I got too heavy, we settled here, and Al works the shows on the island."

Her husband, the examination of his throat and chest completed, returned to the kitchen from the bedroom without bothering to throw his robe over his undershirt and trousers. I was impressed by his shoulders, which were embroidered like tapestry with writhing tattooed dragons, their tails looping up around his wiry corded neck.

"How you like it here, kid?" he demanded.

"I like it fine."

"Doc says I'm going to live for a while," he announced to his wife and to me.

"Not if you don't change jobs," my uncle grunted, but that seemed to make no particular impression. Mr. Alvarez stepped jerkily to the closet and fetched out a long package, a broom handle maybe, wrapped in flannel.

"You didn't take the boy to the sideshow yet, did you, Doc?"

Uncle Dan shook his head. "Give us a chance. He hasn't even been to Bedloe's Island yet, to the Statue of Liberty."

"Aw, the Statue of Liberty. Let me show you something, kid." He unwrapped the flannel with a flourish and exposed a glittering sword, wonderfully filigreed all along the blade.

Before any of us could say a word Mr. Alvarez snapped to attention as though he were presenting arms at court, then raised his walnut-brown sinewy arms and brought the point of the sword to his lips. He bent his grizzled head back farther than I had ever seen anyone do and slipped the sword into his open mouth and down his gullet, inch by inch, then foot by foot. You could actually see it going down from the outside, his bare neck working and swelling as it contained the cold steel.

Mrs. Alvarez sat at the kitchen table, placid and proud. "Pretty good, huh? Here, take along some cookies in wax paper. You'll get hungry later."

Mr. Alvarez brought up the sword as deliberately and delicately as he had slid it down, clicked his heels, and bowed. "You get the point?" he asked, and laughed with a hoarse bark.

"That's the most amazing thing I ever saw," I said honestly.

"I can do that with almost any type sword. Except one that's too curved, like a scimitar." Skimitar, he pronounced it. "I can do it with a rapier, even with a saber. You got to keep a straight passage, see, the head has got to be straight back. It's all in the head, am I right or wrong, Doc?"

Mr. Alvarez gave me the sword to examine. "You come to the show, kid, and you'll be able to see right through me. I swallow an electrified sword, it's got little bulbs on it. I stand in front of a black curtain and you can see the bulbs inside me just like my backbone was lit up."

He was chuckling all the way to the door. "See you in the freak show."

In the car my uncle sighed, his hands hanging over the steering wheel for a moment before he stepped on the starter. "Nice people, aren't they?"

"You bet."

"He's got an ulcerated throat. It's a precancerous condition, really. You can't go on insulting the body indefinitely, Charley boy. But his wife can't work anymore, and he doesn't know how to do anything else. Well, I thought you'd enjoy meeting them."

We did visit the freak show a few nights later. I gaped at the tattooed lady's bluish hide, blurred like an old map, and stared in uncomfortable awe at the seminude form of the half man, half woman, not wholly convinced by Uncle Dan's explanation of glandular pathology. My parents would never have taken me there, either as a favor or an object lesson, and I did not dare to ask Uncle Dan what he had in mind, if anything, besides entertainment.

The Fat Lady was off that night because of a toothache. But since she too was a patient of Uncle Dan's, next morning I found myself riding with her and my uncle in an old panel truck from her flat in Brighton over to the dentist's, on Linden Boulevard in Flatbush. Uncle Dan and I sat in front with the driver, her brother-in-law, who was all business; Smiling Sally herself was spread out, like some giant growth, all over a plank fixed to the bed of the truck for her. From time to time a groan would issue from that vast heap of flesh, and her massive arm would rise slowly, alarmingly, reaching out to my uncle for comfort.

Uncle Dan was to give her the anesthetic, but before the extraction we had to get her into the office of his colleague, Dr. Otto Reinitz, whose first-floor office fortunately had French windows. No sooner had we begun preparations to transport Sally through the window to the dentist than the envious neighborhood kids began to gather, picking their noses and pointing at the groaning circus queen.

First we had to rig up a kind of staging with a block and tackle, like the bos'n's chair used by sign painters, and then, supervised by her sweating but experienced brother-in-law, we hoisted unsmiling Sally aboard and on into the office of the waiting Dr. Reinitz, a skinny man with an eyeshade and the biggest Adam's apple I had ever seen. We pushed the sofa from the waiting room into the office so that Sally could recline on it within reach of the dentist's forceps.

When the job was done and Sally came back to life, she became a person for me. I had no idea how old she was, maybe twenty-five, maybe forty-five, but beneath all of that fat there beat the heart of a flirt. She smiled winsomely, bravely making light of her pain, she looked sidelong at me, she squeezed my hand.

"That's some assistant, Doc," she said to my uncle. "A regaleh doll. How old are you, sonny? Old enough for the girls?"

I knew the answer to the first question, if not to the second, and she rewarded me with an inscribed postcard photo in a glassine envelope, displaying her in a grotesque tentlike puffed-sleeve party dress, bobby socks, and Mary Janes, which she took from the purse that dangled like a toy doll's from the rings of flesh at her wrist. SMILING SALLY, 649 LBS. OF JOLLITY, it said.

"I get a quarter for these at the freak show," she told me. "For you, nothing. Someday you'll grow up to be a big doctor like your uncle."

That morning, I thought maybe I would. There were others my uncle attended whose lives had also been tarnished, some in ways I would not dare to mention when I returned home. In Greenpoint, just across the East River from Lower Manhattan, on Noble Street (the name has stuck in my mind), I waited in a candy store while Uncle Dan administered sedation in the flat upstairs to a screaming woman whose son's body had just been brought back from Red Hook, where rival mobsters had put three bullets in the back of his head. From there we drove in silence, around the Navy Yard, over to a portion of Sands Street which no longer even exists, teetering shacks aswarm with prostitutes.

I waited in the car, my face on fire, trying not to stare back at the bored, gum-chewing girls waving at me from behind lace-curtained windows. When my uncle came out, he tossed his satchel on the back seat and gave my bony shoulder a squeeze.

"The more trouble I see," he said, "the hungrier I get. Let's grab a bite in Borough Hall before I get stuck with my office hours."

He had to file some papers and pick up vaccines in downtown Brooklyn too, so we parked on Montague Street and had a businessman's lunch in a real bar, where I watched salesmen matching each other for drinks by rolling dice from a cup.

"Nothing like that in Dunkirk," I assured my uncle.

"Charley boy," he laughed, "you could say the same thing about Sands Street, in spades."

On the way back to the car, cutting across the open square in front of Borough Hall, we came upon a circle of lunch-hour loungers listening to a sidewalk speaker. I thought at first that he was selling razor blades or carrot slicers, the kind of pitchman that my father always referred to as cheap, cutthroat competition, but then as I pushed my way through I saw that he was black, and that he displayed nothing but a stick of yellow chalk.

He was a skinny, solemn man, conservatively dressed, but with eyes bulbous and roving like those of a rearing stallion. The bony, imperious hand that held the chalk slid occasionally to his mouth to wipe the spittle from his lips.

"Ich bin a shvartser id!" he cried.

Out of the corner of his mouth Uncle Dan explained, "He's telling them he's a black Jew."

"I do not preach the New Testament," the orator shouted in English. "Let us speak only of the wonders concealed in the Old. Let us confine ourselves only to the Pentateuch. Those of you who paid attention in *heder* will recall where it says . . ." and he lapsed into Hebrew.

His accent brought grins from the crowd; but suddenly he squatted and began to print characters on the street, in the space before us. His calligraphy, stark and sharp and yellow, stood out on the black street like the brilliant mysterious border of an Oriental rug. Drawing with nervous rapidity, he continued to scream at us as he stooped over his chalk, lecturing in English, quoting in Hebrew. Swiftly a pattern emerged as he whirled and twisted on his haunches: The mysterious phrases intersected at their center to form—"Inevitably!" he cried out, enraptured, the sweat of persuasion dripping down his cheeks—a cross.

"What I tell you?" a tubby man beside me demanded of his companion. "He's a *meshummad,* like I said."

"To be a *meshummad,* you got to be a Jew to start out. Otherwise, how can you change over? Nah, he's a missionary, an agitator. He comes downtown to convert."

Some of the crowd were muttering angrily, others turning their backs in disgust, a few (like Uncle Dan) chuckling, as the black orator called after us, flailing his long arms, white cuffs dangling over his wrists, "It is written in our own Book! We must admit the Christ to our hearts!"

And in the course of that week I saw signs and portents, cabalic symbols chalked on the city streets and tattooed on the shoulders of beings who ate cold steel; I rode with lunatics, moved from murderers to fallen women, accepted an inscribed photo from the fattest woman in the world, and one morning Van Mungo, the great Dodger pitcher, my hero long before I had come to Brooklyn, and my uncle's friend, rumpled my hair and autographed a baseball for me to take home, where I could varnish it to protect his signature and display it to the doubters of Dunkirk.

What is more, during Uncle Dan's office hours I lolled on the beach with *Official Detective* magazines from his waiting room that were forbidden me at home, surrounded by the undressed throngs come in their thousands from every stifling flat in New York, from every darkened corner of the world, actually, to sun themselves at my side; I learned the sweet subtleties of bluff and deception, kibitzing at the weekly session of my uncle's poker club, attended by the cadaverous dentist, Dr. Reinitz, and three Coney Island businessmen; and I was not just allowed but encouraged to stay up practically all night for the great flashy Mardi Gras parade, blinking sleepy-eyed at the red rows of fire engines rolling glossily along streets sparkling like Catherine wheels. It was the greatest week of my life.

But if my uncle graced my childhood, he also—one bitter wintry evening some ten years later—illumined my adulthood. When the destroyer escort on which I had been pitching miserably through the north Atlantic on wartime convoy duty paused in the dead of night in Gravesend Bay before nosing on up through the Narrows to the Navy Yard, I wangled my way ashore and hurried directly to my Uncle Dan. After all those black nights blinking at meandering merchant vessels groping toward their own destruction, Coney Island was startling, even in the dimout. But it had changed. Icy and inhospitable in the off-season, its faded invitations to dead pleasures creaked in the winter wind, and its empty, empty streets were rimmed with frost and frozen grime.

My uncle was not at home. "But you go on over to the Turkish bath," his housekeeper said to me. "You remember where it is, right down the block. He's playin' poker there with his club, Dr. Reinitz and all of them."

Already a little let down, I shivered along the barren streets and shouldered on into the hot, dank sanctuary of the bathhouse. There, seated around a card table messy with poker chips, sandwich ends, French fries on wax paper, and beer in paper cups, were my Uncle Dan and his fellow bachelors, their bare skulls and shoulders shining wetly under the brilliant light of a hundred-watt bulb that hung straight down from a cord. The cadaverous Dr. Reinitz was naked save for clogs and a Turkish towel across his lap, but I recognized him at once by his Adam's apple and his green eyeshade, which apparently he never discarded; instead of his swiveled drill he held three cards in his hand, but he had changed in no essential aspect.

Uncle Dan was half draped in a bed sheet, roughly like a Roman senator, except that you don't think of Romans as clenching cigars. The fringe of hair on his chest had turned white, and his paunch was twice what I had remembered it to be. He glanced up at me coolly, with a weary casualness more startling than the collapse of his looks.

"Look who's here. How are you, Charley boy? Gentlemen, you remember my nephew. Otto, Oscar—"

I nodded.

"Here, pull up a chair." The one named Oscar extended his hand and showed me two rings. "Hey, Jake, bring another corned beef. And a beer. Never saw a sailor didn't like beer."

"You been overseas?" Dr. Reinitz inquired incuriously.

"I've been back and forth," I muttered. "On convoy duty. Halifax. Scotland. Murmansk."

"You don't say. I was in Archangel once myself. Very drab. You could see daylight right through the chinks in the log cabins."

"Well," said Uncle Dan, "main thing is you're back in New York safe and sound. What are you going to do with your leave—paint the town red?"

"Paint the town red?" I cried, hoping desperately that he would do for me, one last time, what he had when I was thirteen.

I had been seasick and frightened for a long time. I had been knocked off my feet by depth charges, I had been nauseated by the twilight farewell of a helpless wallowing Hog Island veteran of the first war, flaring briefly against the horizon like a struck match and then pointing its bow at the sky like an accusing finger before sinking beneath the sea, leaving nothing but a few screaming men and the junky debris of war.

Now I was appalled by these civilians and their unrationed self-satisfaction, and most of all by my uncle himself. I was heartsick with disappointment. Like a boy crudely misunderstood by a girl he has romanticized, I wanted only to flee. Then I saw that my uncle wore a queer expression that I would never have identified with him, and so found incomprehensible: At that moment I took it to be a look of envy, embedded in the puffy used-up features of one seemingly beyond anything but an evening of cards with his similars in a Turkish bath. And I could think of nothing to say except to repeat, "Paint the town red?"

He shook his head slowly. And slowly, as he turned the cigar between his lips, an old glint came back to his eyes. Passing his index finger across his whitening mustache to brush it into place, he murmured, "I know what you mean, Charley boy. But I wasn't worried about you for a minute. You're bigger now than I ever was. I'm the one that's been going down, here, little by little, and with no lifesaver either." Ignoring those about us, who had suddenly ceased to exist either as his friends or my antagonists, he paused for a moment in order that the words that followed, more shocking to me than his appearance, might bar the door forever to my childish demands on him. "I'm the one who could use some help now."

THE TREE OF LIFE

In the summer of my thirty-first year, I found myself living alone in a rural slum, in a Mexican village outside Oaxaca called San Felipe. My wife had left me in Taxco and I was having a bad time of it, what with self-pity and lack of funds. Although I had failed to persuade her, I was still trying to convince myself that I had a distinct talent as a potter. What was happening to me was that, with no wife, no children, and no great originality, I was slowly being overwhelmed by the terror of growing old to no purpose, of gradual annihilation by the meaningless declension from a life that in my heart I despised but still feared to let go of. In between throwing and firing pots, I played dominoes with a Mexican linoleum salesman I knew, at the sidewalk café in front of the Hotel Marques des Valle in the main plaza of Oaxaca.

One afternoon, as I was washing down my tequila with a swallow of sangrita, a perfectly enormous American automobile, its windows ablaze with Mammoth Cave, Blue Ridge, and *turista* stickers, rolled to a stop at the curb, over at the far end of the plaza. There was no one in the car but the big-bellied driver, who wriggled out slowly, like a snake easing himself free of his skin.

"Good God," I said.

"What about him?" Julio glanced at me drowsily. "Jus' one more tourist, no?"

"No," I said. "It's my Coney Island uncle."

And as I sat there, all but paralyzed, watching my uncle make his way gingerly around the square with that blind, groping uneasiness peculiar to the American away from his homeland for the first time, I saw not this aging man, with the outsized cigar and dark glasses, the outrageous Hawaiian sport shirt over the great soft paunch that spelled lassitude more than stateliness, but rather the stocky, self-assured bachelor who had been the favorite uncle of my boyhood. How I had admired him! And how good he had been to me!

Although more than ten years had passed since he and I had been in close communion, what I remembered now was not our last, wartime encounter, when I had been a frightened sailor back from Murmansk and he a philosophical civilian physician, relaxing with his cronies over a poker game in a Coney Island bathhouse; nor even the wonderful week I had spent with him on his medical rounds as an adolescent in flight from my parents' failing hardware store in Dunkirk, New York, during the depression. No, what I would always associate ineradicably with him was the healing visit he had paid me during a terrible period of childhood disillusion.

One summer afternoon when I was seven or eight, my Irish setter Ryan and I had gotten caught in an unexpected rainstorm on our way home from the lake. At the front door I knelt to wipe him off and discovered that the dog's eyes and nose were running and that he was breathing jaggedly through the mouth, his sides heaving as though he had run all the way. Mother refused to listen to my pleas. She threw the dog out of the house and threw me into a hot tub.

Next day the vet told us that Ryan had pneumonia. My mother was contrite and let him into the house, but it was a little late, for the pneumonia was simply a secondary result of distemper, about which we could do nothing but wait.

I wrote, or rather printed, a letter to Uncle Dan in Brooklyn, since I thought he ought to know what had happened. He was the one who had given me the dog for a present, on my first day of kindergarten; and besides he was a big-city doctor. Uncle Dan sent me a picture postcard of the Hotel St. George (World's Biggest), and advised me to hope for the best.

We all did, but one sultry afternoon Ryan went into convulsions. Mother ran to the hardware store to get help while I called the vet. I had been feeling queer for some hours, almost as if I'd had a premonition; by the time the dog was taken away I had a raging fever and was aching not just in the region of my heart but all over, as if I were being squeezed in one of the steel vises in the back of Father's store.

Mother's hair, usually coiled so neatly at the nape of her neck, was coming down; as she bent over me a hairpin dangled limply, like a worm from a leaf; and as she unbuttoned me tears were running down her cheeks, leaving shiny tracks in her face powder. I was crying too, but I couldn't even tell whether it was because poor Ryan, his hindquarters quivering uncontrollably, had been taken from me, or because I myself was suddenly in such pain as I had never known before.

It turned out that I had rheumatic fever. As I lay fretful and languid in my sloping-eaved little room at the back of the second floor, mesmerized for days on end by the coffee-colored stains where the chimney flashing had curled back and allowed the snow to seep through the wallpaper, I sipped juice through a straw and whined for my dog who could have comforted me at the foot of the bed. But I did not rage against my parents, or even blame them, until Ronnie, the big kid from down the block, came to bring me some Don Sturdy books and laughed in my face when I told him about my folks putting Ryan out to board in the country.

"Put him away is what you mean."

I stared at him and his grinning buck-toothed superiority.

"The vet chloroformed him. They always do. Ryan is dead, that's what."

"Mommy!" I cried. "Mommy, come here!"

Frightened by the anguish in my voice, my mother hurried into the room. She collided in the doorway with Ronnie, who mumbled something about having to be going and left her to cope with the terrible suspicion he had aroused in my heart.

Yes, she said, reaching across the bed for my hand, which I withdrew and hid, clenched, under the covers, it was true. Ryan was dead. They had had to put him away.

"But why did you lie to me?" I sobbed. "Why did you lie?"

"We didn't mean to." She tried to stroke my hair, but I turned my head aside. "We didn't want to hurt you, when you were so sick. If you'd been well, we'd have told you. Your father was just waiting—"

I pulled the pillow over my head and refused to listen to any more.

Instead of getting better, I grew worse. By the next day I was out of my head, and I thought I heard Mother discussing me with Uncle Dan, who was almost five hundred miles away. But I was not wholly mistaken, for in her fright Mother had turned to her brother the doctor, calling him for advice on the long-distance telephone, which was something we did only in extreme emergencies.

It seemed to me only moments later, although I suppose it was the next day, that Uncle Dan was standing at the side of my bed, his cigar drooping beneath his big mustache, his watch chain glinting in a double arc across his vest. He hauled out the gold turnip watch that had been his father's, my grandfather's, and took firm hold of my wrist.

"What do you say, Charley boy?" he demanded. "Giving the folks a hard time?"

"They killed Ryan," I whispered.

"That's right. They did. But it had to be done. It's my business, you can believe me when I tell you. It would have been cruel to keep that dog alive. Even a miracle wouldn't have saved him."

"They should have told me."

Uncle Dan smiled, showing me his discolored teeth that were supposed to be shaped like mine. "They should have. But people don't always know what's best for a sick person. Not even parents. Come on, swallow this, and I'll tell you something." He waved his fat cigar at me as though it were a wand. "You turn around and go to sleep, and in the morning there'll be a different kind of miracle in the yard, right outside your window. Is it a deal?"

I could barely nod, for already I was slipping off to sleep.

When I woke again, I was alone in my room, it was morning, the sun was already hot and bright on the patchwork quilt folded at the foot of my bed, and a whole flock of robins were talking to one another in the old apple tree, a branch of which brushed my windowpane. As I came awake I remembered Uncle Dan's promise, of a miracle outside my window, and I squatted on my knees by the casement to see if it had happened yet.

For a moment I was disappointed. Through the thick foliage of the tree which my father's father had planted at the turn of the century, all the familiar objects in our yard—the hollyhocks, the red pump set in the concrete lid of the well cover, the bird bath bordered with petunias, my little two-wheeler lying on its side rusting in the damp grass—looked just as they had when Ryan and I had chased each other round and round the doghouse Father had built for him.

But then, as my eye was distracted by the birds whirring about their nests in the twisted arms of the apple tree, I realized that it was not just the ripening Baldwins among which they fluttered and sang. No, there were oranges hanging from the tree too! And lemons! It wasn't possible, but why else were the birds crying out so passionately?

"Plums," I said aloud, "and pears. And there's a whole bunch of bananas!"

"That only makes six different kinds, counting the apples," remarked my uncle from behind me. "There must be more than that. I promised you a real miracle, not just a plain ordinary one."

"Uncle Dan, how did they *get* there?"

"Just go ahead and count."

"There's some grapes over there, and a bunch of cherries. That's eight different kinds of fruit. And what are those little green things?"

"Look like quince, but I'm no expert, Charley boy. In Coney I buy my fruit from Giuseppe at the corner stand. You spotted nine, now what about the other branch? Take a good look."

"I see a cantaloupe, and some tangerines, a lot of tangerines. That makes eleven different kinds of fruit. Eleven! And there's even some tomatoes, down there near that nest. Except that tomatoes are vegetables."

"Wrong again. Don't they teach you kids anything in Dunkirk? Tomatoes are a fruit, they're a member of the berry family, like grapes or bananas. And that makes twelve fruits, and that's your miracle." Uncle Dan's eyes were glittering, blacker than I had ever seen them, and the flesh around them was unusually dark and shadowed. "That plain old apple tree turned into a tree of life."

"A tree . . . ?"

"Sometimes I think you don't know anything at all, Charley boy." Uncle Dan pushed open my window very wide. "Reach out and pick yourself a fruit."

I glanced at the doorway behind him, at Father in his dangling suspenders and collarless shirt, at Mother wiping her hands tremulously on a dish towel.

"Go ahead. If I say to do it, it's okay."

My parents made no move to stop me, so I scrambled onto the sill, leaned far out, and picked myself a plum. As I bit into it, after rubbing it on my pajama sleeve, my uncle gave me a tremendous squeeze.

"There," he said. "Now. You've eaten of the tree of life. If you read your Bible, Book of Genesis in the Old Testament, Book of Revelation in the New Testament, you'd know what that means."

"My father claims you said the Bible is a pack of lies."

My father's face flamed. He had always supported Mother's insistence that I attend Sunday school regularly, and I had heard him charge his doctor brother-in-law with being a heathen.

Uncle Dan said easily, "We're not going to get into a discussion about that now. It's a known medical fact that when you eat of the tree of life, regardless of what you think happened in the Garden of Eden, it makes you immortal. I promise you, you'll be here long after the rest of us are gone. So why not start getting well, Charley boy?"

I did, of course. My uncle might not have been an outstanding physician, but he knew, even though he never fathered a son, what could turn the trick with a small boy. He must have been up the better part of the night in that old Baldwin apple tree, teetering wearily from Father's extension ladder while he fastened all that fancy fruit outside my window, but it was good medicine, because the next thing I can remember, he was gone and I was well and pumping my box scooter through the streets of Dunkirk.

And now here he was, an old man, peering up and down the streets, while I—I had to force myself to raise my arm and call out, "Uncle Dan, here I am," for I was ashamed of his seeing me. My chinos were stained with clays and glazes, my leather sandals were torn, I needed a shave, my hand shook. What could he think, if he too remembered me from those dead days as the fresh-faced boy who could be solaced for the loss of a pet with fairy trees?

But he strolled up to me with his old equanimity, as if it were only since breakfast that we hadn't seen each other. He waved the cigar confidently, as though it were the old magic wand with which he could change me back to what I had once been.

"How've you been, Charley boy? Had a feeling I'd find you here."

"I bet you did," I said. "Word gets around. But what brings you down here?" I could not get used to him in this context, or in any outside of that which I had always associated with him—it was like meeting your barber, out of uniform, at the movies.

"It was time," he said vaguely. "It was time. Am I interrupting anything?"

I introduced him to Julio, whose English was not good, and over a bottle of dark Mexican beer he explained to us leisurely that it was hotter than the hinges of hell in Brooklyn, that his poker partner Oscar ("You remember Oscar, Charley boy?"), with whom he had planned to go on a cruise, had died, and that he had simply closed the office and started driving.

"I may just keep right on going to Guatemala, if my tires and my spirits hold up," he said, smiling.

But I knew that wasn't so. I felt that he had come to see me, although I wasn't sure why, and I observed that beneath the heartiness his skin was worse than white; it was yellowed and greasy.

"I hear there's some nice ruins around here," he said. "I'll just go on inside and check in—figured I'd stay for a couple days?" His voice went up on the last words, as though he feared that I might discourage him or indicate my unwillingness to have him around.

"I live out of town a ways," I said, "and it's just a dump, or I'd invite you to stay with me."

"Oh, I didn't mean—"

"But I'll be happy to take you to Mitla and Monte Alban, and any place else that appeals to you. I'm not very busy these days."

"Me either, Charley boy." Uncle Dan flashed the old smile as he arose. "Nice to have met you, Julio."

When we drove out to the great ruins in Uncle Dan's air-conditioned monster the following morning, I began to think that perhaps I had been reading things into his appearance that weren't there. He poked around dutifully, asked me to photograph him blinking in the bright sun with his arms around a pair of ragged Indian kids, and haggled over some fake Mixtec relics with the women who peddled them in baskets outside the church at Mitla; but he said nothing to indicate that he wanted anything other than this.

What was more, he displayed no curiosity about my personal situation, after he had made sure that he wouldn't be putting me out by making me his guide. We did not talk about our relatives, as we used to occasionally when I was a boy, except that in the town of Mitla he did shop for rebozos. "I've got to bring something home for your aunts. Let's pick out a couple nice quiet ones, not too loud."

In the home of a family of weavers, standing spread-legged on the dirt floor with his cigar stuck in his mouth. trying out his Brooklyn Spanish on an old crone and a mostly naked youngster, Uncle Dan pointed at a small placard tacked to the door, below a faded movie poster of Cantinflas as a comic bullfighter.

"Say, Charley boy, translate this for me, would you?"

"This is a Catholic home," I read. "Protestant propaganda is inadmissible and unwelcome here."

"I'll be damned." He thought for a while. "All my life I lived in New York, and I never once saw a sign like that."

The next day Uncle Dan asked, almost shyly, if it would be possible for me to drive to the coast with him. I suppose the fact that I was somewhat taken aback must have shown in my face.

"Not Acapulco," he added hastily. "Too far. Besides, everybody says it's Miami all over again. I was thinking, It would be fun to see an unspoiled place before it gets taken over. Someone told me Puerto Angel is like that, not like Coney, just a quiet beach, with palm trees and tropical fruits, and hardly anybody there. We could make it in less than a day from Oaxaca, they say."

"I've never been, myself." I paused and stared at him, but he looked back at me blandly, expectantly. "Sure, let's go."

We made it to Pachutla in something like five hours in that monstrous car, with me driving and Uncle Dan relaxing, ignoring the hairpin turns and enjoying the wild landscape, the ravines and chasms that gaped on either hand. From Pachutla we had maybe another half hour to reach the Pacific, and I hesitated to press on to Puerto Angel, filled suddenly with a queer foreboding.

But Uncle Dan was a good traveling companion, uncomplaining about discomforts that he had surely never been exposed to in all his life. He ate wretched food and red-hot food, filthy chicken wings and ulcerating tacos, he laughed at indescribably dirty toilets and no toilets at all, he didn't mind the heat that boiled up as we descended, for he was eager to get to the sea. So we jounced over the potholed road that was an insult even to jeeps, and at last we swung round the last bend and beheld the blue body of the Pacific.

"Like stout Cortez, that's how I feel," laughed Uncle Dan, patting his belly. "Just like stout Cortez."

"Except that it was really Balboa."

"Well, whoever. You know something, Charley boy? I never saw the Pacific Ocean before. Come on, let's hit the beach."

But when we got there I could have wept for my Uncle Dan. His tropical paradise consisted of a modern school, a few stone buildings, and for the rest a row of wobbling wooden shacks tenanted not only by human beings but cats, dogs, chickens, and pigs. The beach was strewn with refuse, alive with litters of squealing piglets slithering back and forth, and black with their excrement. And the heat fell on us as though it had been waiting, venomous and smothering, for us to emerge from the air-cooled car.

"Buck up, Charley boy." Uncle Dan rapped me lightly on the biceps. "Don't feel guilty. Imagine how *I* feel, dragging you off to this."

We made our way around a corner of the village and cut across a dried-up stream and a bend of hill to what had looked from the distance like a mirage but turned out to be exquisitely real. A heavenly beach, curving away from the midden of the village, where we undressed and lay on our backs, utterly alone, with our feet in the bluest, most caressing water anywhere in the world. We were wary, paddling through the water, of sting rays, and an occasional shark, but no matter. There were no pigs, there were no people. We might have been the first human beings ever to trace our toeprints in that crystalline sand.

"I want to tell you something, Charley boy," my uncle said at last. "I imagine that when you were a kid, you used to envy me."

"Well, I admired you. You were good to me."

"But I wasn't to myself. I should have married, I should have—oh, done any number of things. We're all cowards in one way or another. And then, you know, these last few years, after all the old urgencies were burned out, the chasing after women, running to make a buck, wishing for things that weren't going to be, like eminence in the profession or adventures away from home, I found that just being alive was like finding a treasure every morning."

He rolled over on his big stomach and spoke with his mouth inches from the fine white sand. "The trouble was that just when I thought I had it made, a new fear came at me—the fear of death, something I'd never understood in all my years of practice. You remember, when you were a little boy I told you that you were immortal . . . well, I never really believed it myself, maybe because I wasn't a small-town kid and I'd never tasted of the tree of life the way you did. Or maybe because when you grow up in New York there's no innocence for you to lose."

He paused. I said, as casually as I could, "And now?"

Uncle Dan startled me with his loud, almost raucous laugh. "I'm glad I came down here, that's all. I got caught up a little. You can't have everything, but what a shame if you never get to reach for it! That's the only thing I'd regret. There's really nothing to be afraid of in the reaching, you know? You strain your engine to reach paradise, and when you get there, all sweaty and out of breath, you find that the little piggies have beaten you to the beach. And there isn't a damn thing wrong with that —it's all part of the game. Don't you think it's worth a lot to find that out? Life is great, and you've got to grab for it every morning. But what good would it be if you knew it was going to be yours forever?"

Next morning, after a crazy night barricaded against the invading pigs in a cubicle of one of the beachfront shacks that called itself a hotel, Uncle Dan and I crawled into his car and headed back for Oaxaca. We drove in silence all the way, both of us staring into the green depths of the ravines and breathing more deeply as we climbed into the pure mountain air. I knew that my uncle was dying, but I wasn't sure that he had come, as he had claimed on the beach at Puerto Angel, just to find out certain things for himself.

Now that he is gone, though, I feel fairly certain—even though he never asked me about myself, either to commiserate or to condemn—that Uncle Dan made his last trip as much to communicate with me one last time, to show me another path, as to please himself or to assuage his own yearning heart.

Shortly after he drove away, leaving me to stare at myself in the cracked mirror of my Mexican lodging place, I threw off my self-pity as you would cast away a soiled and worn-out coat, and returned to the United States, to a better and more reasoned kind of life. And when I visited his resting place in a crowded and unlovely corner of a Queens cemetery—for one morning before my return Uncle Dan had died quietly in his office, without making any particular fuss—I took along a small arborvitae, and when no one was looking I planted the tree of life quickly and gently on his grave.